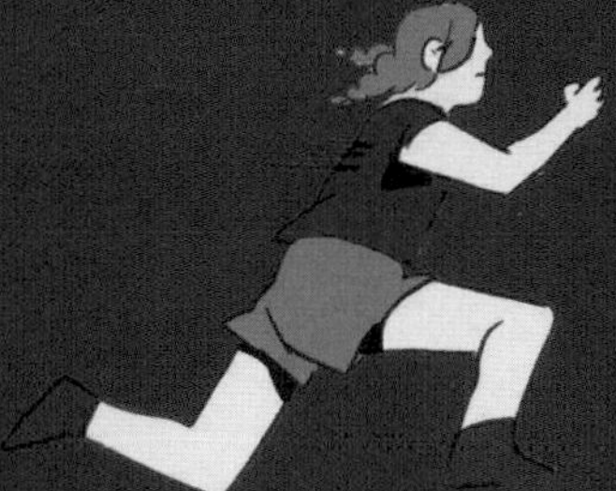

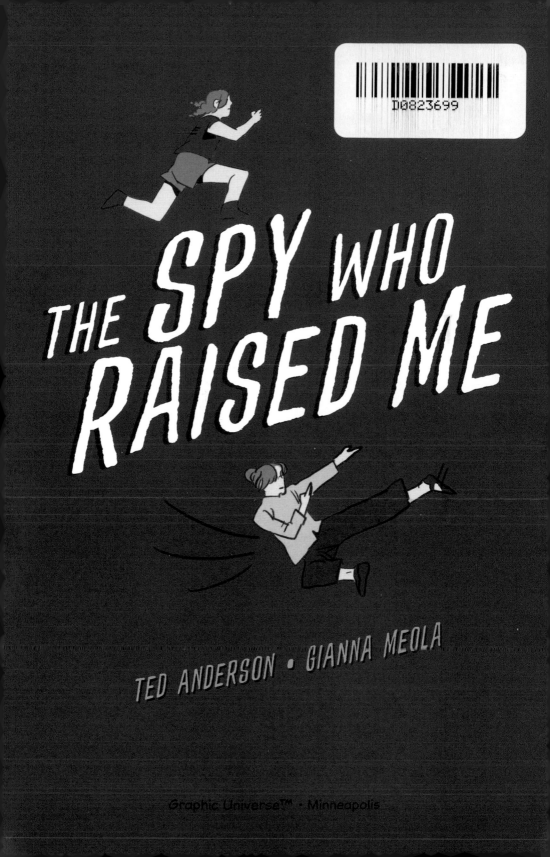

THE SPY WHO RAISED ME

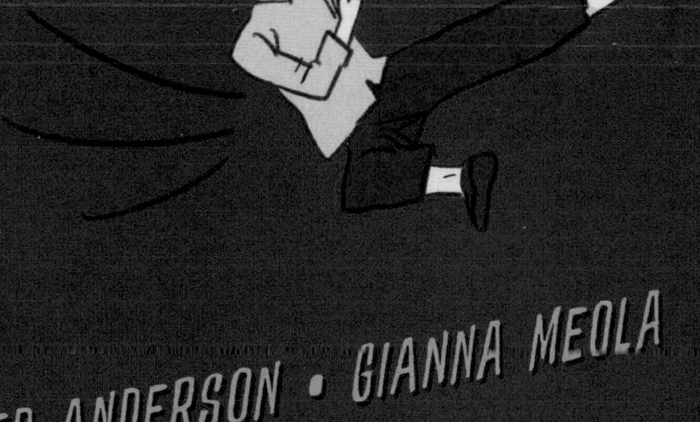

TED ANDERSON • GIANNA MEOLA

Graphic Universe™ • Minneapolis

For my parents, who only ever brainwashed me the normal way
—T.A.

Thanks to Alex
—G.M.

Graphic Universe™
An imprint of Lerner Publishing Group, Inc.
241 First Avenue North
Minneapolis, MN 55401 USA

For reading levels and more information, look up this title at www.lernerbooks.com.

Main body text set in CCDaveGibbonsLower.
Typeface provided by Comicraft.

Library of Congress Cataloging-in-Publication Data

Names: Anderson, Ted, 1985– author. | Meola, Gianna, illustrator.
Title: The spy who raised me / Ted Anderson, Gianna Meola.
Description: Minneapolis : Graphic Universe, [2021] | Audience: Ages 13–18 | Audience: Grades 10–12 | Summary: "Josie Black can infiltrate any building and move like a martial artist. But no one told her that. When she discovers her mom programmed her to be a special operative, spy family drama breaks out." —Provided by publisher.
Identifiers: LCCN 2019040559 (print) | LCCN 2019040560 (ebook) | ISBN 9781541532403 (library binding) | ISBN 9781541599505 (ebook)
Subjects: LCSH: Graphic novels. | CYAC: Graphic novels. | Spies—Fiction. | Families—Fiction.
Classification: LCC PZ7.7.A49 Sp 2021 (print) | LCC PZ7.7.A49 (ebook) | DDC 741.5/973—dc23

LC record available at https://lccn.loc.gov/2019040559
LC ebook record available at https://lccn.loc.gov/2019040560

Manufactured in the United States of America
2-51552-35713-8/10/2021

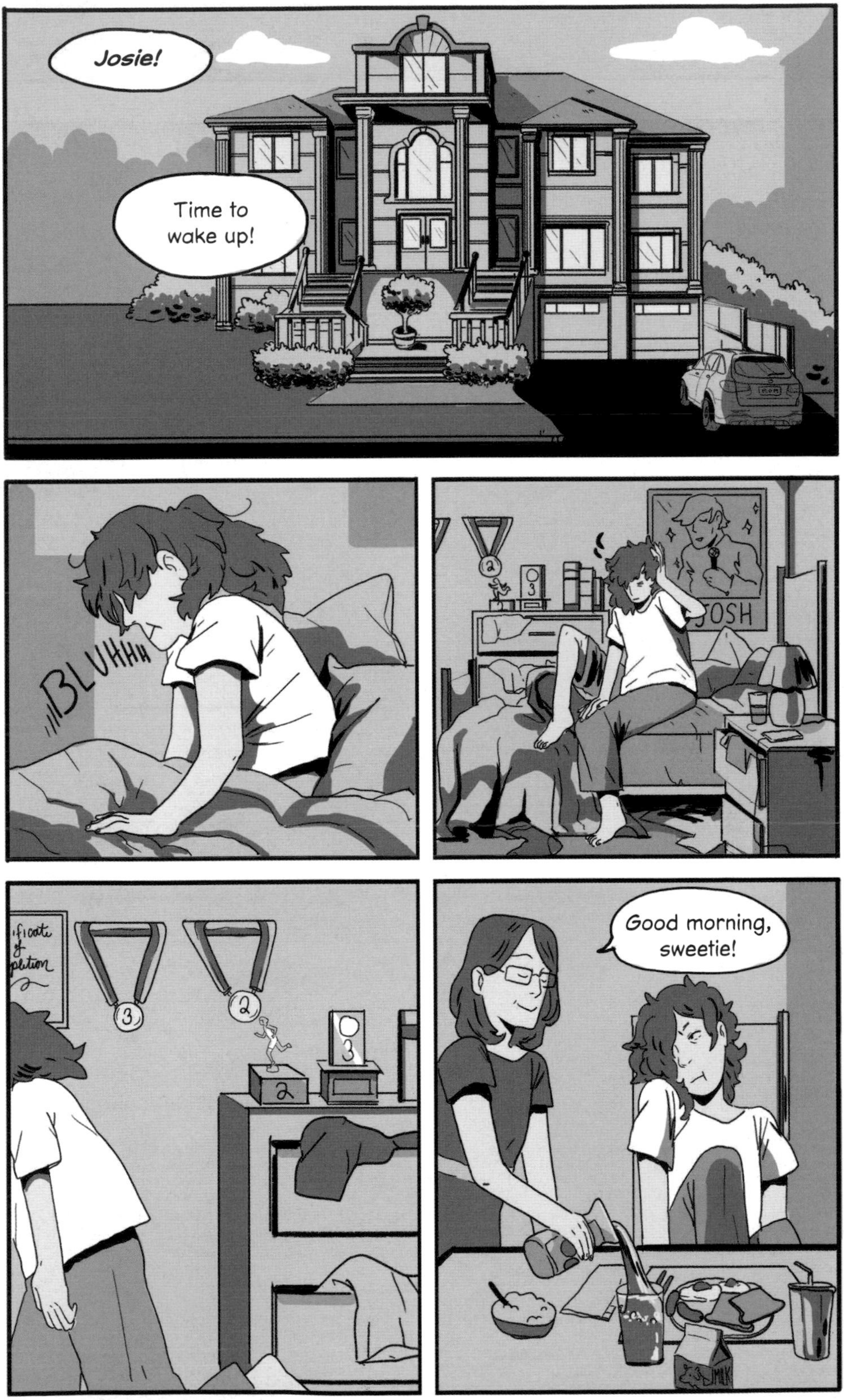
Josie!
Time to wake up!
BLUHHH
JOSH
Good morning, sweetie!

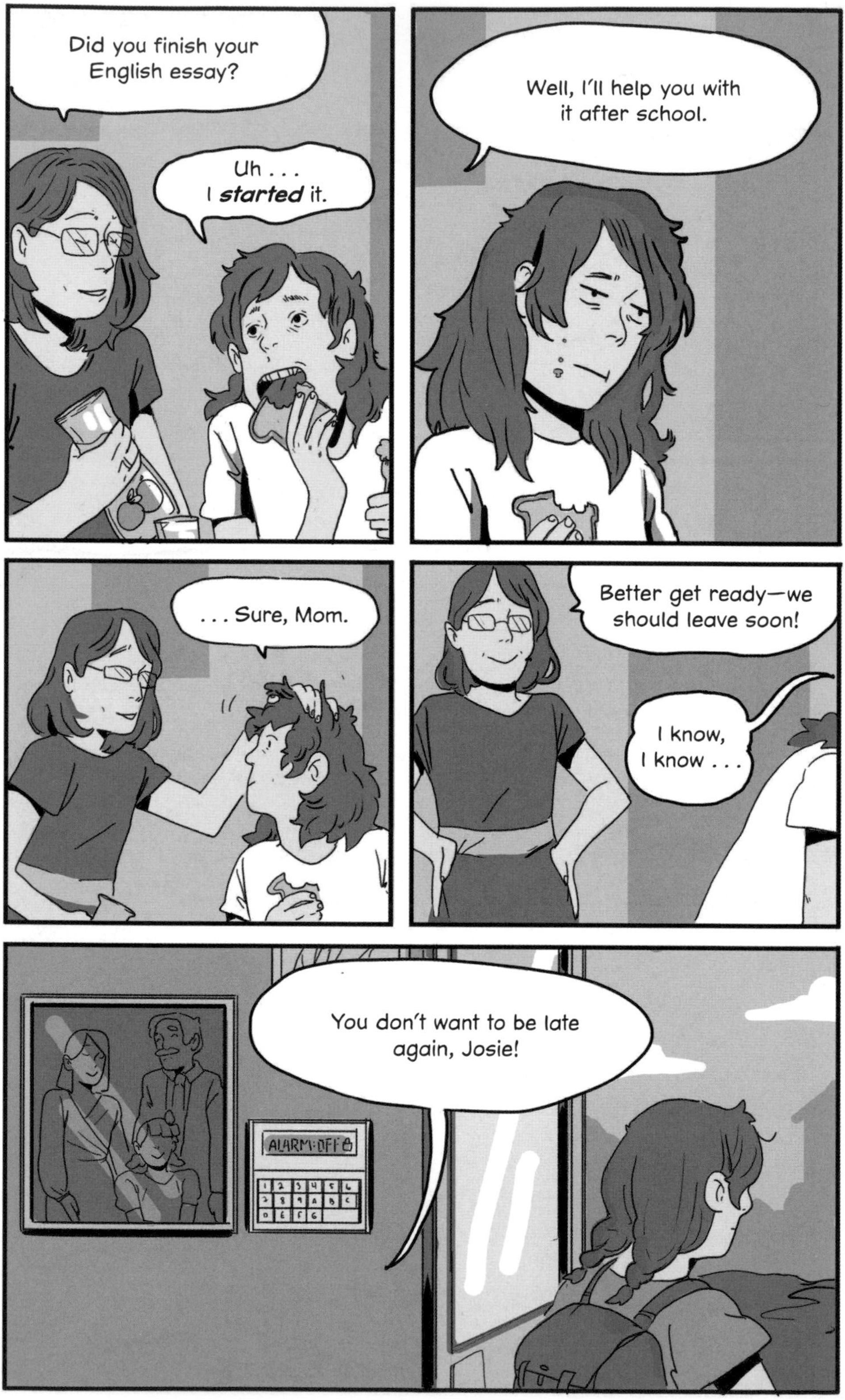
Did you finish your English essay?
Uh . . . I *started* it.
Well, I'll help you with it after school.
. . . Sure, Mom.
Better get ready—we should leave soon!
I know, I know . . .
ALARM: OFF
You don't want to be late again, Josie!

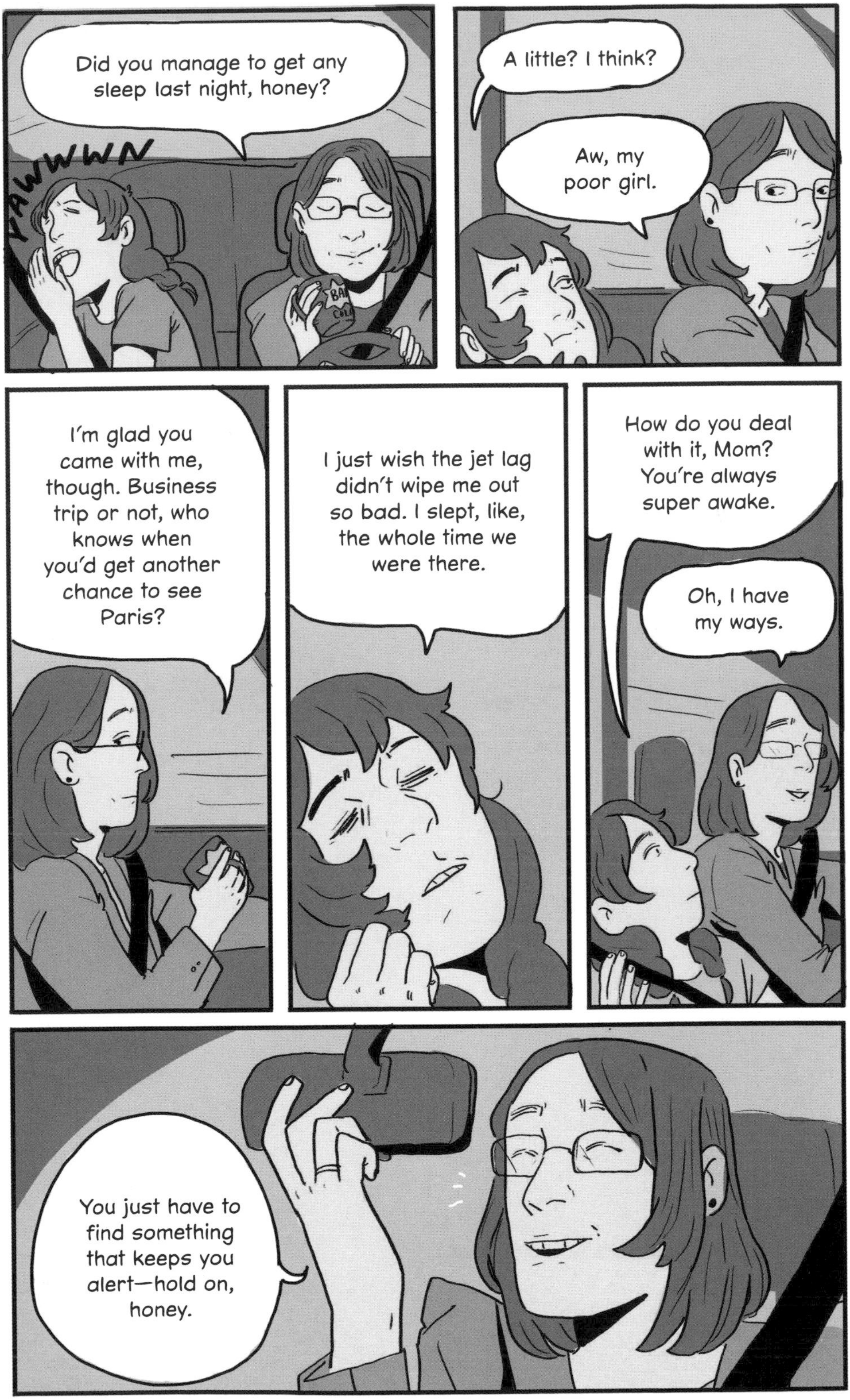
Did you manage to get any sleep last night, honey?
YAWWWN
A little? I think?
Aw, my poor girl.
I'm glad you came with me, though. Business trip or not, who knows when you'd get another chance to see Paris?
I just wish the jet lag didn't wipe me out so bad. I slept, like, the whole time we were there.
How do you deal with it, Mom? You're always super awake.
Oh, I have my ways.
You just have to find something that keeps you alert—hold on, honey.

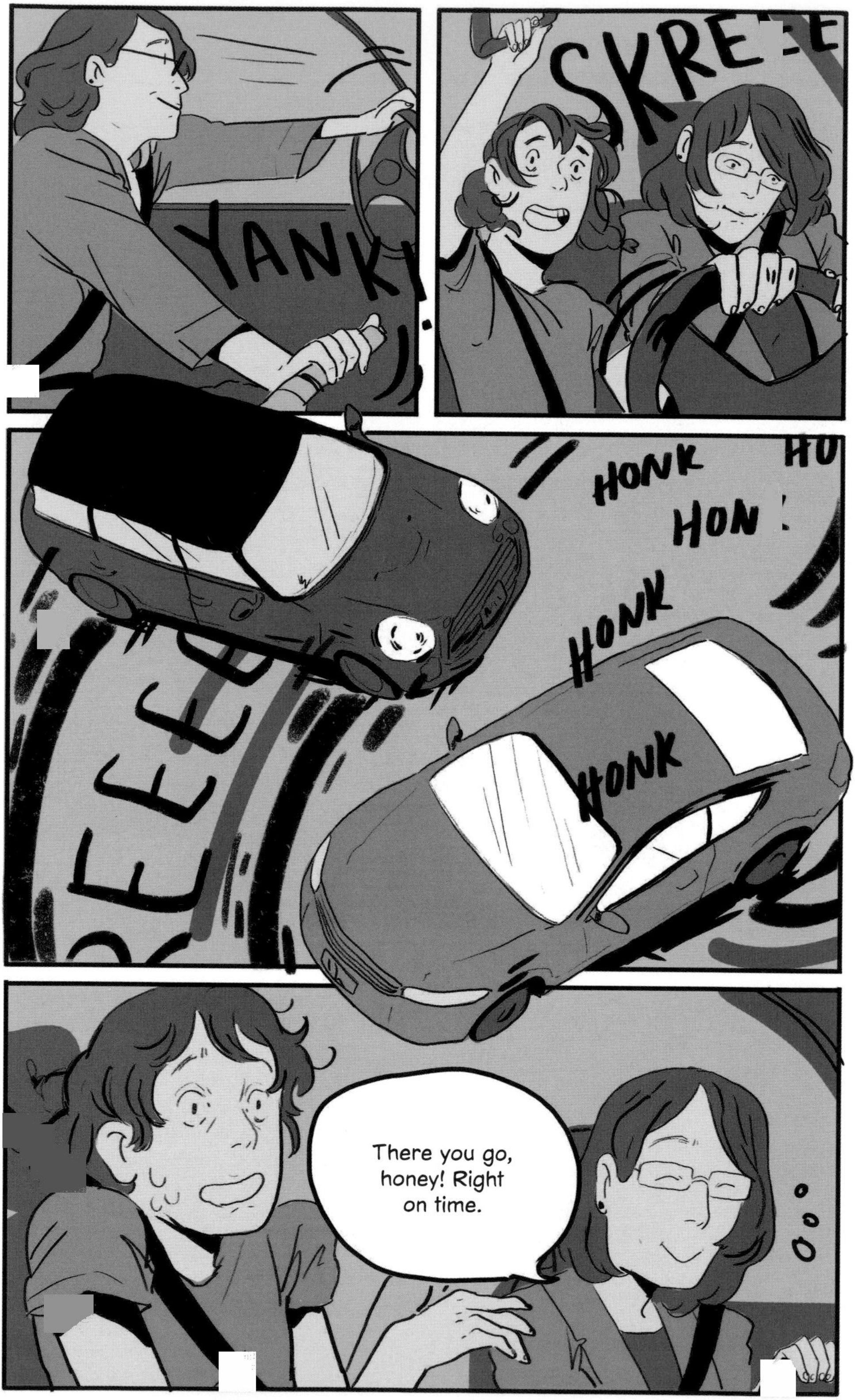
YANK!
SKREEE
HONK
HONK
HONK
HONK
HONK
There you go, honey! Right on time.

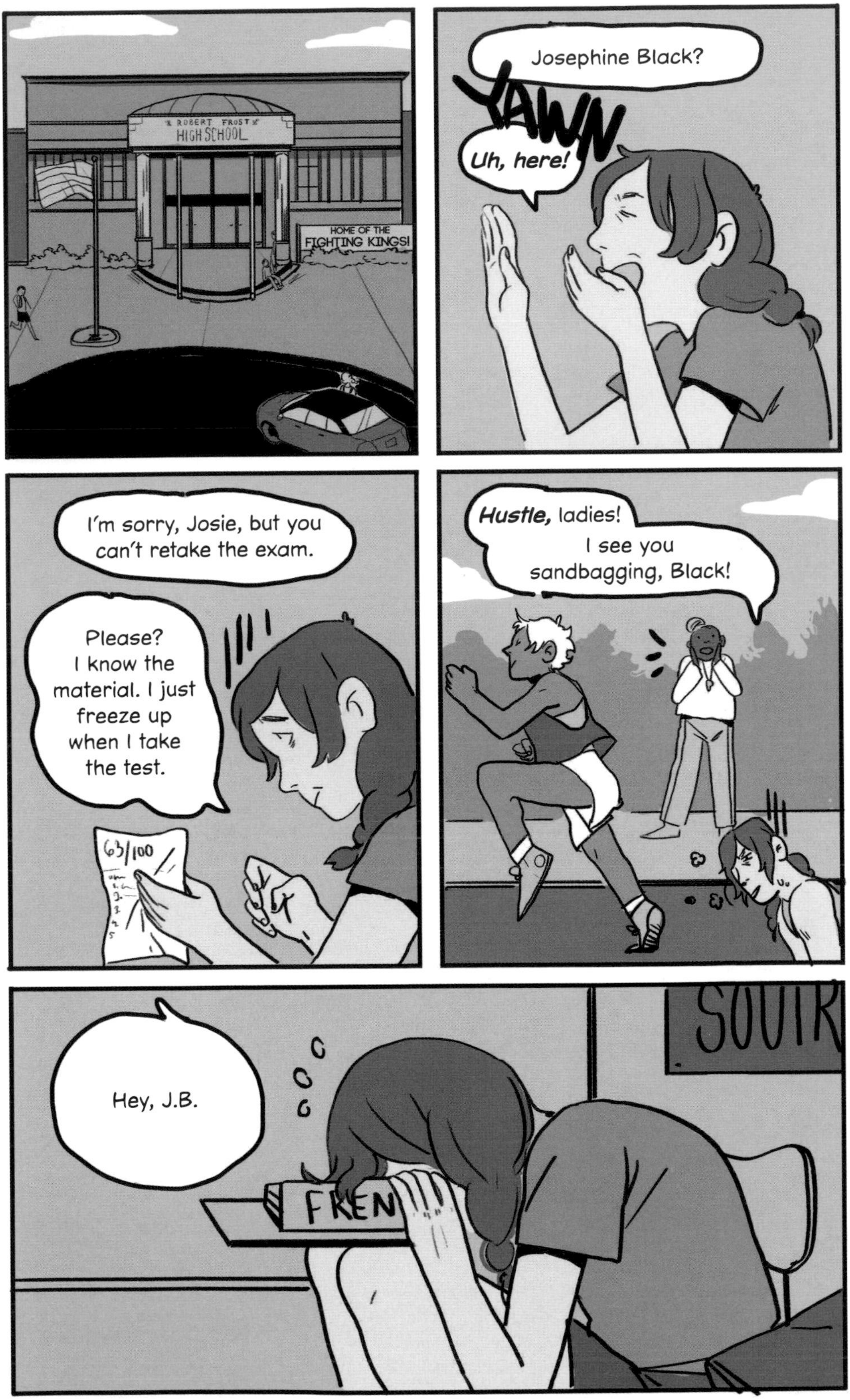
ROBERT FROST
HIGH SCHOOL
HOME OF THE
FIGHTING KINGS!
Josephine Black?
YAWN
Uh, here!
I'm sorry, Josie, but you can't retake the exam.
Please? I know the material. I just freeze up when I take the test.
63/100
Hustle, ladies!
I see you sandbagging, Black!
SQUIR
FREN
Hey, J.B.

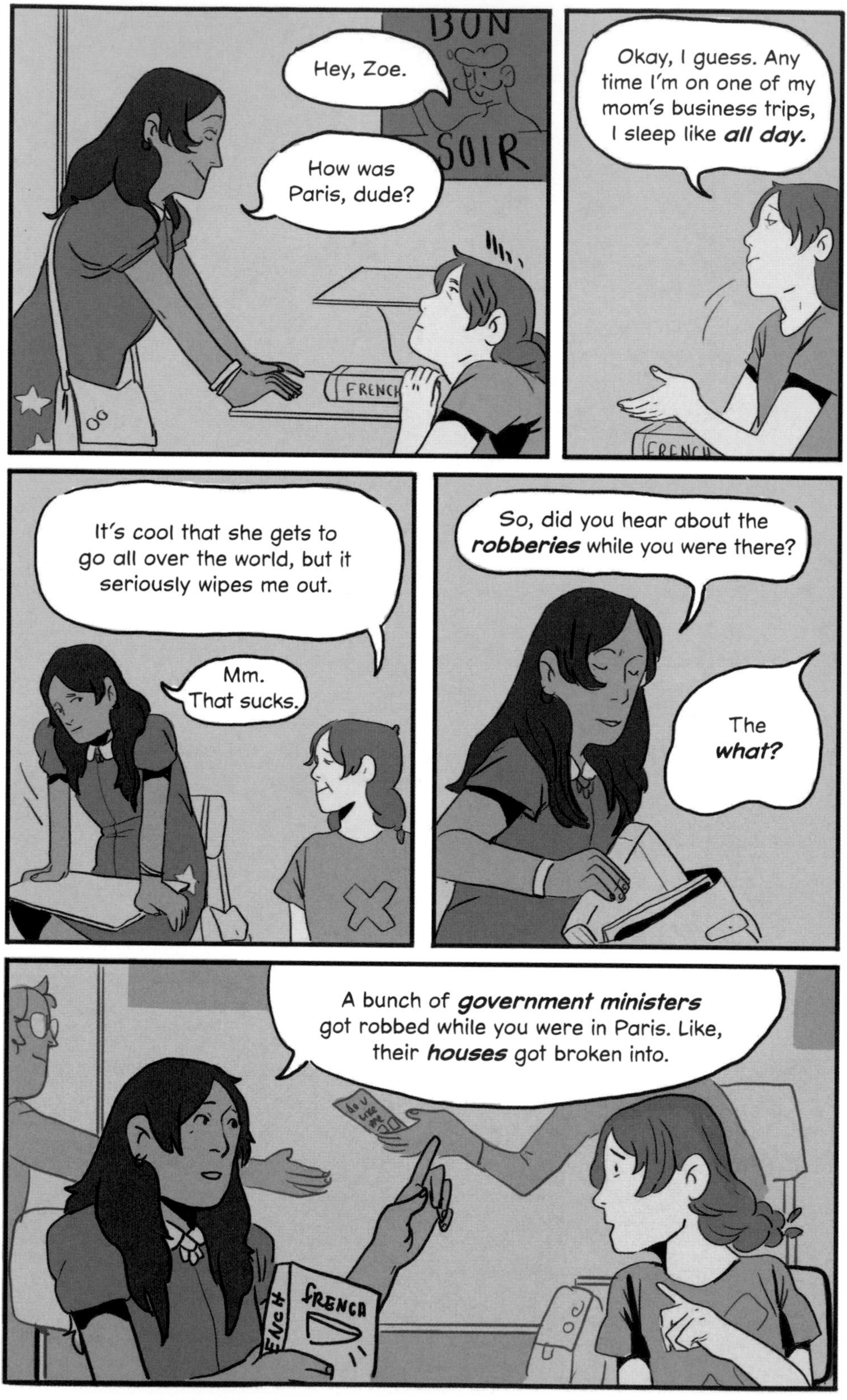
BON
SOIR
Hey, Zoe.
How was Paris, dude?
FRENCH
Okay, I guess. Any time I'm on one of my mom's business trips, I sleep like ***all day.***
It's cool that she gets to go all over the world, but it seriously wipes me out.
Mm. That sucks.
So, did you hear about the ***robberies*** while you were there?
The ***what?***
A bunch of ***government ministers*** got robbed while you were in Paris. Like, their ***houses*** got broken into.
FRENCH

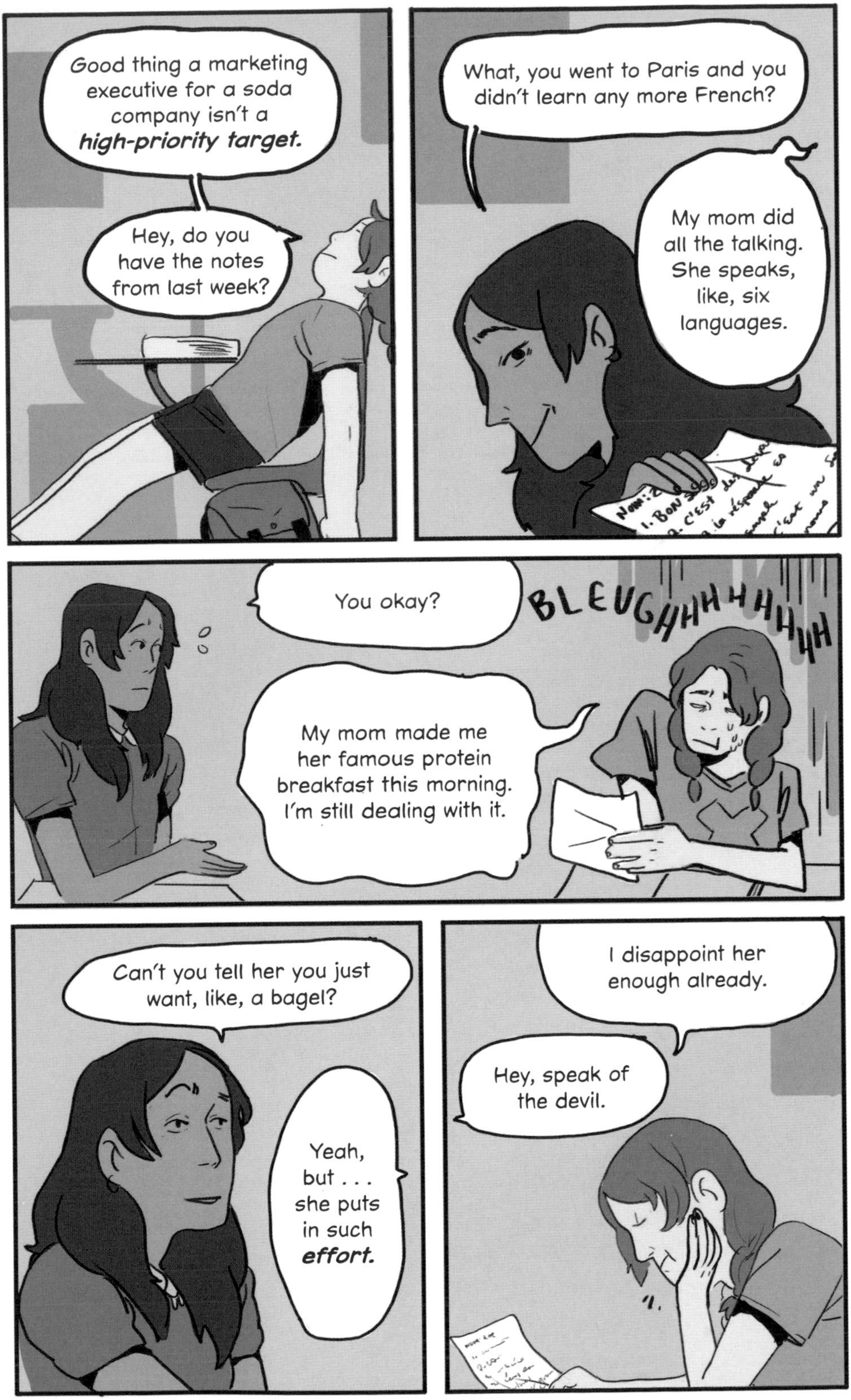
Good thing a marketing executive for a soda company isn't a ***high-priority target.***
Hey, do you have the notes from last week?
What, you went to Paris and you didn't learn any more French?
My mom did all the talking. She speaks, like, six languages.
You okay?
BLEUGHHHHHHHH
My mom made me her famous protein breakfast this morning. I'm still dealing with it.
Can't you tell her you just want, like, a bagel?
Yeah, but . . . she puts in such ***effort.***
I disappoint her enough already.
Hey, speak of the devil.

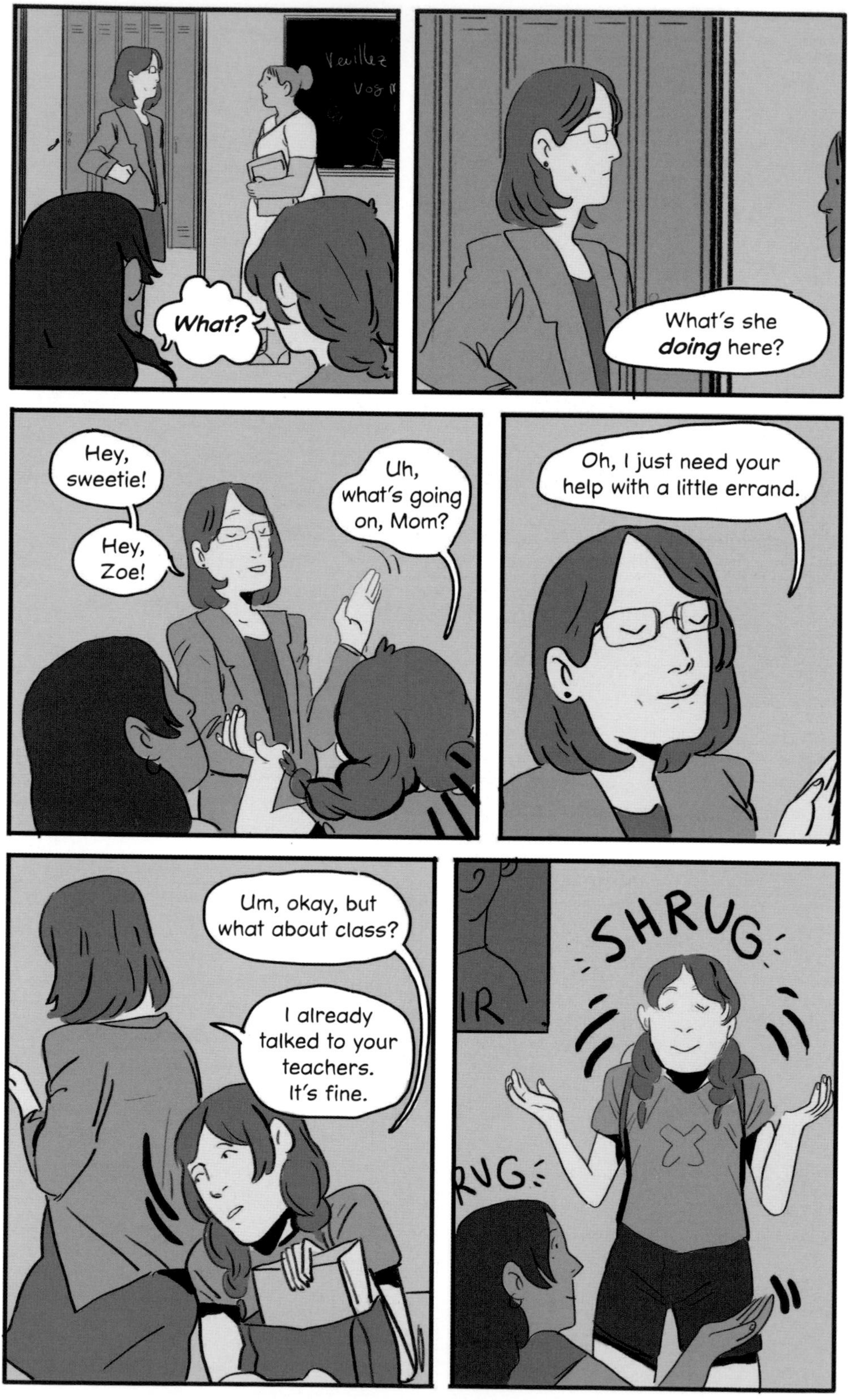
Veuillez
What?
What's she *doing* here?
Hey, sweetie!
Hey, Zoe!
Uh, what's going on, Mom?
Oh, I just need your help with a little errand.
Um, okay, but what about class?
I already talked to your teachers. It's fine.
SHRUG
RUG

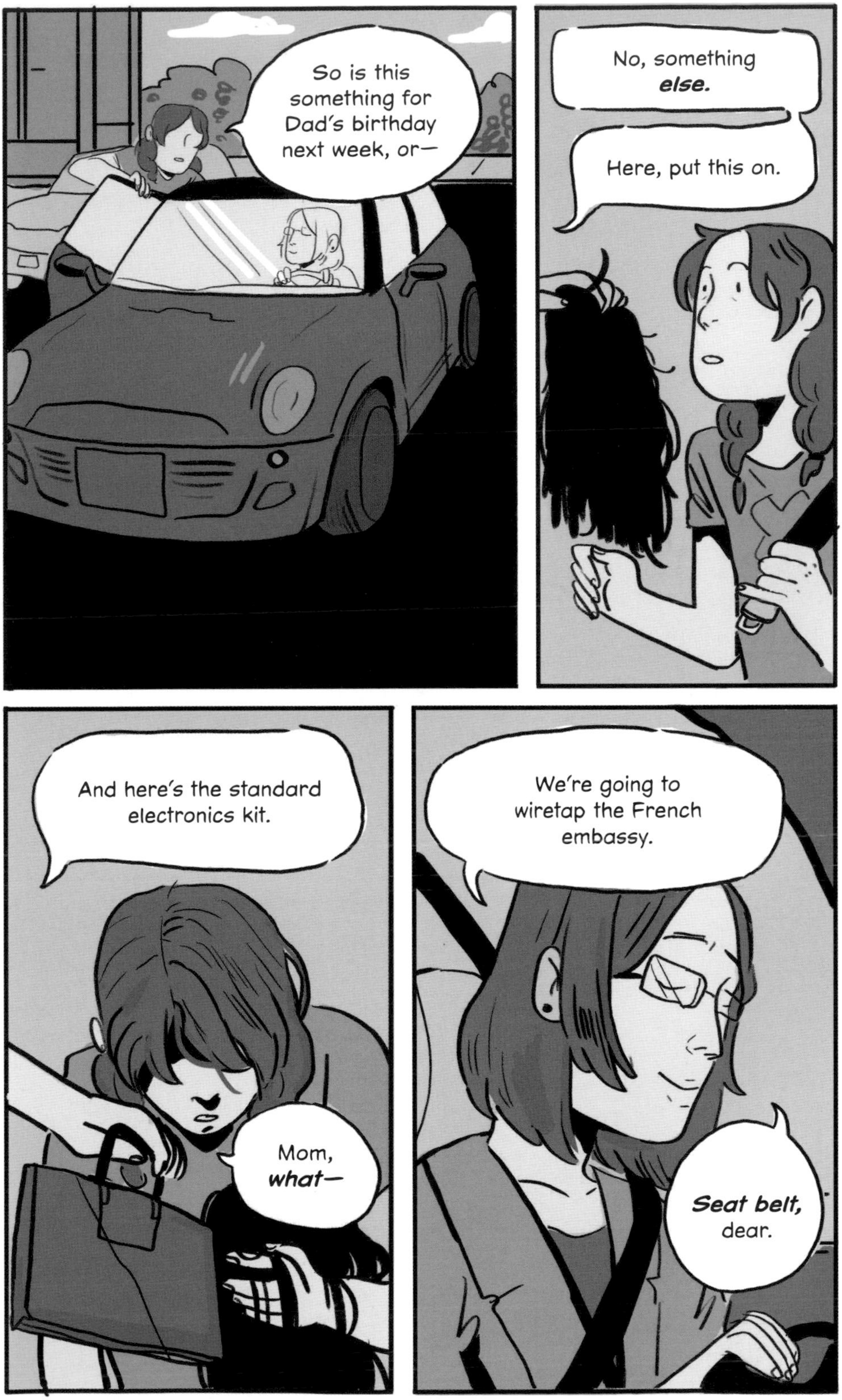
So is this something for Dad's birthday next week, or—
No, something *else.*
Here, put this on.
And here's the standard electronics kit.
Mom, *what—*
We're going to wiretap the French embassy.
Seat belt, dear.

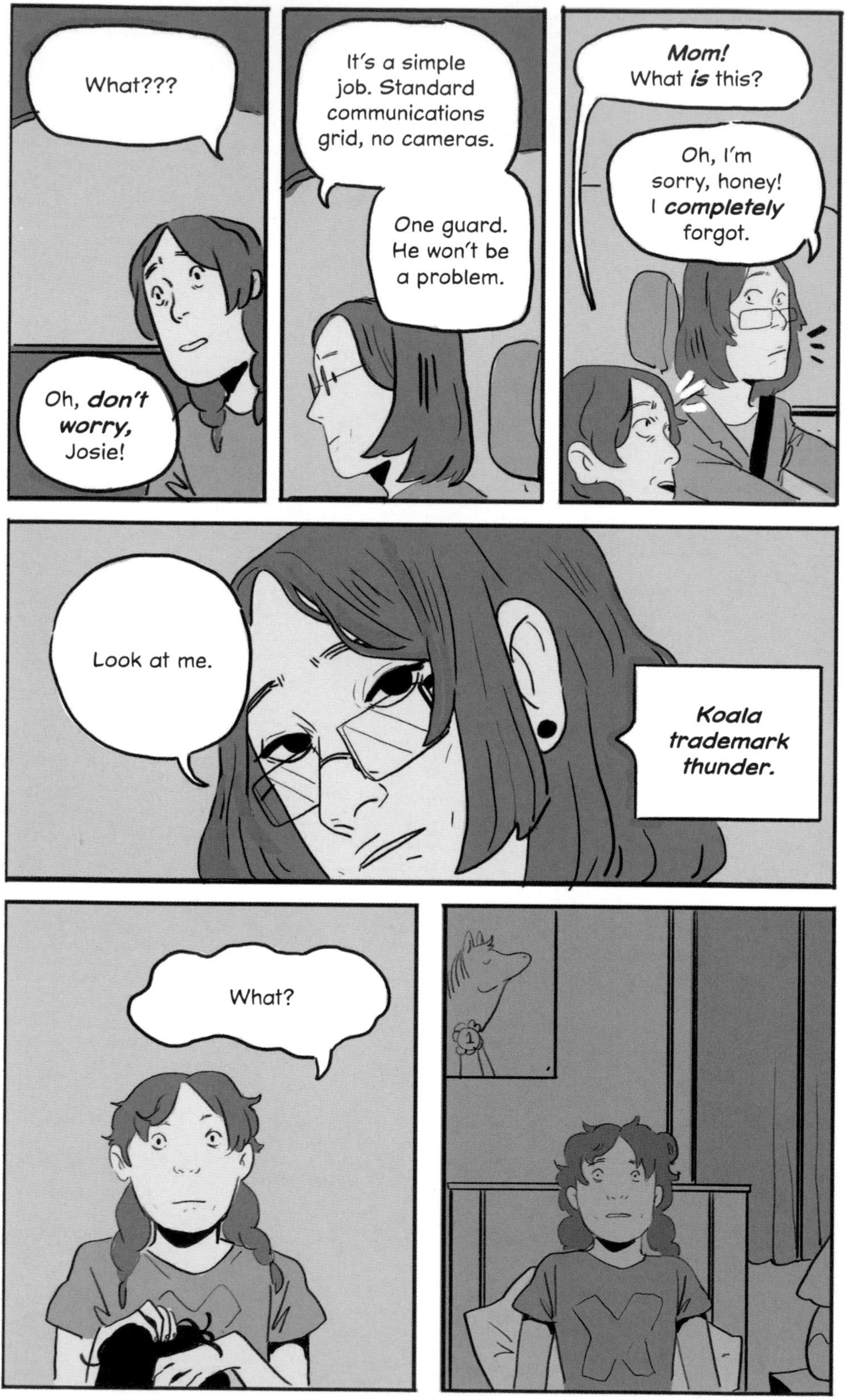
What???
Oh, *don't worry,* Josie!
It's a simple job. Standard communications grid, no cameras.
One guard. He won't be a problem.
Mom! What *is* this?
Oh, I'm sorry, honey! I *completely* forgot.
Look at me.
Koala trademark thunder.
What?

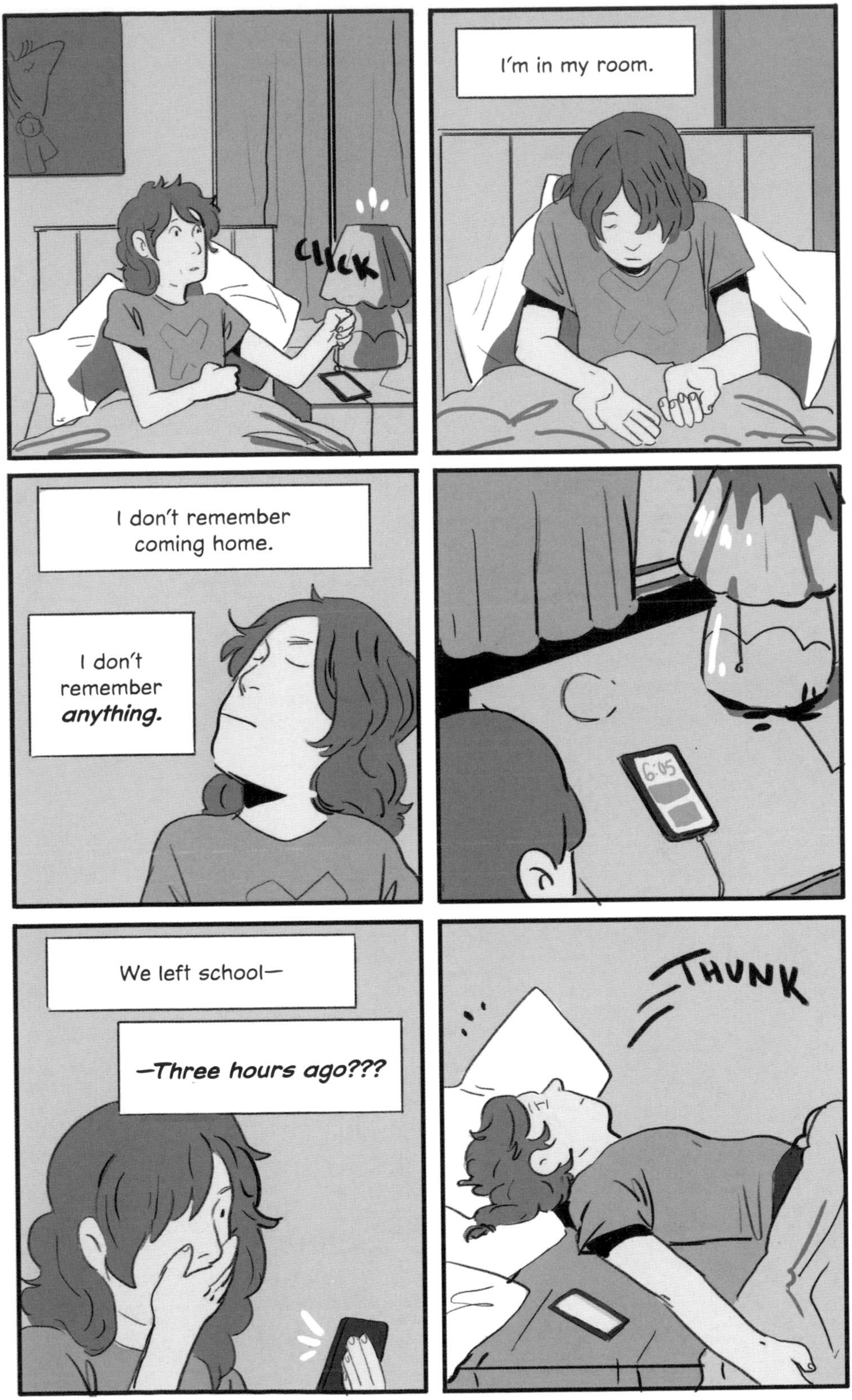
CLICK
I'm in my room.
I don't remember coming home.
I don't remember *anything.*
6:05
We left school—
—Three hours ago???
THUNK

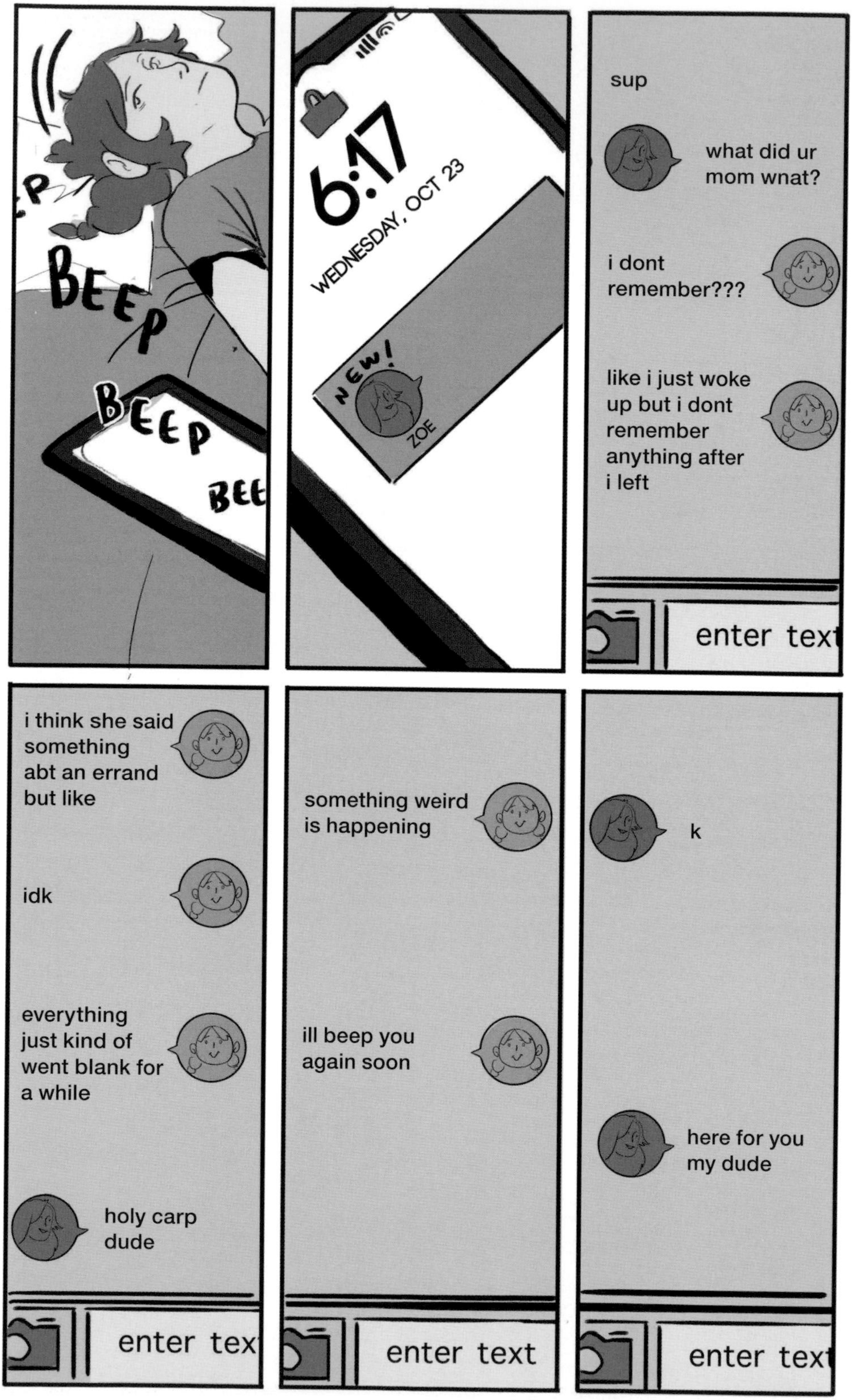

BEEP
BEEP
BEEP
BEE
6:17
WEDNESDAY, OCT 23
NEW!
ZOE
sup
what did ur mom wnat?
i dont remember???
like i just woke up but i dont remember anything after i left
enter text
i think she said something abt an errand but like
idk
everything just kind of went blank for a while
holy carp dude
enter text
something weird is happening
ill beep you again soon
enter text
k
here for you my dude
enter text

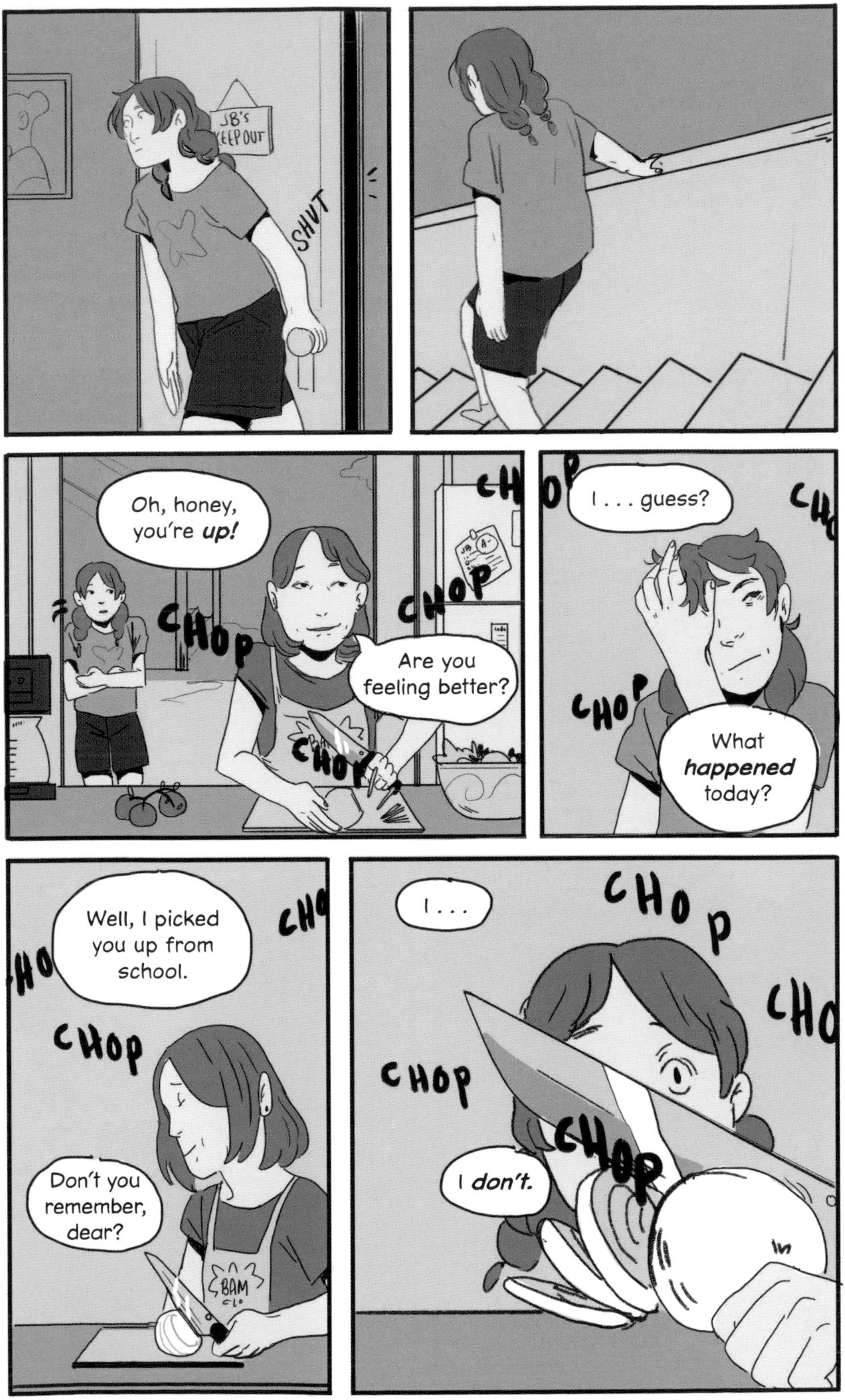
JB's KEEP OUT
SHUT
Oh, honey, you're *up!*
CHOP
CHOP
CHOP
Are you feeling better?
CHOP
I . . . guess?
CHOP
What *happened* today?
Well, I picked you up from school.
CHOP
Don't you remember, dear?
BAM
I . . .
CHOP
CHOP
CHOP
I *don't.*

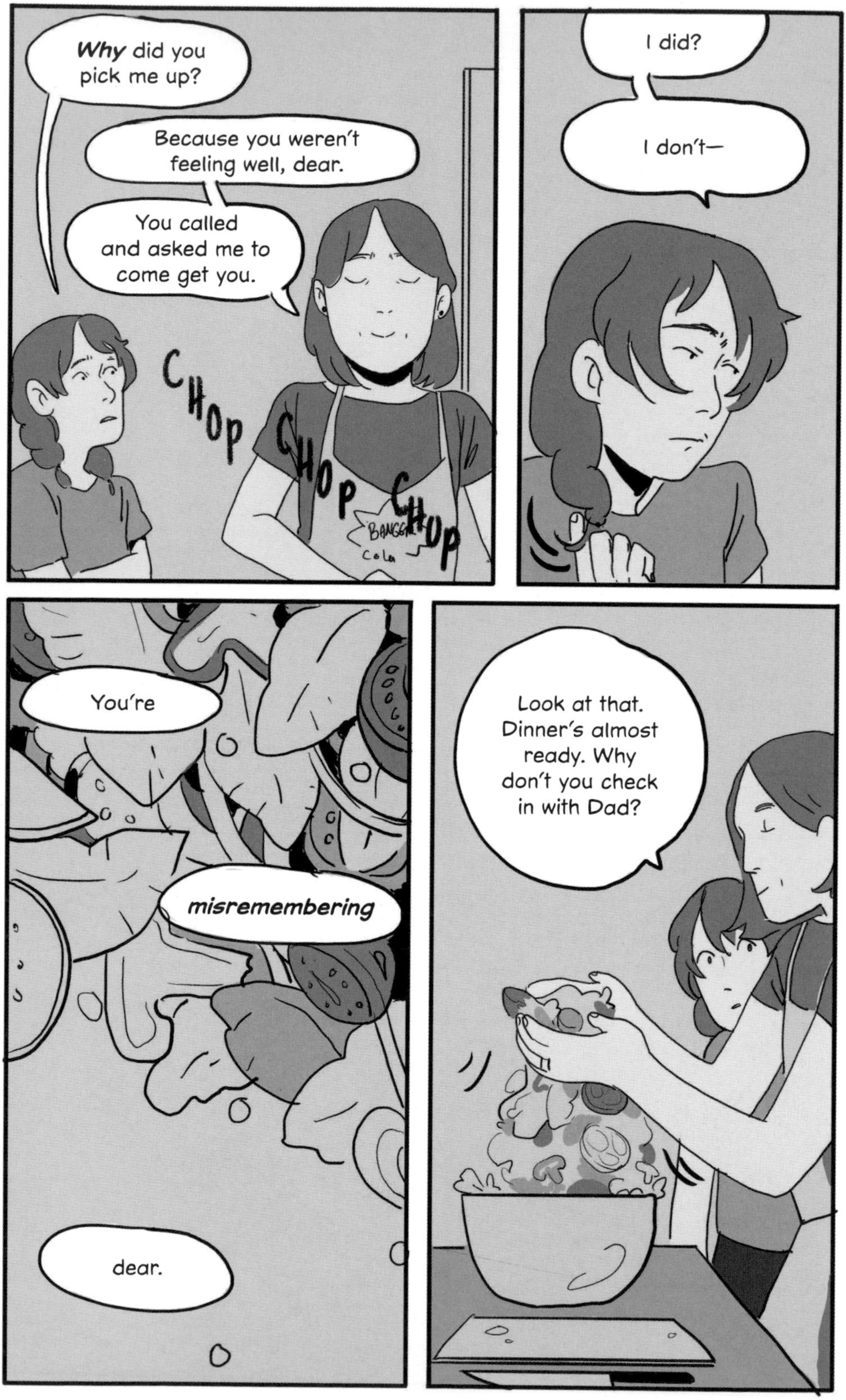

Why did you pick me up?
Because you weren't feeling well, dear.
You called and asked me to come get you.
CHOP CHOP CHOP
BANG
Cola
I did?
I don't—
You're
misremembering
dear.
Look at that. Dinner's almost ready. Why don't you check in with Dad?

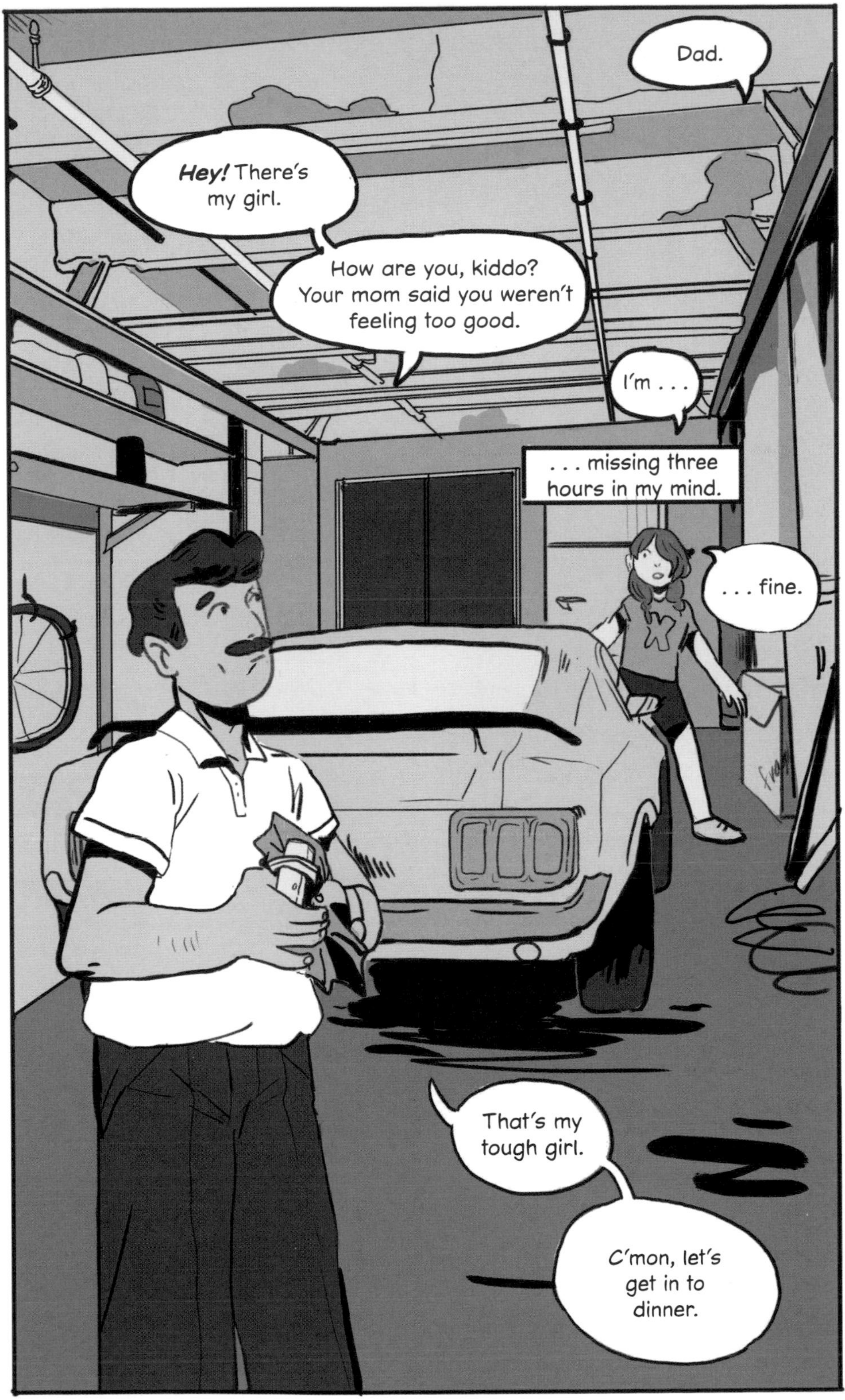
Dad.
Hey! There's my girl.
How are you, kiddo? Your mom said you weren't feeling too good.
I'm . . .
. . . missing three hours in my mind.
. . . fine.
That's my tough girl.
C'mon, let's get in to dinner.

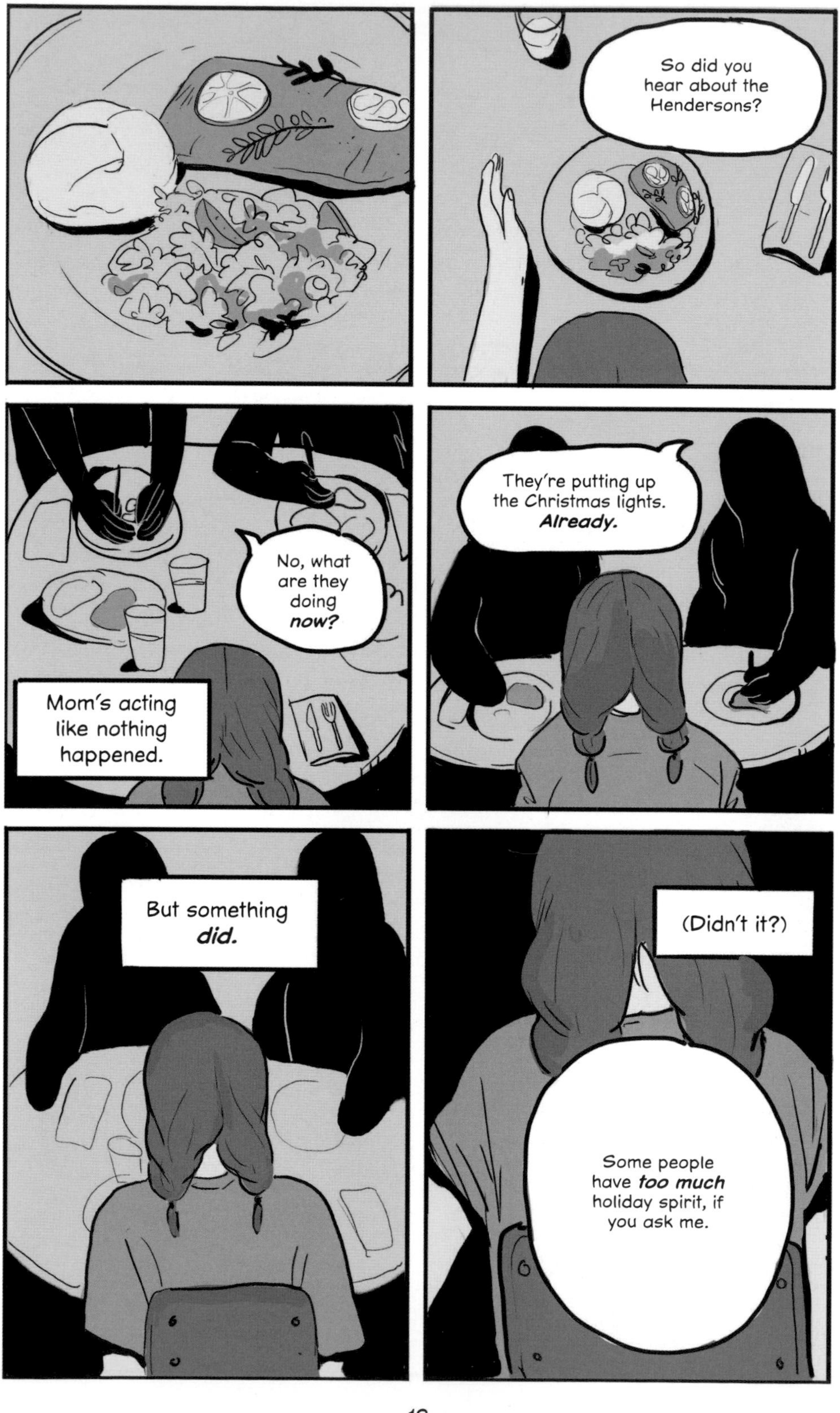
So did you hear about the Hendersons?
No, what are they doing *now?*
Mom's acting like nothing happened.
They're putting up the Christmas lights. ***Already.***
But something ***did.***
(Didn't it?)
Some people have ***too much*** holiday spirit, if you ask me.

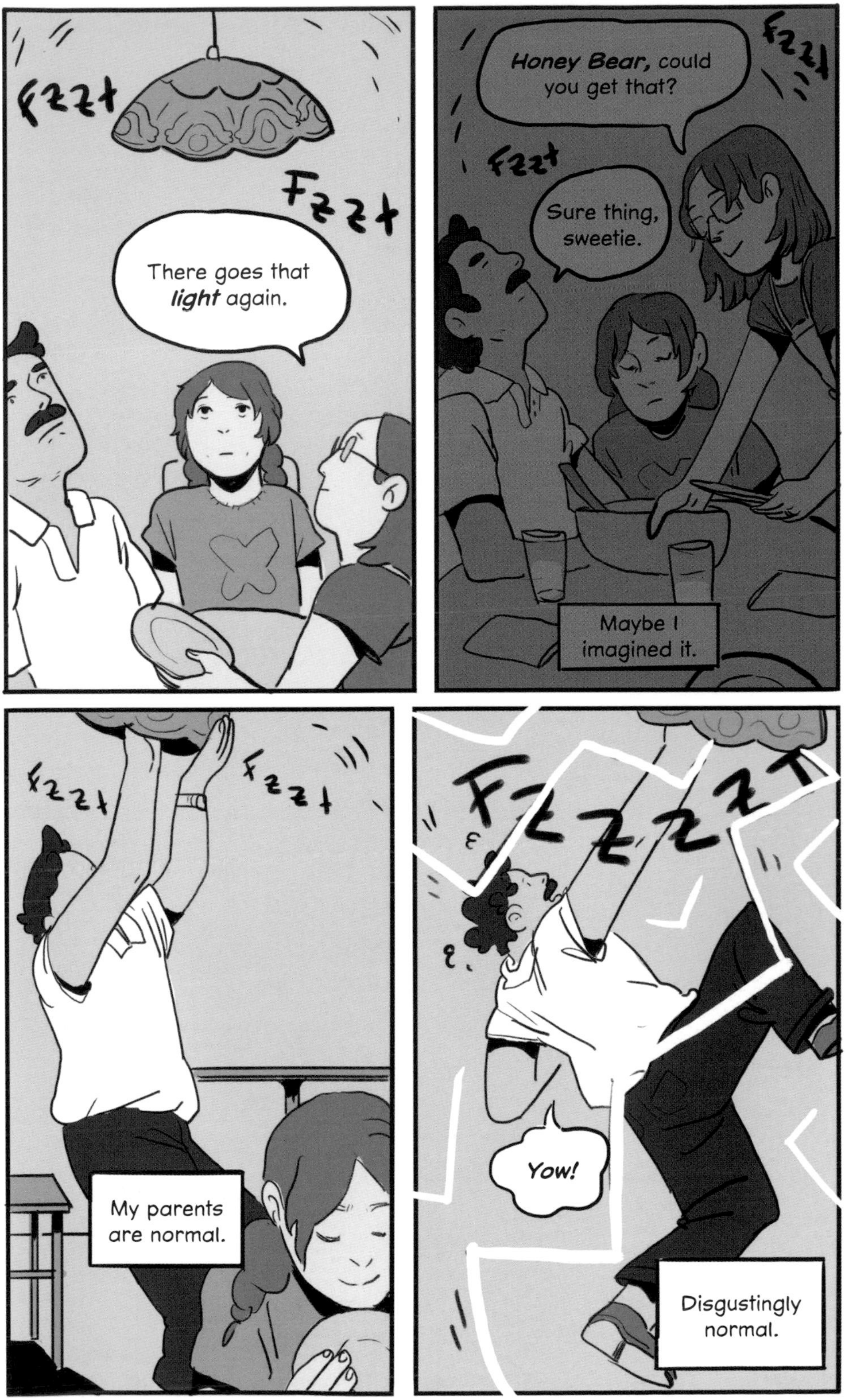

FZZT
FZZT
There goes that *light* again.
Honey Bear, could you get that?
FZZT
FZZT
Sure thing, sweetie.
Maybe I imagined it.
FZZT
FZZT
My parents are normal.
FZZZZZT
Yow!
Disgustingly normal.

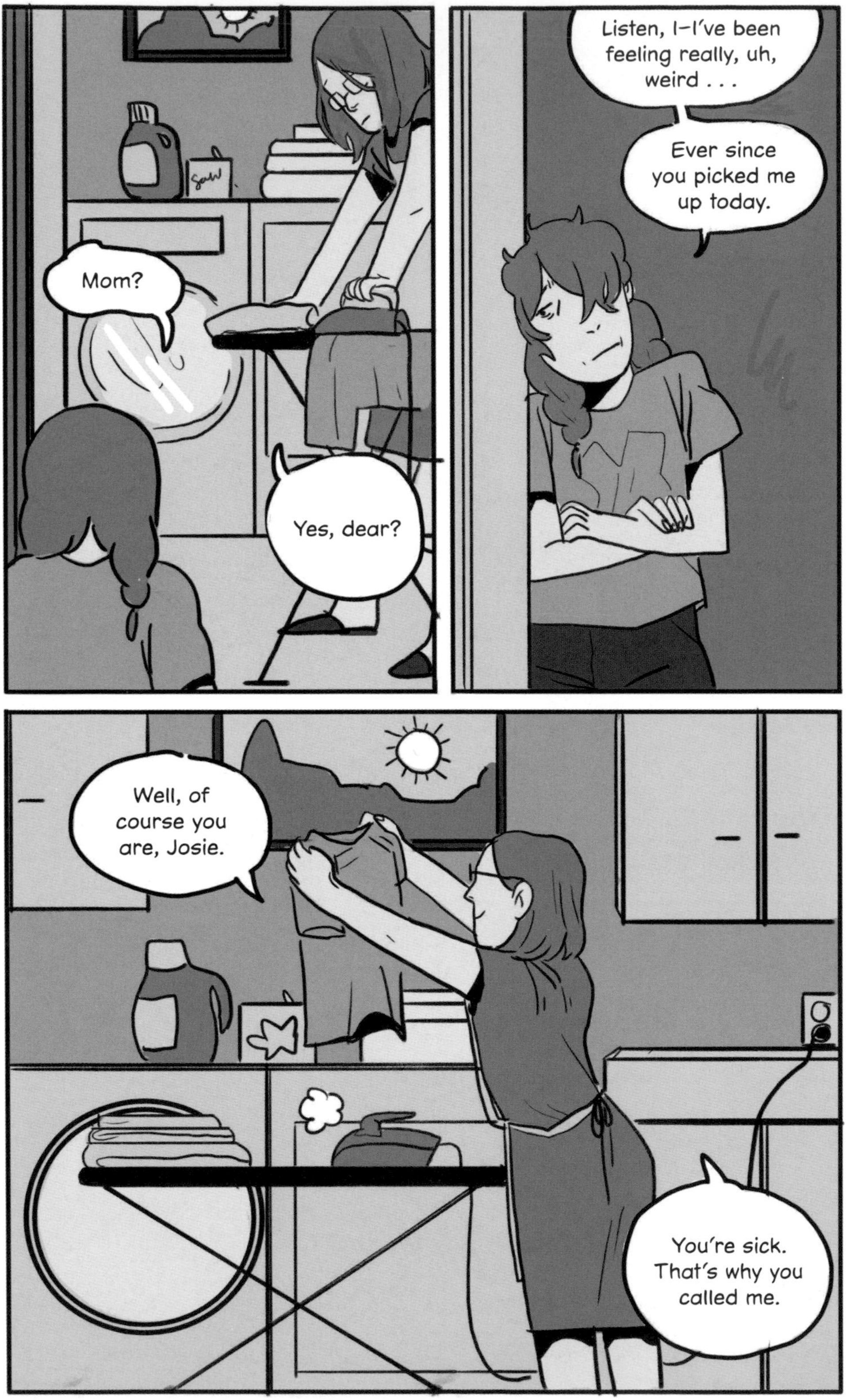
Mom?
Yes, dear?
Listen, I–I've been feeling really, uh, weird . . .
Ever since you picked me up today.
Well, of course you are, Josie.
You're sick. That's why you called me.

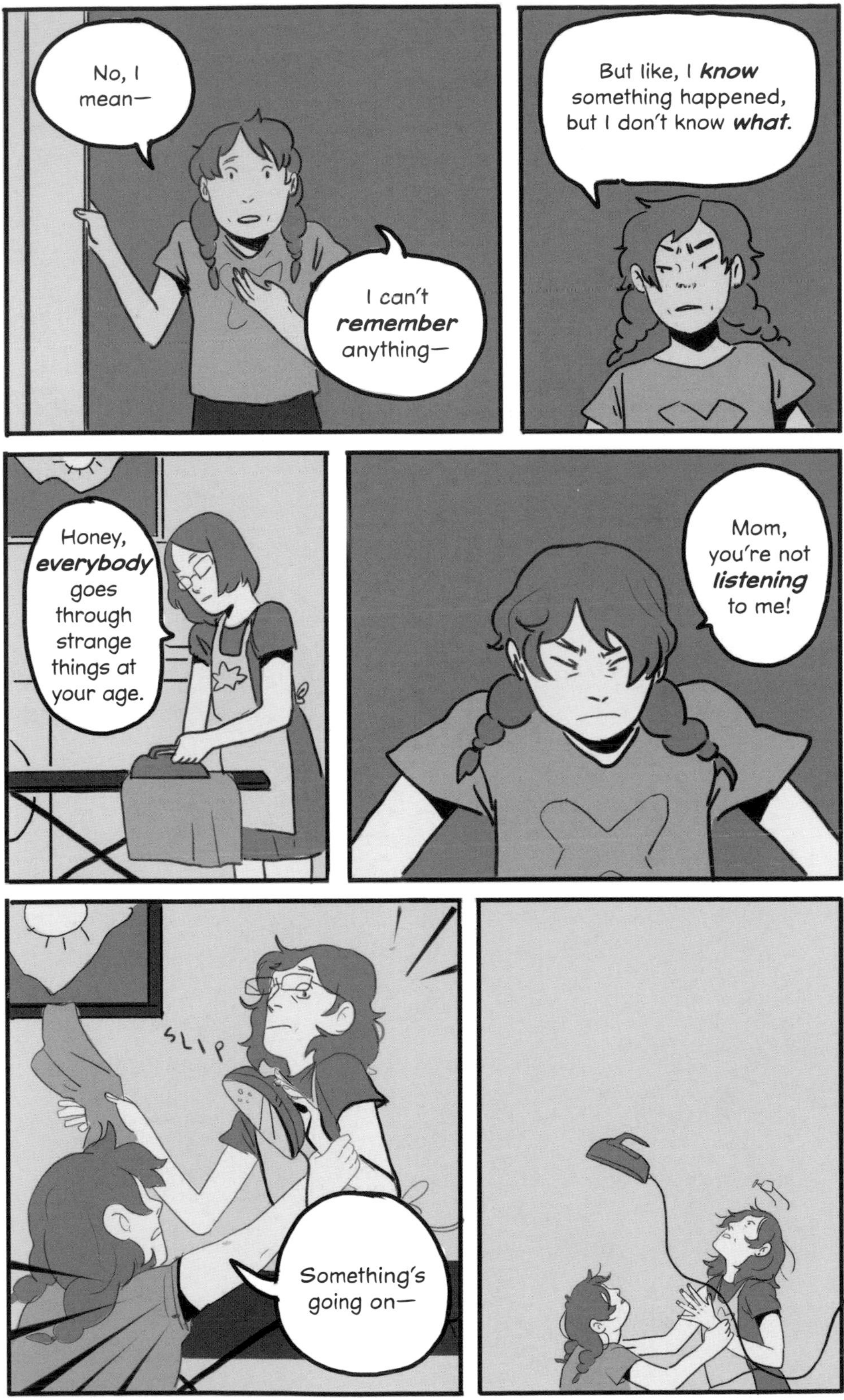
No, I mean—
I can't **remember** anything—
But like, I **know** something happened, but I don't know **what**.
Honey, **everybody** goes through strange things at your age.
Mom, you're not **listening** to me!
SLIP
Something's going on—

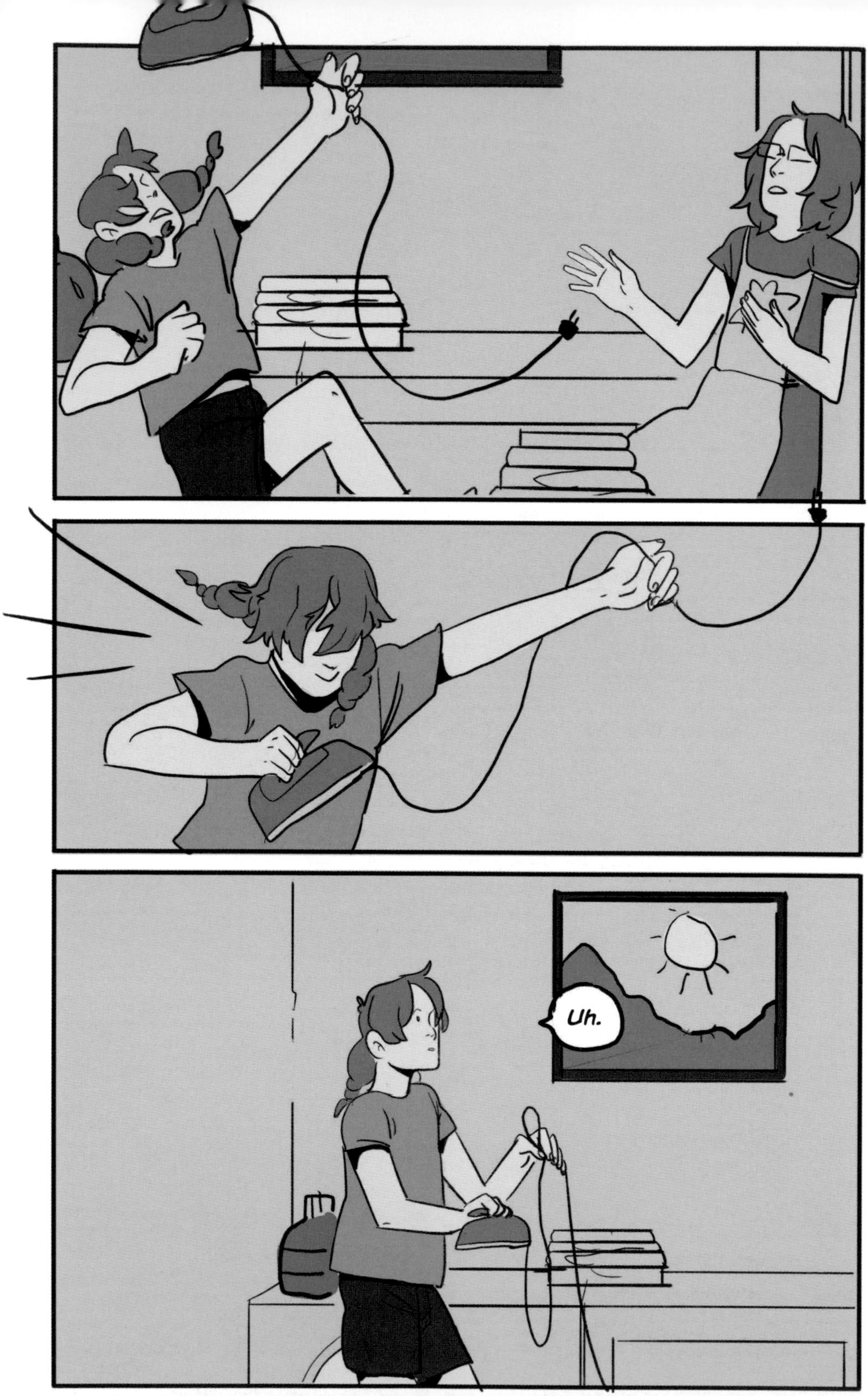
Uh.

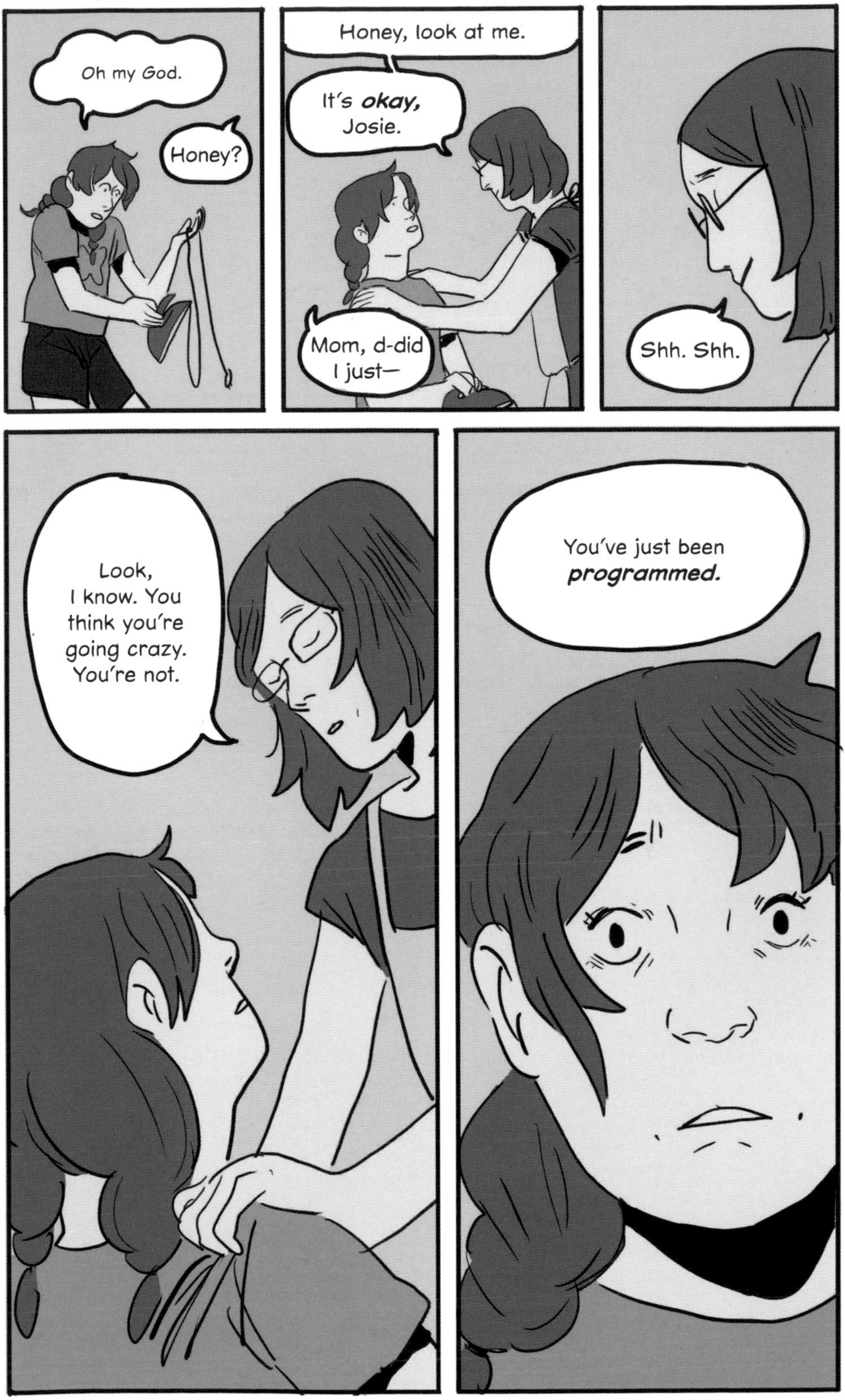
Oh my God.
Honey?
Honey, look at me.
It's **okay,** Josie.
Mom, d-did I just—
Shh. Shh.
Look, I know. You think you're going crazy. You're not.
You've just been ***programmed.***

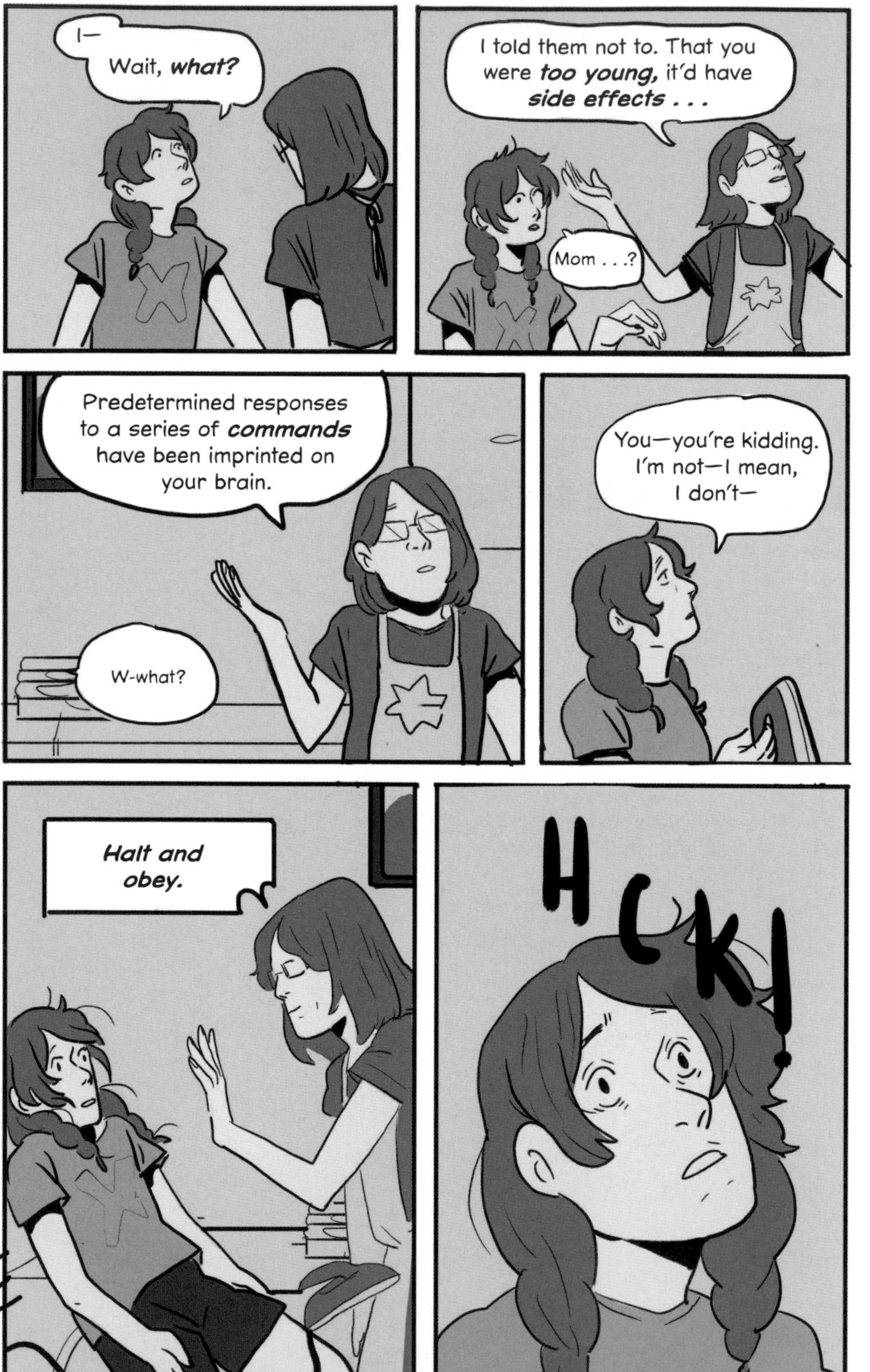
I—
Wait, what?
I told them not to. That you were too young, it'd have side effects . . .
Mom . . .?
Predetermined responses to a series of commands have been imprinted on your brain.
W-what?
You—you're kidding. I'm not—I mean, I don't—
Halt and obey.
HCK!

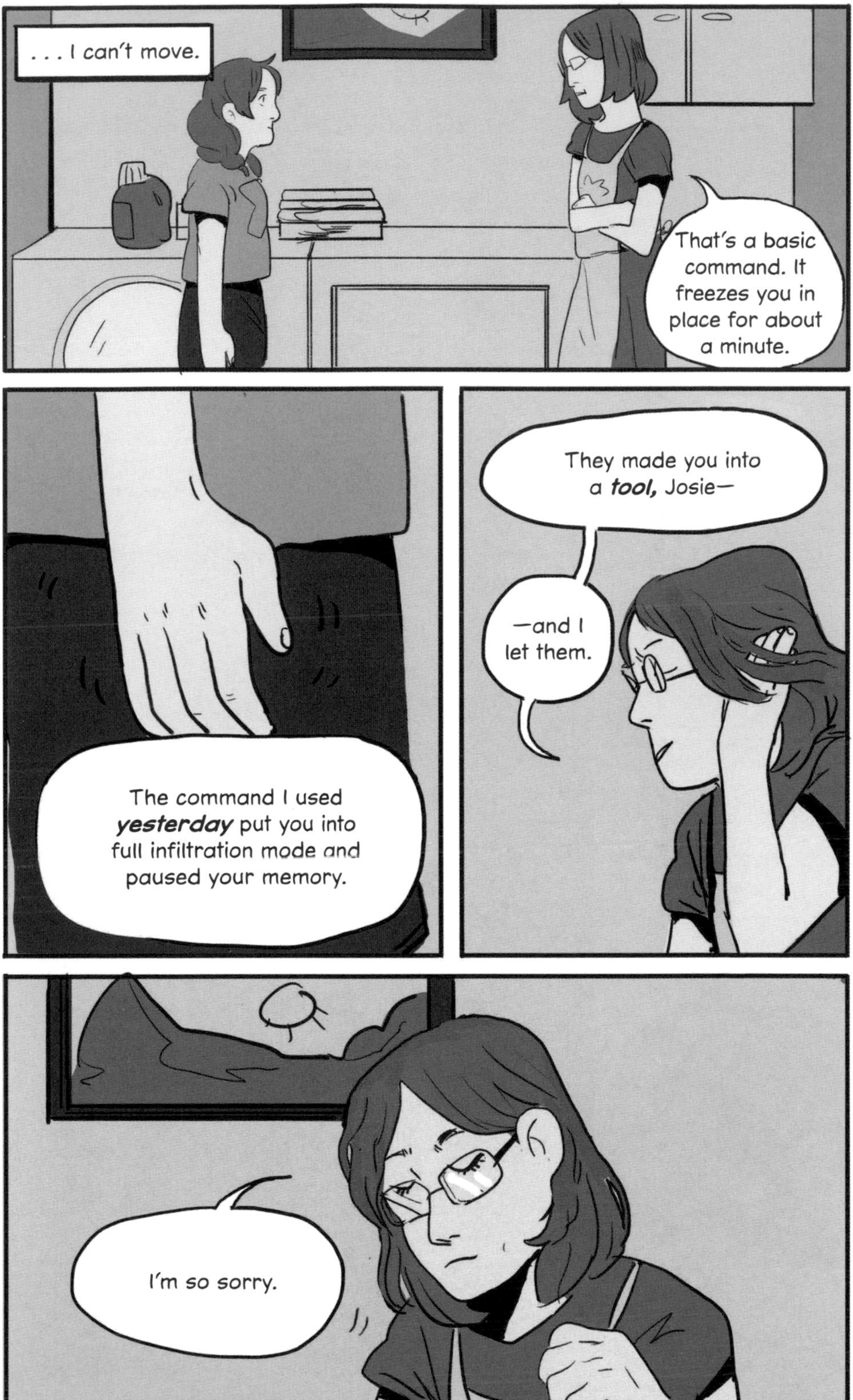
. . . I can't move.
That's a basic command. It freezes you in place for about a minute.
The command I used *yesterday* put you into full infiltration mode and paused your memory.
They made you into a *tool,* Josie—
—and I let them.
I'm so sorry.

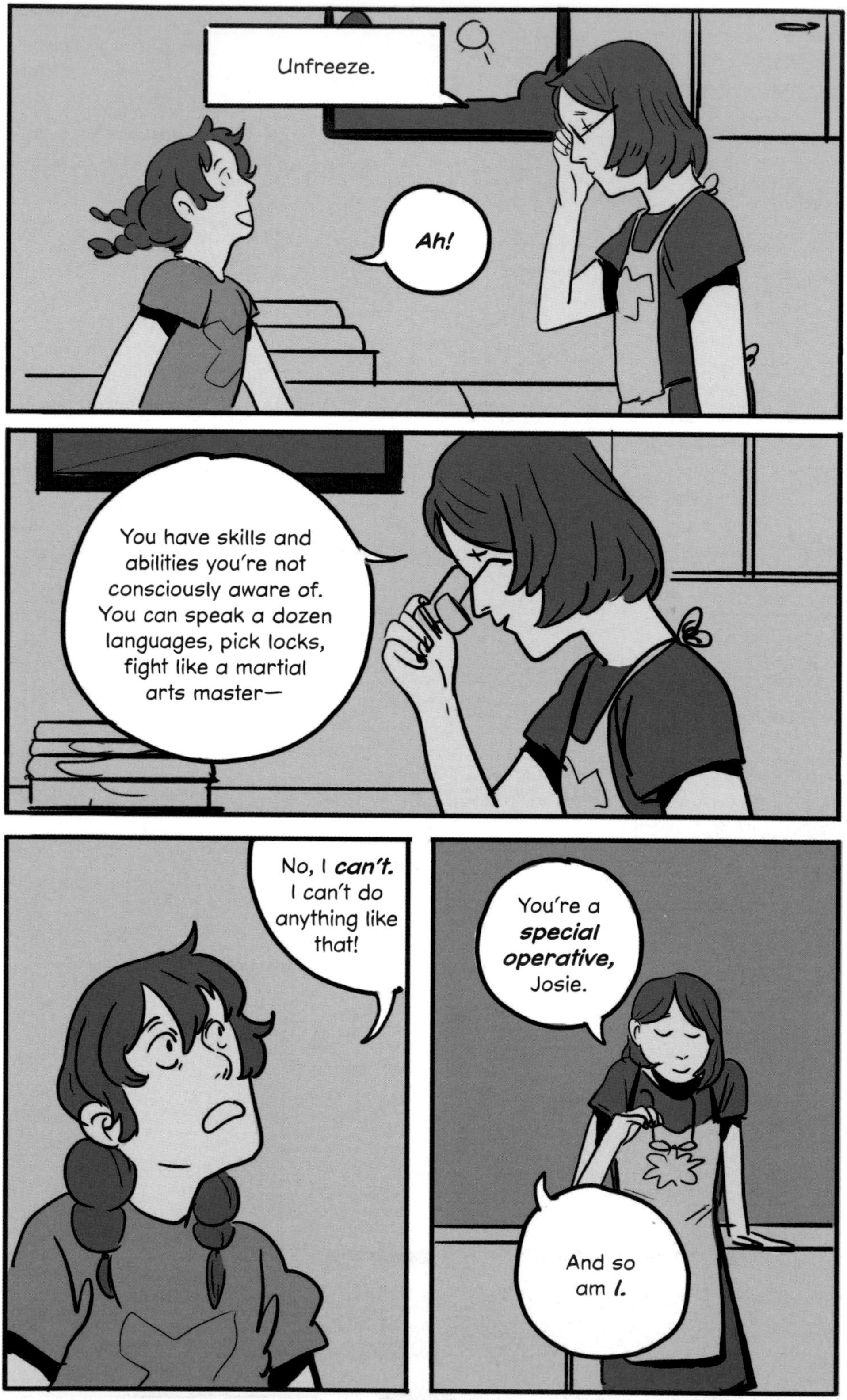
Unfreeze.
Ah!
You have skills and abilities you're not consciously aware of. You can speak a dozen languages, pick locks, fight like a martial arts master—
No, I *can't.* I can't do anything like that!
You're a ***special operative,*** Josie.
And so am *I.*

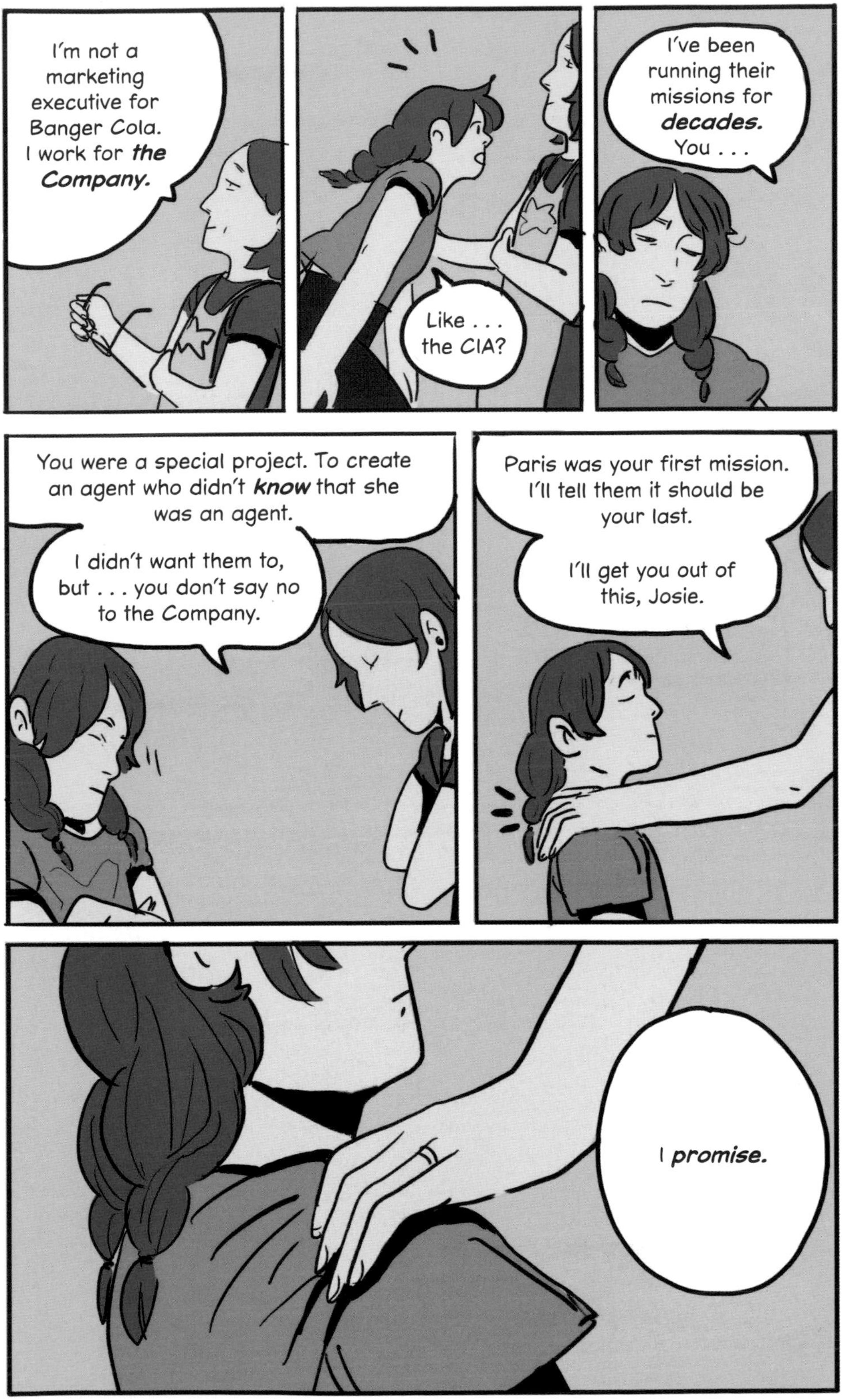
I'm not a marketing executive for Banger Cola. I work for ***the Company.***
Like . . . the CIA?
I've been running their missions for ***decades.*** You . . .
You were a special project. To create an agent who didn't ***know*** that she was an agent.
I didn't want them to, but . . . you don't say no to the Company.
Paris was your first mission. I'll tell them it should be your last.
I'll get you out of this, Josie.
I ***promise.***

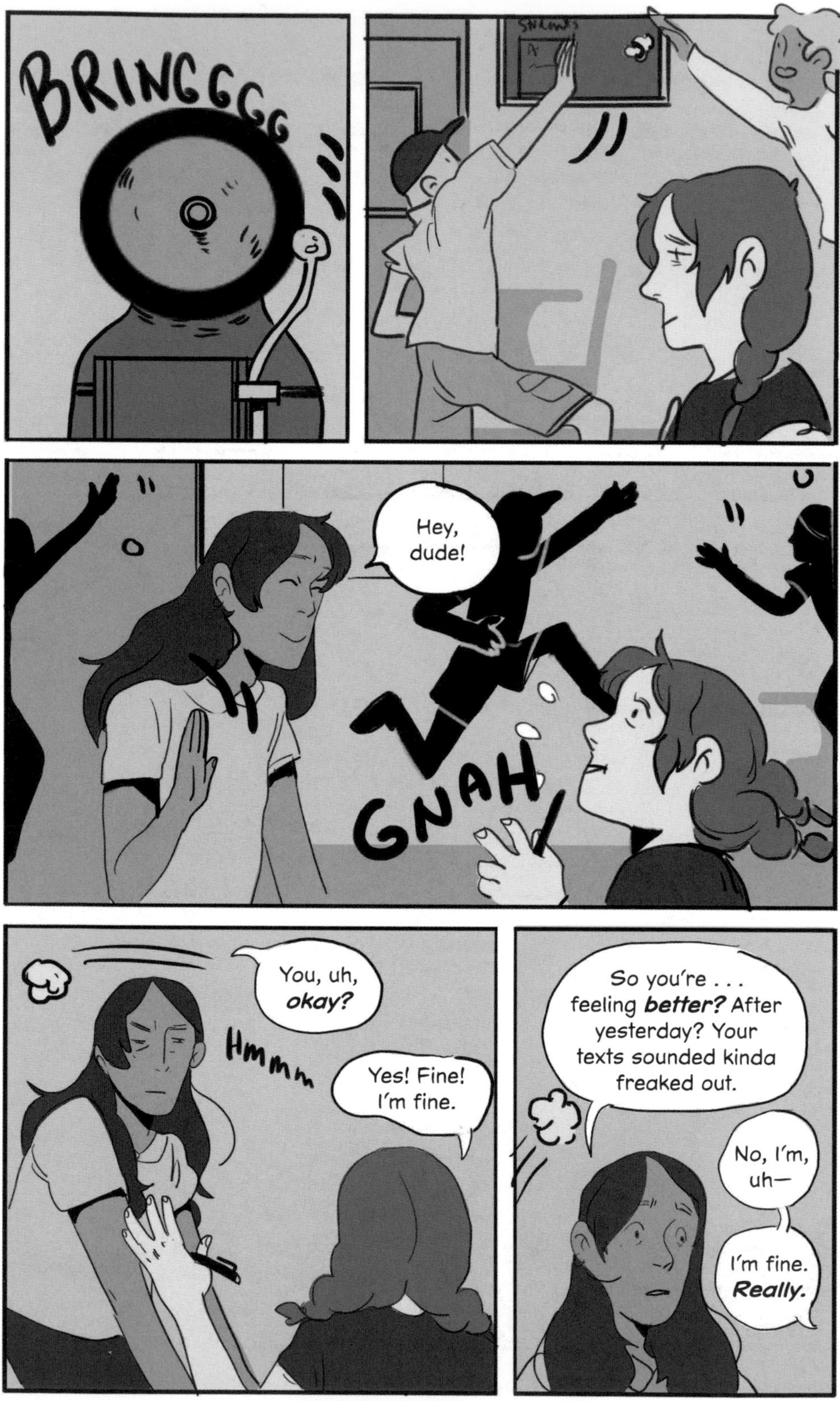
BRINGGGG
Hey, dude!
GNAH
You, uh, *okay?*
Hmmm
Yes! Fine! I'm fine.
So you're . . . feeling **better?** After yesterday? Your texts sounded kinda freaked out.
No, I'm, uh—
I'm fine. ***Really.***

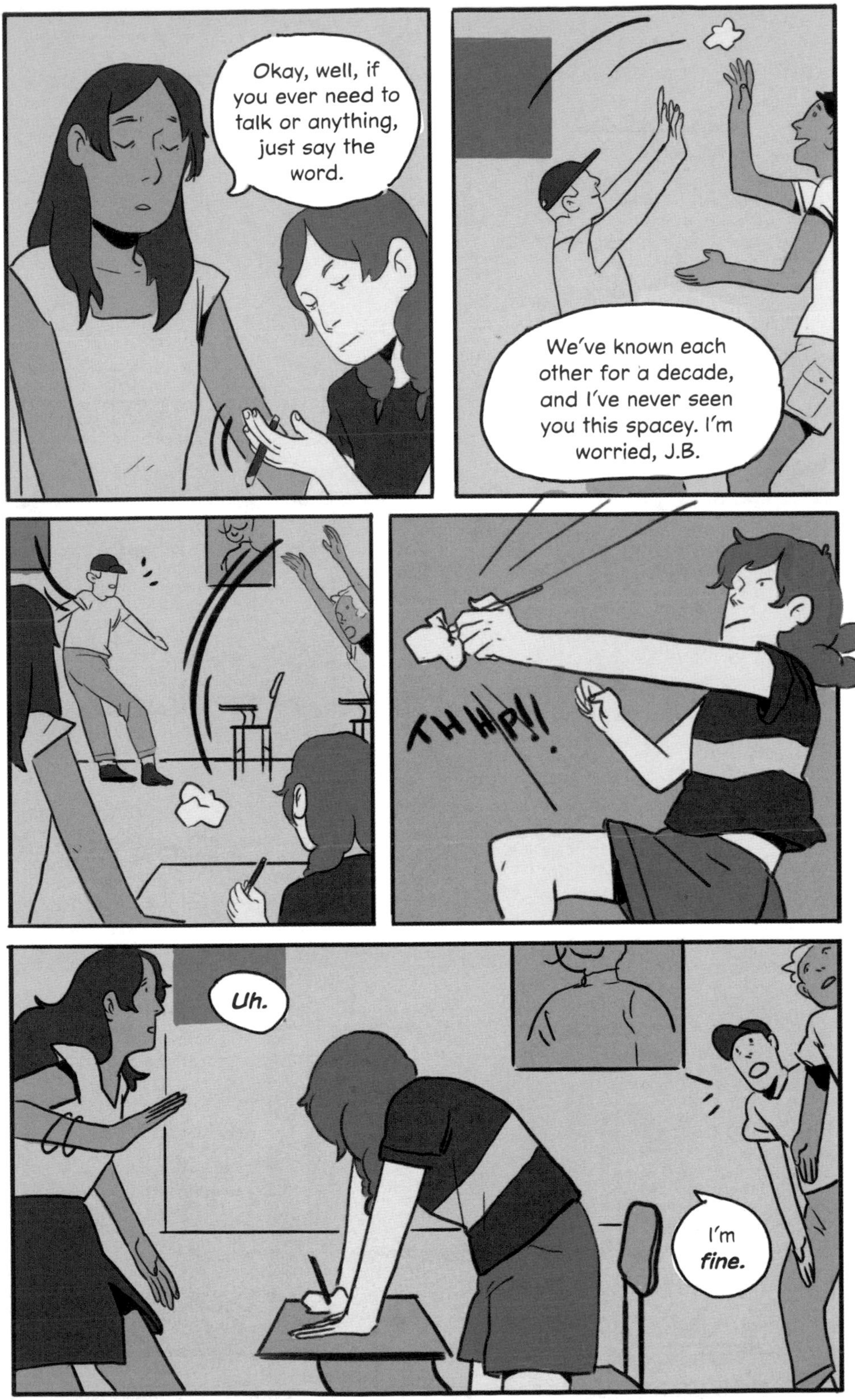
Okay, well, if you ever need to talk or anything, just say the word.
We've known each other for a decade, and I've never seen you this spacey. I'm worried, J.B.
THHP!!
Uh.
I'm fine.

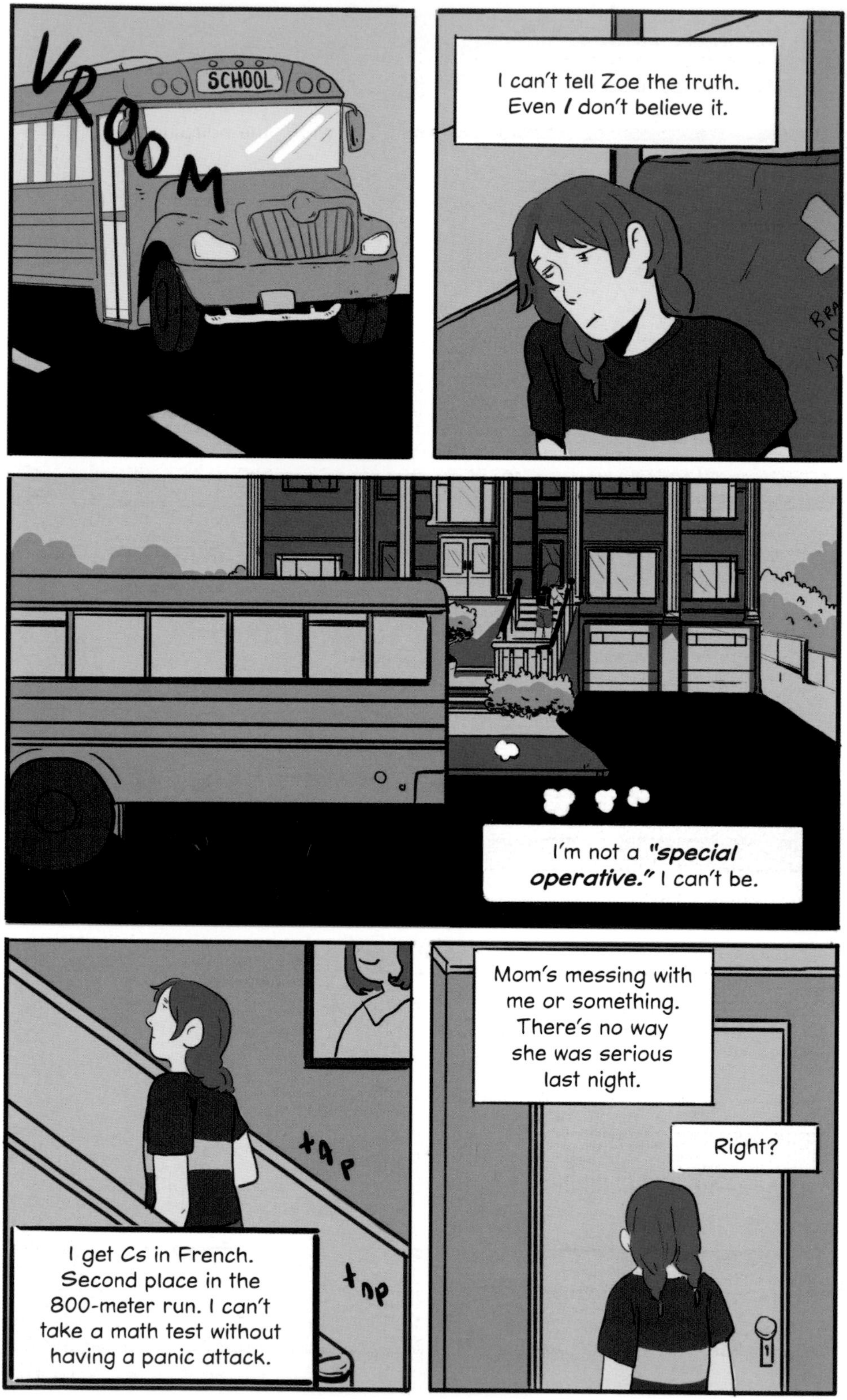
VROOM
SCHOOL
I can't tell Zoe the truth. Even *I* don't believe it.
I'm not a ***"special operative."*** I can't be.
I get Cs in French. Second place in the 800-meter run. I can't take a math test without having a panic attack.
tap
tap
Mom's messing with me or something. There's no way she was serious last night.
Right?

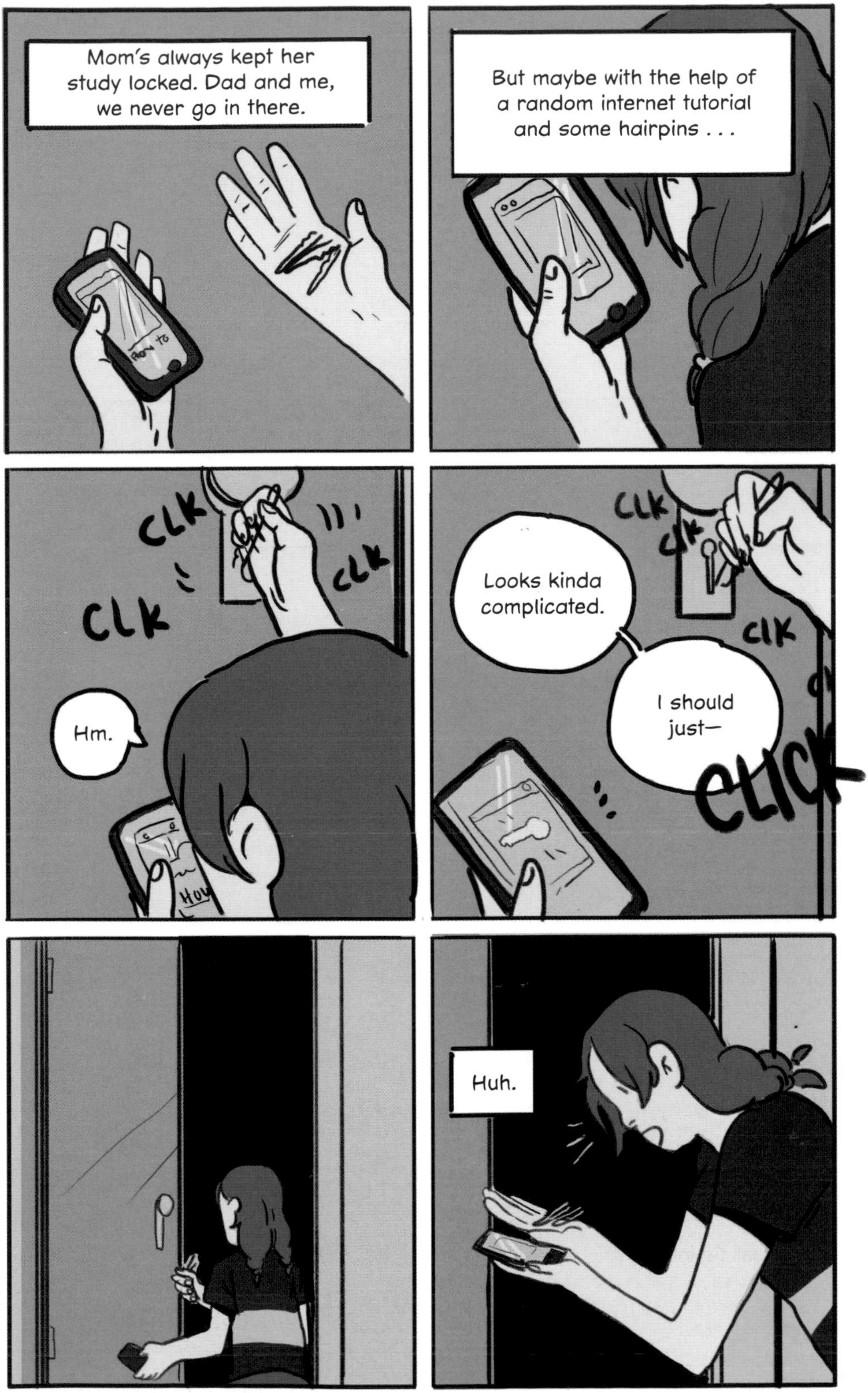

Mom's always kept her study locked. Dad and me, we never go in there.
But maybe with the help of a random internet tutorial and some hairpins . . .
CLK
CLK
CLK
Hm.
CLK
Looks kinda complicated.
CLK
I should just—
CLICK
Huh.

Dang. Locked.

Let's see if my magic spy fingers know how to **hack!**

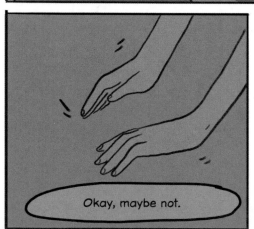

Okay, maybe not.

But if that's a backup drive, maybe I can plug it into another computer . . .

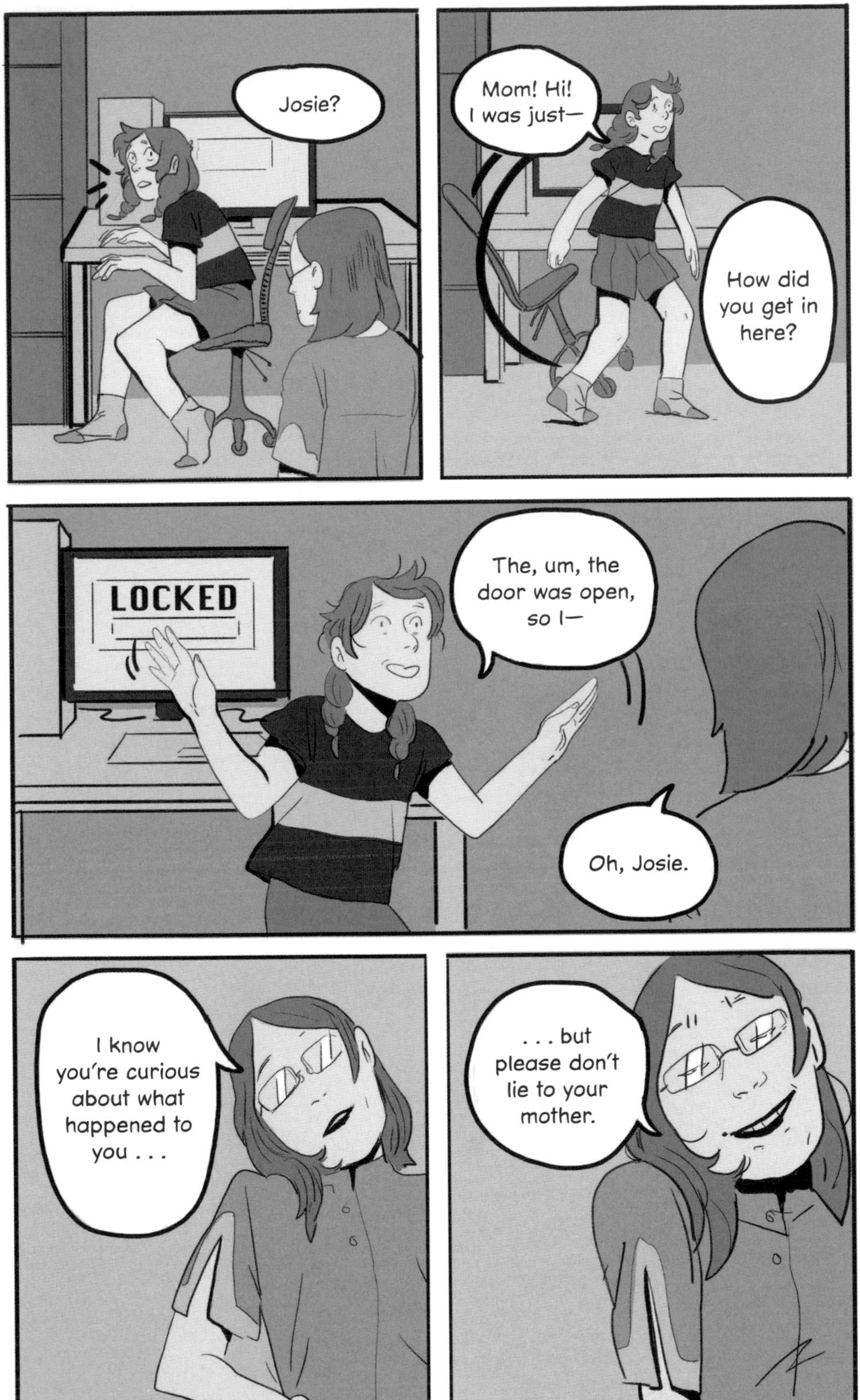
Josie?
Mom! Hi! I was just—
How did you get in here?
LOCKED
The, um, the door was open, so I—
Oh, Josie.
I know you're curious about what happened to you . . .
. . . but please don't lie to your mother.

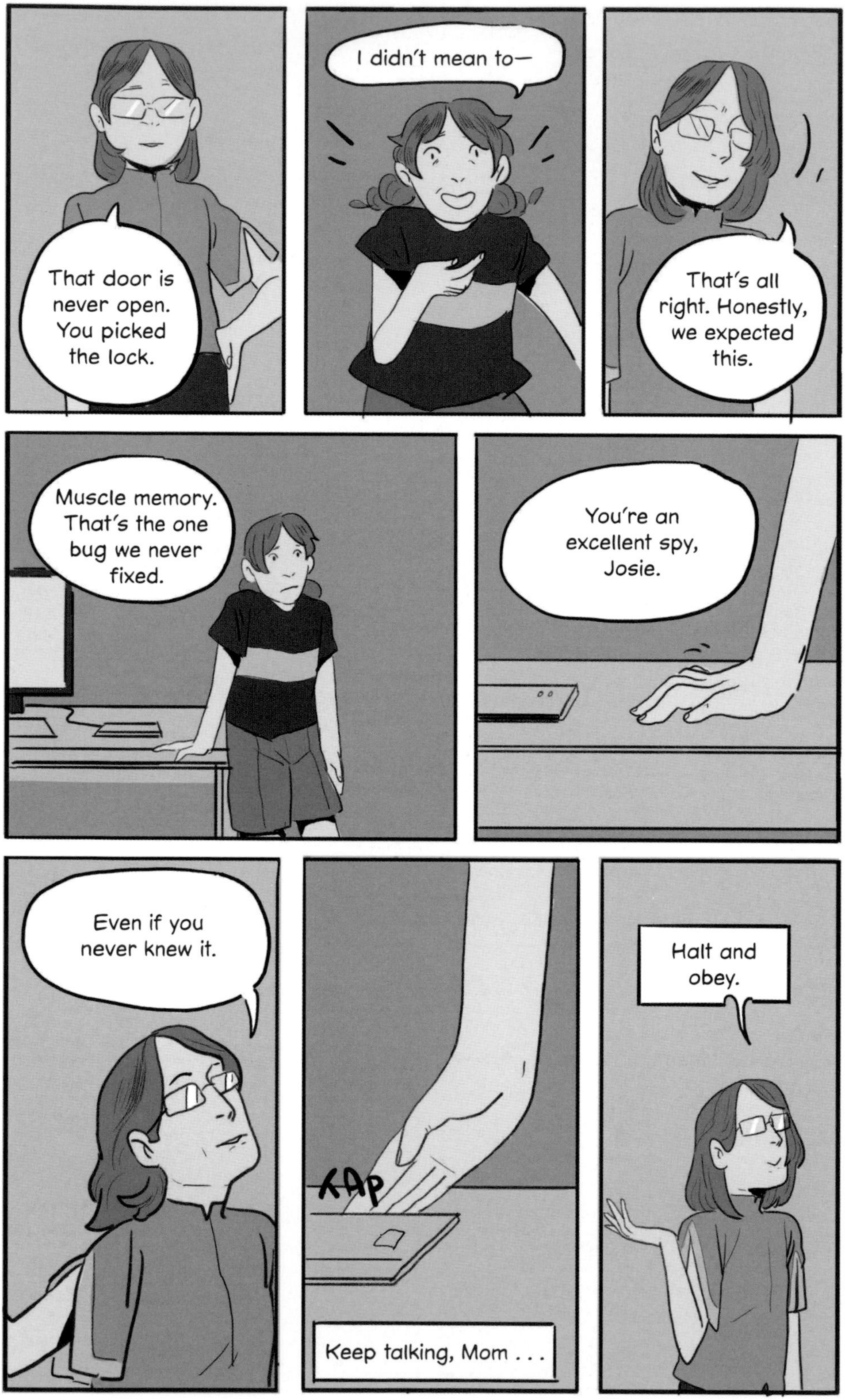
That door is never open. You picked the lock.
I didn't mean to—
That's all right. Honestly, we expected this.
Muscle memory. That's the one bug we never fixed.
You're an excellent spy, Josie.
Even if you never knew it.
KAP
Keep talking, Mom . . .
Halt and obey.

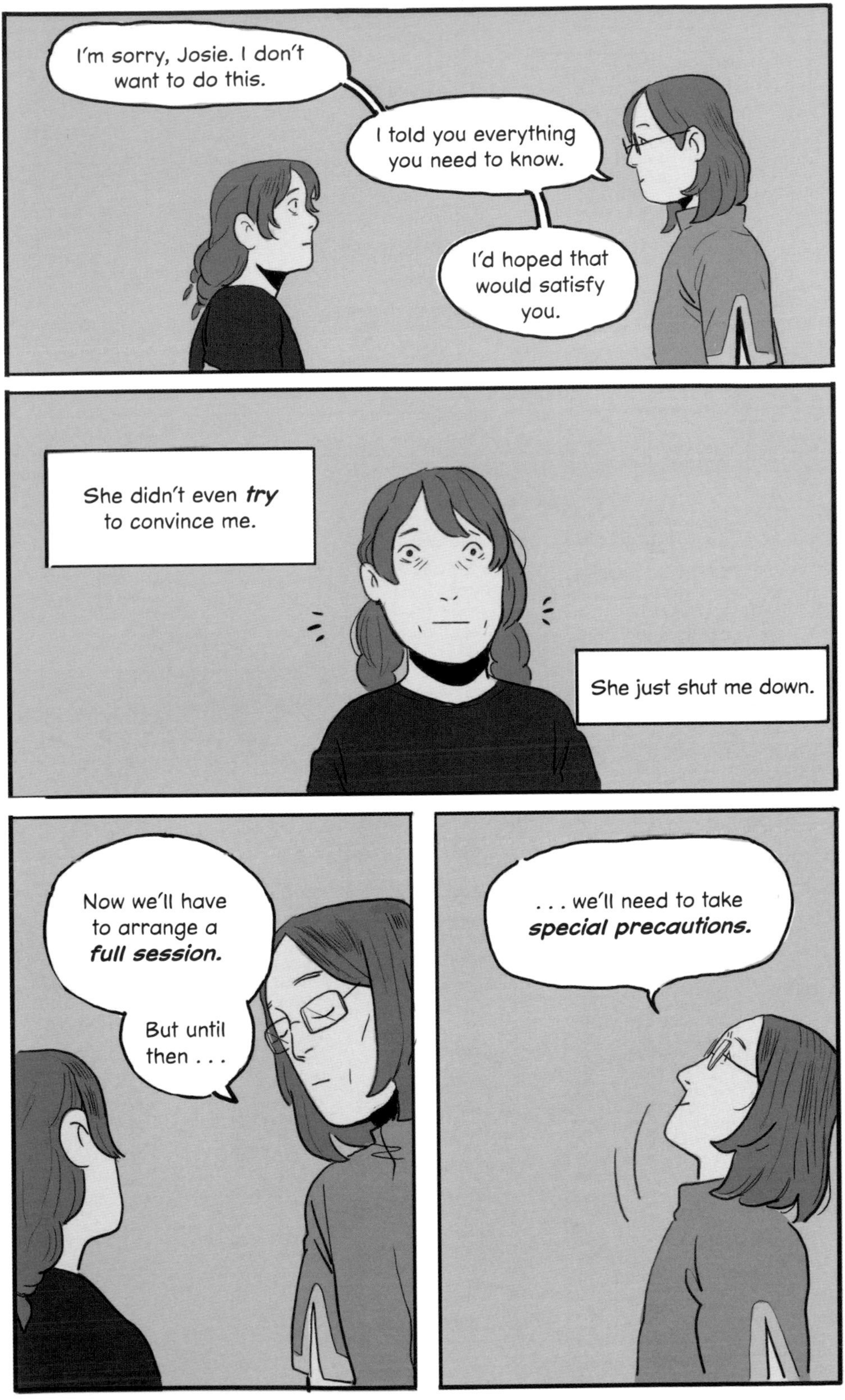
I'm sorry, Josie. I don't want to do this.
I told you everything you need to know.
I'd hoped that would satisfy you.
She didn't even *try* to convince me.
She just shut me down.
Now we'll have to arrange a ***full session.***
But until then . . .
. . . we'll need to take ***special precautions.***

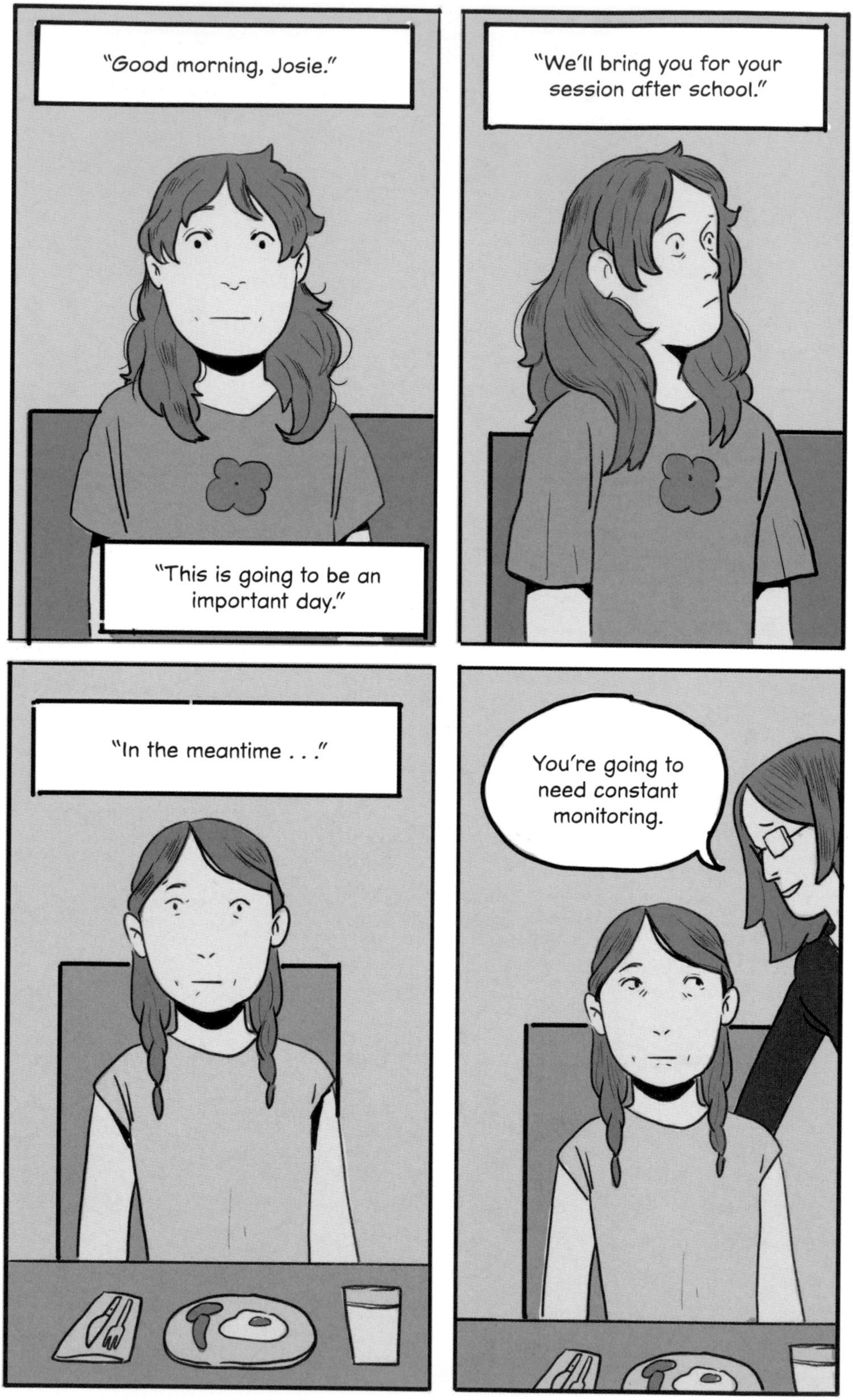
"Good morning, Josie."
"This is going to be an important day."
"We'll bring you for your session after school."
"In the meantime . . ."
You're going to need constant monitoring.

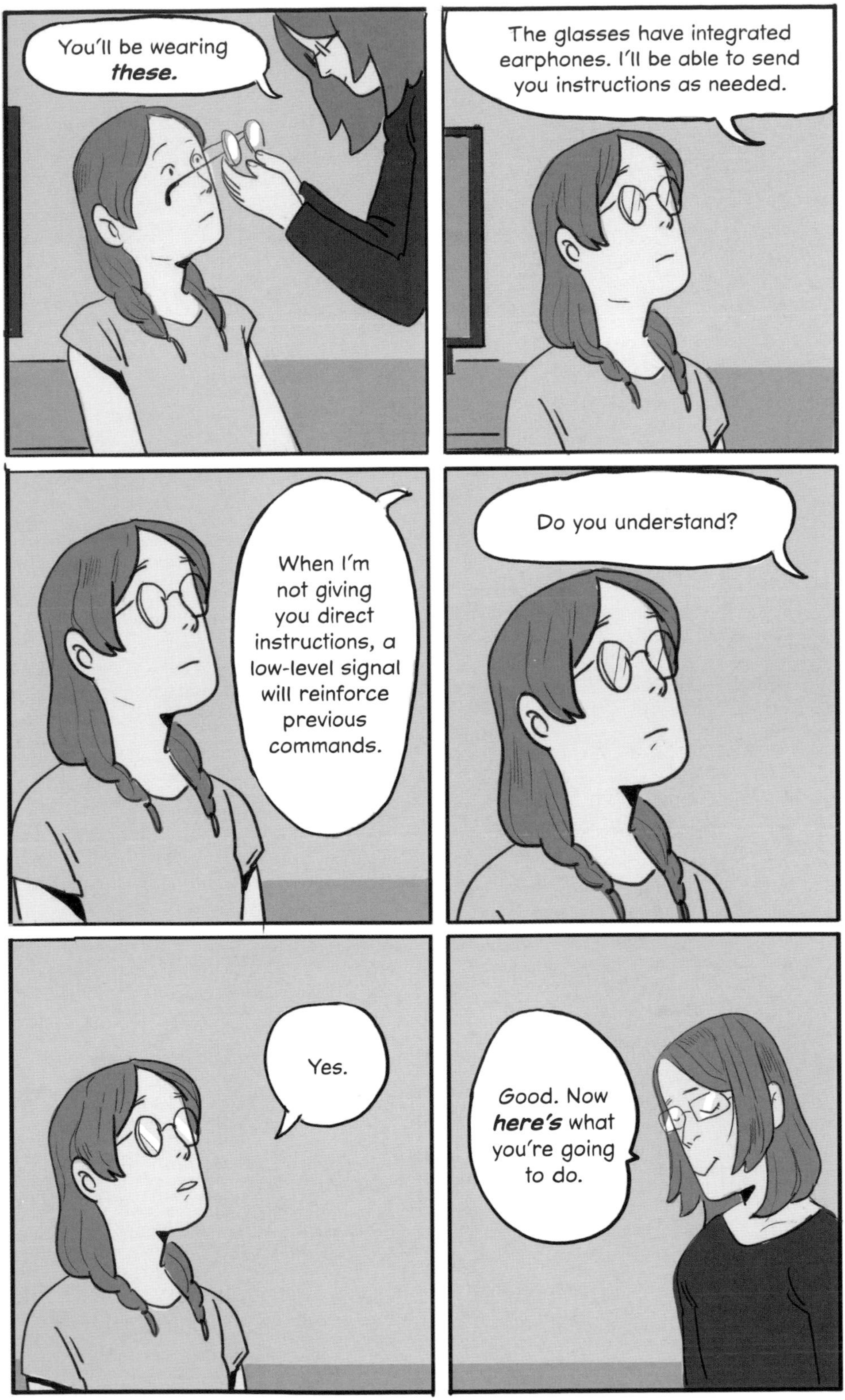
You'll be wearing *these.*
The glasses have integrated earphones. I'll be able to send you instructions as needed.
When I'm not giving you direct instructions, a low-level signal will reinforce previous commands.
Do you understand?
Yes.
Good. Now *here's* what you're going to do.

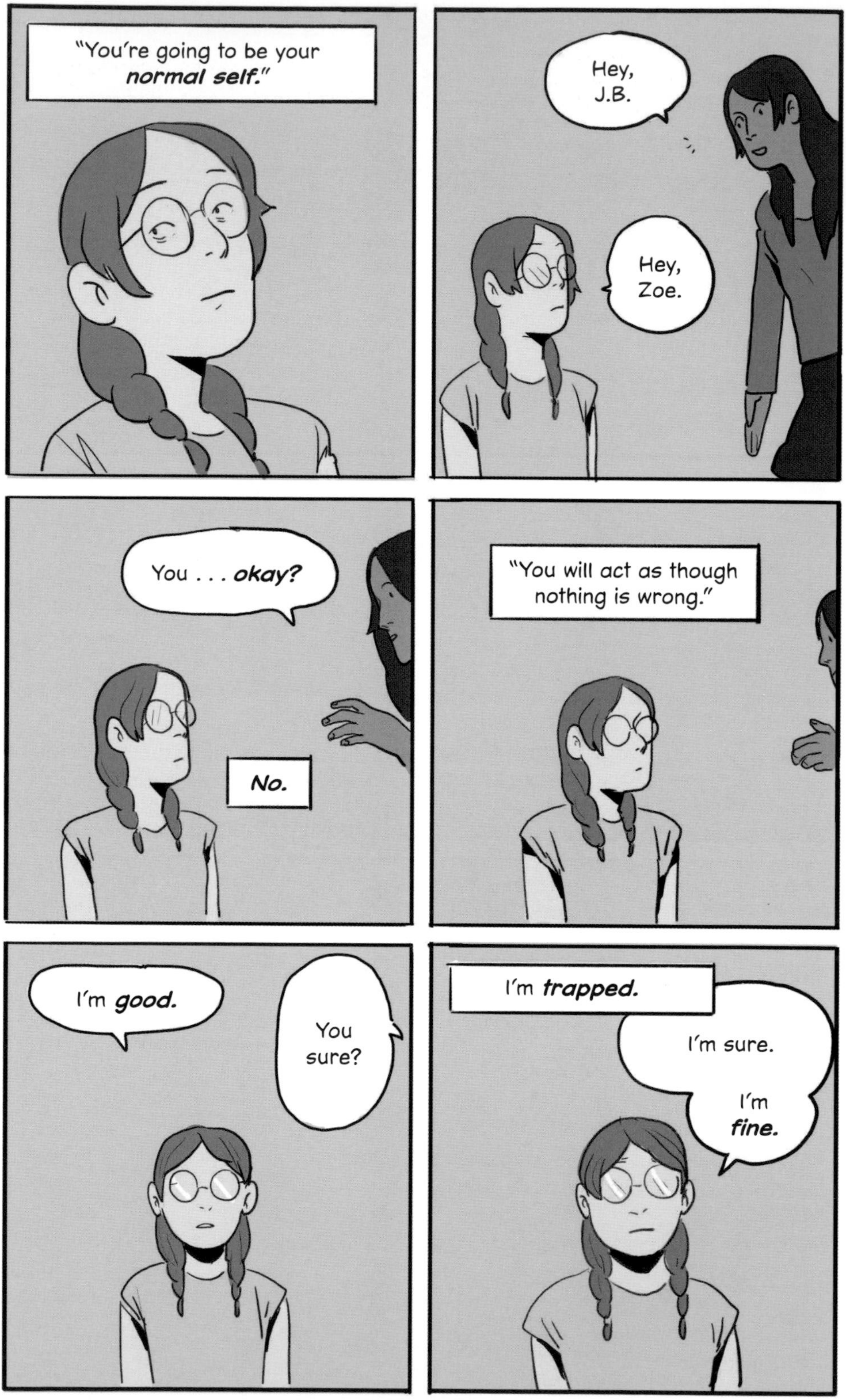
"You're going to be your **normal self.**"
Hey, J.B.
Hey, Zoe.
You . . . **okay?**
No.
"You will act as though nothing is wrong."
I'm **good.**
You sure?
I'm **trapped.**
I'm sure.
I'm **fine.**

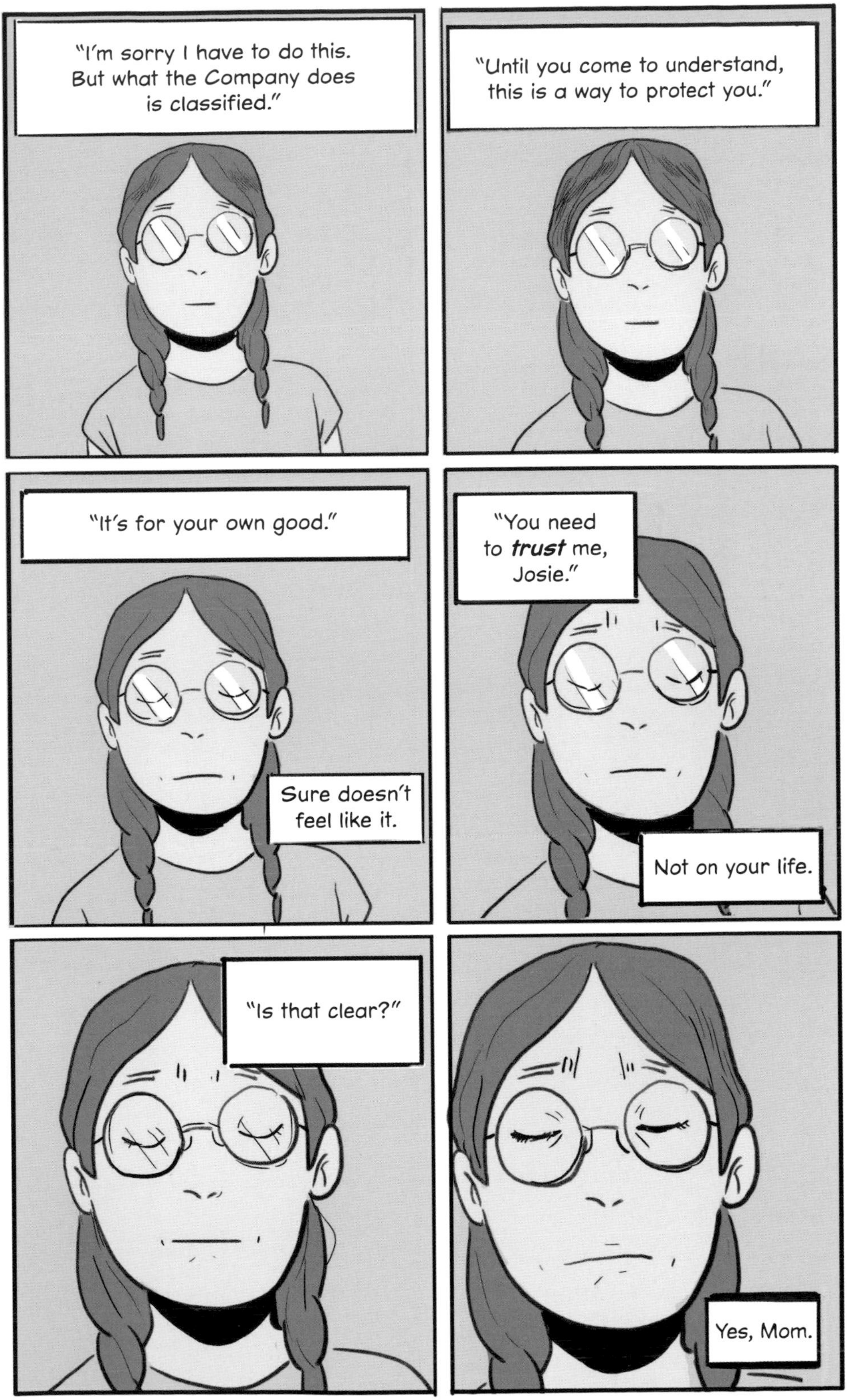
"I'm sorry I have to do this. But what the Company does is classified."
"Until you come to understand, this is a way to protect you."
"It's for your own good."
Sure doesn't feel like it.
"You need to **trust** me, Josie."
Not on your life.
"Is that clear?"
Yes, Mom.

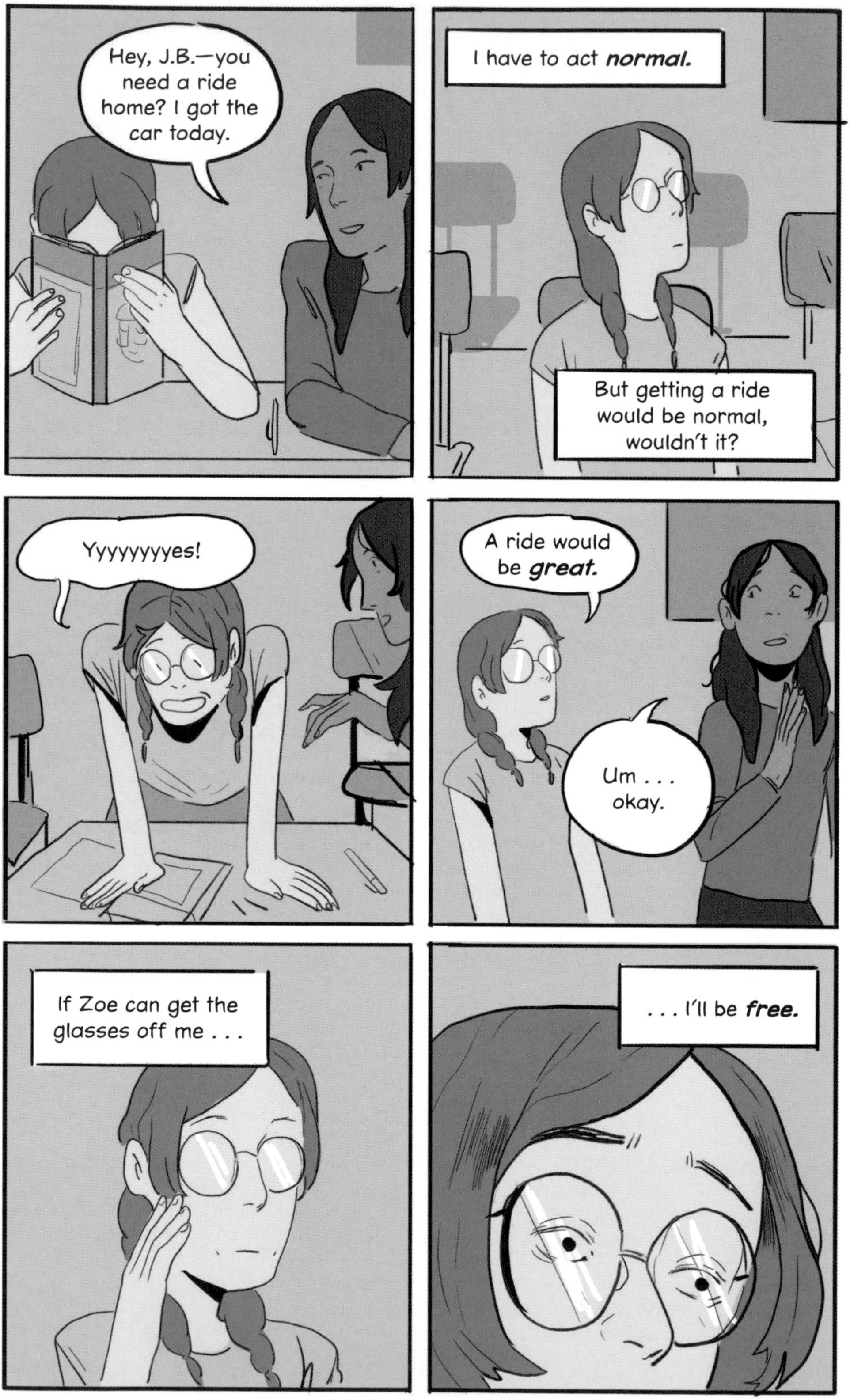
Hey, J.B.—you need a ride home? I got the car today.
I have to act ***normal.***
But getting a ride would be normal, wouldn't it?
Yyyyyyyyes!
A ride would be ***great.***
Um . . . okay.
If Zoe can get the glasses off me . . .
. . . I'll be ***free.***

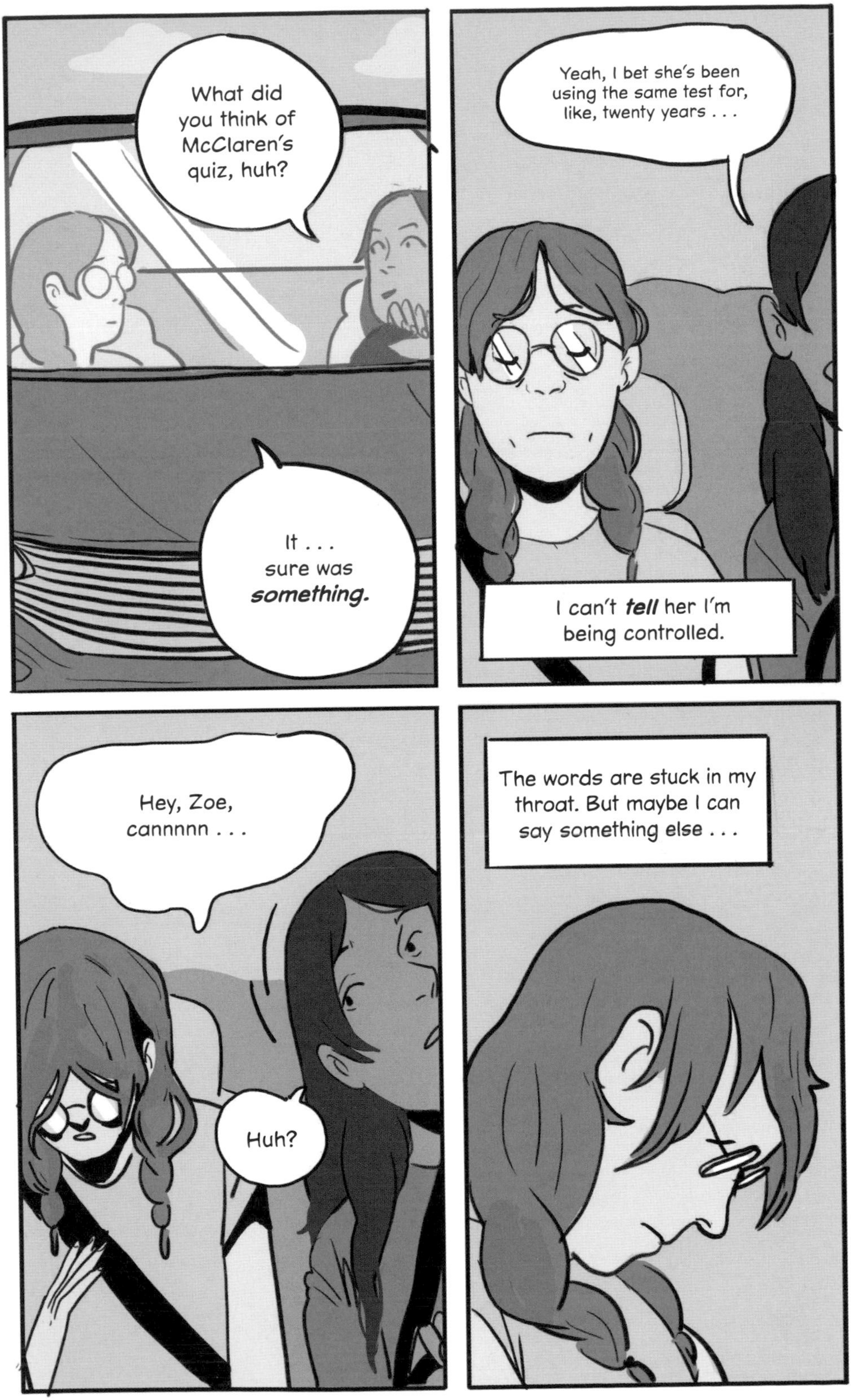
What did you think of McClaren's quiz, huh?
It . . . sure was *something.*
Yeah, I bet she's been using the same test for, like, twenty years . . .
I can't *tell* her I'm being controlled.
Hey, Zoe, cannnnn . . .
Huh?
The words are stuck in my throat. But maybe I can say something else . . .

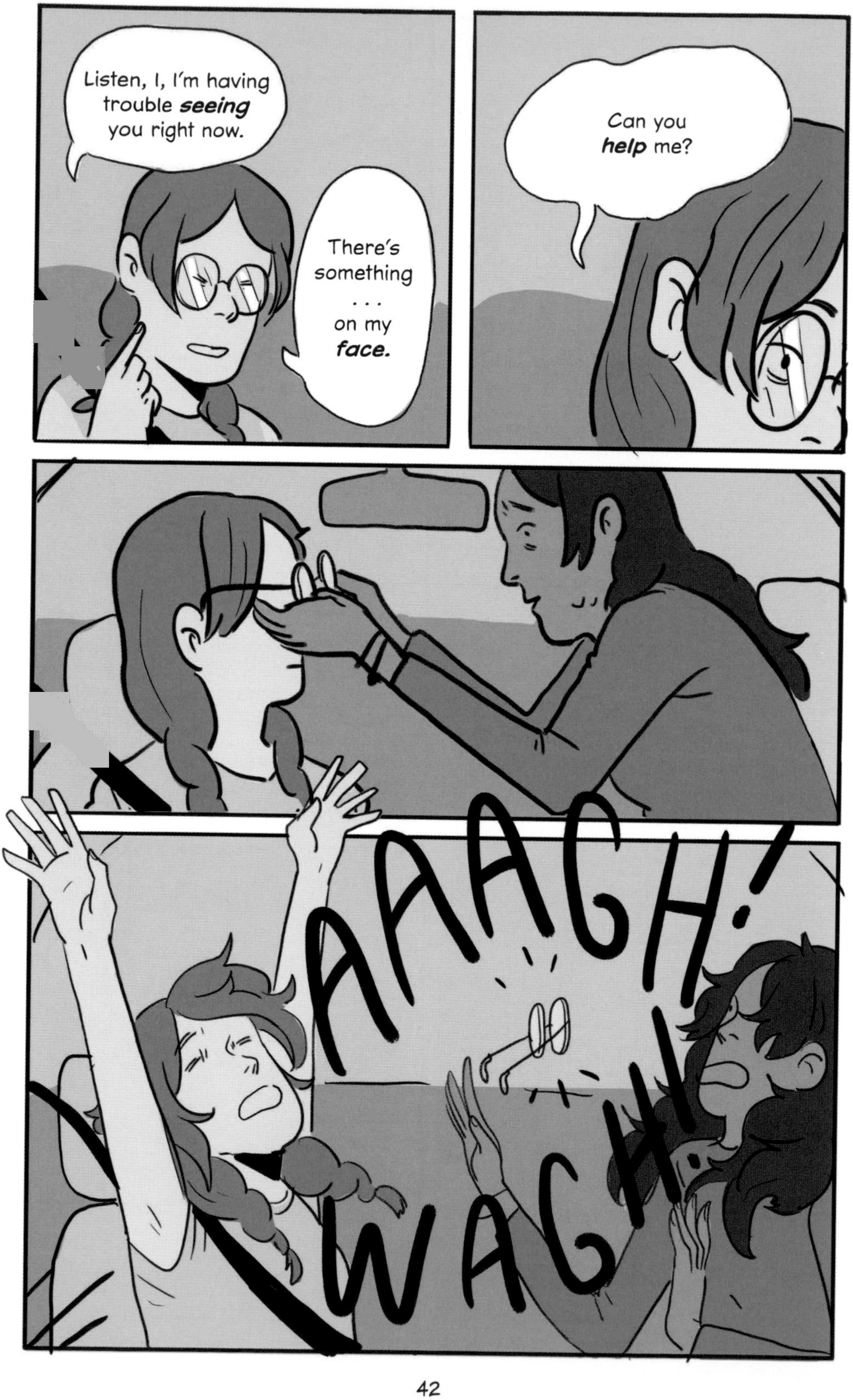
Listen, I, I'm having trouble ***seeing*** you right now.
There's something . . . on my ***face.***
Can you ***help*** me?
AAAGH!
WAGH!

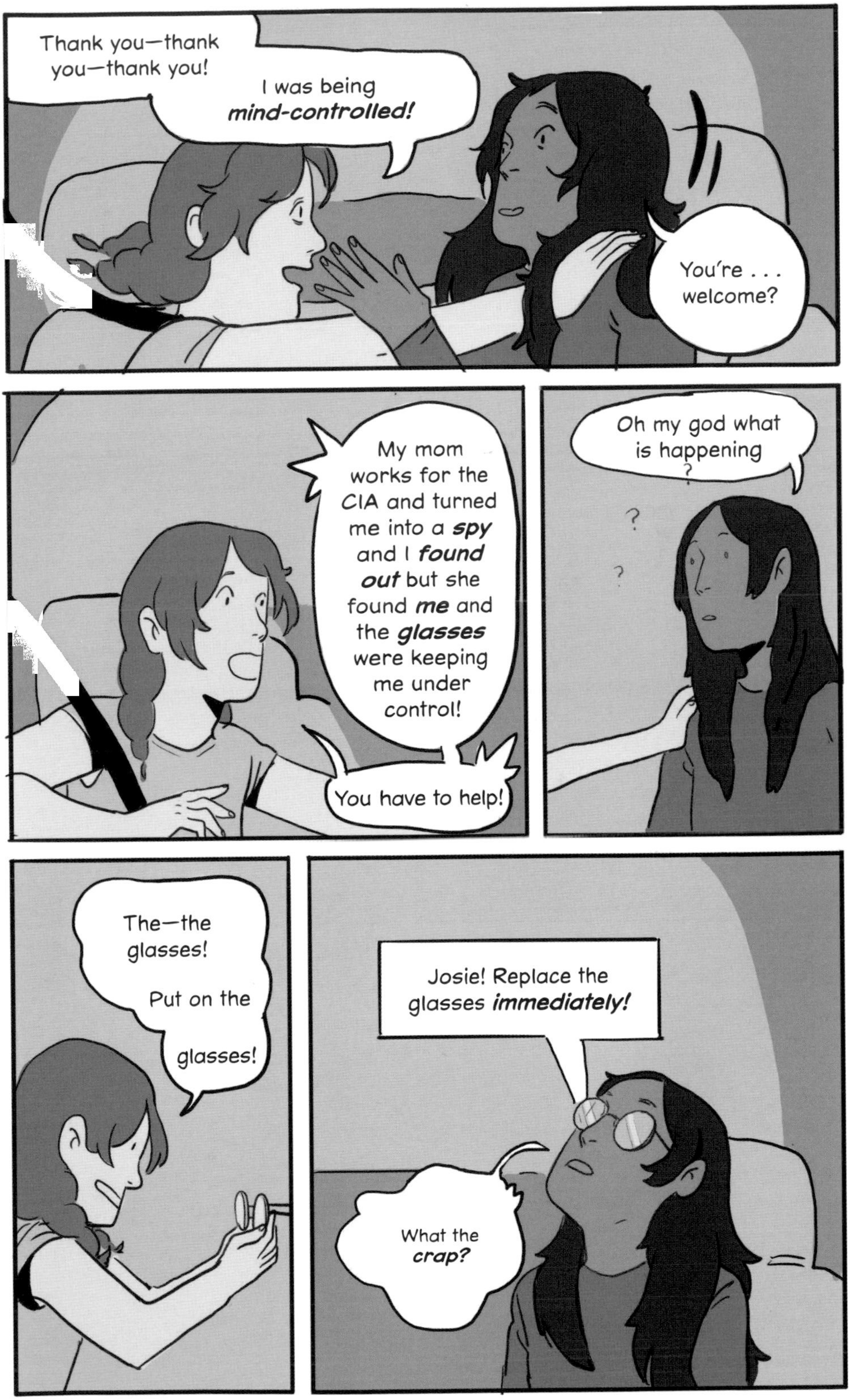
Thank you—thank you—thank you!
I was being ***mind-controlled!***
You're . . . welcome?
My mom works for the CIA and turned me into a ***spy*** and I ***found out*** but she found ***me*** and the ***glasses*** were keeping me under control!
You have to help!
Oh my god what is happening
?
?
?
The—the glasses!
Put on the
glasses!
Josie! Replace the glasses ***immediately!***
What the ***crap?***

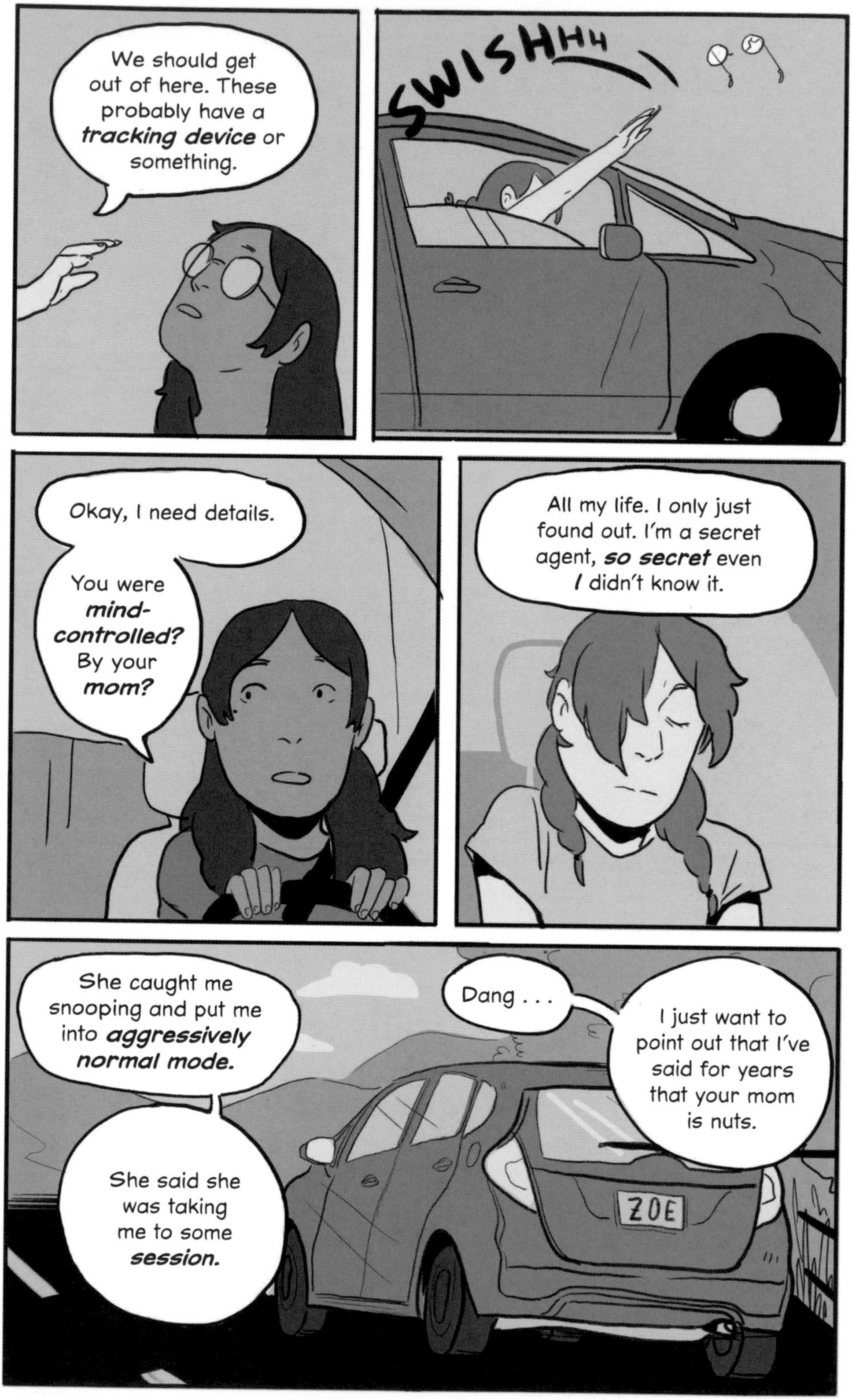
We should get out of here. These probably have a *tracking device* or something.
SWISHHH
Okay, I need details.
You were *mind-controlled?* By your *mom?*
All my life. I only just found out. I'm a secret agent, *so secret* even *I* didn't know it.
She caught me snooping and put me into *aggressively normal mode.*
She said she was taking me to some *session.*
Dang . . .
I just want to point out that I've said for years that your mom is nuts.
ZOE

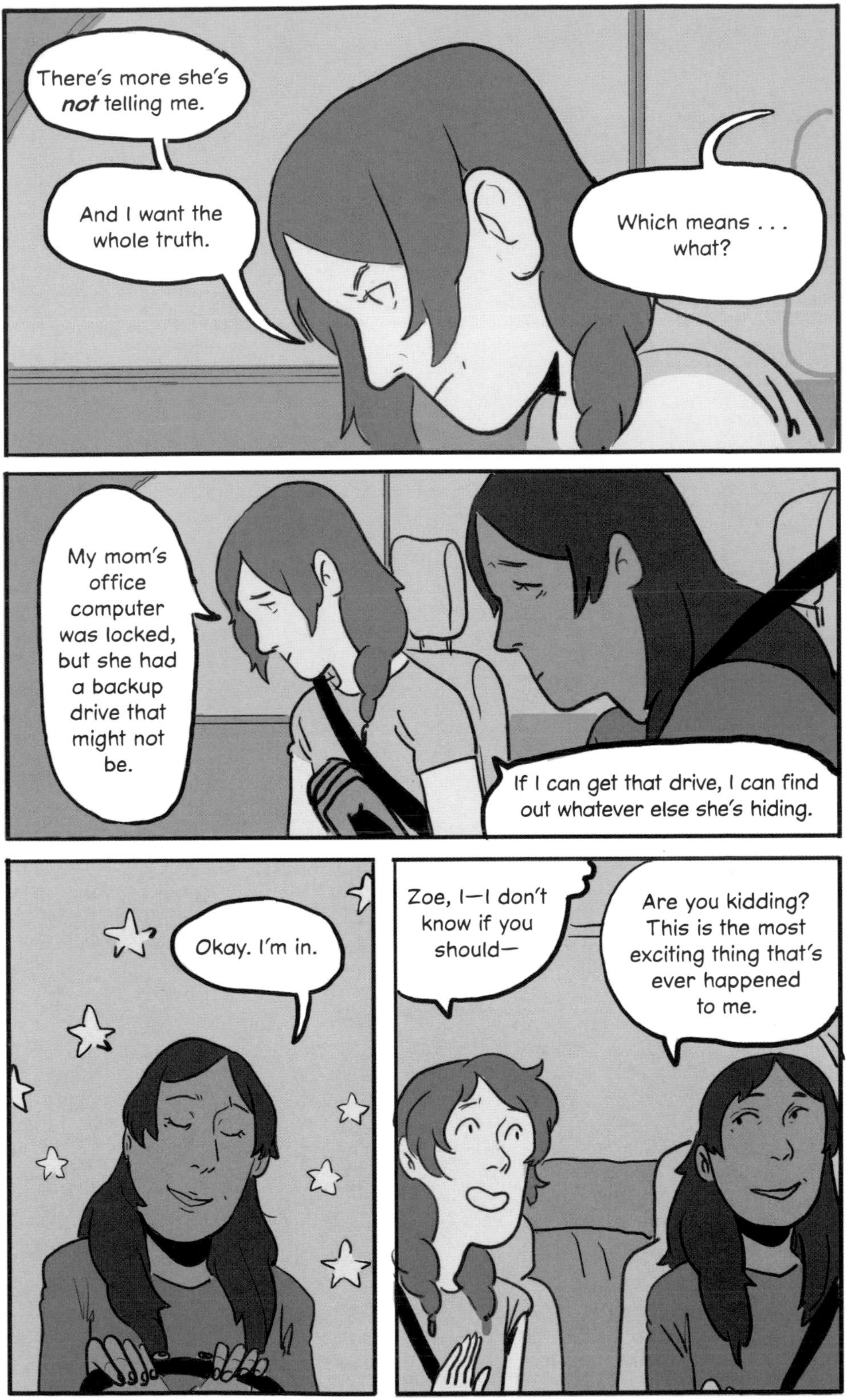
There's more she's *not* telling me.
And I want the whole truth.
Which means . . . what?
My mom's office computer was locked, but she had a backup drive that might not be.
If I can get that drive, I can find out whatever else she's hiding.
Okay. I'm in.
Zoe, I—I don't know if you should—
Are you kidding? This is the most exciting thing that's ever happened to me.

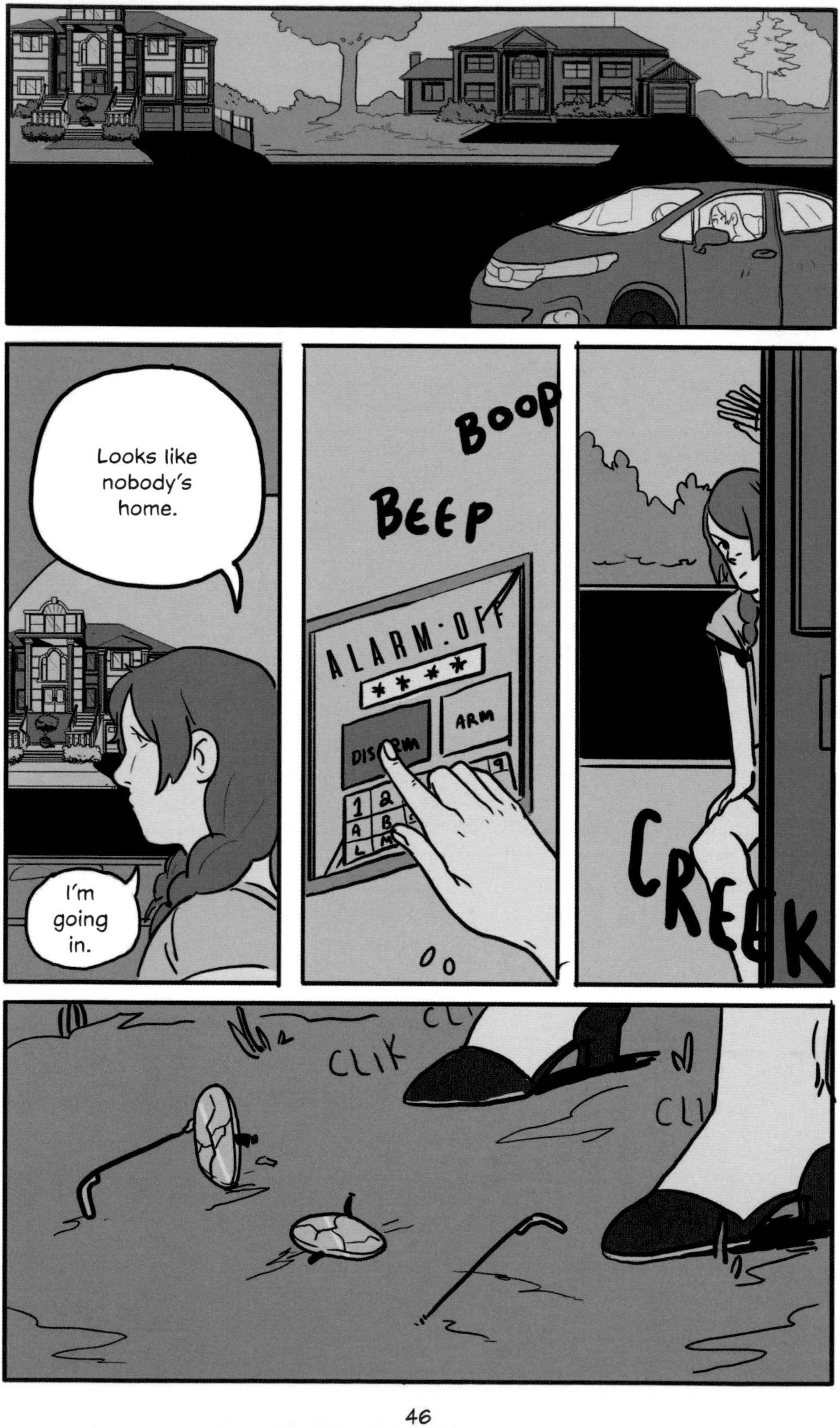
Looks like nobody's home.
I'm going in.
BOOP
BEEP
ALARM: OFF
ARM
CREEK
CLIK
CLIK
CLI

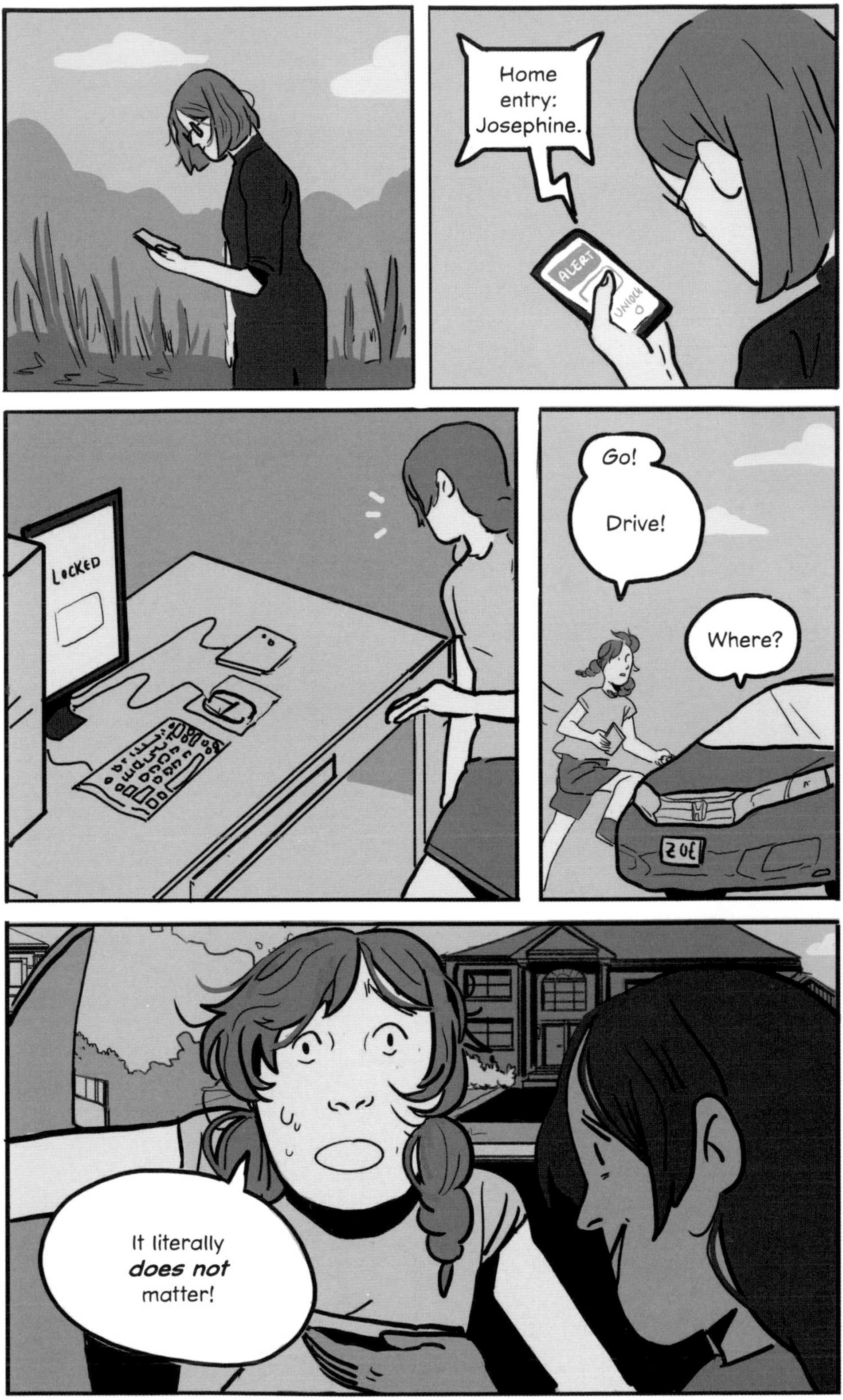
Home entry: Josephine.
ALERT
UNLOCK
LOCKED
Go! Drive!
Where?
It literally ***does not*** matter!

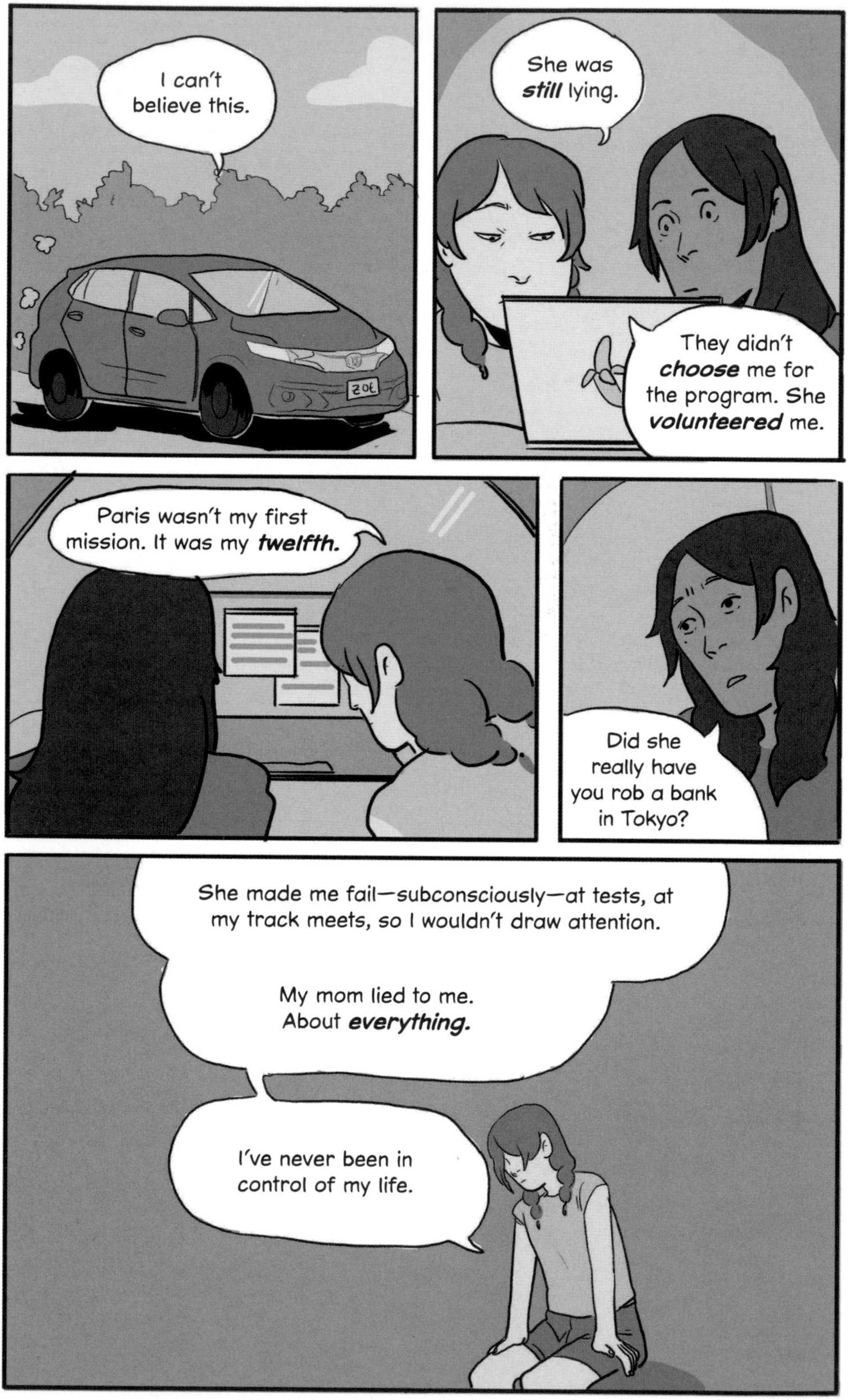
I can't believe this.
She was *still* lying.
They didn't *choose* me for the program. She *volunteered* me.
Paris wasn't my first mission. It was my *twelfth.*
Did she really have you rob a bank in Tokyo?
She made me fail—subconsciously—at tests, at my track meets, so I wouldn't draw attention.
My mom lied to me. About *everything.*
I've never been in control of my life.

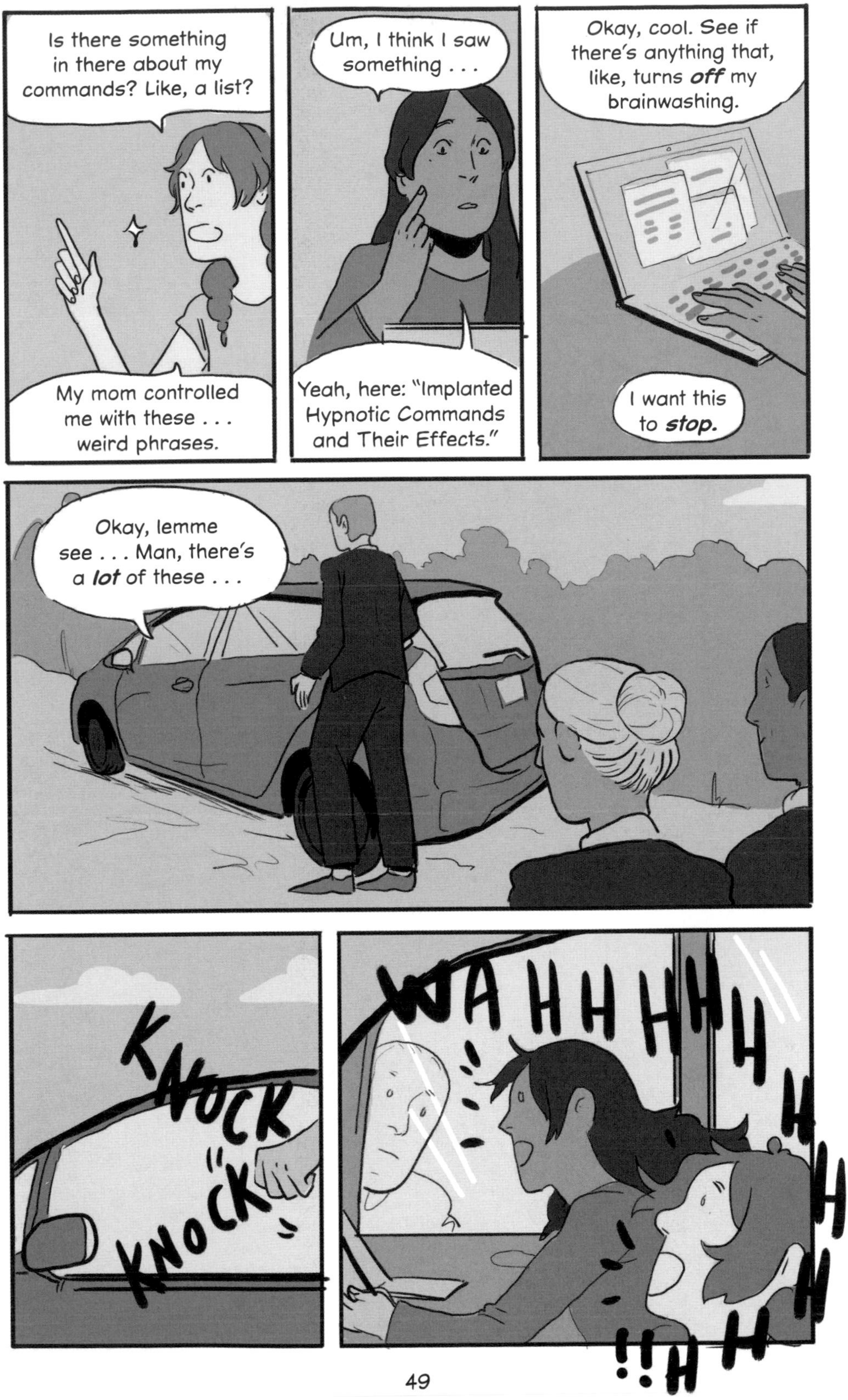

Is there something in there about my commands? Like, a list?
My mom controlled me with these . . . weird phrases.
Um, I think I saw something . . .
Yeah, here: "Implanted Hypnotic Commands and Their Effects."
Okay, cool. See if there's anything that, like, turns ***off*** my brainwashing.
I want this to ***stop.***
Okay, lemme see . . . Man, there's a ***lot*** of these . . .
KNOCK
KNOCK
WAHHHHHHHHHHHH!!

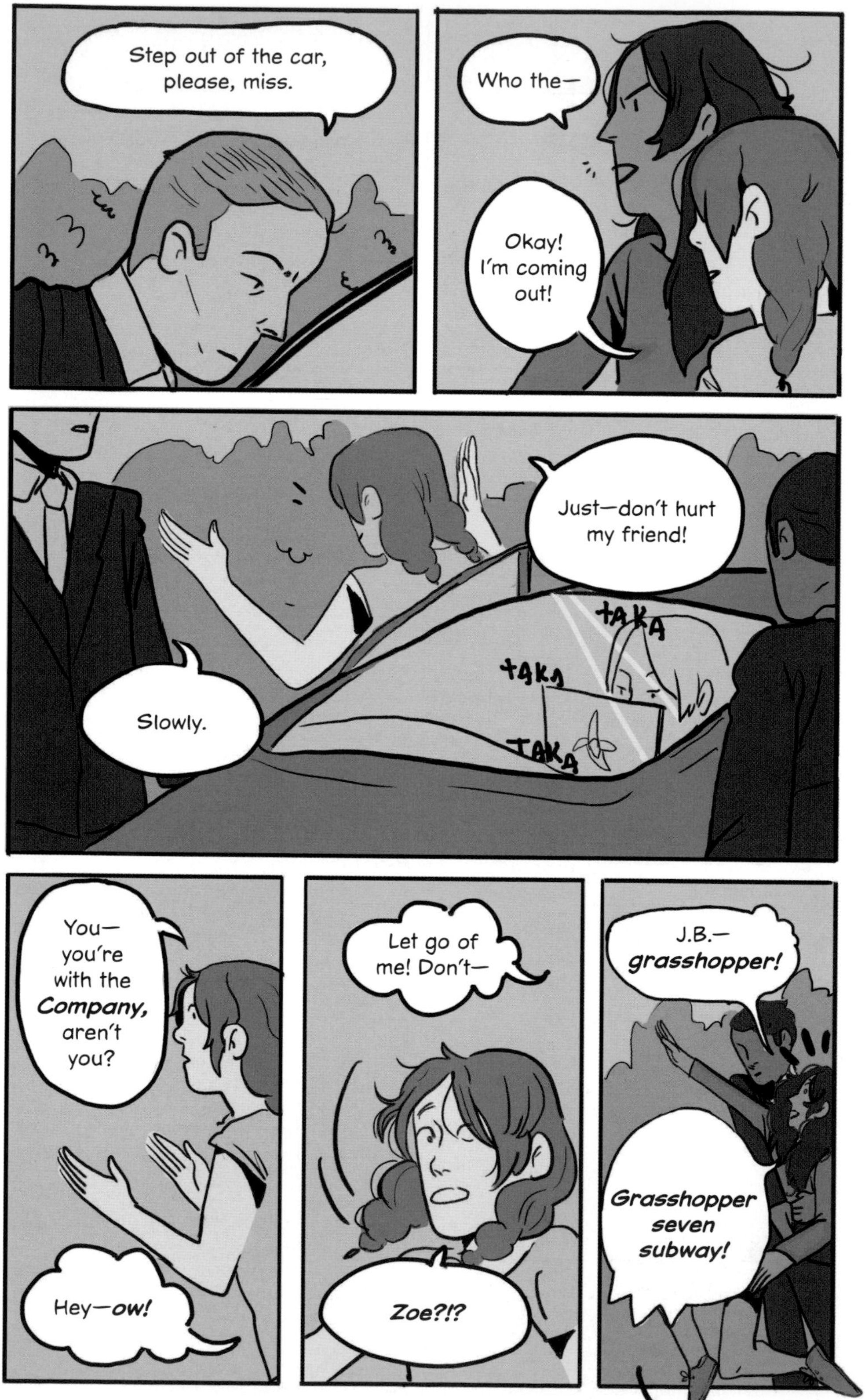
Step out of the car, please, miss.
Who the—
Okay! I'm coming out!
Just—don't hurt my friend!
TAKA
TAKA
TAKA
Slowly.
You—you're with the *Company,* aren't you?
Hey—*ow!*
Let go of me! Don't—
Zoe?!?
J.B.—*grasshopper!*
Grasshopper seven subway!

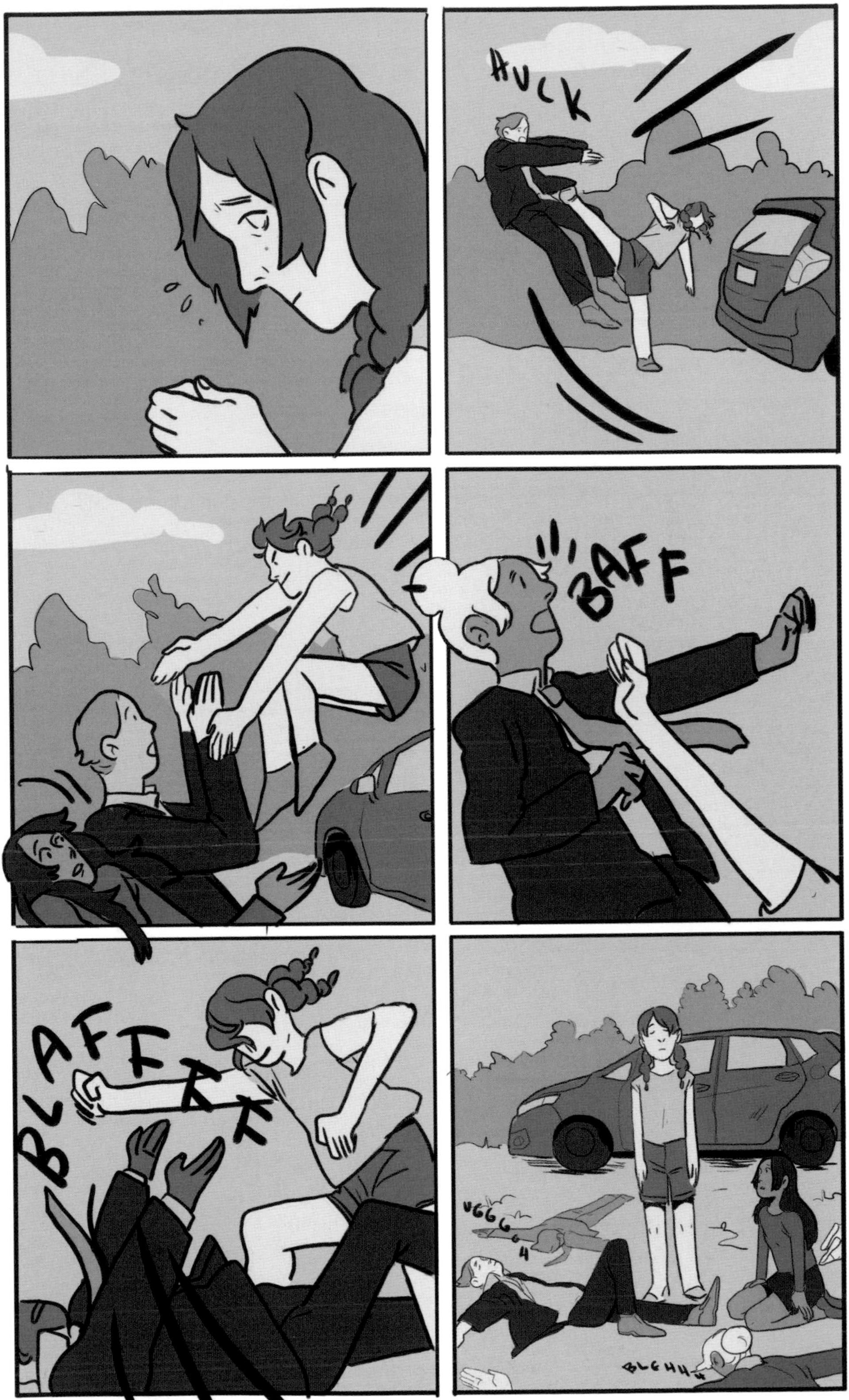
HUCK
BAFF
BLAFF
UGGGH
BLGHHH

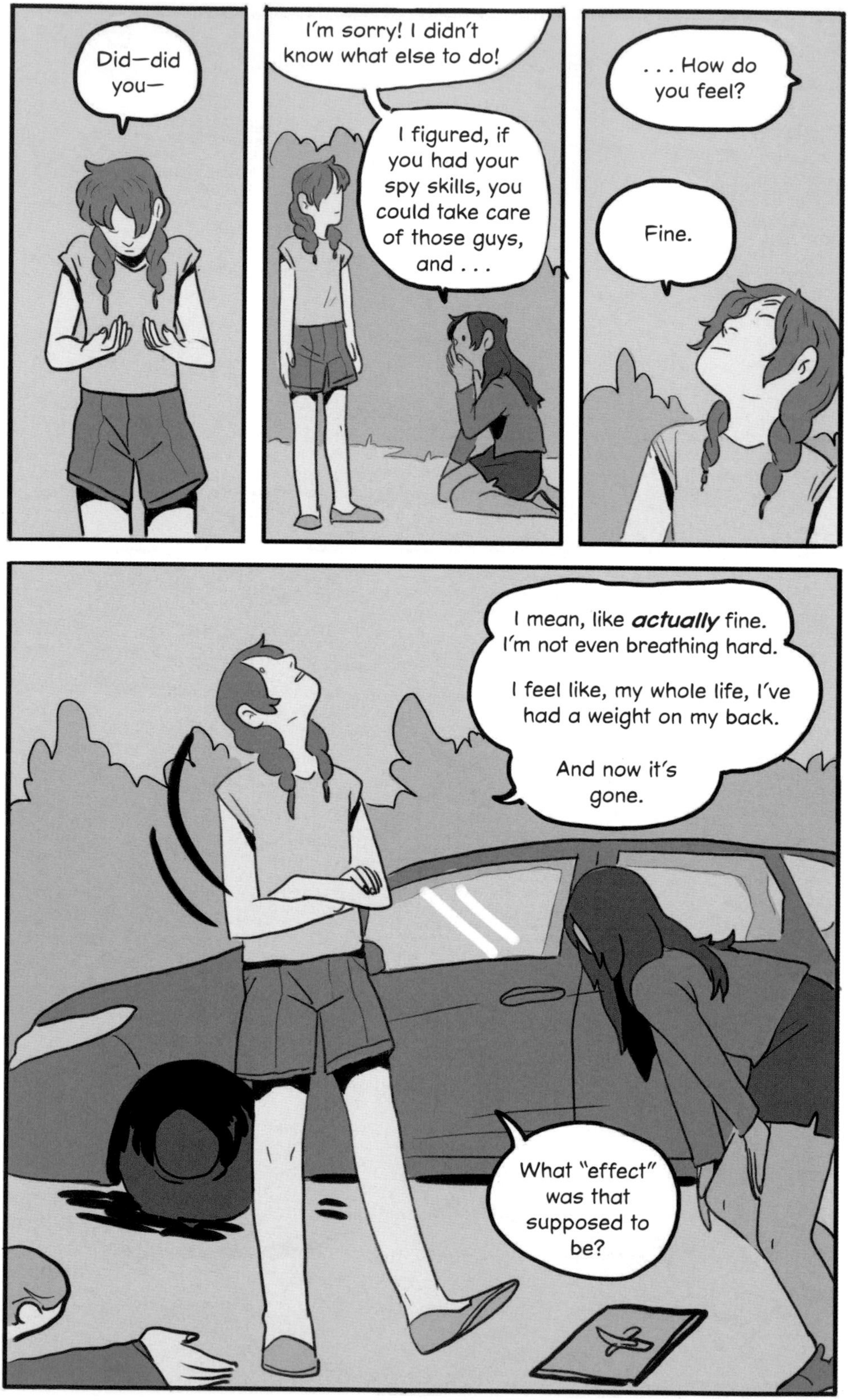
Did—did you—
I'm sorry! I didn't know what else to do!
I figured, if you had your spy skills, you could take care of those guys, and . . .
. . . How do you feel?
Fine.
I mean, like *actually* fine. I'm not even breathing hard.
I feel like, my whole life, I've had a weight on my back.
And now it's gone.
What "effect" was that supposed to be?

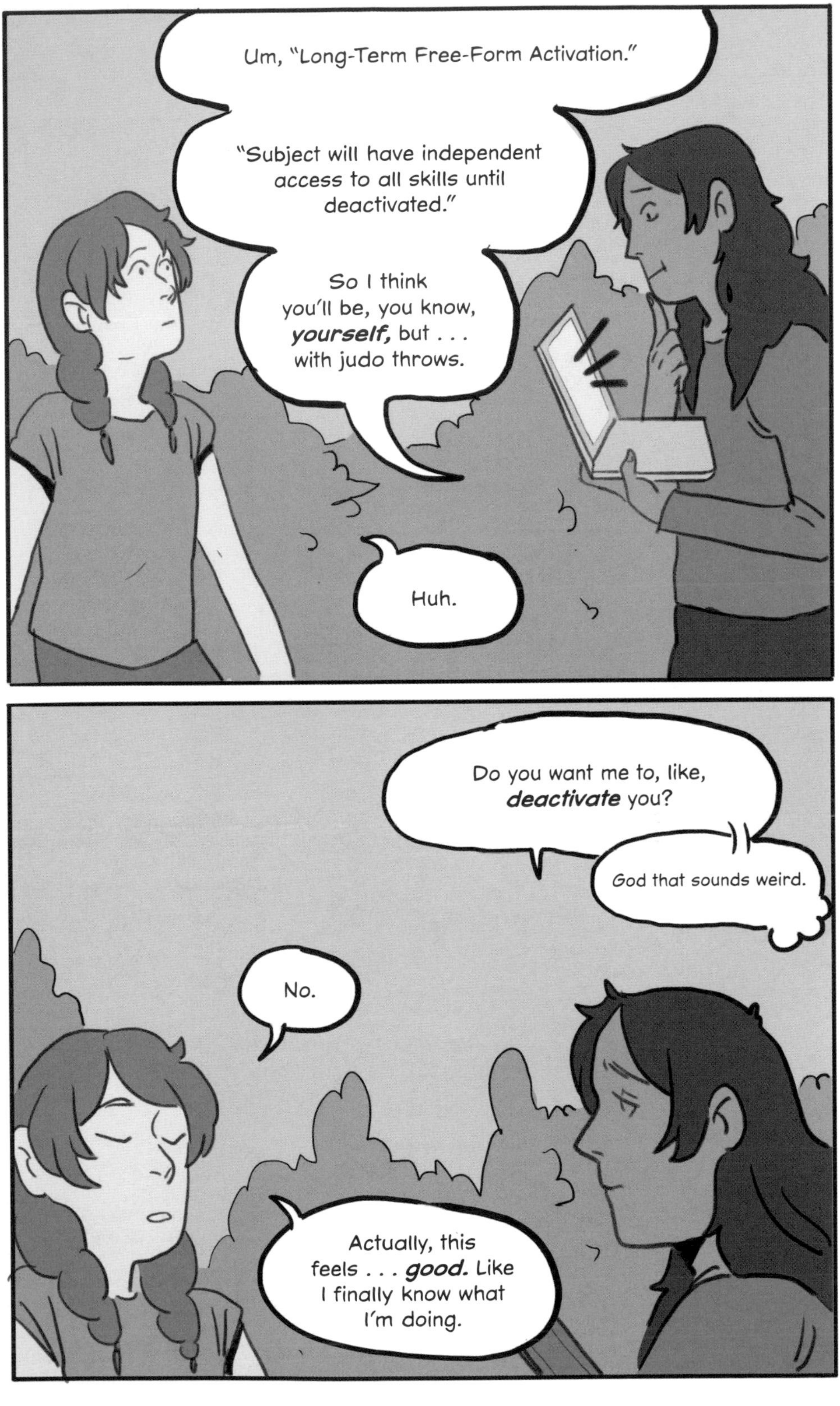
Um, "Long-Term Free-Form Activation."
"Subject will have independent access to all skills until deactivated."
So I think you'll be, you know, ***yourself,*** but . . . with judo throws.
Huh.
Do you want me to, like, ***deactivate*** you?
God that sounds weird.
No.
Actually, this feels . . . ***good.*** Like I finally know what I'm doing.

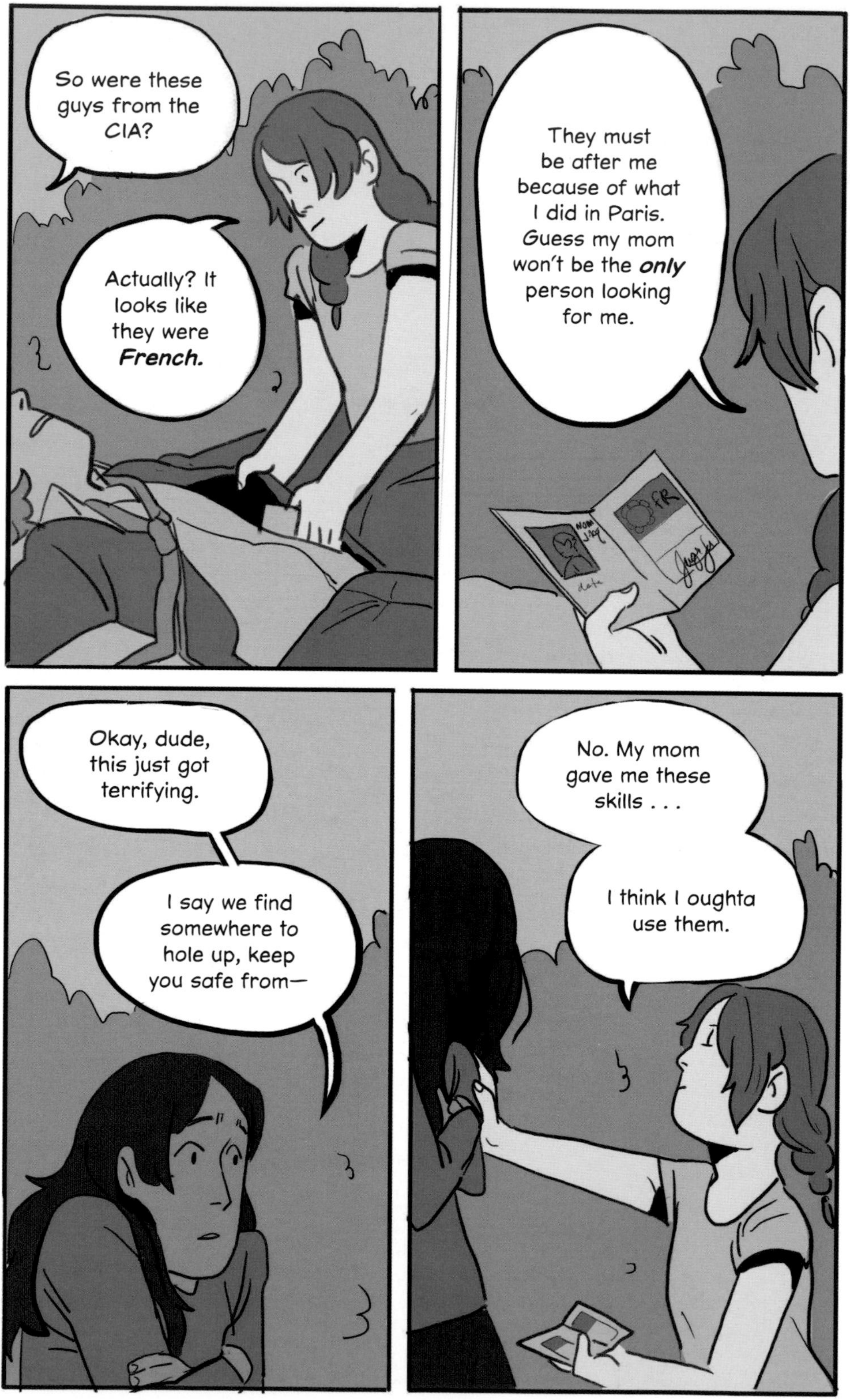

So were these guys from the CIA?
Actually? It looks like they were ***French.***
They must be after me because of what I did in Paris. Guess my mom won't be the ***only*** person looking for me.
Okay, dude, this just got terrifying.
I say we find somewhere to hole up, keep you safe from—
No. My mom gave me these skills . . .
I think I oughta use them.

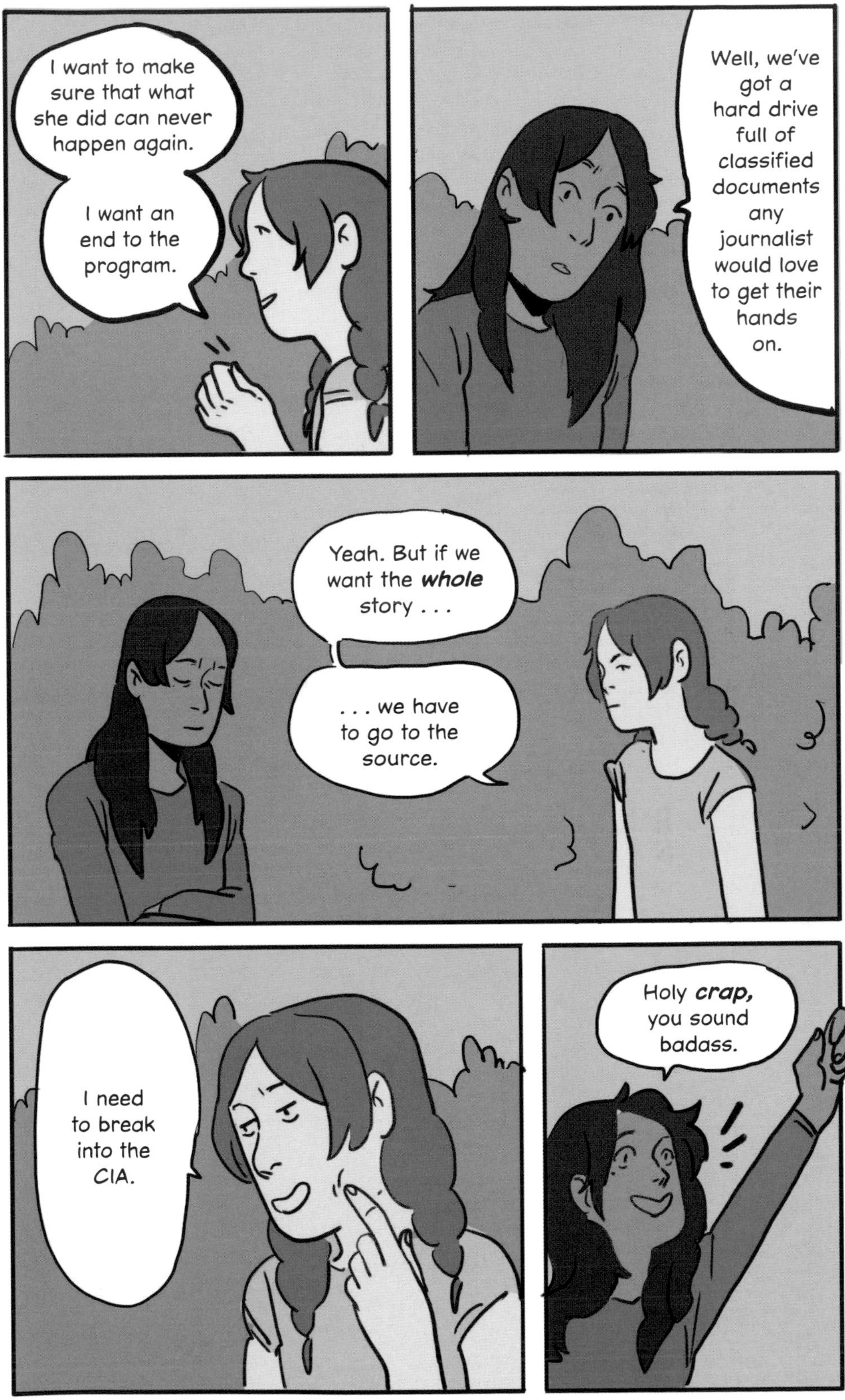
I want to make sure that what she did can never happen again.
I want an end to the program.
Well, we've got a hard drive full of classified documents any journalist would love to get their hands on.
Yeah. But if we want the ***whole*** story . . .
. . . we have to go to the source.
I need to break into the CIA.
Holy ***crap,*** you sound badass.

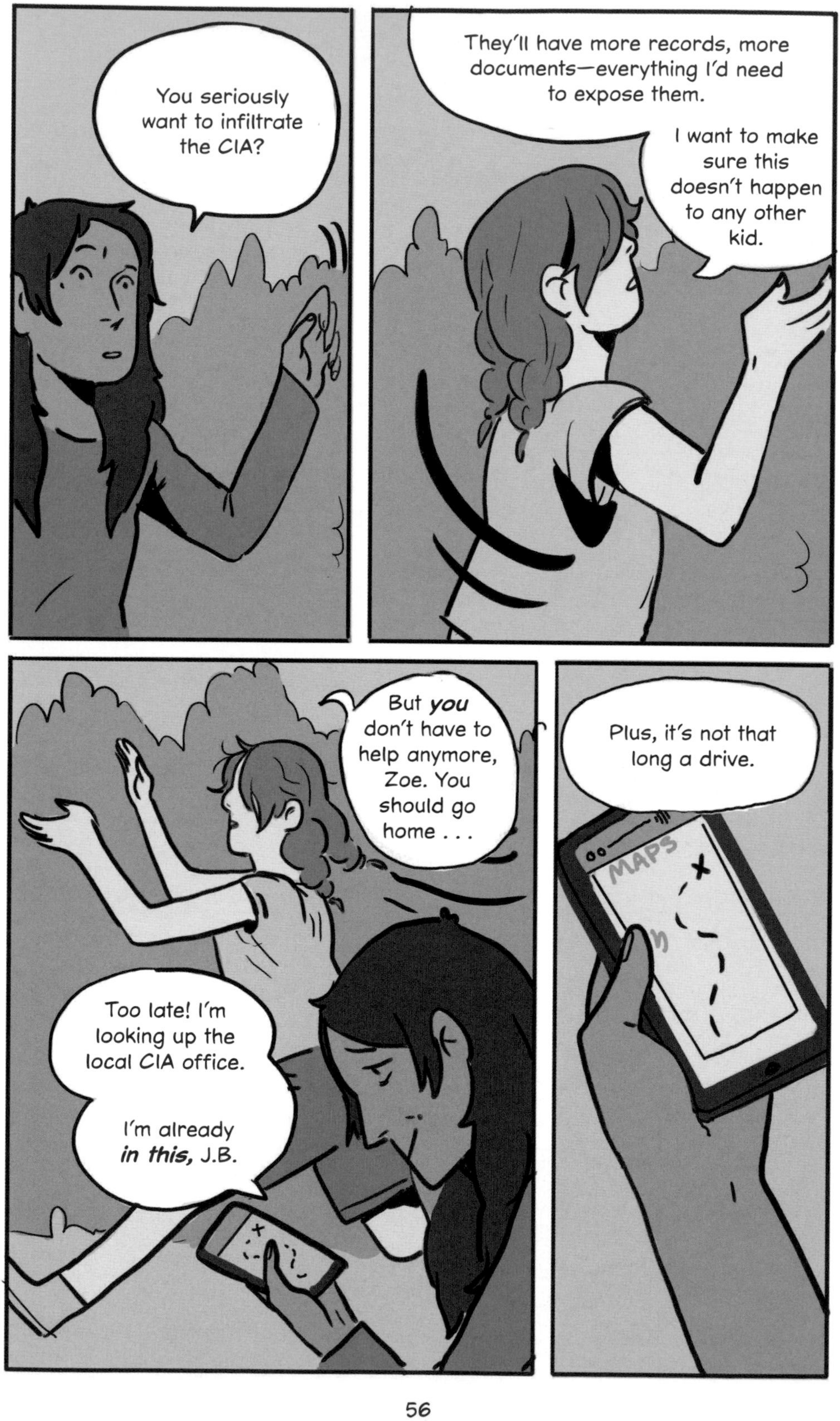
You seriously want to infiltrate the CIA?
They'll have more records, more documents—everything I'd need to expose them.
I want to make sure this doesn't happen to any other kid.
But *you* don't have to help anymore, Zoe. You should go home . . .
Too late! I'm looking up the local CIA office.
I'm already ***in this,*** J.B.
Plus, it's not that long a drive.
MAPS

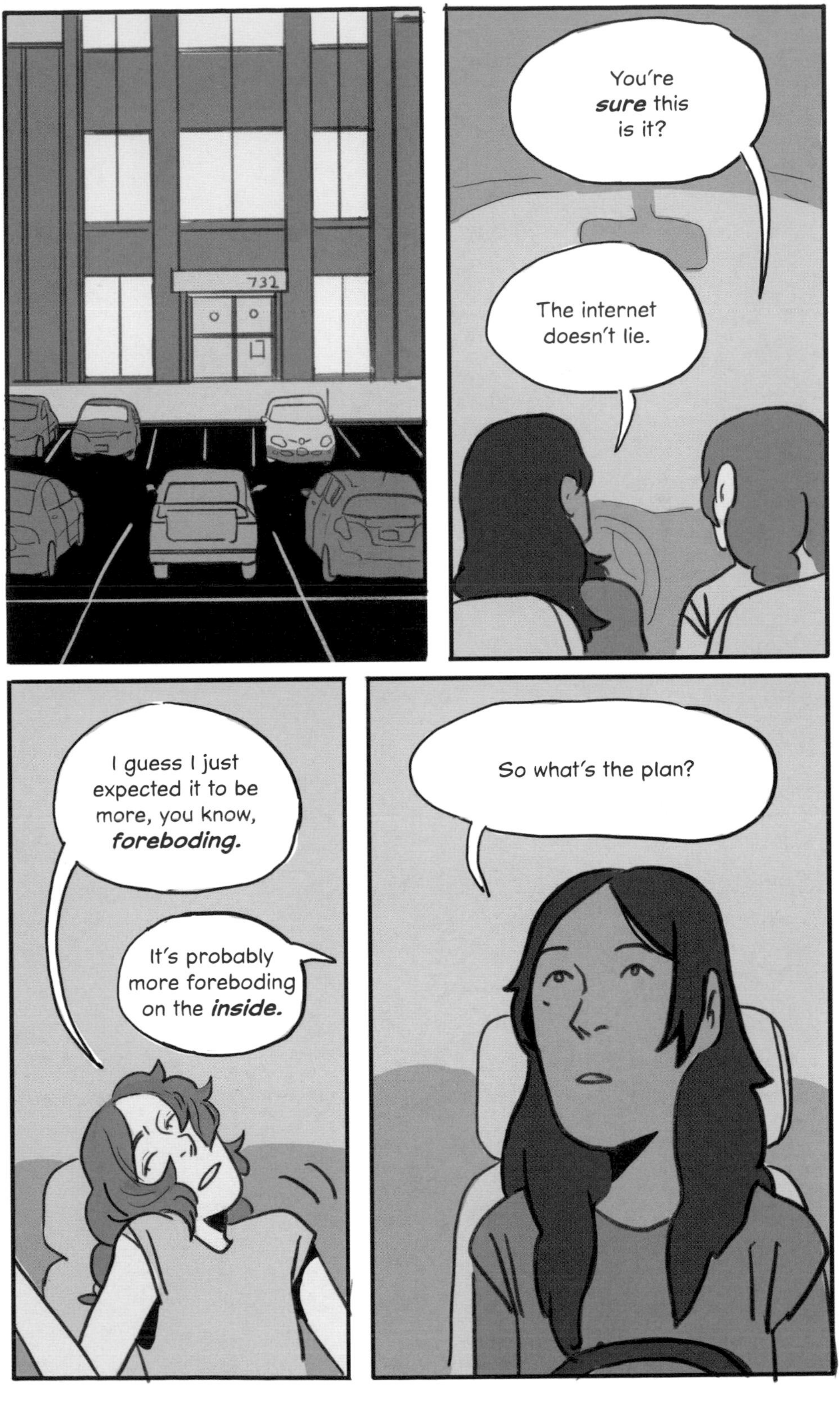
You're *sure* this is it?
The internet doesn't lie.
I guess I just expected it to be more, you know, *foreboding.*
It's probably more foreboding on the *inside.*
So what's the plan?

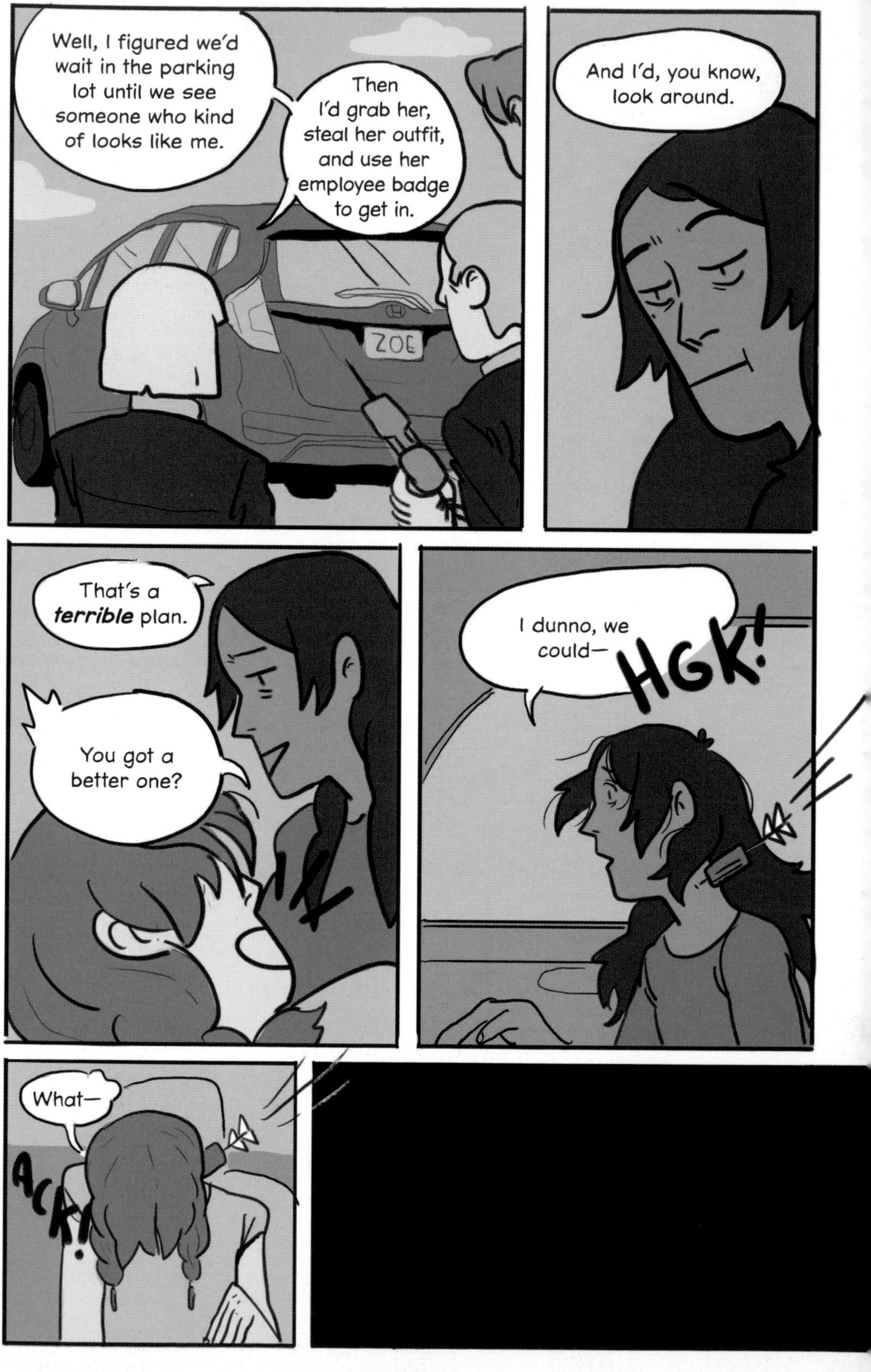
Well, I figured we'd wait in the parking lot until we see someone who kind of looks like me.
Then I'd grab her, steal her outfit, and use her employee badge to get in.
ZOE
And I'd, you know, look around.
That's a ***terrible*** plan.
You got a better one?
I dunno, we could—
HGK!
What—
ACK!

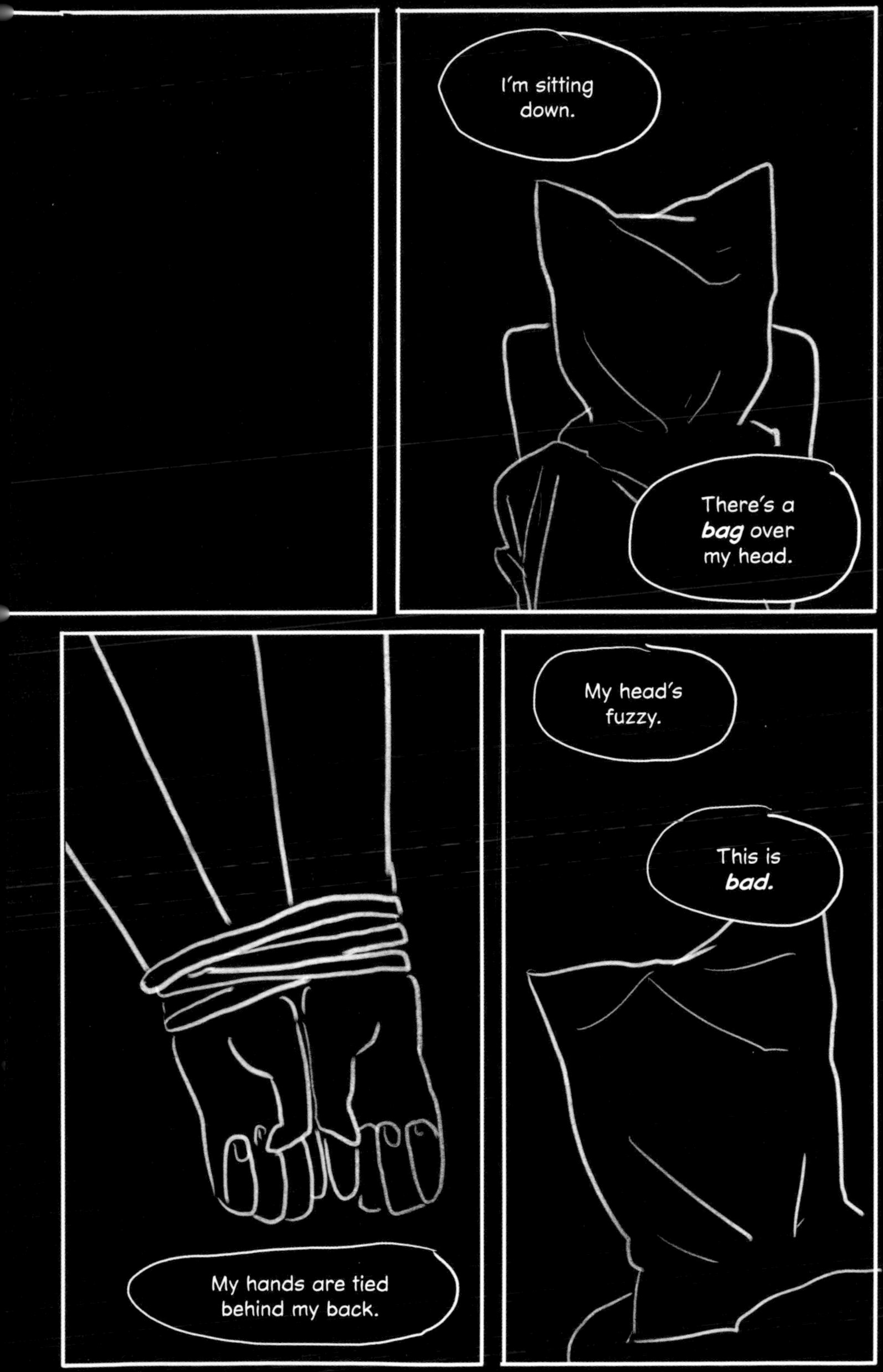

I'm sitting down.
There's a **bag** over my head.
My hands are tied behind my back.
My head's fuzzy.
This is **bad.**

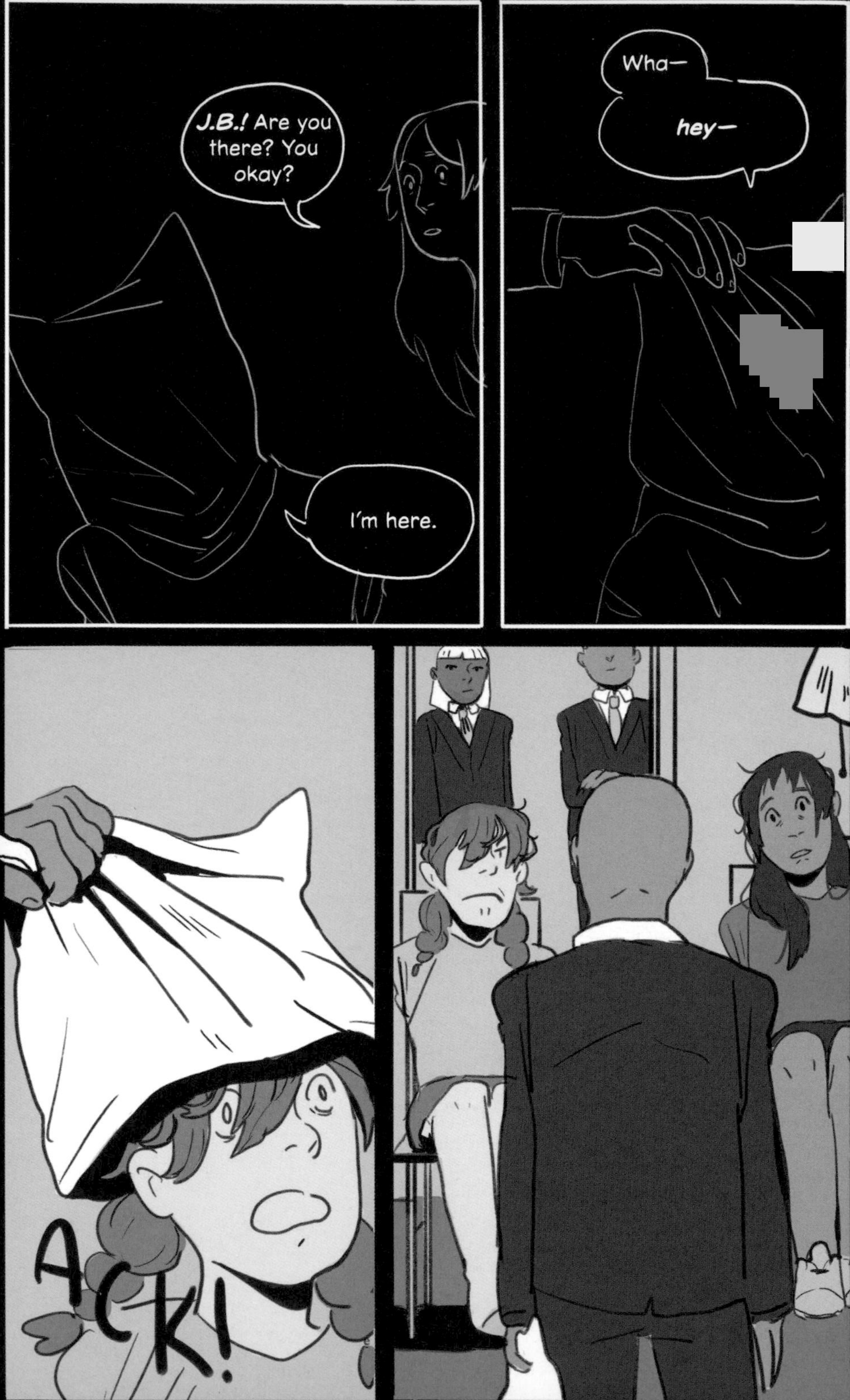
J.B.! Are you there? You okay?
I'm here.
Wha—
hey—
ACK!

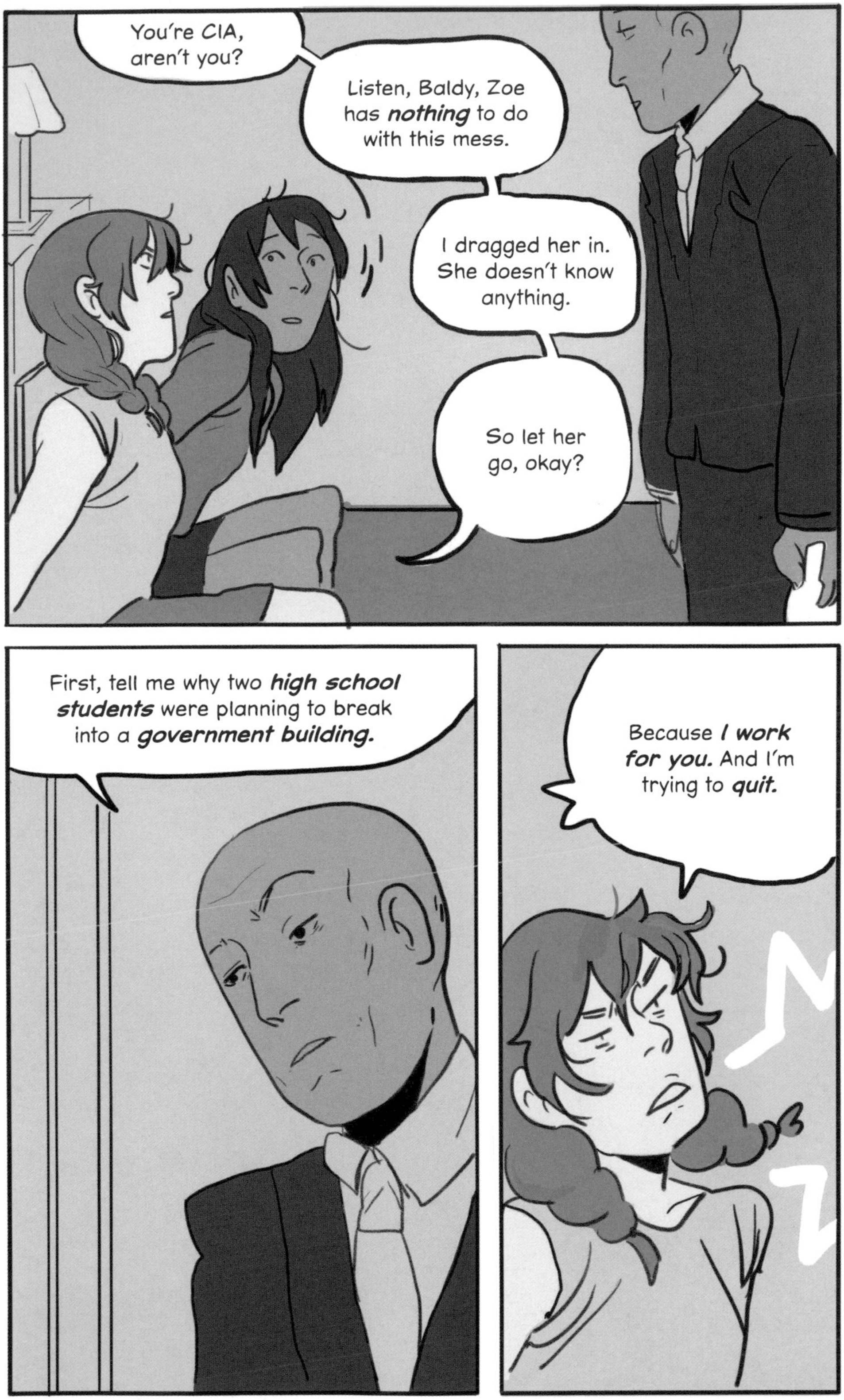
You're CIA, aren't you?
Listen, Baldy, Zoe has **nothing** to do with this mess.
I dragged her in. She doesn't know anything.
So let her go, okay?
First, tell me why two **high school students** were planning to break into a **government building.**
Because **I work for you.** And I'm trying to **quit.**

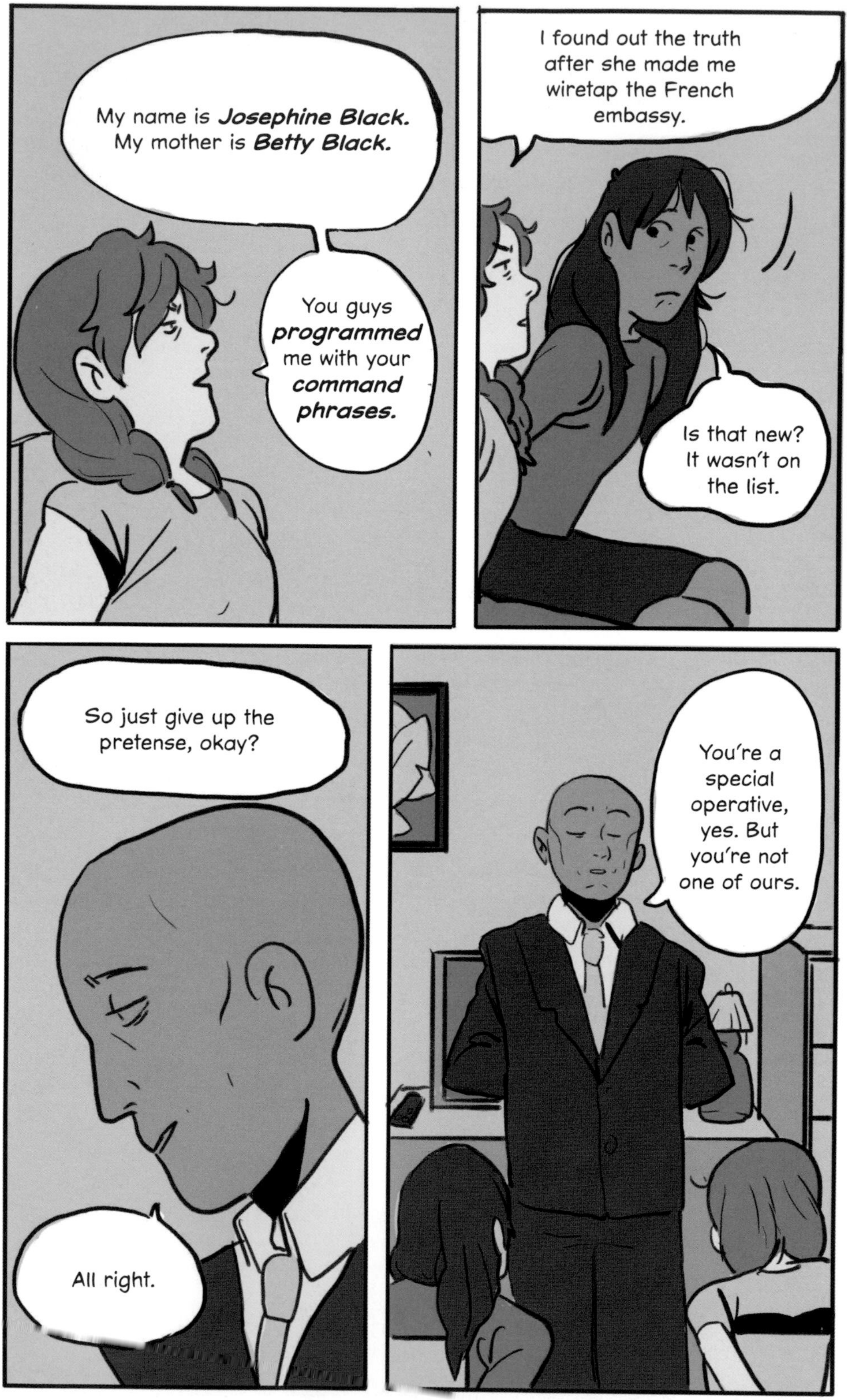
My name is *Josephine Black.* My mother is *Betty Black.*
You guys **programmed** me with your **command phrases.**
I found out the truth after she made me wiretap the French embassy.
Is that new? It wasn't on the list.
So just give up the pretense, okay?
All right.
You're a special operative, yes. But you're not one of ours.

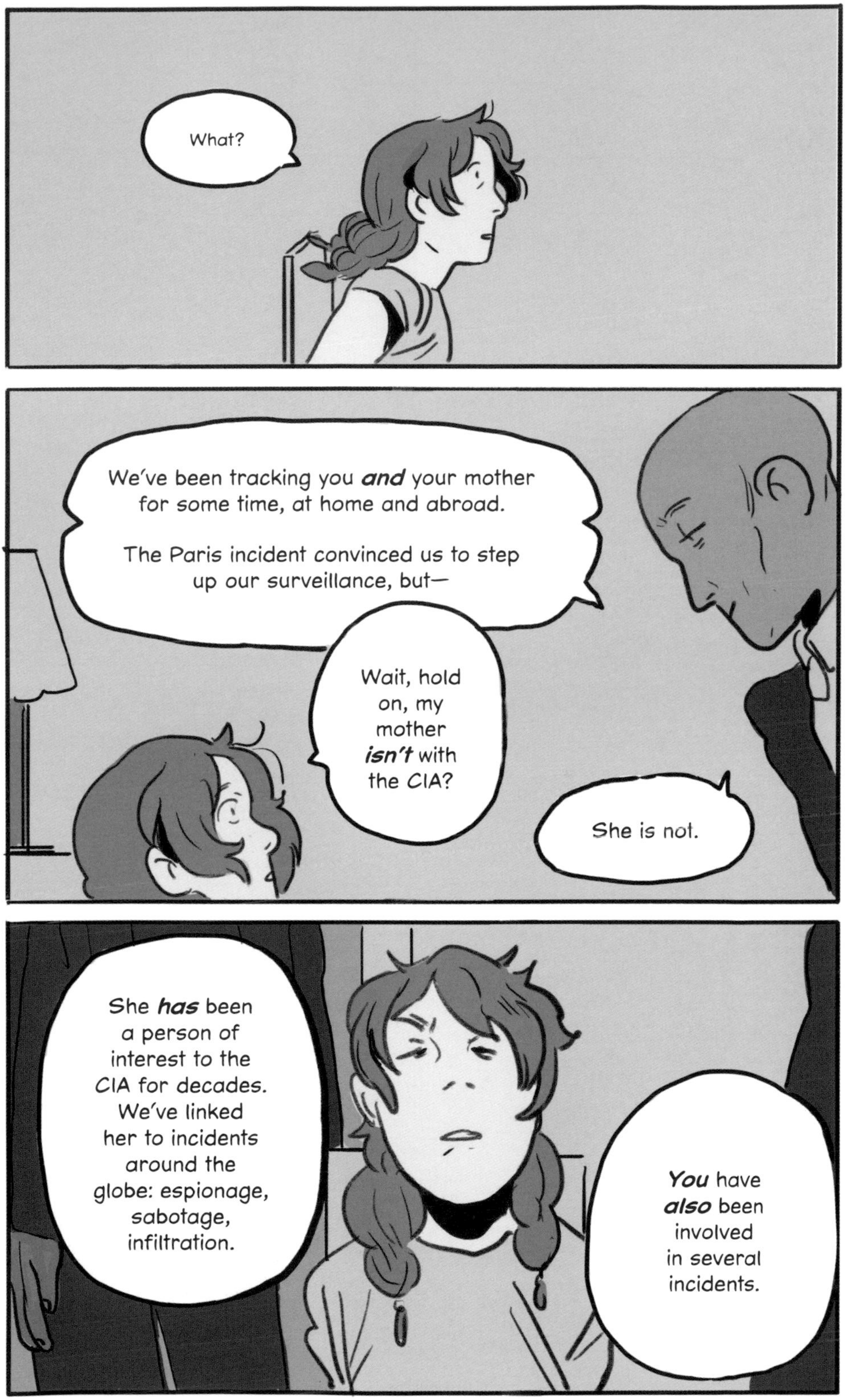

What?
We've been tracking you ***and*** your mother for some time, at home and abroad.
The Paris incident convinced us to step up our surveillance, but—
Wait, hold on, my mother ***isn't*** with the CIA?
She is not.
She ***has*** been a person of interest to the CIA for decades. We've linked her to incidents around the globe: espionage, sabotage, infiltration.
You have ***also*** been involved in several incidents.

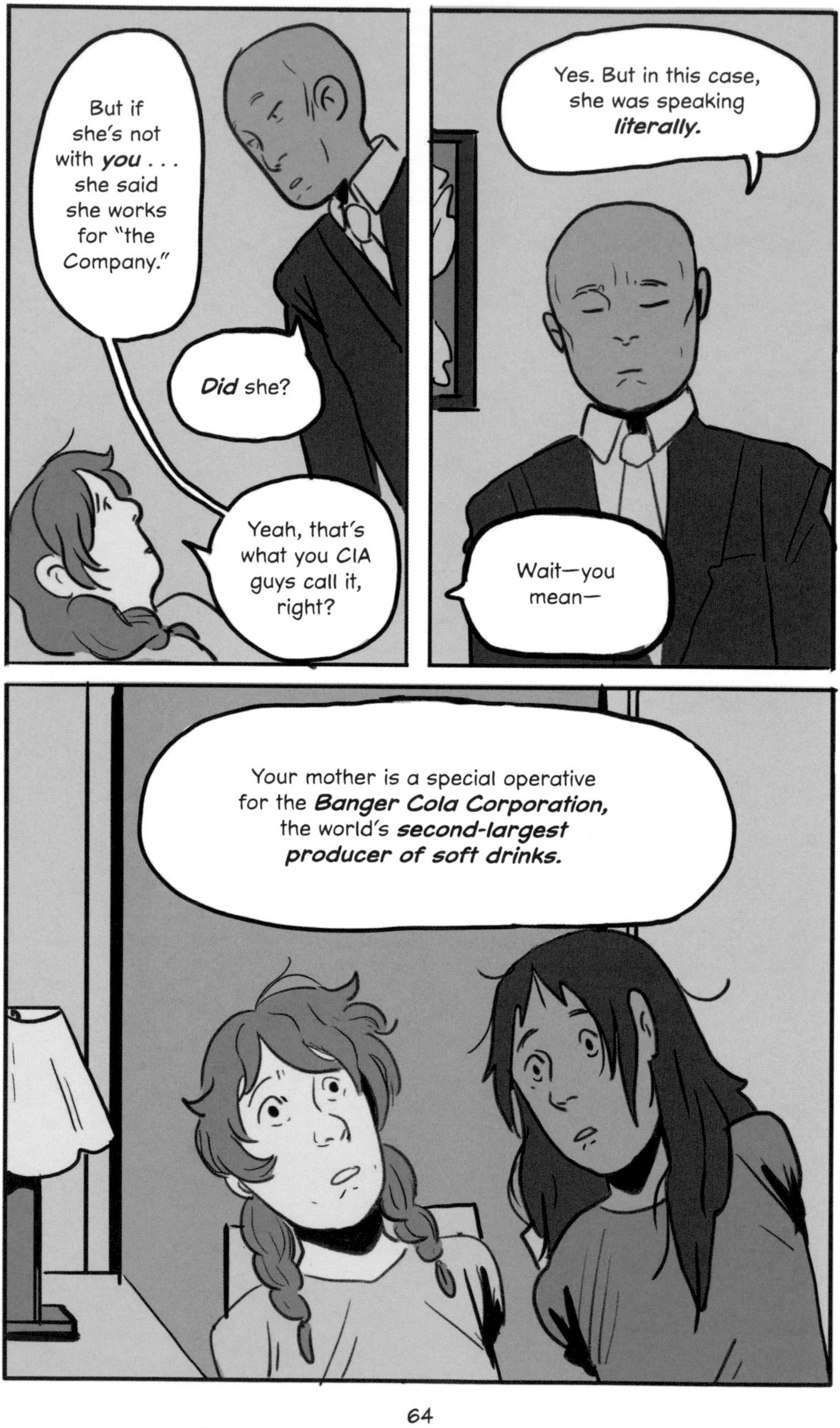
But if she's not with ***you . . .*** she said she works for "the Company."
Did she?
Yeah, that's what you CIA guys call it, right?
Yes. But in this case, she was speaking ***literally.***
Wait—you mean—
Your mother is a special operative for the ***Banger Cola Corporation,*** the world's ***second-largest producer of soft drinks.***

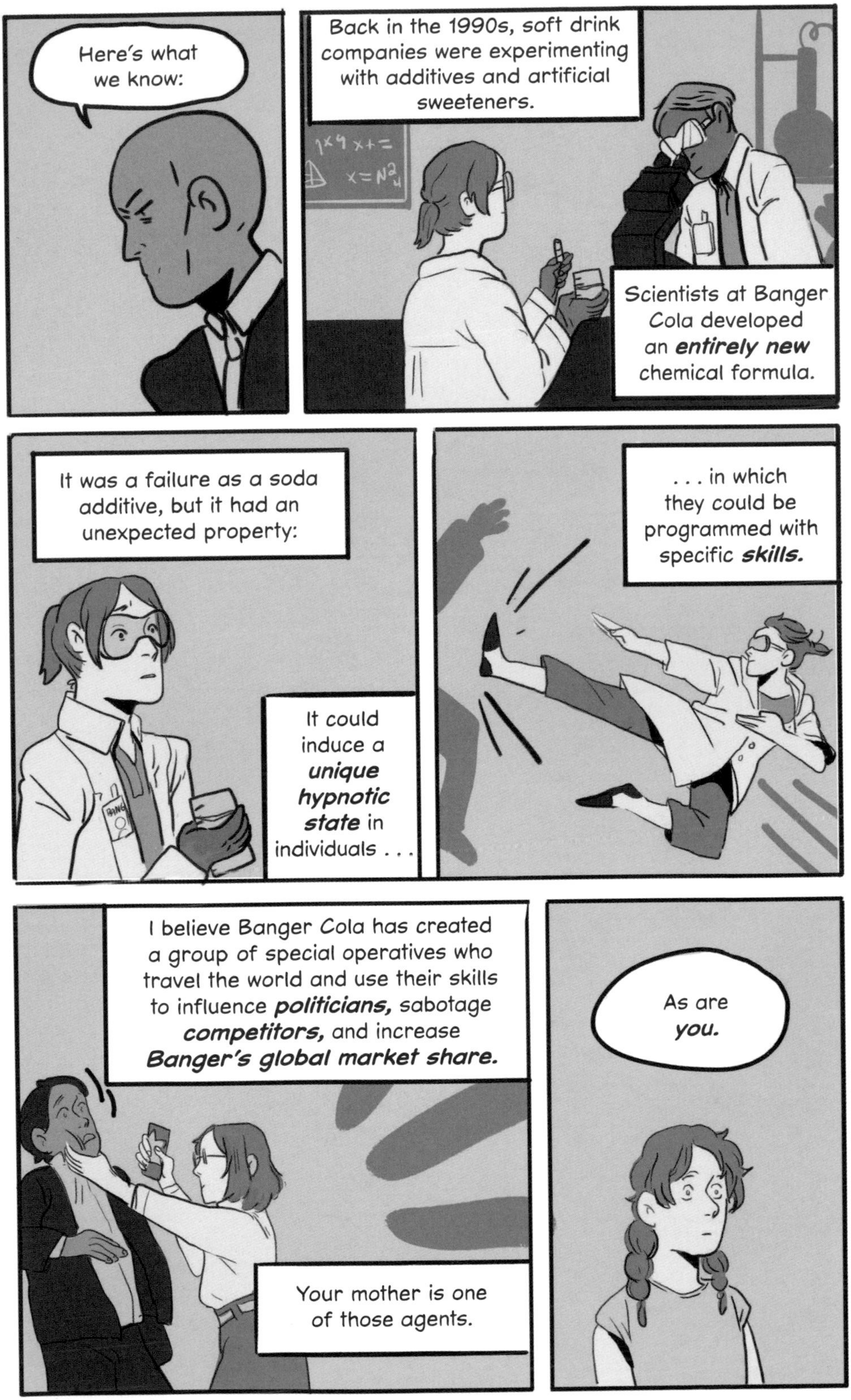
Here's what we know:
Back in the 1990s, soft drink companies were experimenting with additives and artificial sweeteners.
Scientists at Banger Cola developed an ***entirely new*** chemical formula.
It was a failure as a soda additive, but it had an unexpected property:
It could induce a ***unique hypnotic state*** in individuals . . .
. . . in which they could be programmed with specific ***skills.***
I believe Banger Cola has created a group of special operatives who travel the world and use their skills to influence ***politicians,*** sabotage ***competitors,*** and increase ***Banger's global market share.***
Your mother is one of those agents.
As are ***you.***

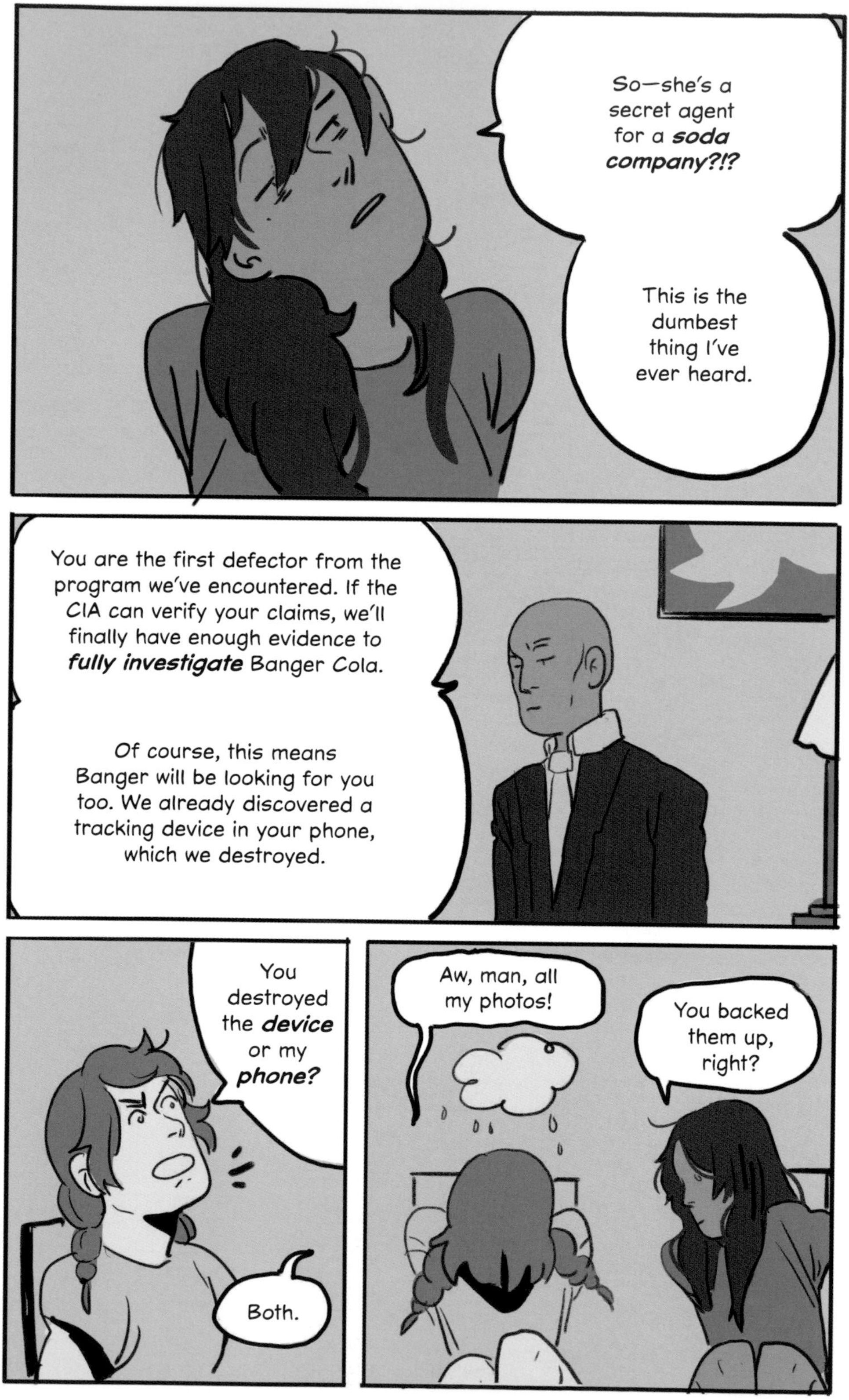
So—she's a secret agent for a ***soda company?!?***
This is the dumbest thing I've ever heard.
You are the first defector from the program we've encountered. If the CIA can verify your claims, we'll finally have enough evidence to ***fully investigate*** Banger Cola.
Of course, this means Banger will be looking for you too. We already discovered a tracking device in your phone, which we destroyed.
You destroyed the ***device*** or my ***phone?***
Both.
Aw, man, all my photos!
You backed them up, right?

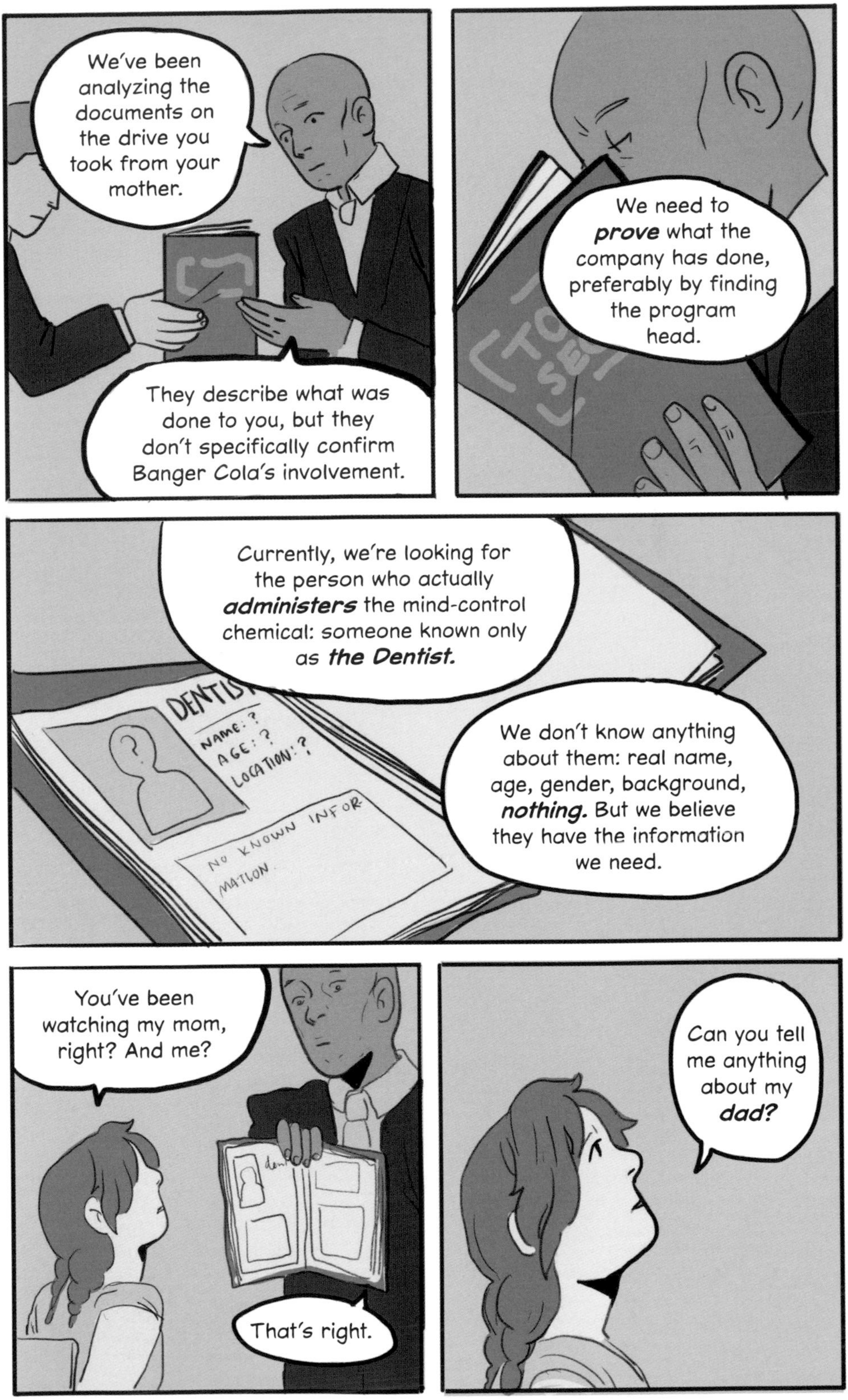
We've been analyzing the documents on the drive you took from your mother.
They describe what was done to you, but they don't specifically confirm Banger Cola's involvement.
We need to ***prove*** what the company has done, preferably by finding the program head.
Currently, we're looking for the person who actually ***administers*** the mind-control chemical: someone known only as ***the Dentist.***
NAME: ?
AGE: ?
LOCATION: ?
NO KNOWN INFOR
MATION.
We don't know anything about them: real name, age, gender, background, ***nothing.*** But we believe they have the information we need.
You've been watching my mom, right? And me?
That's right.
Can you tell me anything about my ***dad?***

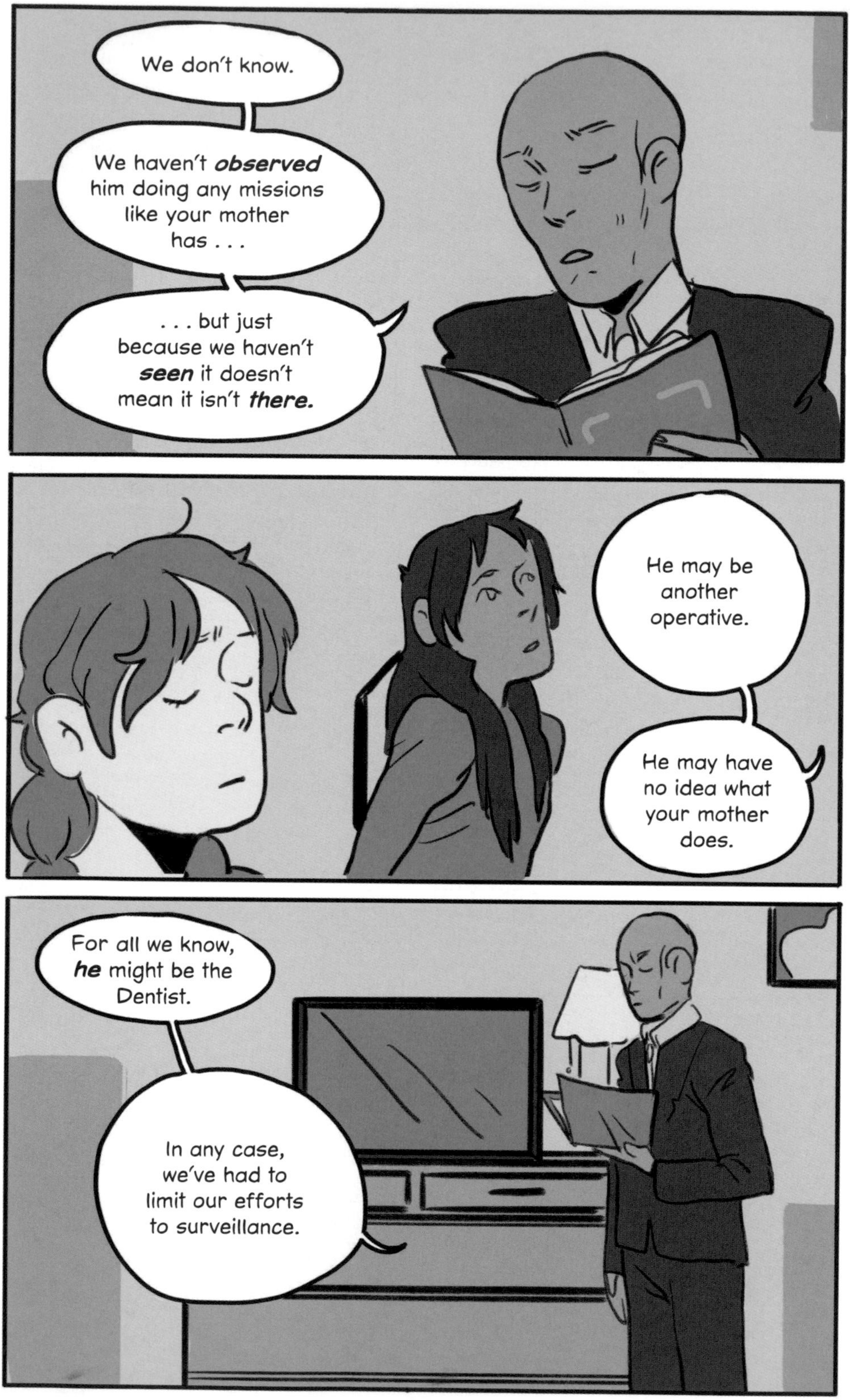
We don't know.
We haven't **observed** him doing any missions like your mother has . . .
. . . but just because we haven't **seen** it doesn't mean it isn't **there.**
He may be another operative.
He may have no idea what your mother does.
For all we know, **he** might be the Dentist.
In any case, we've had to limit our efforts to surveillance.

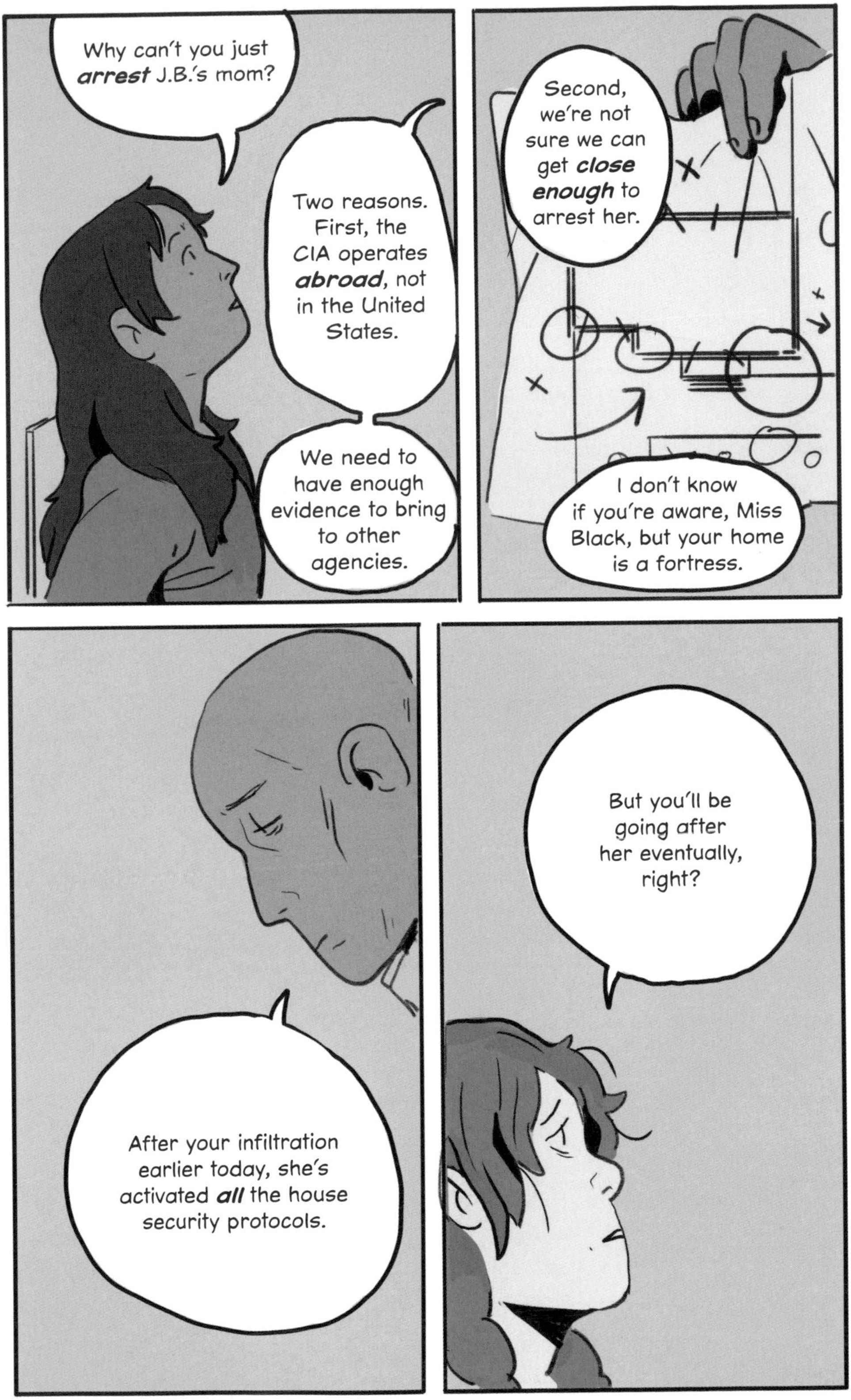
Why can't you just *arrest* J.B.'s mom?
Two reasons. First, the CIA operates *abroad,* not in the United States.
We need to have enough evidence to bring to other agencies.
Second, we're not sure we can get *close enough* to arrest her.
I don't know if you're aware, Miss Black, but your home is a fortress.
After your infiltration earlier today, she's activated *all* the house security protocols.
But you'll be going after her eventually, right?

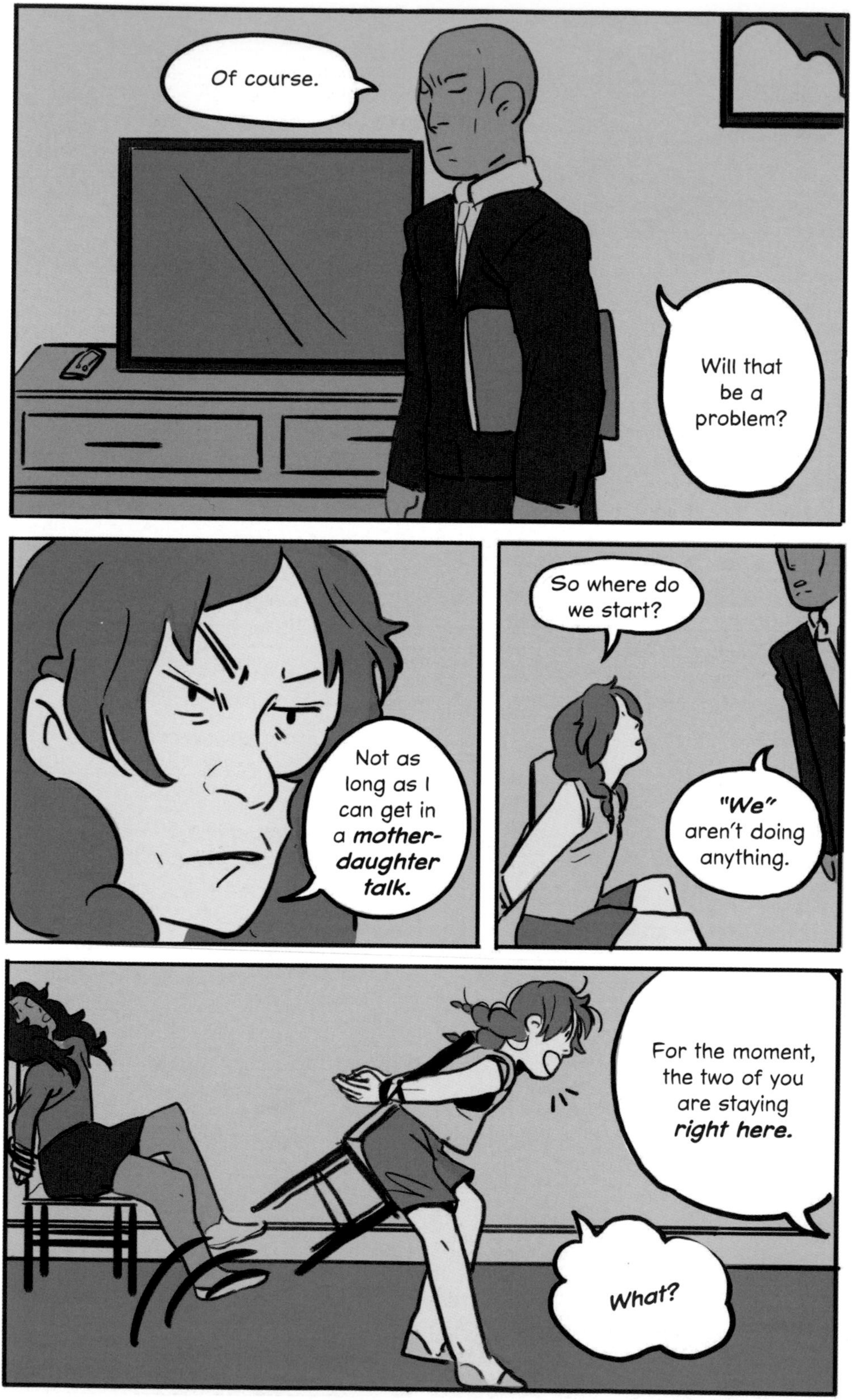
Of course.
Will that be a problem?
Not as long as I can get in a ***mother-daughter talk.***
So where do we start?
"We" aren't doing anything.
For the moment, the two of you are staying ***right here.***
What?

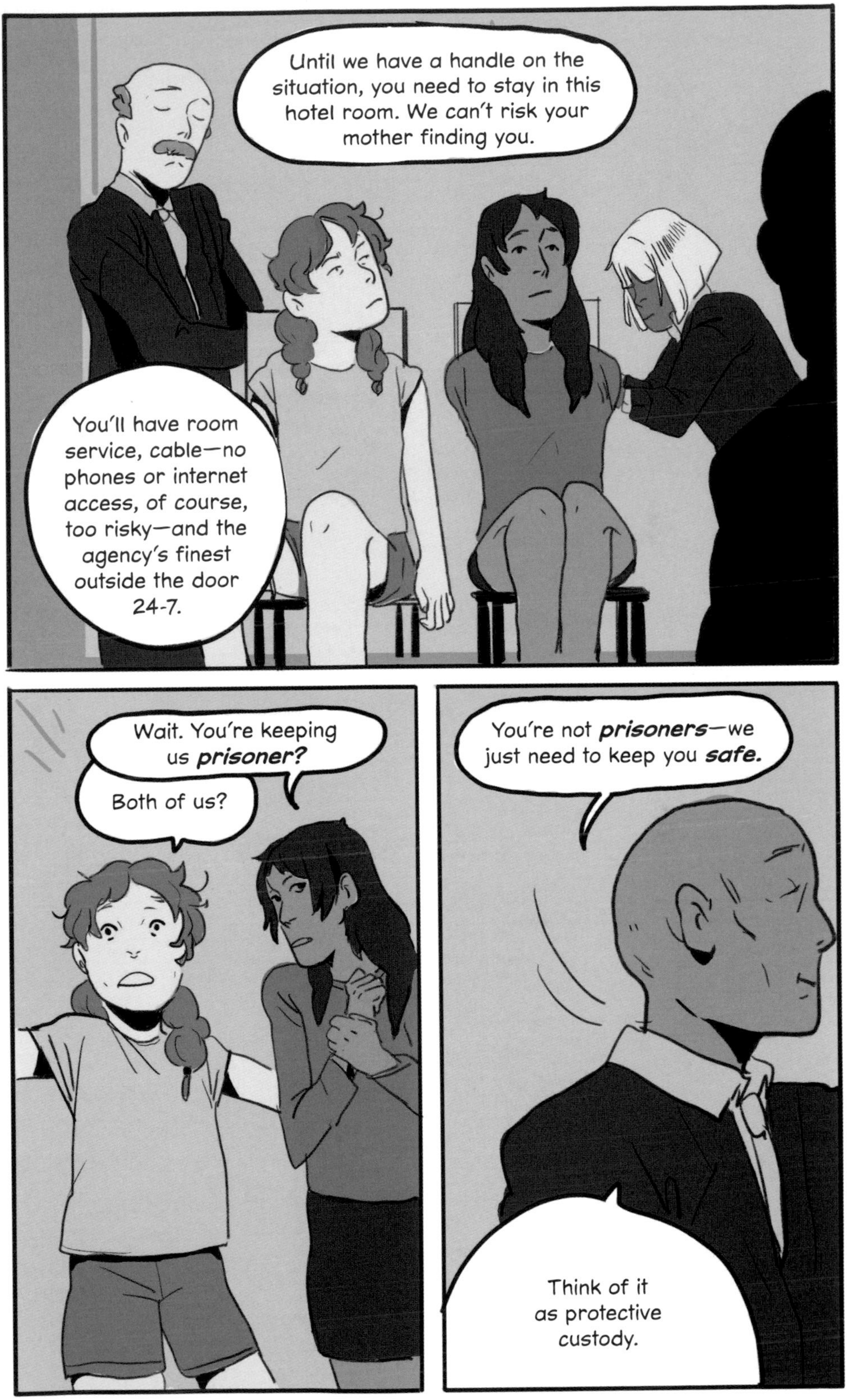
Until we have a handle on the situation, you need to stay in this hotel room. We can't risk your mother finding you.
You'll have room service, cable—no phones or internet access, of course, too risky—and the agency's finest outside the door 24-7.
Wait. You're keeping us **prisoner?**
Both of us?
You're not **prisoners**—we just need to keep you **safe.**
Think of it as protective custody.

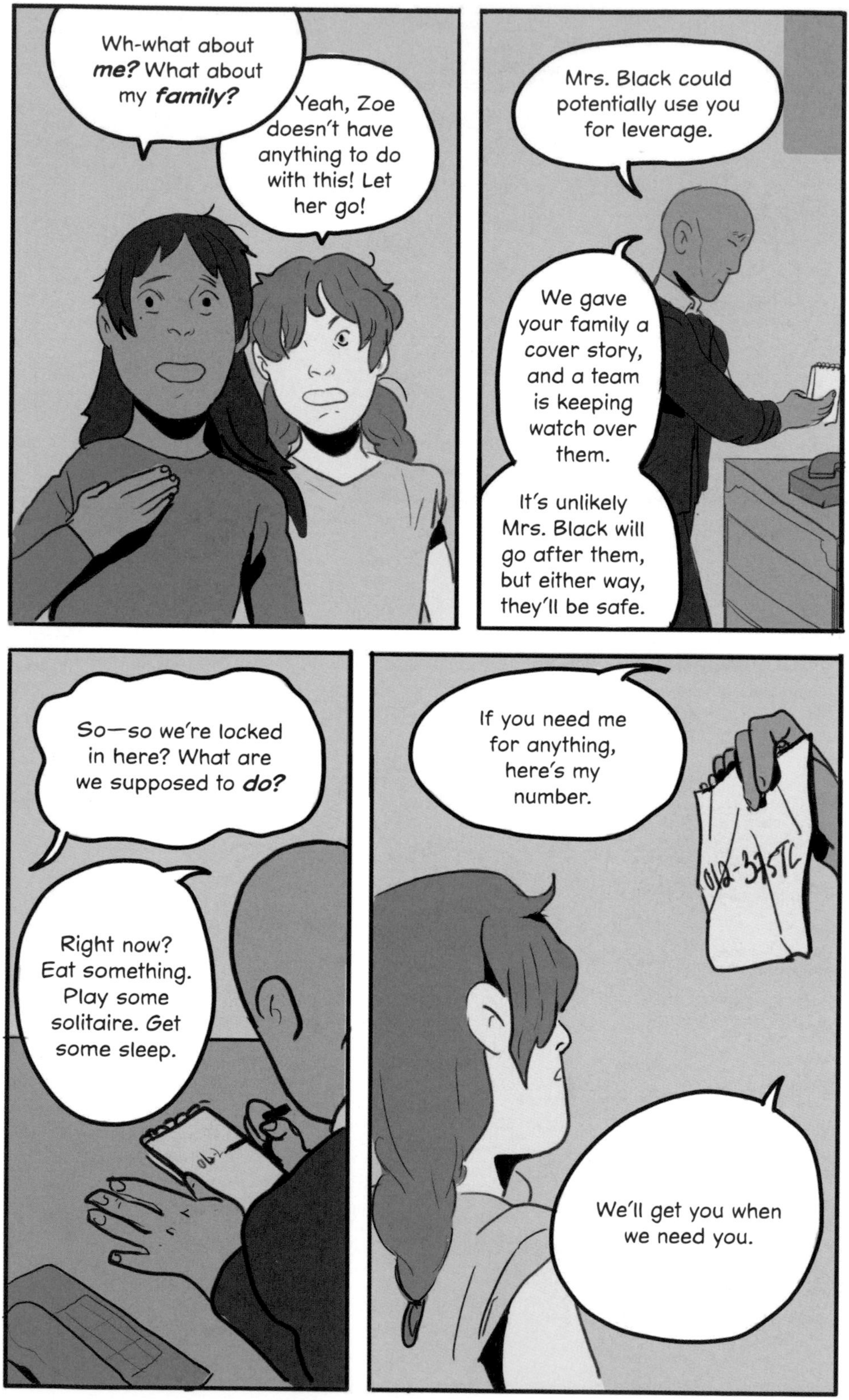
Wh-what about **me?** What about my **family?**
Yeah, Zoe doesn't have anything to do with this! Let her go!
Mrs. Black could potentially use you for leverage.
We gave your family a cover story, and a team is keeping watch over them.
It's unlikely Mrs. Black will go after them, but either way, they'll be safe.
So—so we're locked in here? What are we supposed to **do?**
Right now? Eat something. Play some solitaire. Get some sleep.
If you need me for anything, here's my number.
We'll get you when we need you.

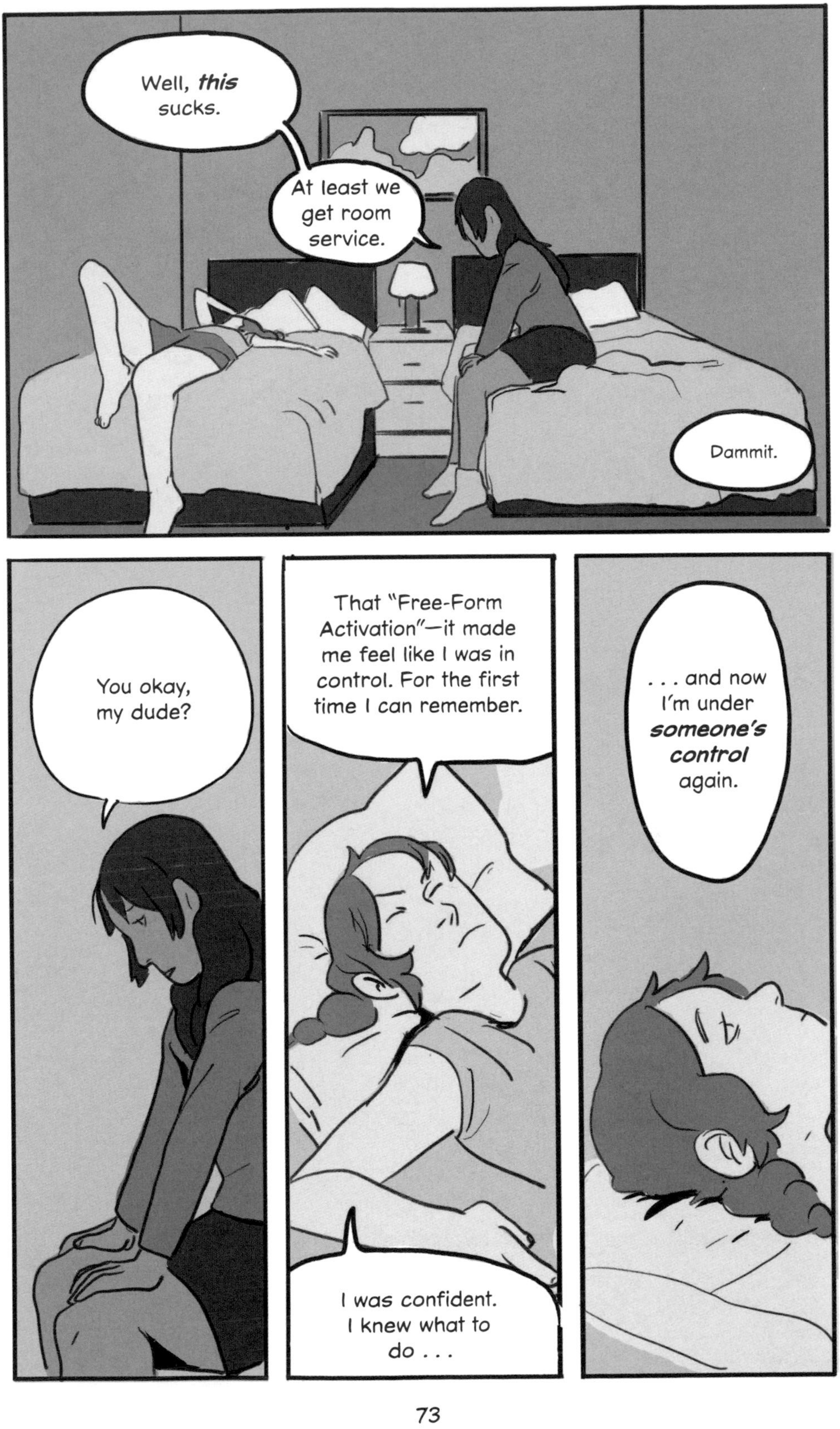
Well, *this* sucks.
At least we get room service.
Dammit.
You okay, my dude?
That "Free-Form Activation"—it made me feel like I was in control. For the first time I can remember.
I was confident. I knew what to do . . .
. . . and now I'm under *someone's control* again.

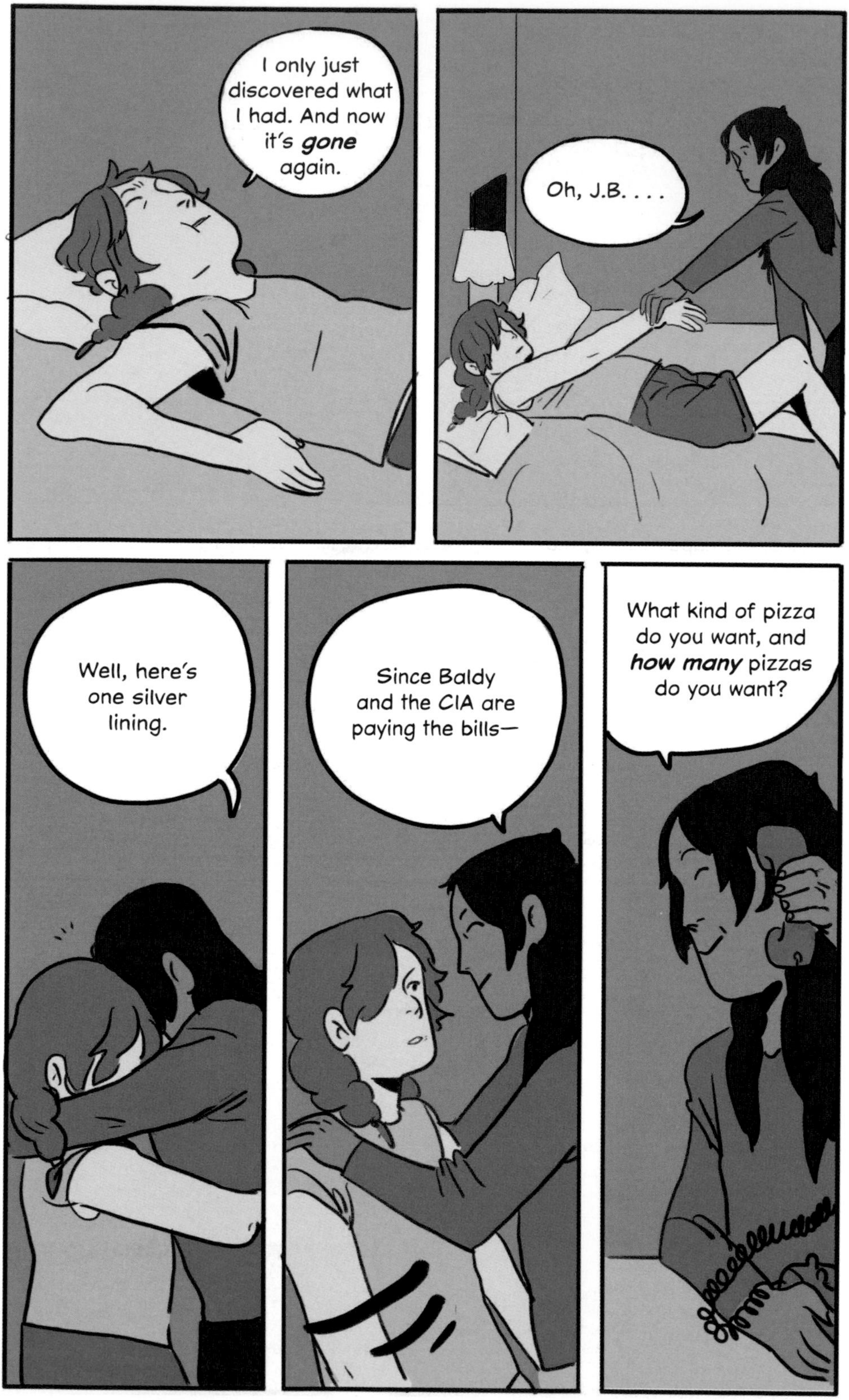
I only just discovered what I had. And now it's ***gone*** again.
Oh, J.B. . . .
Well, here's one silver lining.
Since Baldy and the CIA are paying the bills—
What kind of pizza do you want, and ***how many*** pizzas do you want?

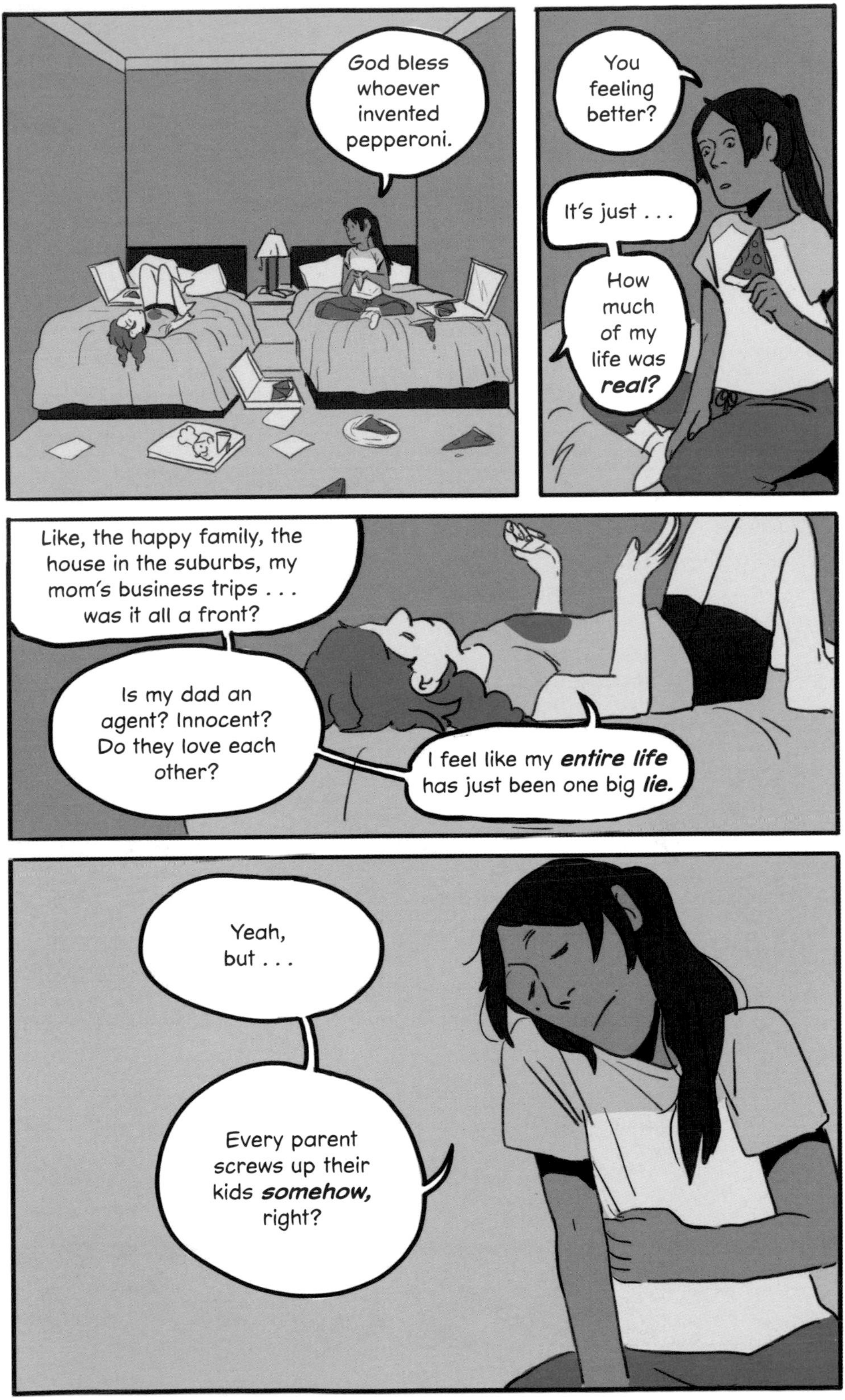
God bless whoever invented pepperoni.
You feeling better?
It's just . . .
How much of my life was ***real?***
Like, the happy family, the house in the suburbs, my mom's business trips . . . was it all a front?
Is my dad an agent? Innocent? Do they love each other?
I feel like my ***entire life*** has just been one big ***lie.***
Yeah, but . . .
Every parent screws up their kids ***somehow,*** right?

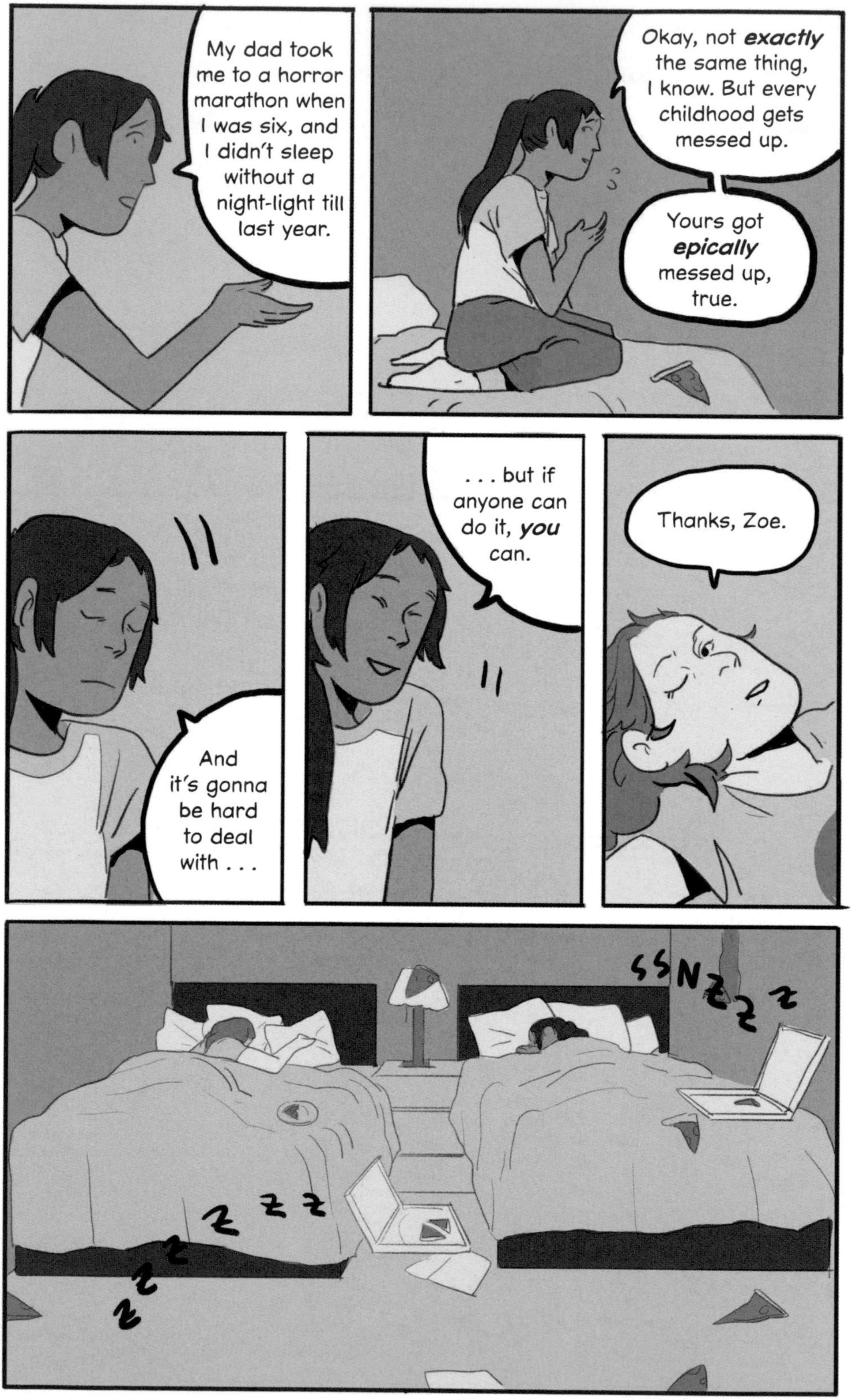

My dad took me to a horror marathon when I was six, and I didn't sleep without a night-light till last year.
Okay, not **exactly** the same thing, I know. But every childhood gets messed up.
Yours got **epically** messed up, true.
And it's gonna be hard to deal with . . .
. . . but if anyone can do it, ***you*** can.
Thanks, Zoe.
SSNZZZ
ZZZZZZ

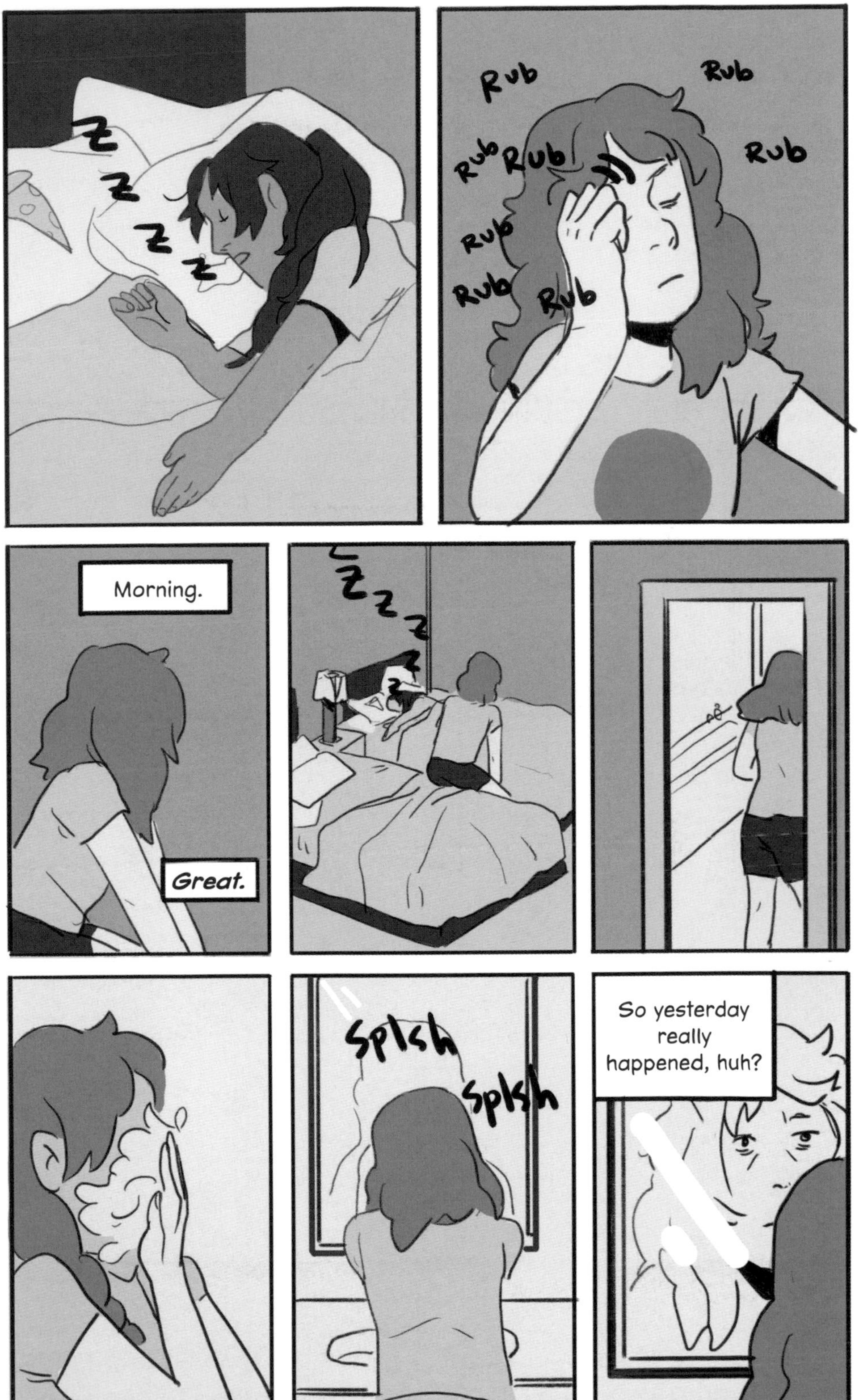
Z
Z
Z
Z
Rub
Rub
Rub
Rub
Rub
Rub
Rub
Rub
Morning.
Great.
Z
Z
Z
Z
Z
Splsh
Splsh
So yesterday really happened, huh?

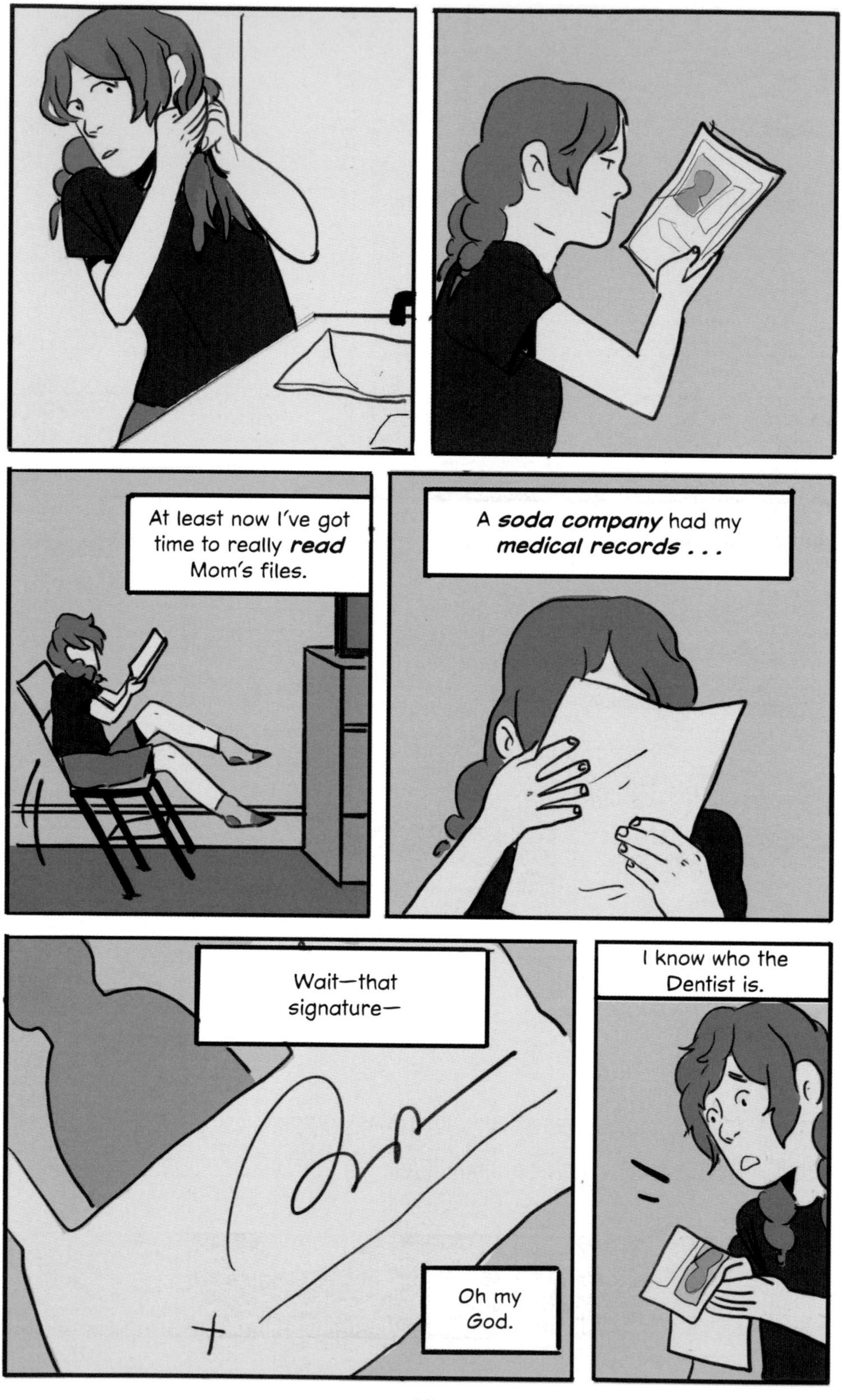

At least now I've got time to really ***read*** Mom's files.
A ***soda company*** had my ***medical records . . .***
Wait—that signature—
Oh my God.
I know who the Dentist is.

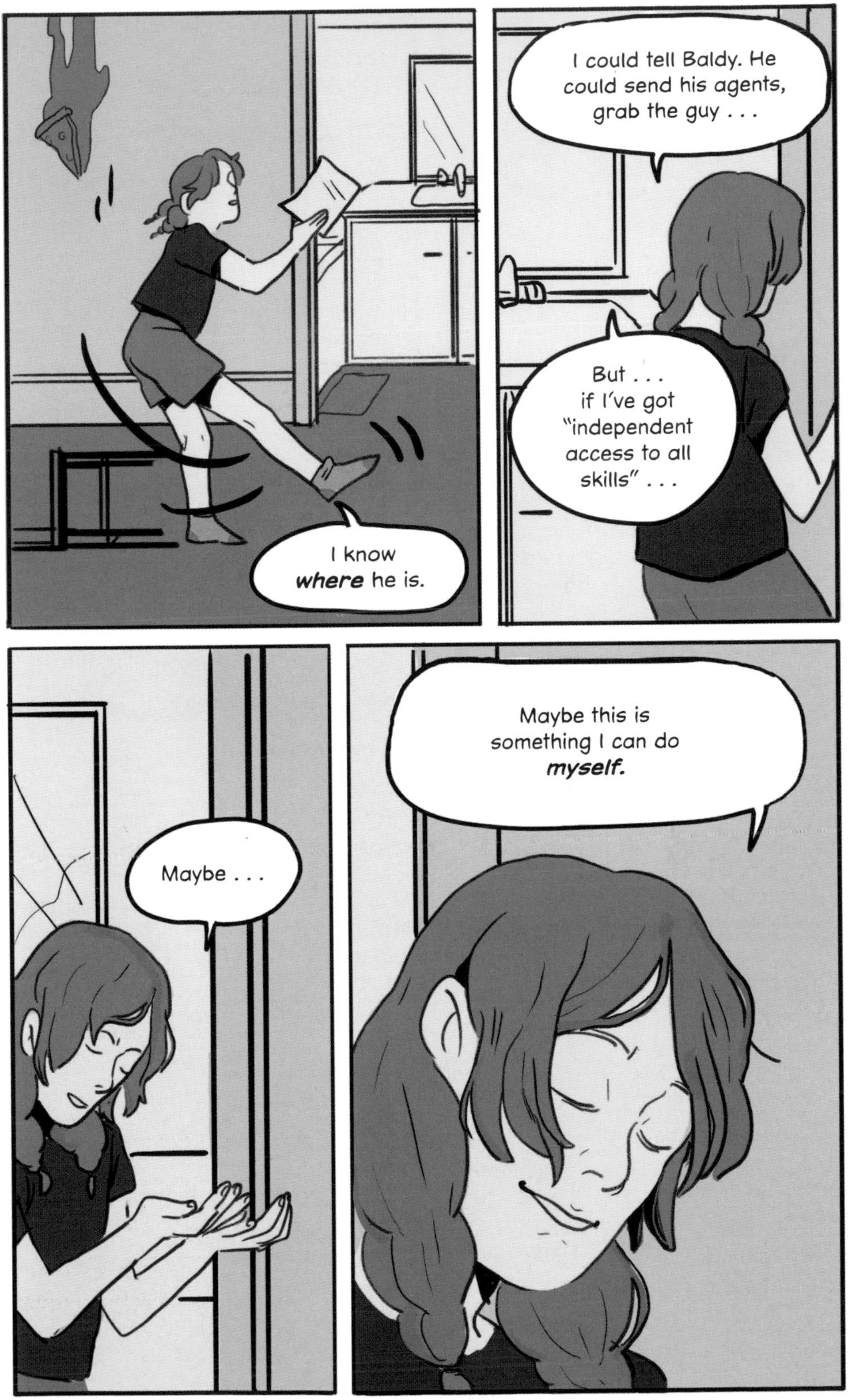
I know *where* he is.
I could tell Baldy. He could send his agents, grab the guy . . .
But . . . if I've got "independent access to all skills" . . .
Maybe . . .
Maybe this is something I can do *myself.*

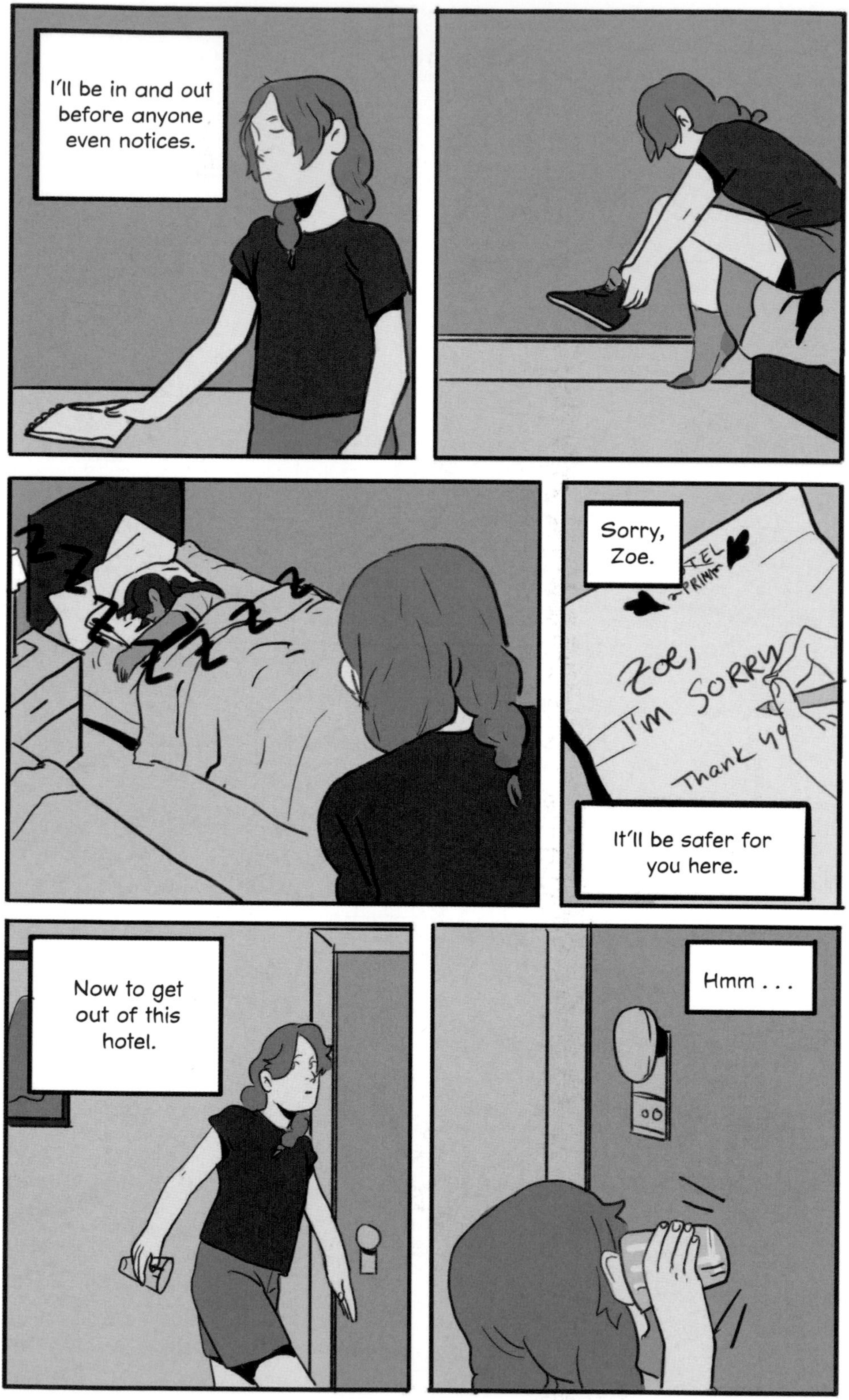
I'll be in and out before anyone even notices.
Sorry, Zoe.
Zoe,
I'm SORRY
It'll be safer for you here.
Now to get out of this hotel.
Hmm . . .

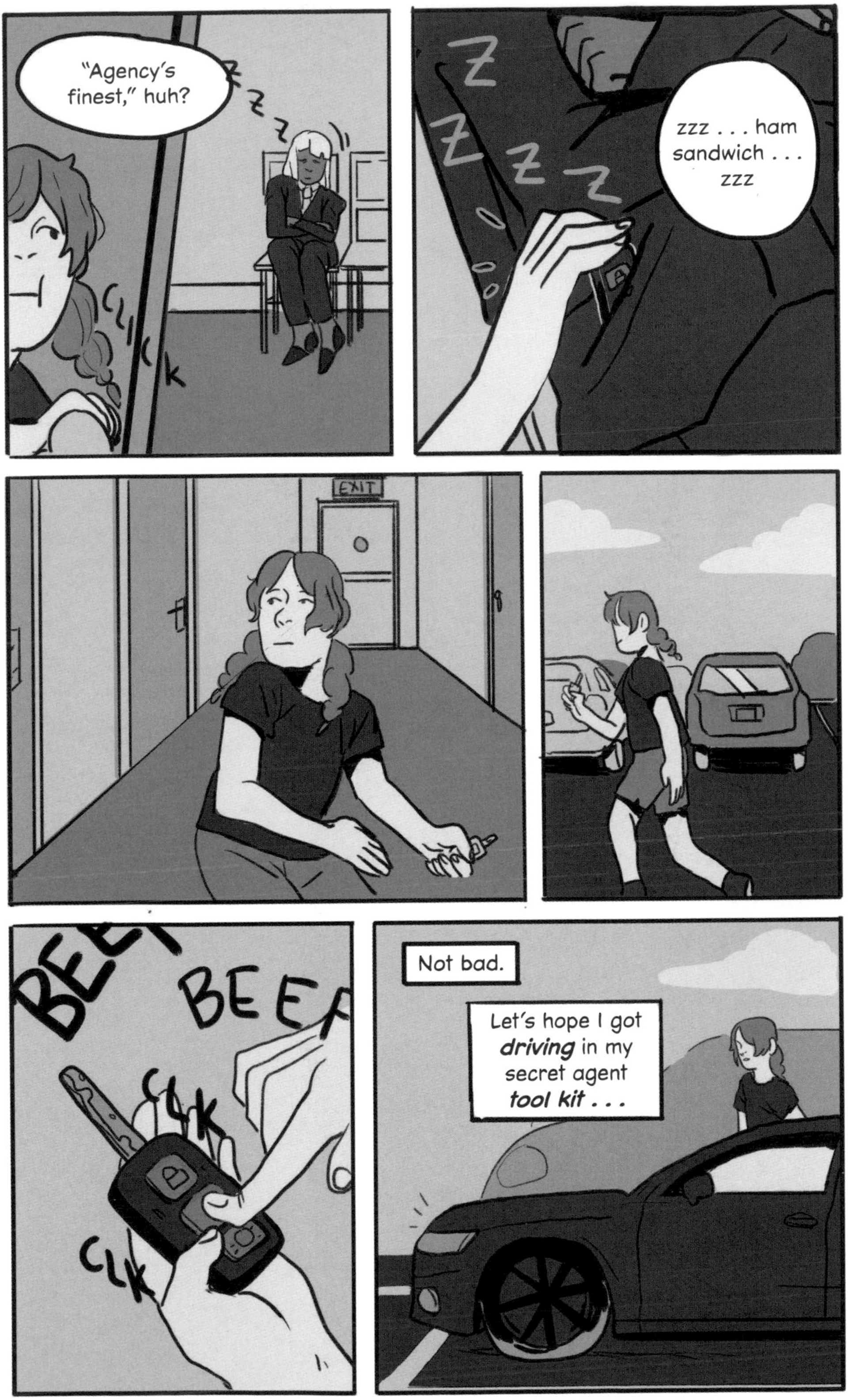
"Agency's finest," huh?
ZZZ
CLICK
zzz . . . ham sandwich . . . zzz
ZZZZ
BEEP
BEEP
CLK
CLK
Not bad.
Let's hope I got **driving** in my secret agent **tool kit . . .**

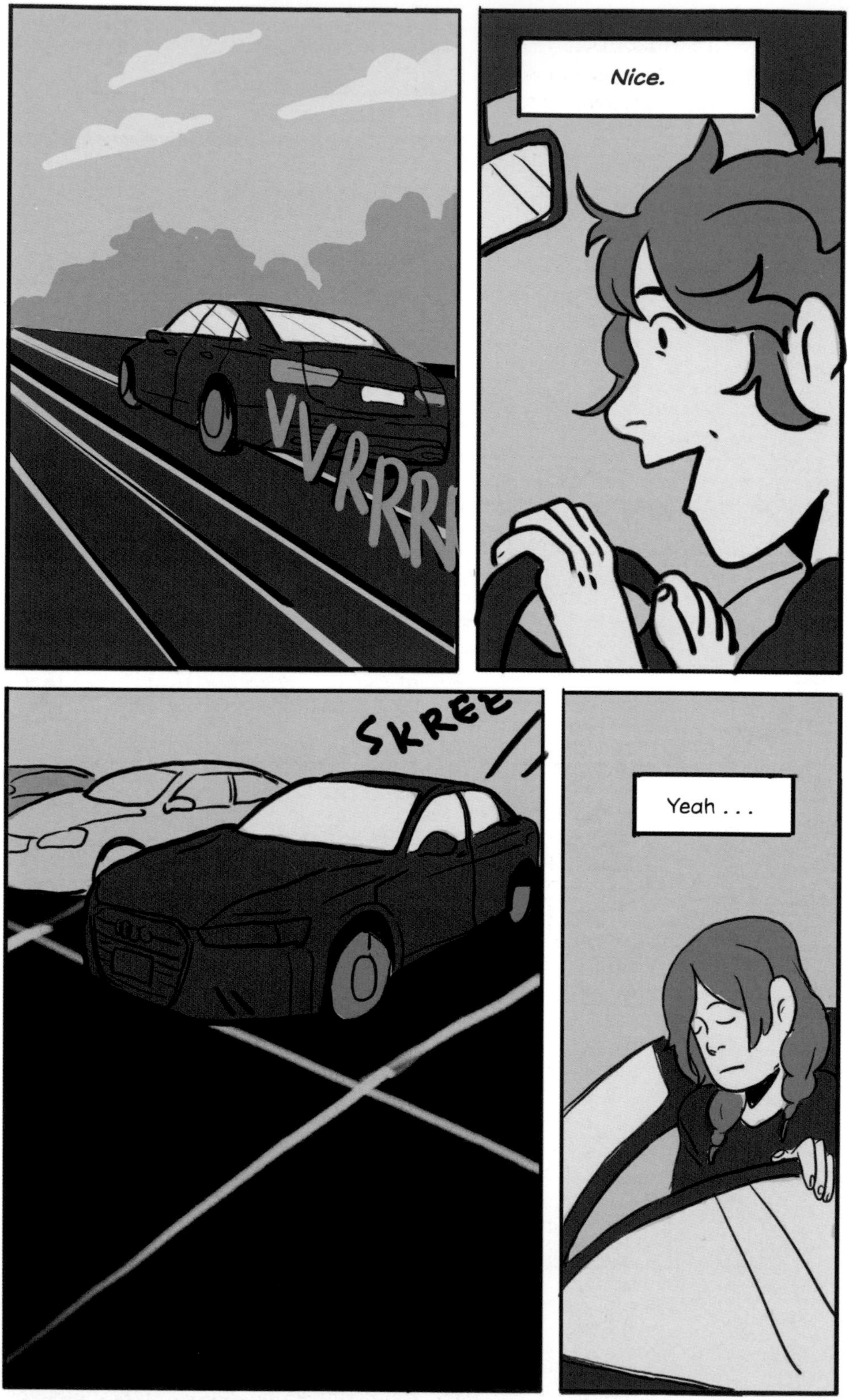
VVRRRR
Nice.
SKREE
Yeah . . .

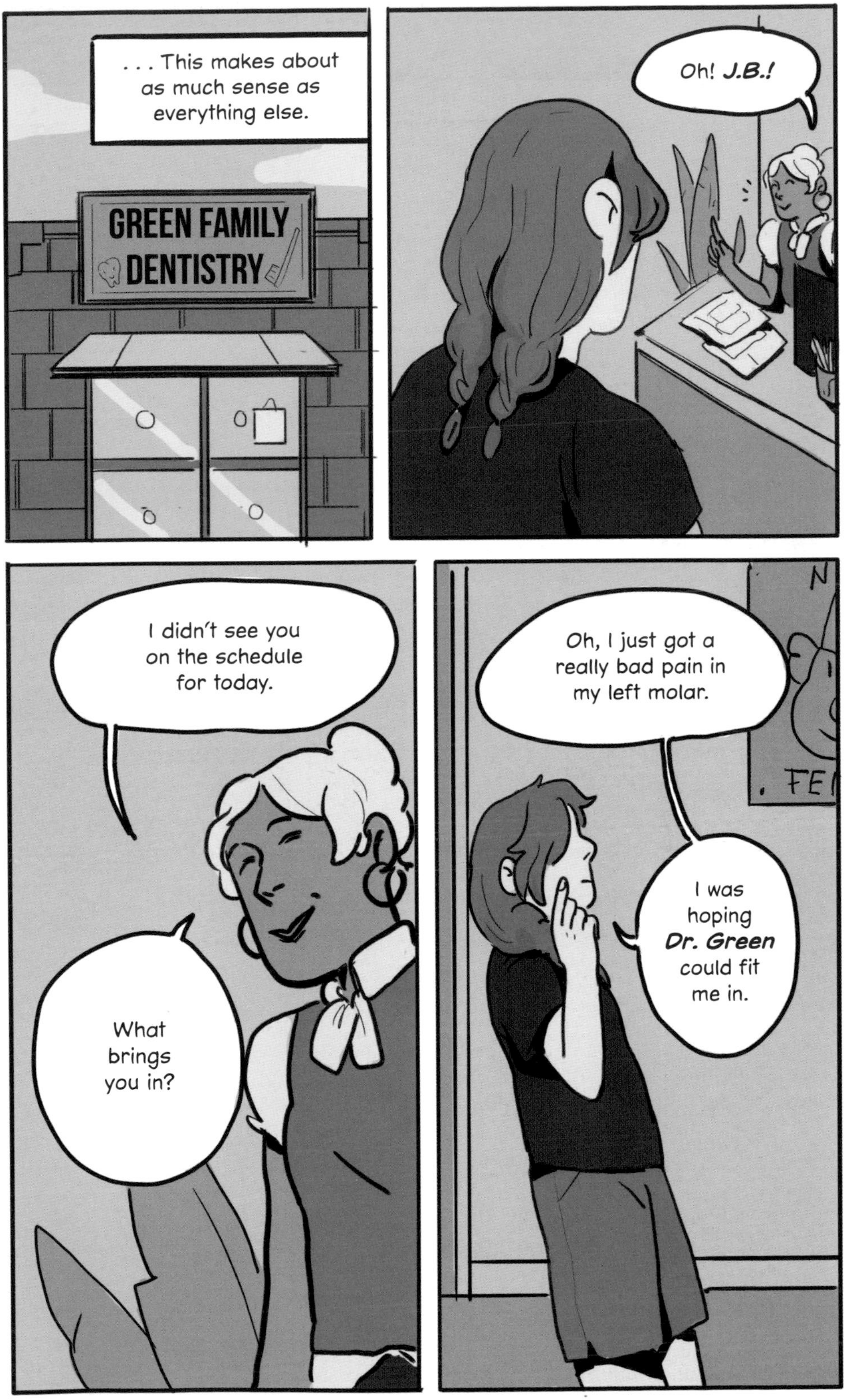
. . . This makes about as much sense as everything else.
GREEN FAMILY DENTISTRY
Oh! J.B.!
I didn't see you on the schedule for today.
What brings you in?
Oh, I just got a really bad pain in my left molar.
I was hoping Dr. Green could fit me in.

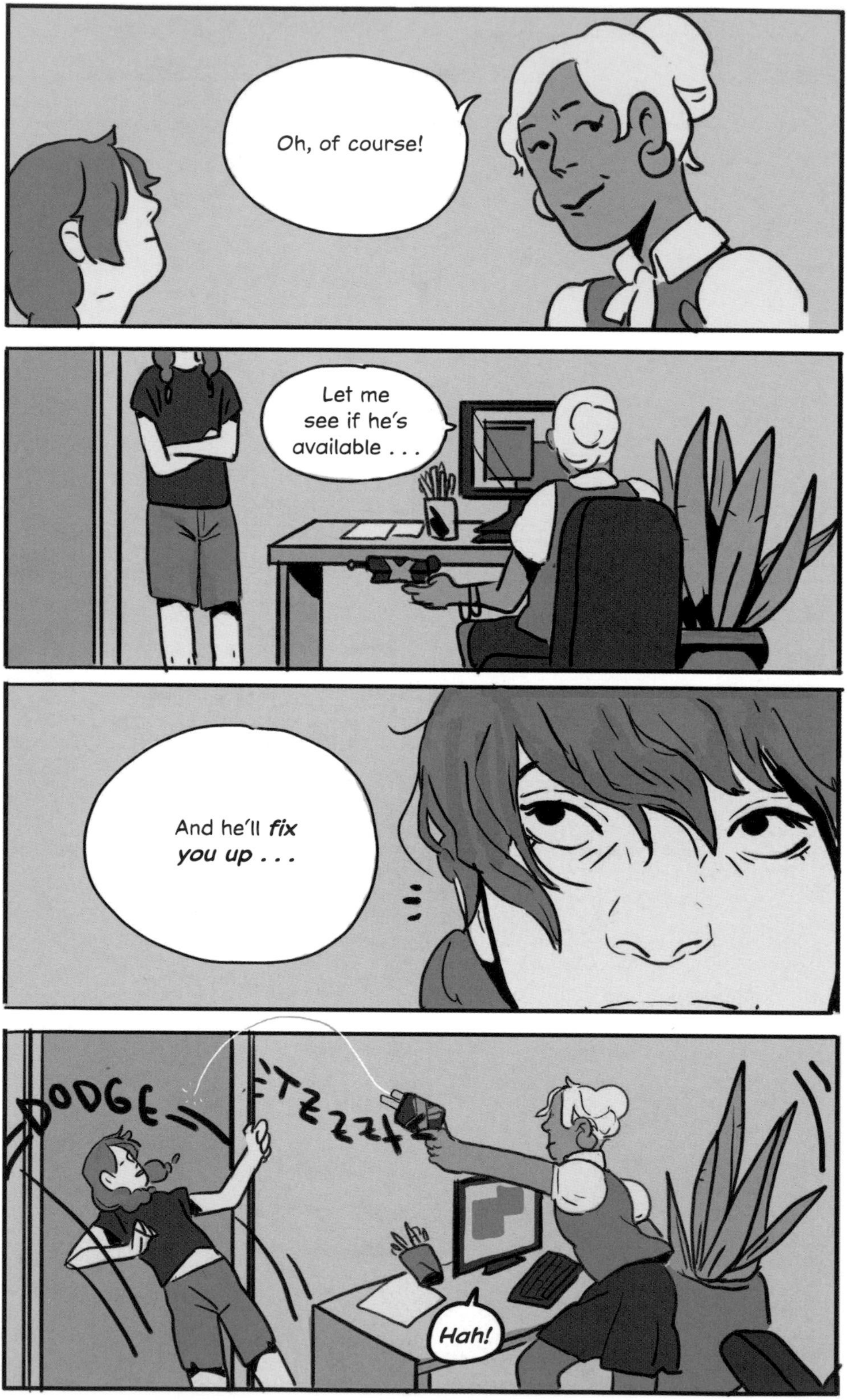
Oh, of course!
Let me see if he's available . . .
And he'll *fix you up . . .*
DODGE
TZZZZT
Hah!

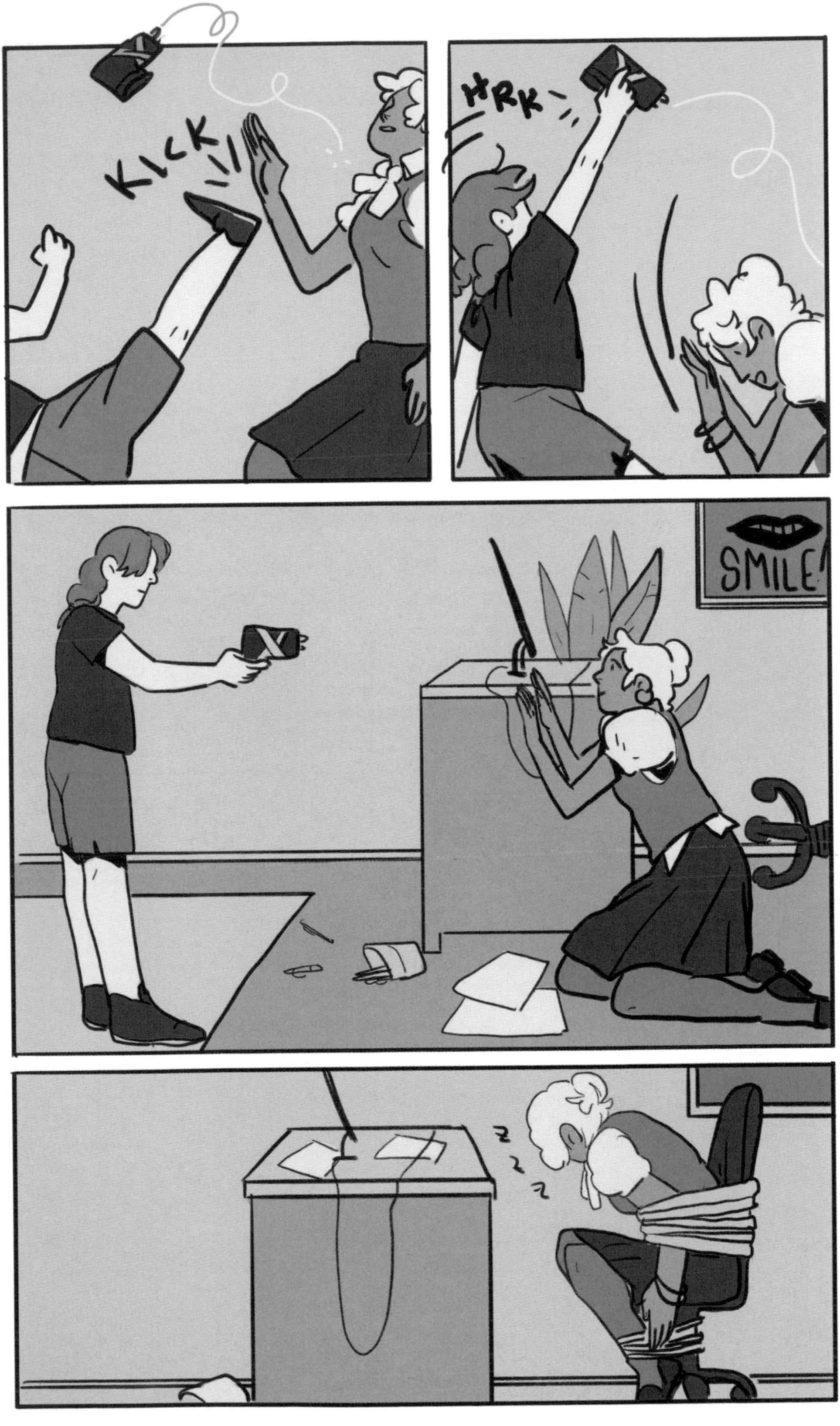
KICK
HRK
SMILE

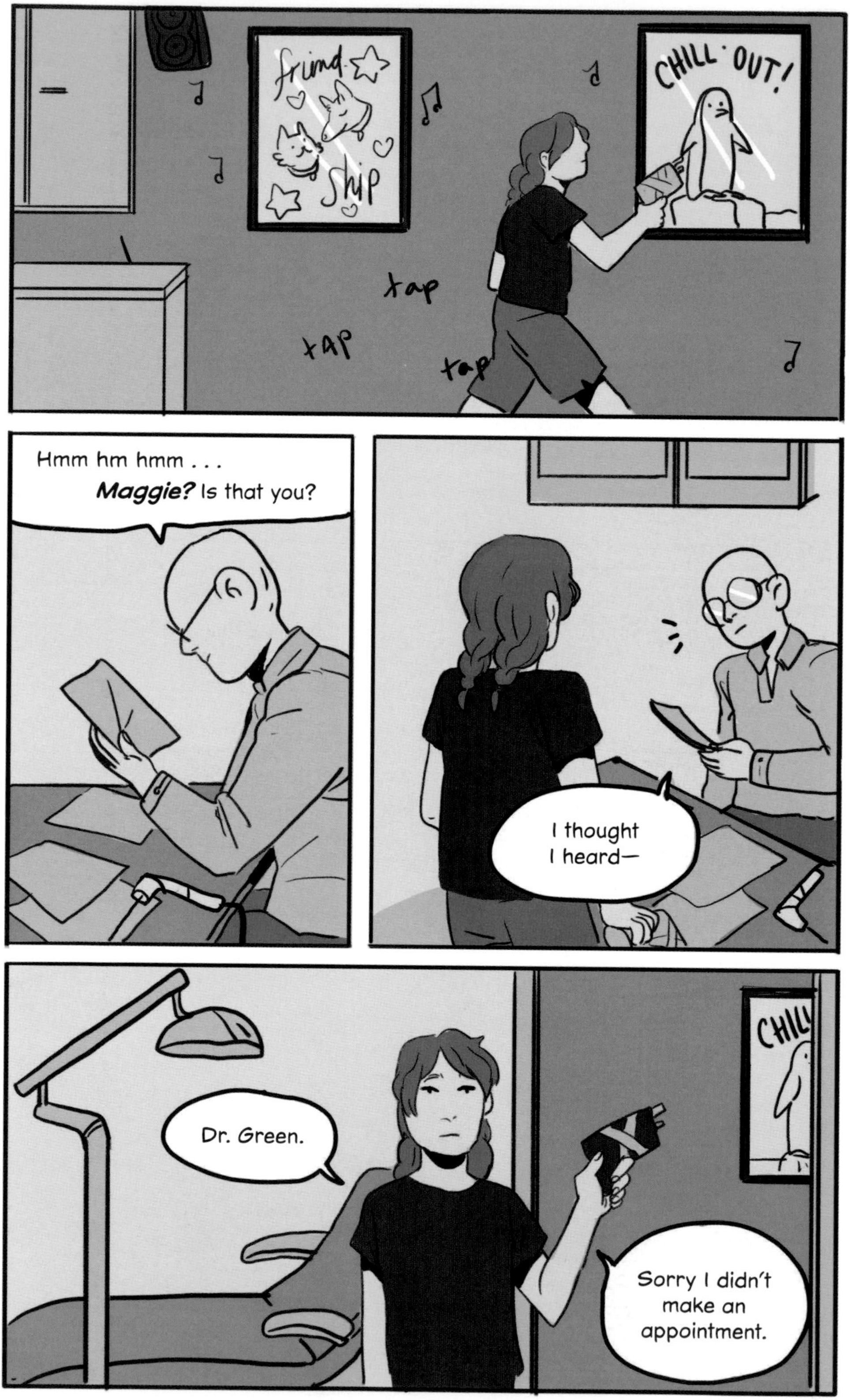
friend-ship
CHILL·OUT!
tap
tap
tap
Hmm hm hmm . . .
Maggie? Is that you?
I thought I heard—
Dr. Green.
Sorry I didn't make an appointment.

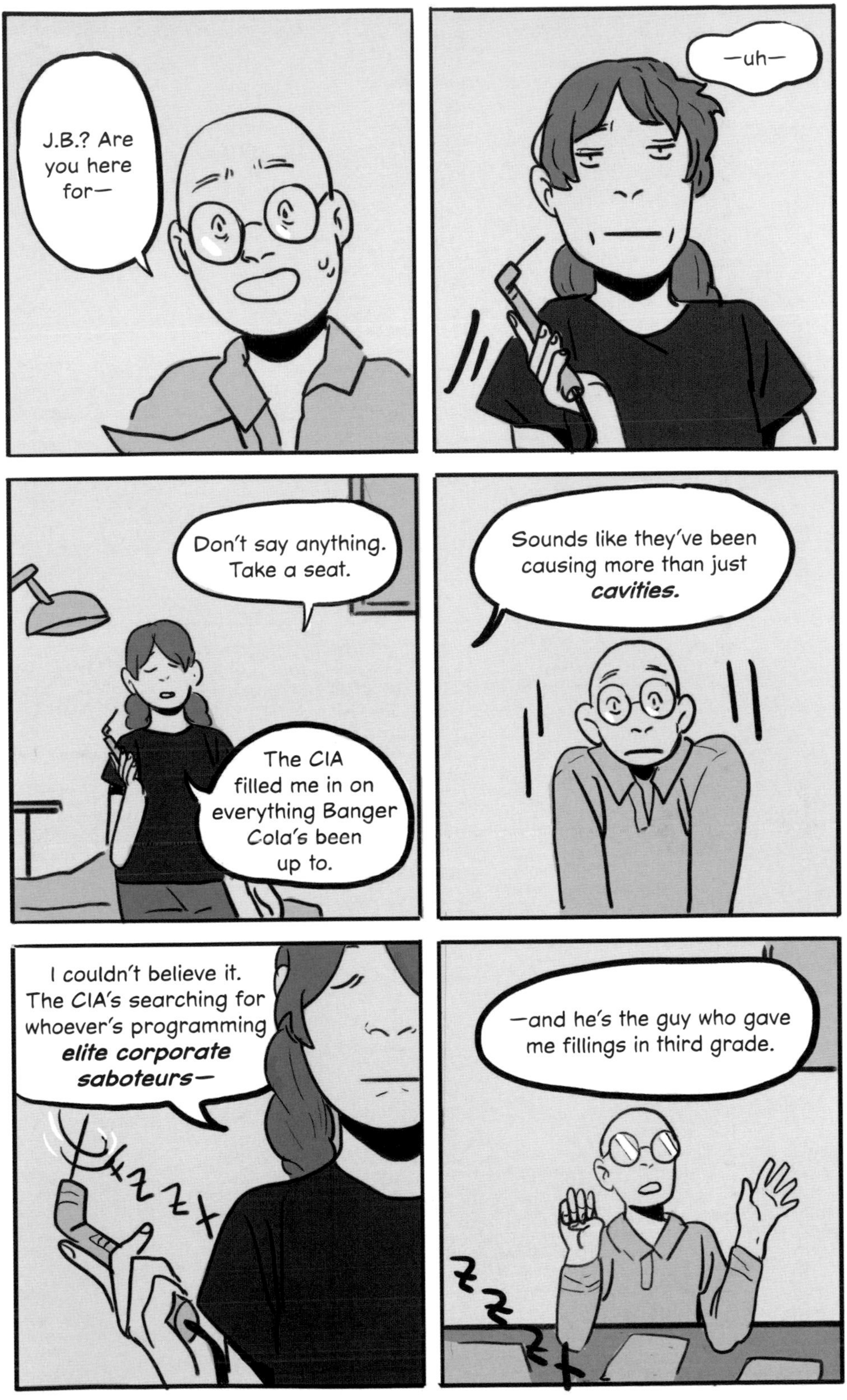
J.B.? Are you here for—
—uh—
Don't say anything. Take a seat.
The CIA filled me in on everything Banger Cola's been up to.
Sounds like they've been causing more than just ***cavities.***
I couldn't believe it. The CIA's searching for whoever's programming ***elite corporate saboteurs***—
—and he's the guy who gave me fillings in third grade.

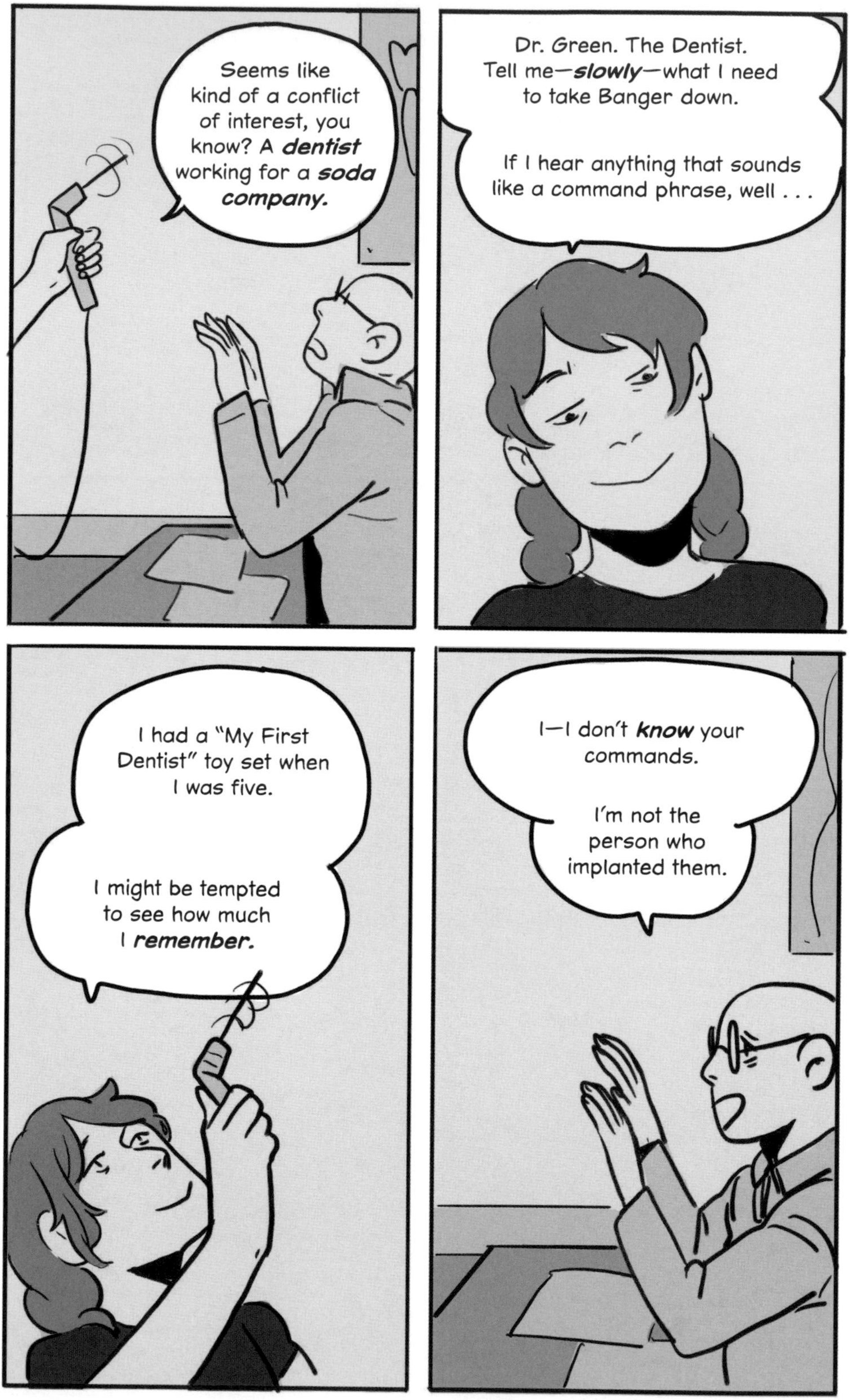
Seems like kind of a conflict of interest, you know? A **dentist** working for a **soda company.**
Dr. Green. The Dentist. Tell me—**slowly**—what I need to take Banger down.
If I hear anything that sounds like a command phrase, well . . .
I had a "My First Dentist" toy set when I was five.
I might be tempted to see how much I **remember.**
I—I don't **know** your commands.
I'm not the person who implanted them.

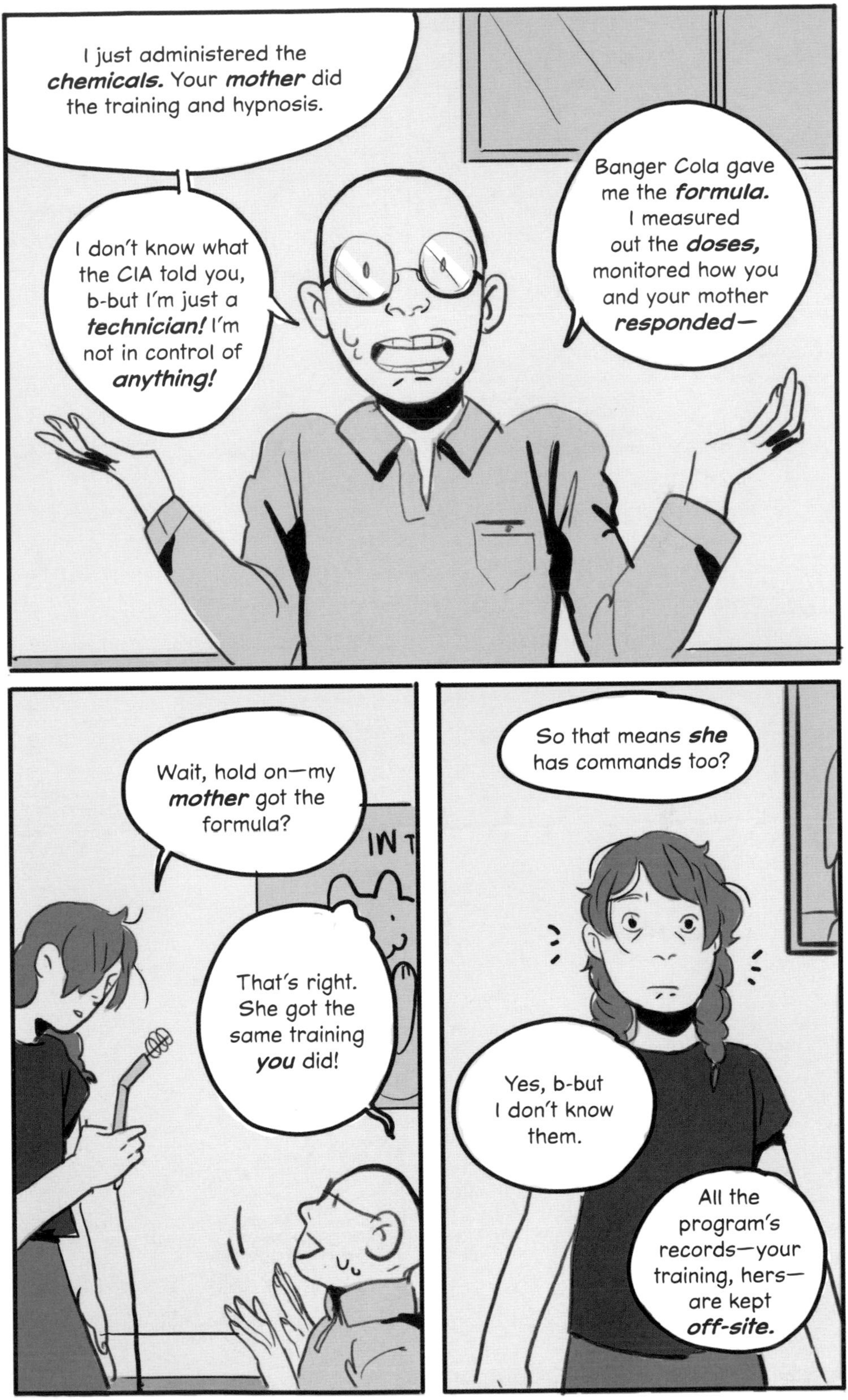
I just administered the ***chemicals.*** Your ***mother*** did the training and hypnosis.
I don't know what the CIA told you, b-but I'm just a ***technician!*** I'm not in control of ***anything!***
Banger Cola gave me the ***formula.*** I measured out the ***doses,*** monitored how you and your mother ***responded—***
Wait, hold on—my ***mother*** got the formula?
That's right. She got the same training ***you*** did!
So that means ***she*** has commands too?
Yes, b-but I don't know them.
All the program's records—your training, hers—are kept ***off-site.***

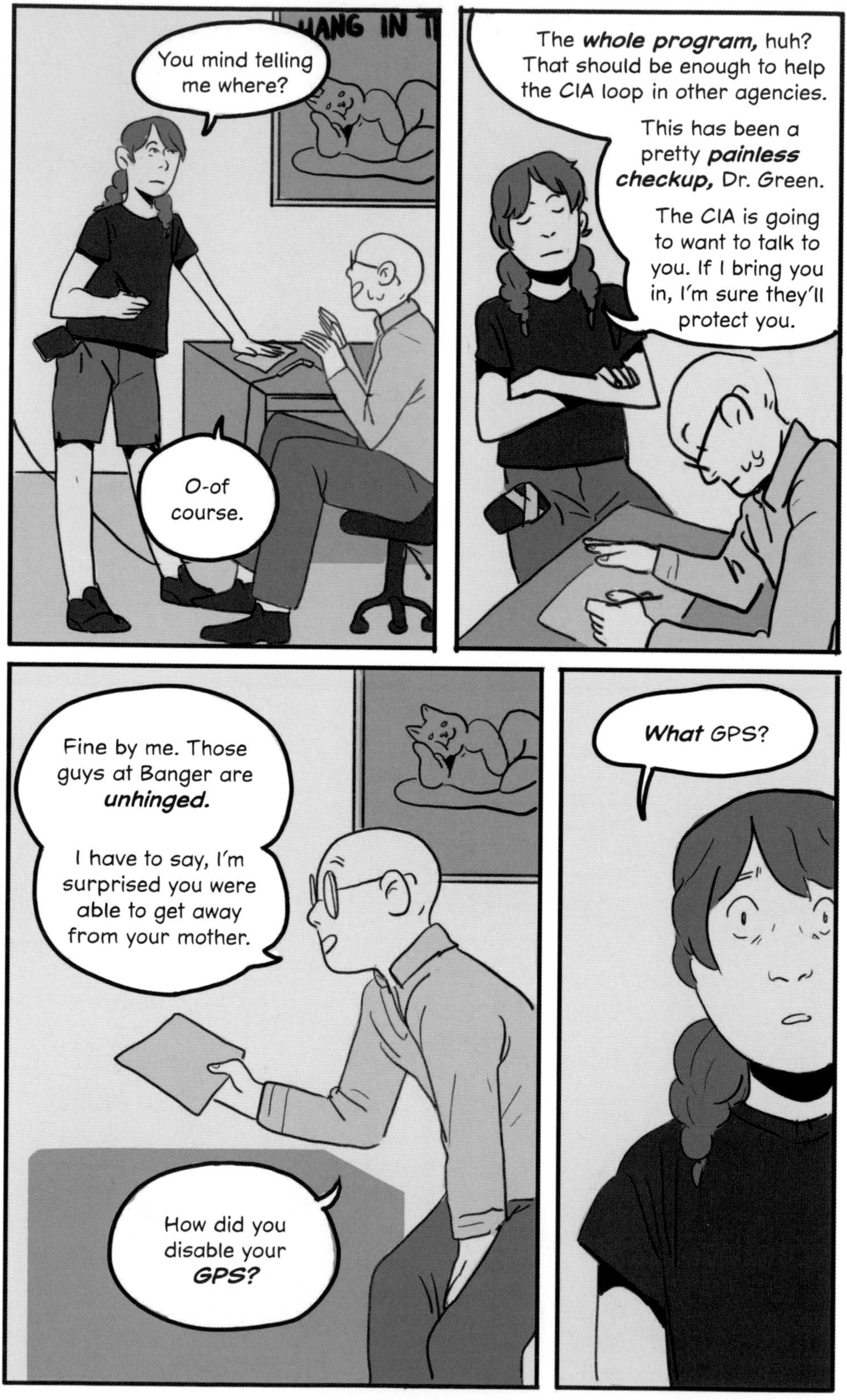
HANG IN T
You mind telling me where?
O-of course.
The *whole program,* huh? That should be enough to help the CIA loop in other agencies.
This has been a pretty *painless checkup,* Dr. Green.
The CIA is going to want to talk to you. If I bring you in, I'm sure they'll protect you.
Fine by me. Those guys at Banger are *unhinged.*
I have to say, I'm surprised you were able to get away from your mother.
How did you disable your *GPS?*
What GPS?

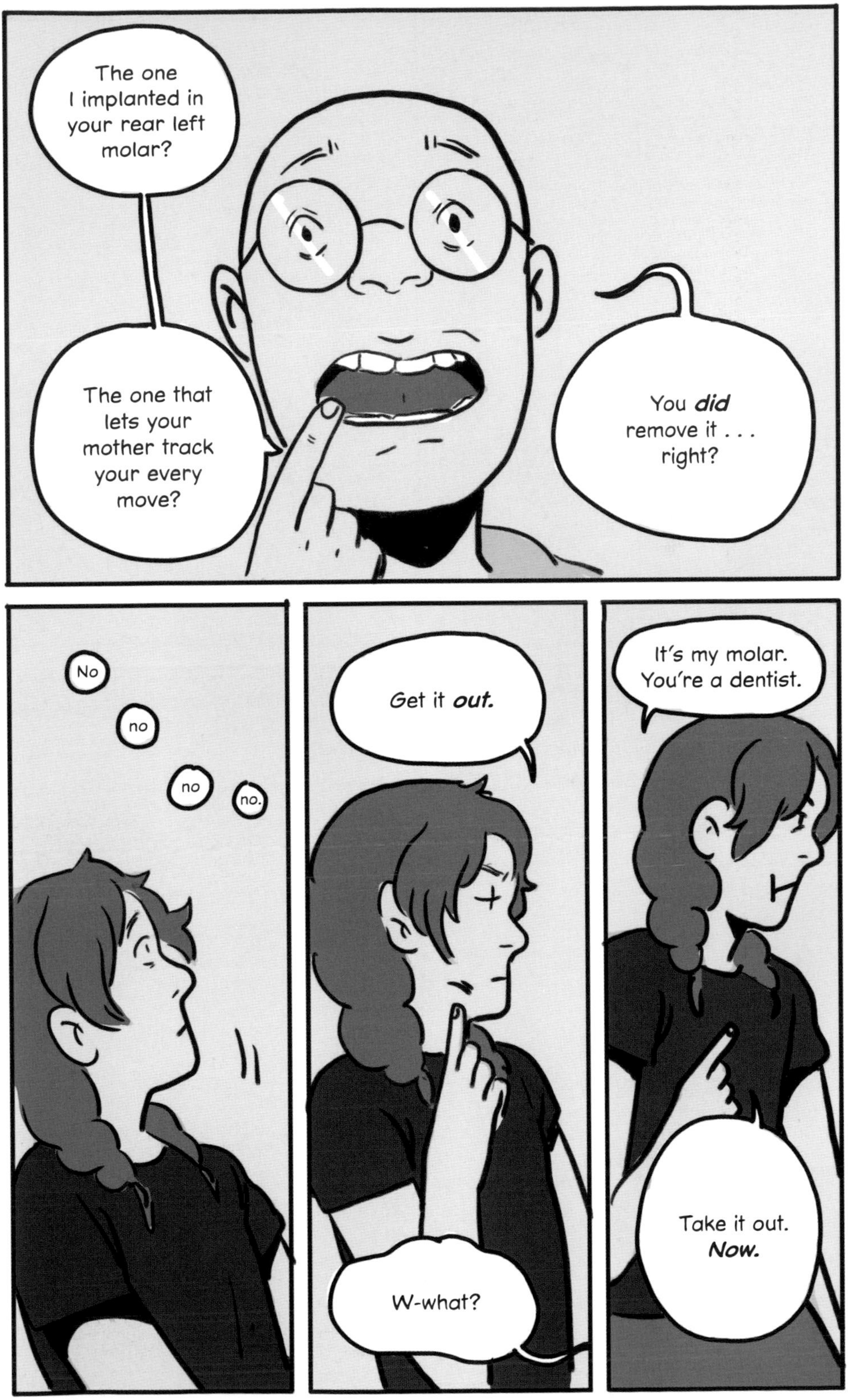
The one I implanted in your rear left molar?
The one that lets your mother track your every move?
You *did* remove it . . . right?
No
no
no
no.
Get it *out.*
W-what?
It's my molar. You're a dentist.
Take it out. *Now.*

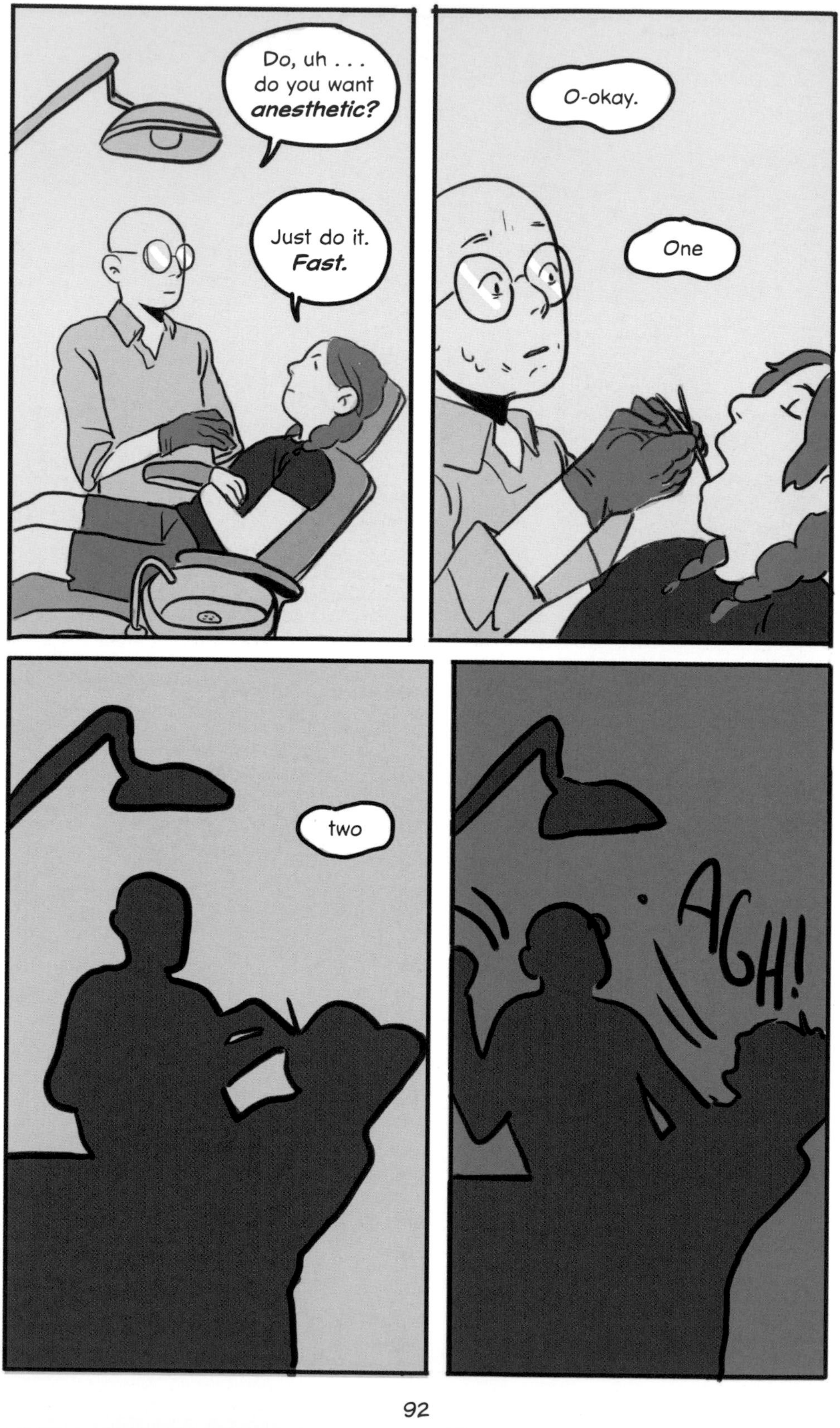
Do, uh . . .
do you want
anesthetic?
Just do it.
Fast.
O-okay.
One
two
AGH!

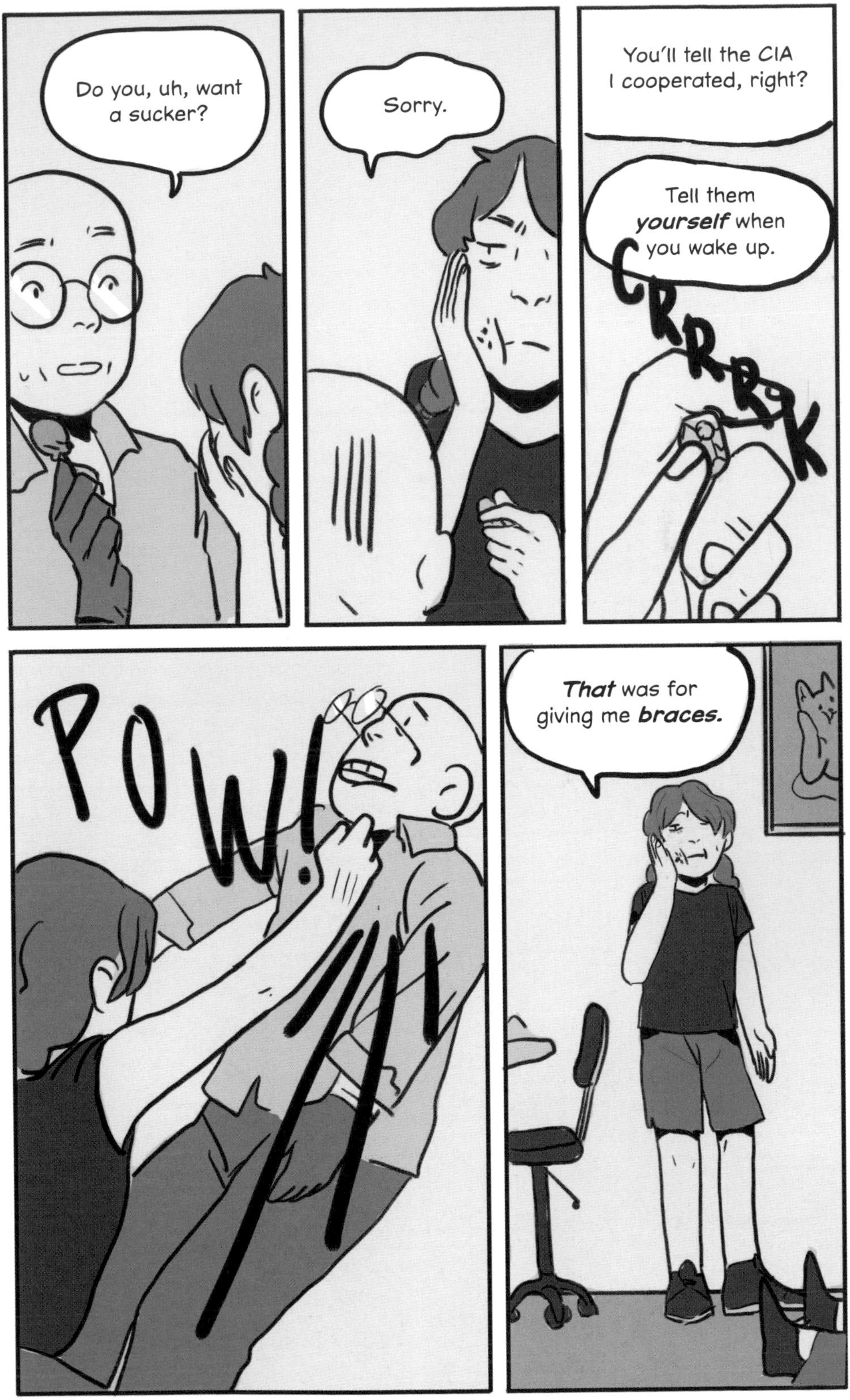
Do you, uh, want a sucker?
Sorry.
You'll tell the CIA I cooperated, right?
Tell them ***yourself*** when you wake up.
CRRRK
POW!
That was for giving me ***braces.***

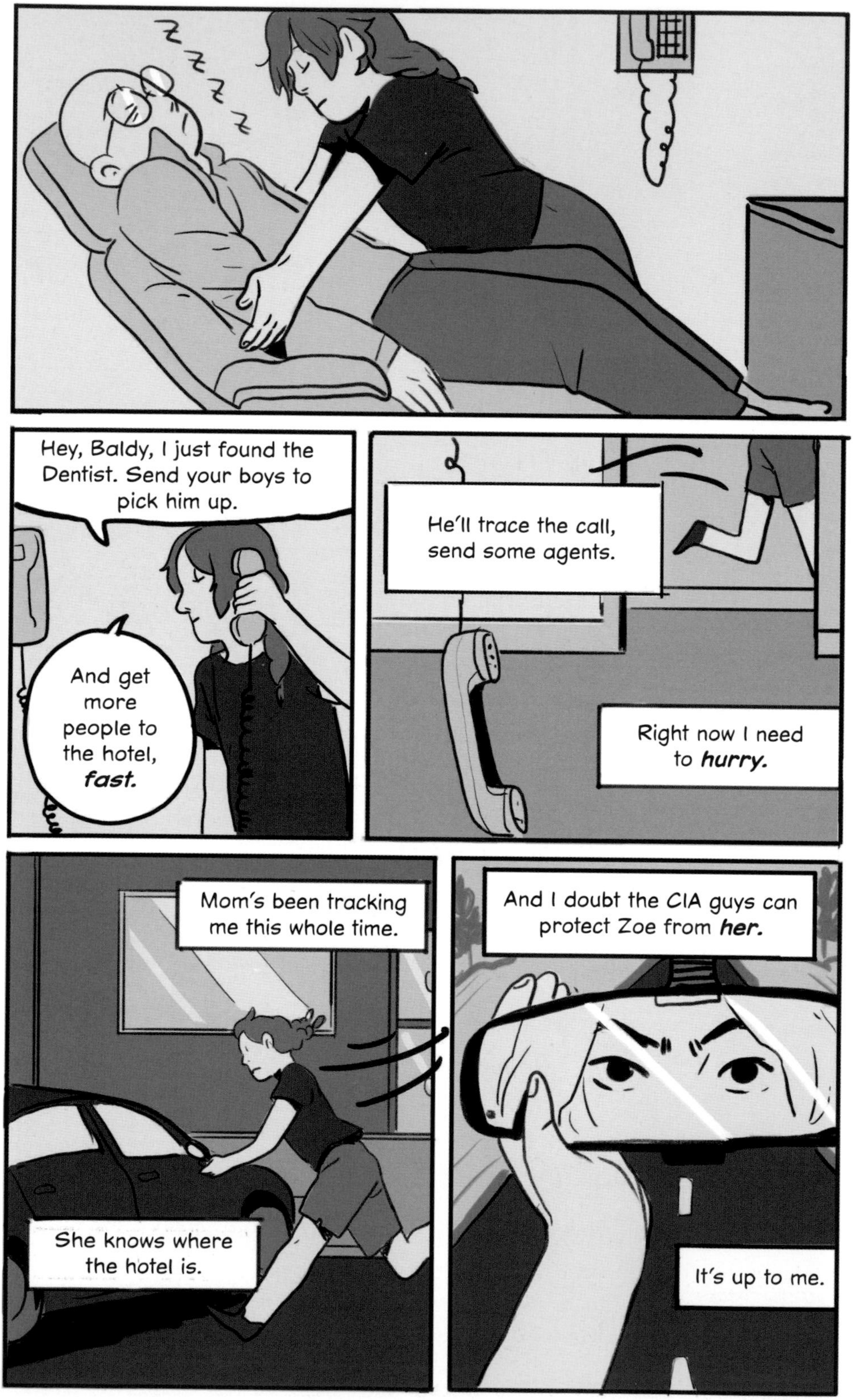
Z Z Z Z Z
Hey, Baldy, I just found the Dentist. Send your boys to pick him up.
And get more people to the hotel, *fast.*
He'll trace the call, send some agents.
Right now I need to *hurry.*
Mom's been tracking me this whole time.
She knows where the hotel is.
And I doubt the CIA guys can protect Zoe from *her.*
It's up to me.

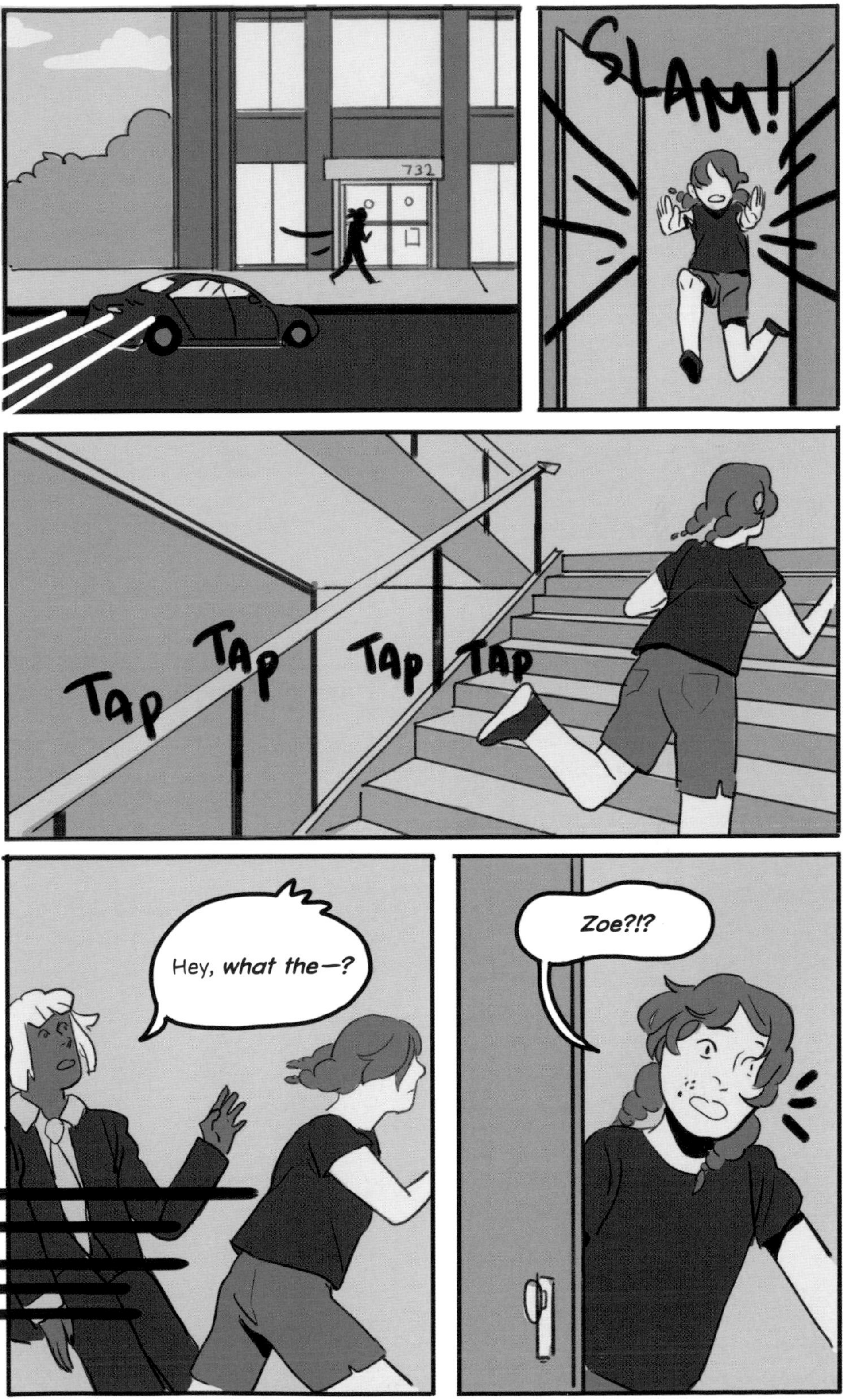
SLAM!
TAP
TAP
TAP
TAP
Hey, what the—?
Zoe?!?

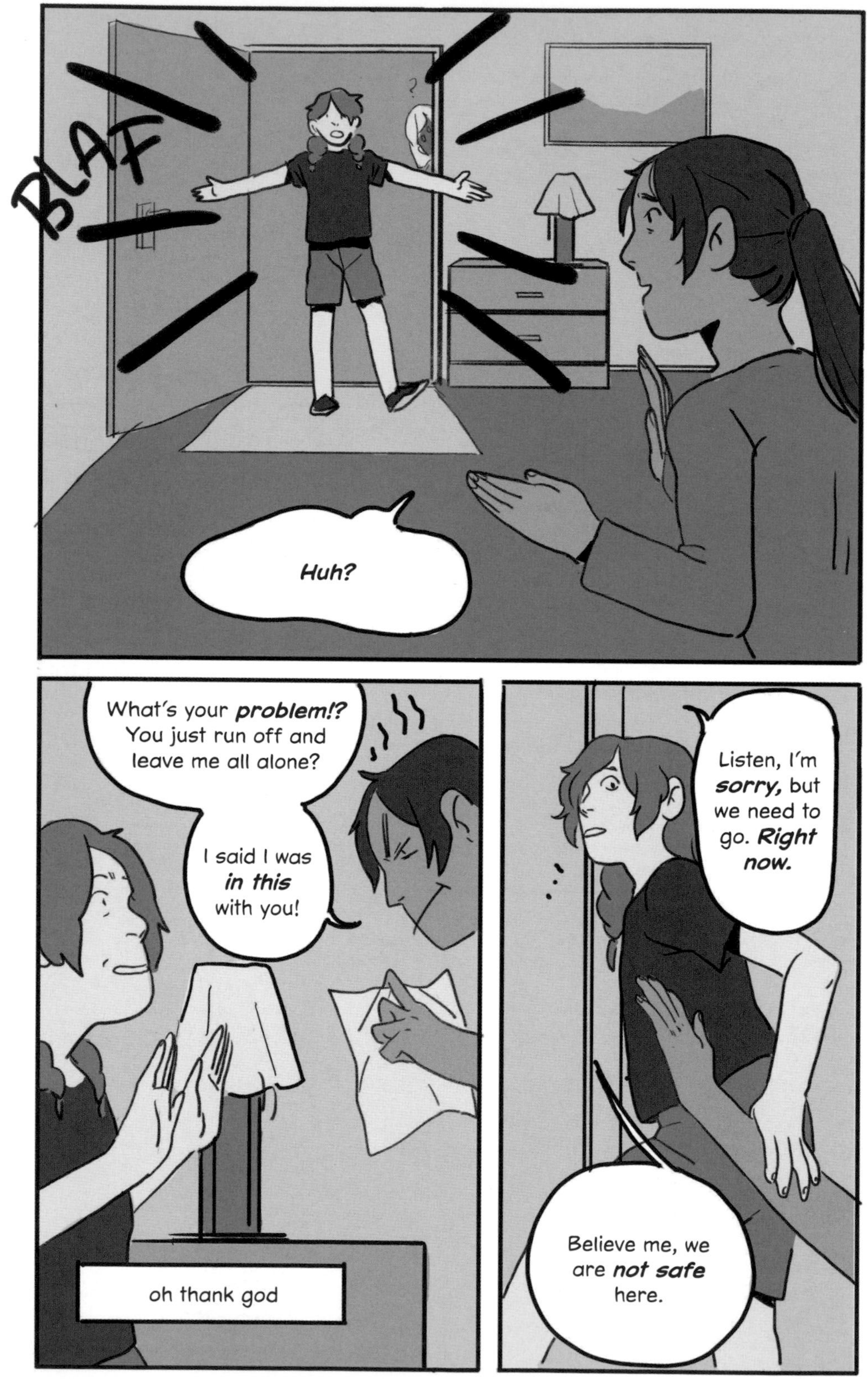
BLAF
Huh?
What's your **problem!?** You just run off and leave me all alone?
I said I was ***in this*** with you!
oh thank god
Listen, I'm ***sorry,*** but we need to go. ***Right now.***
Believe me, we are ***not safe*** here.

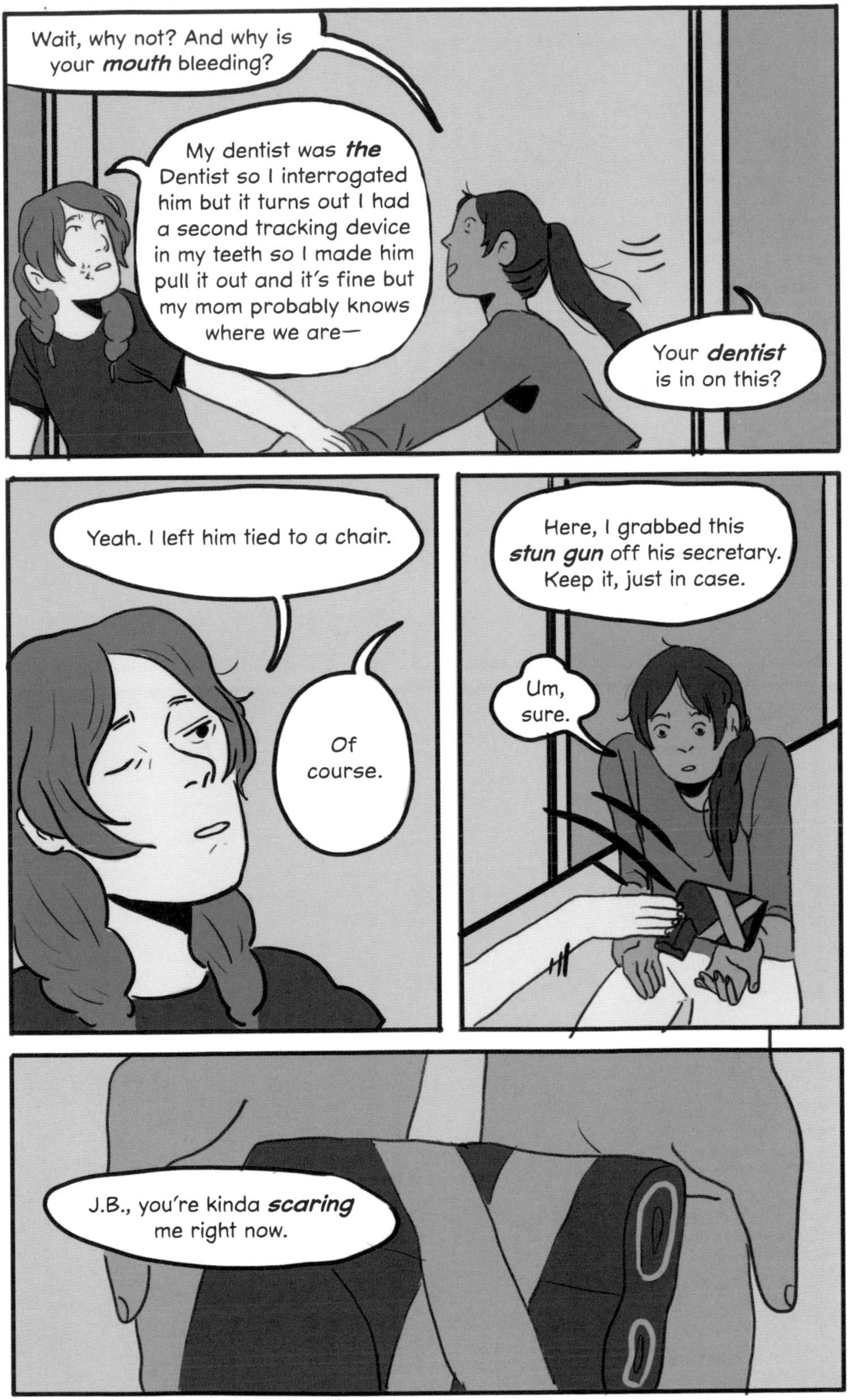
Wait, why not? And why is your *mouth* bleeding?
My dentist was *the* Dentist so I interrogated him but it turns out I had a second tracking device in my teeth so I made him pull it out and it's fine but my mom probably knows where we are—
Your *dentist* is in on this?
Yeah. I left him tied to a chair.
Of course.
Here, I grabbed this *stun gun* off his secretary. Keep it, just in case.
Um, sure.
J.B., you're kinda *scaring* me right now.

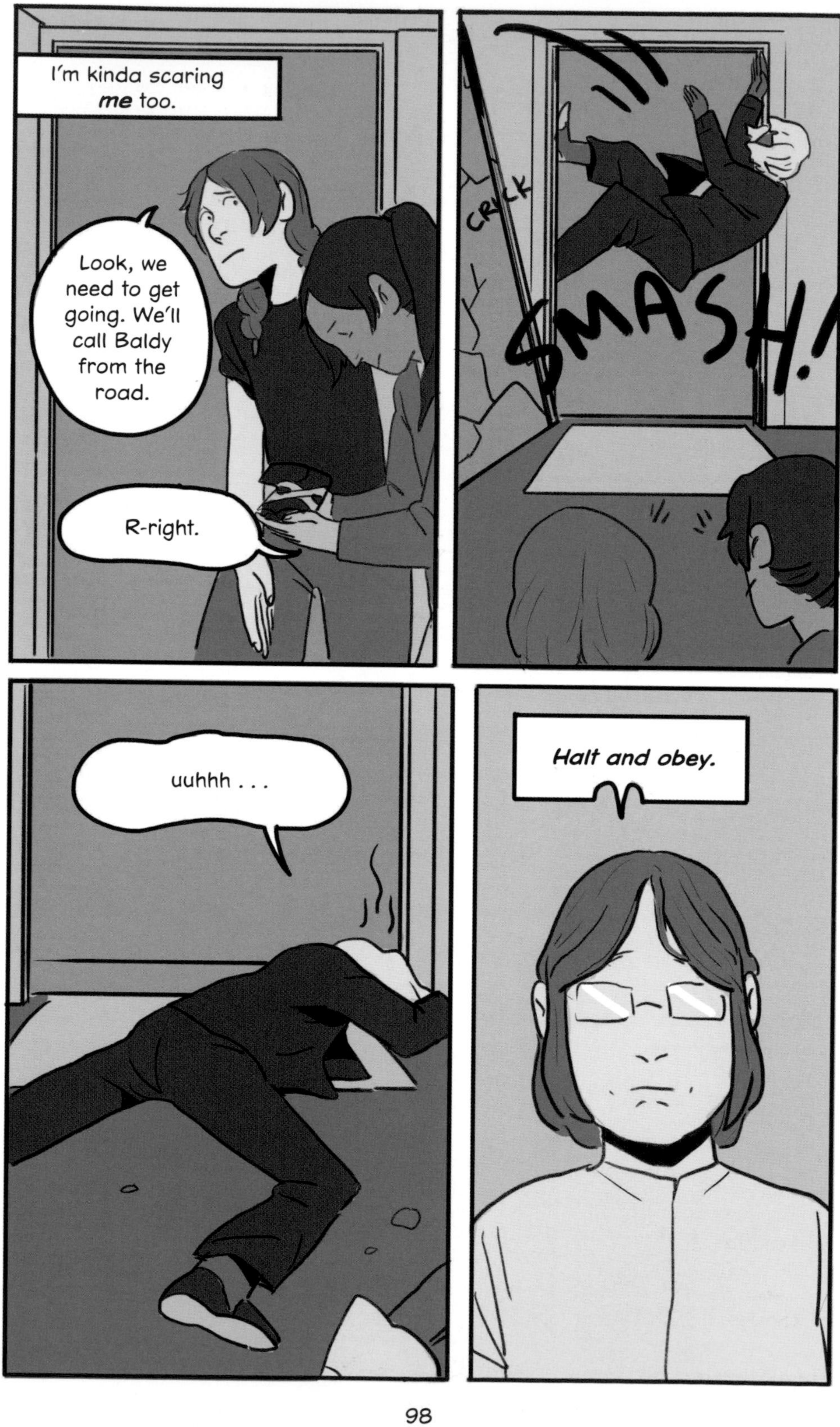
I'm kinda scaring ***me*** too.
Look, we need to get going. We'll call Baldy from the road.
R-right.
CRACK
SMASH!!
uuhhh . . .
Halt and obey.

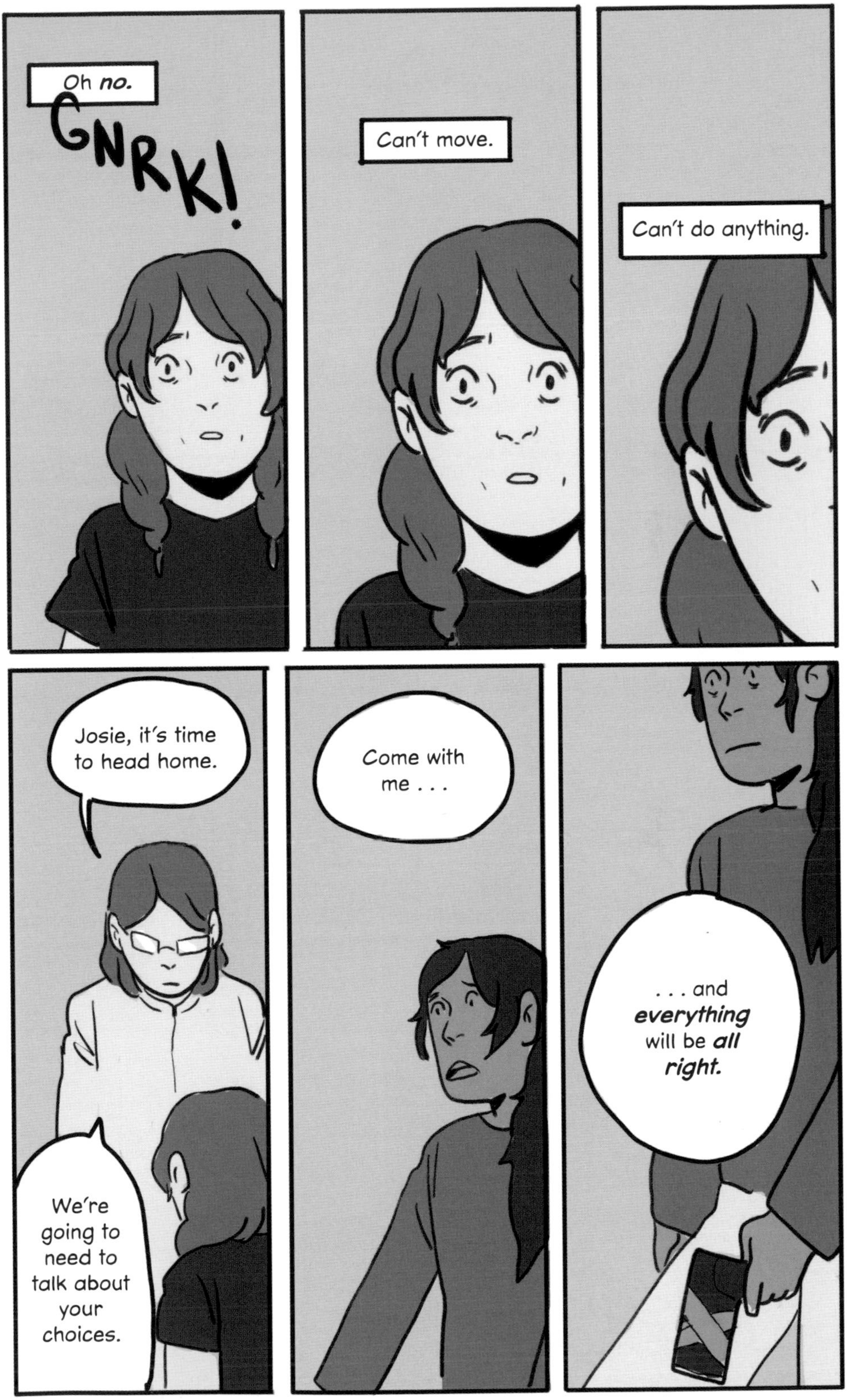
Oh no.
GNRK!
Can't move.
Can't do anything.
Josie, it's time to head home.
We're going to need to talk about your choices.
Come with me . . .
. . . and everything will be all right.

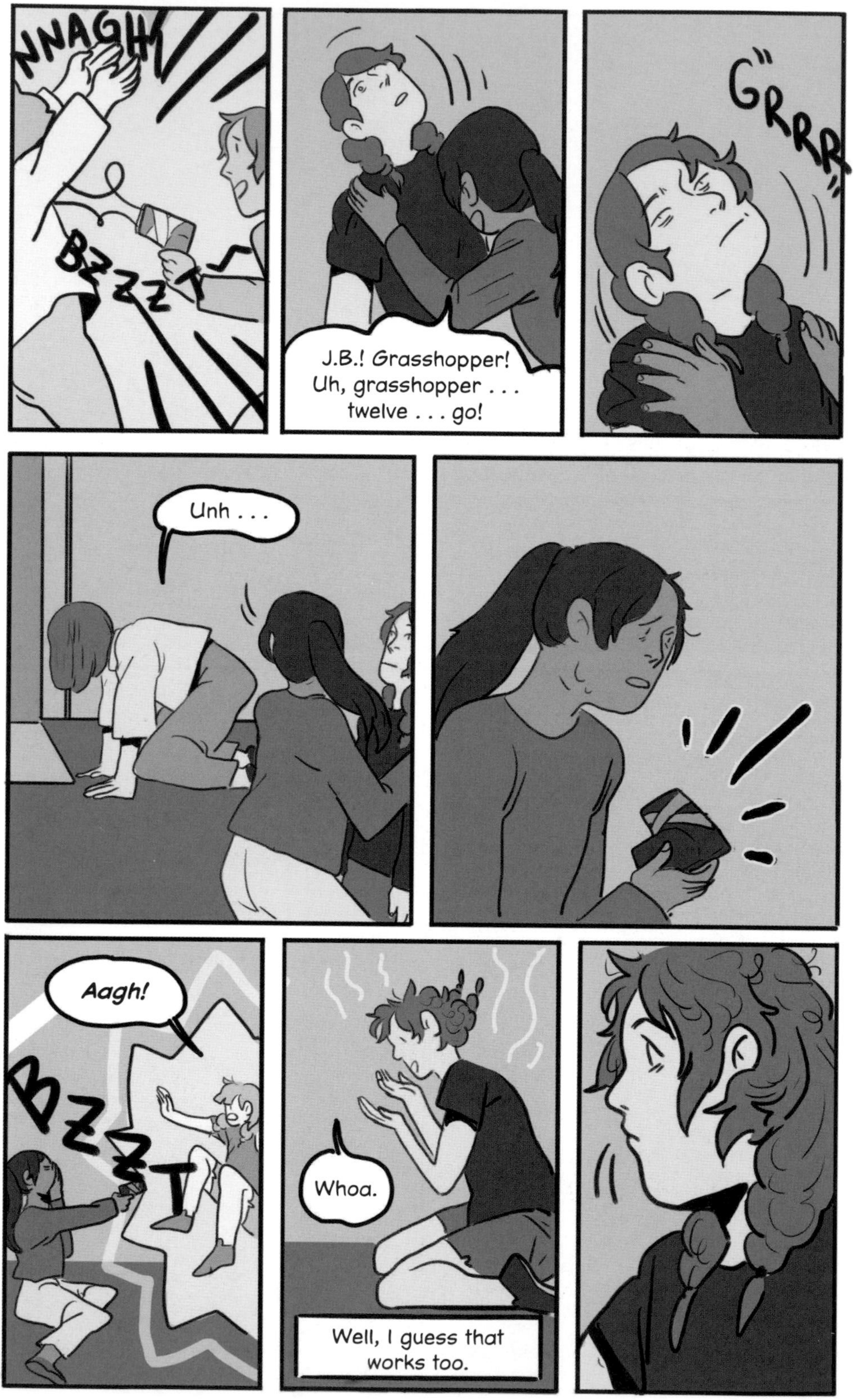
NNAGH
BZZZT
J.B.! Grasshopper! Uh, grasshopper . . . twelve . . . go!
GRRRR
Unh . . .
Aagh!
BZZZT
Whoa.
Well, I guess that works too.

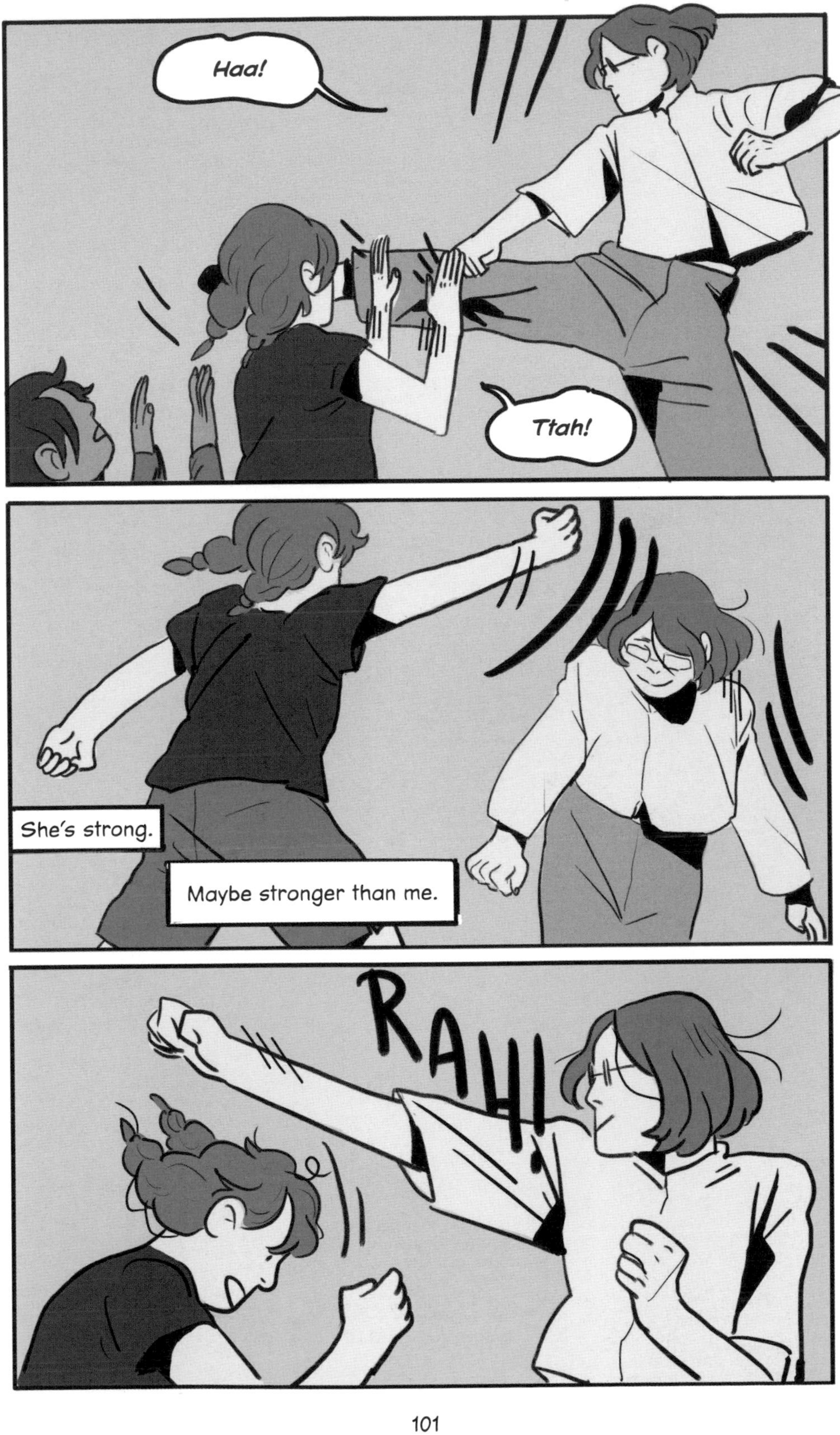
Haa!
Ttah!
She's strong.
Maybe stronger than me.
RAHH!

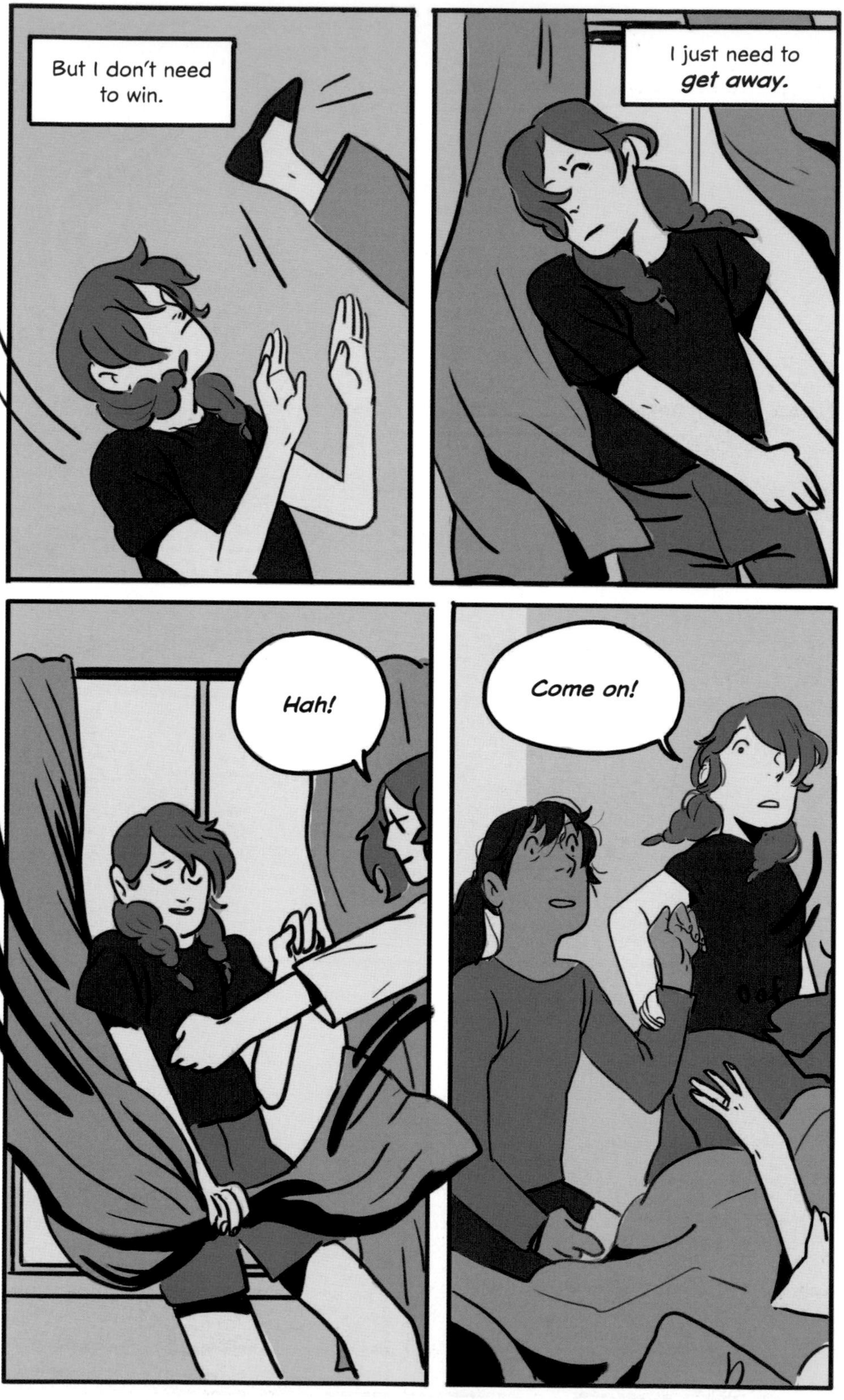
But I don't need to win.
I just need to *get away.*
Hah!
Come on!
oof

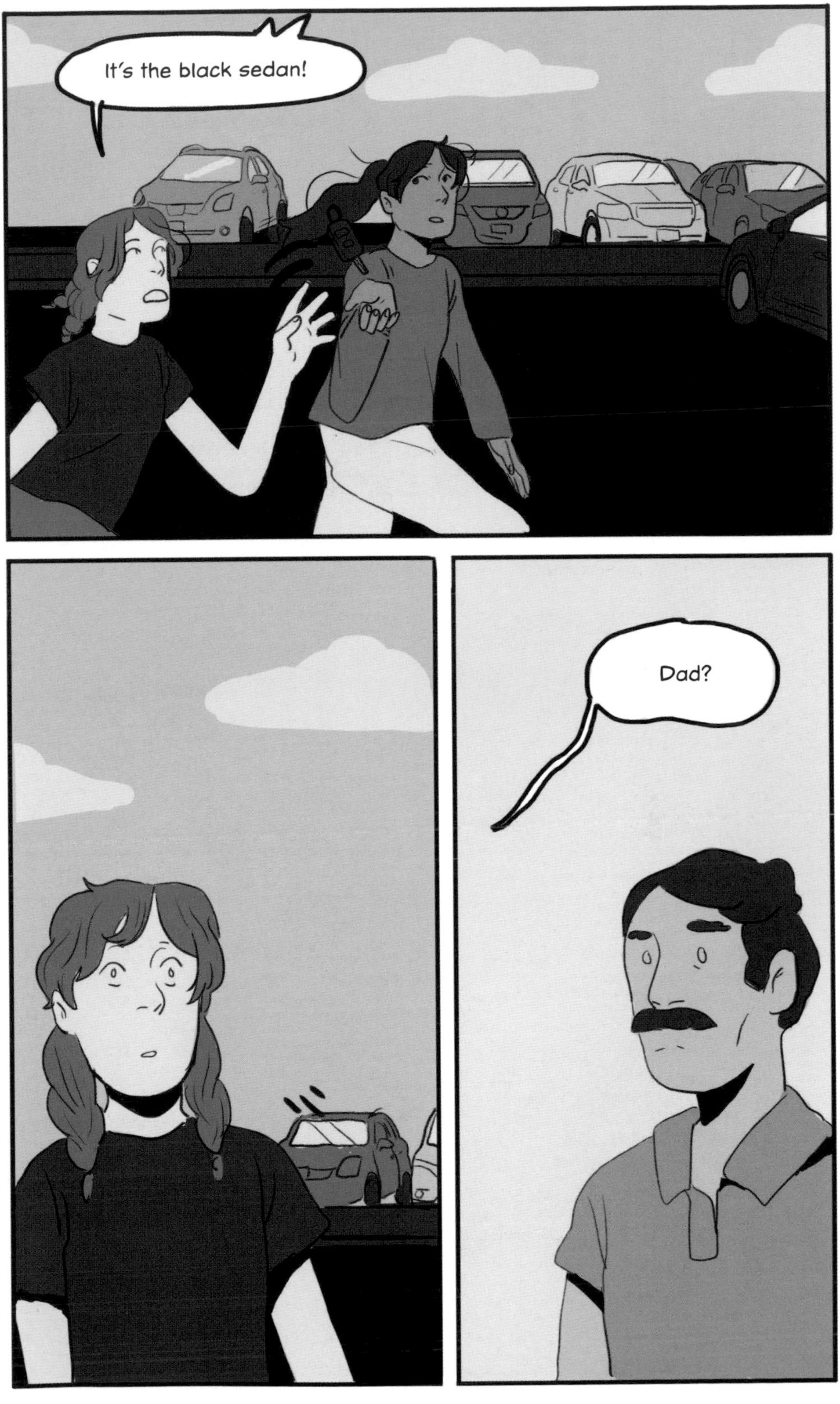
It's the black sedan!
Dad?

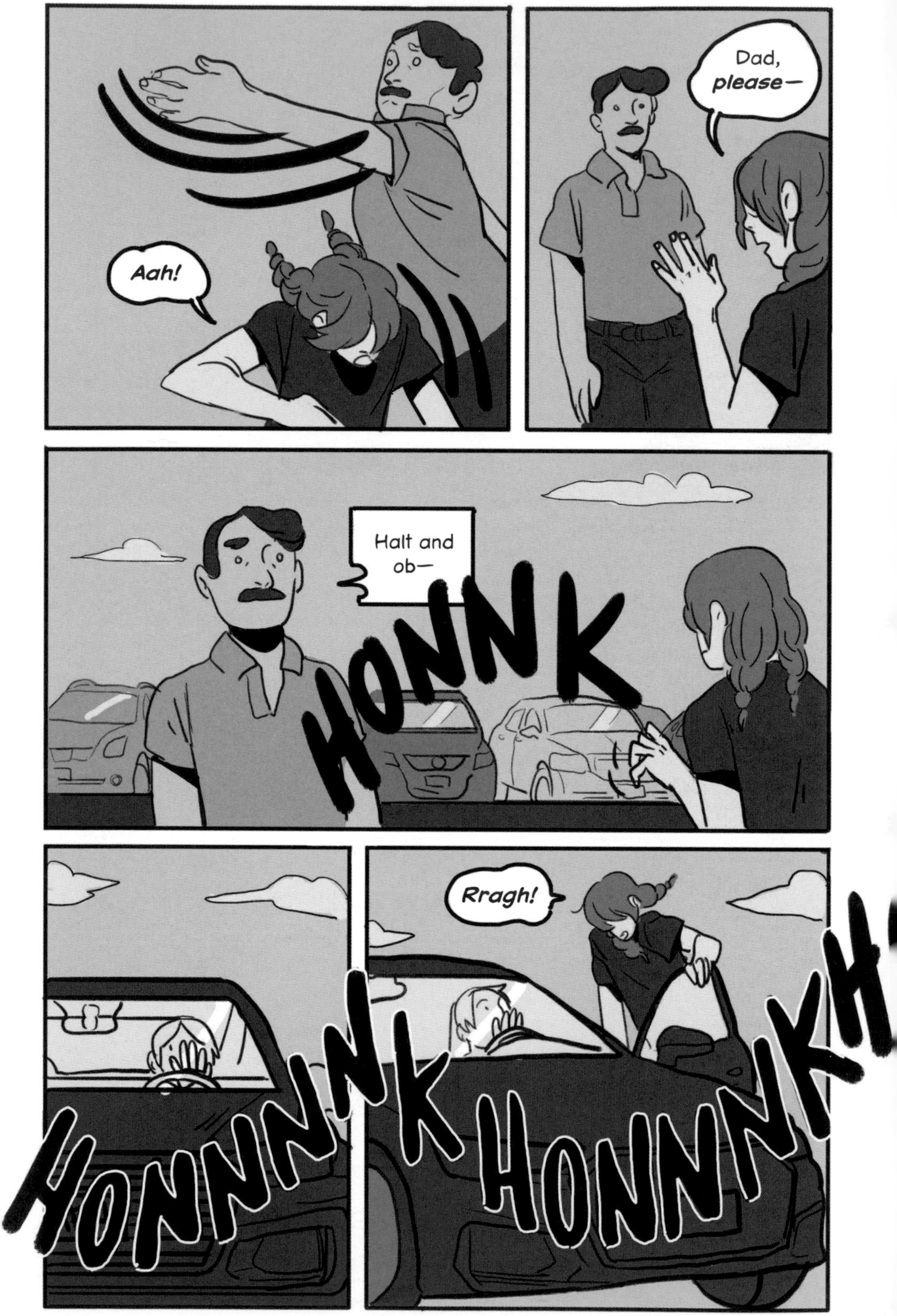
Aah!
Dad,
please—
Halt and
ob—
HONNK
Rragh!
HONNNNK
HONNNNKH

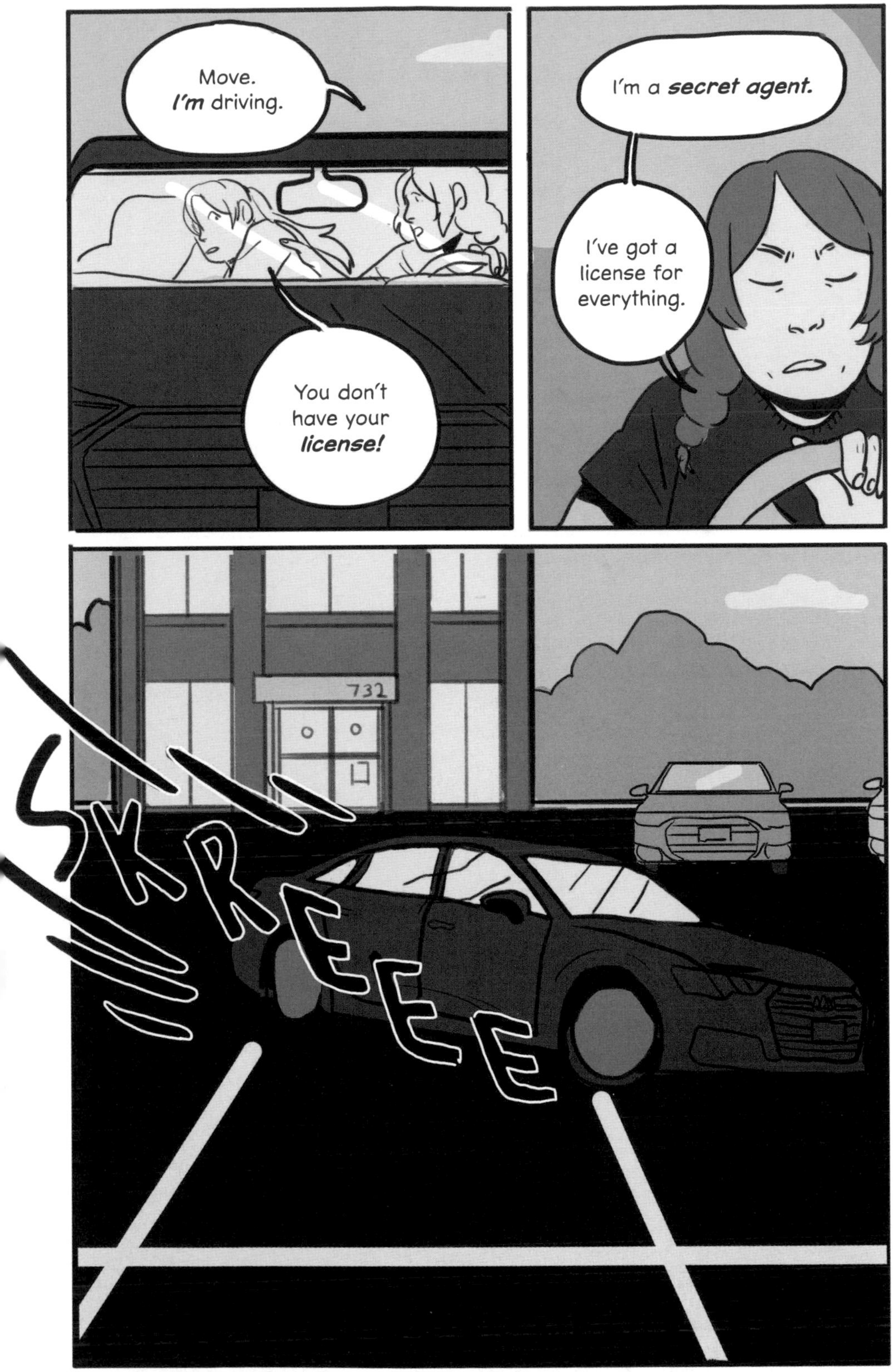
Move. *I'm* driving.
You don't have your ***license!***
I'm a ***secret agent.***
I've got a license for everything.
732
SKREEEE

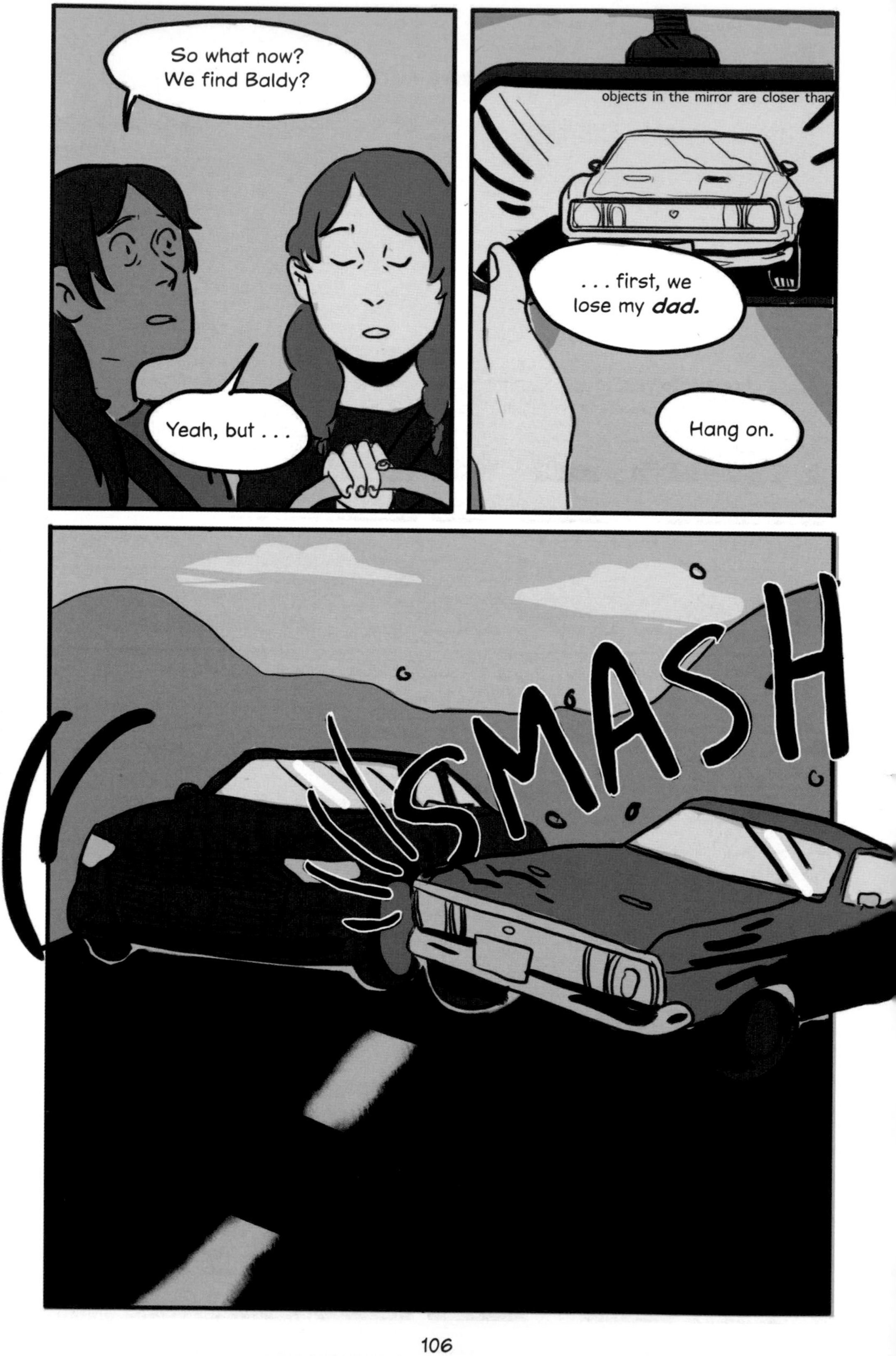
So what now? We find Baldy?
Yeah, but . . .
objects in the mirror are closer tha
. . . first, we lose my *dad.*
Hang on.
SMASH

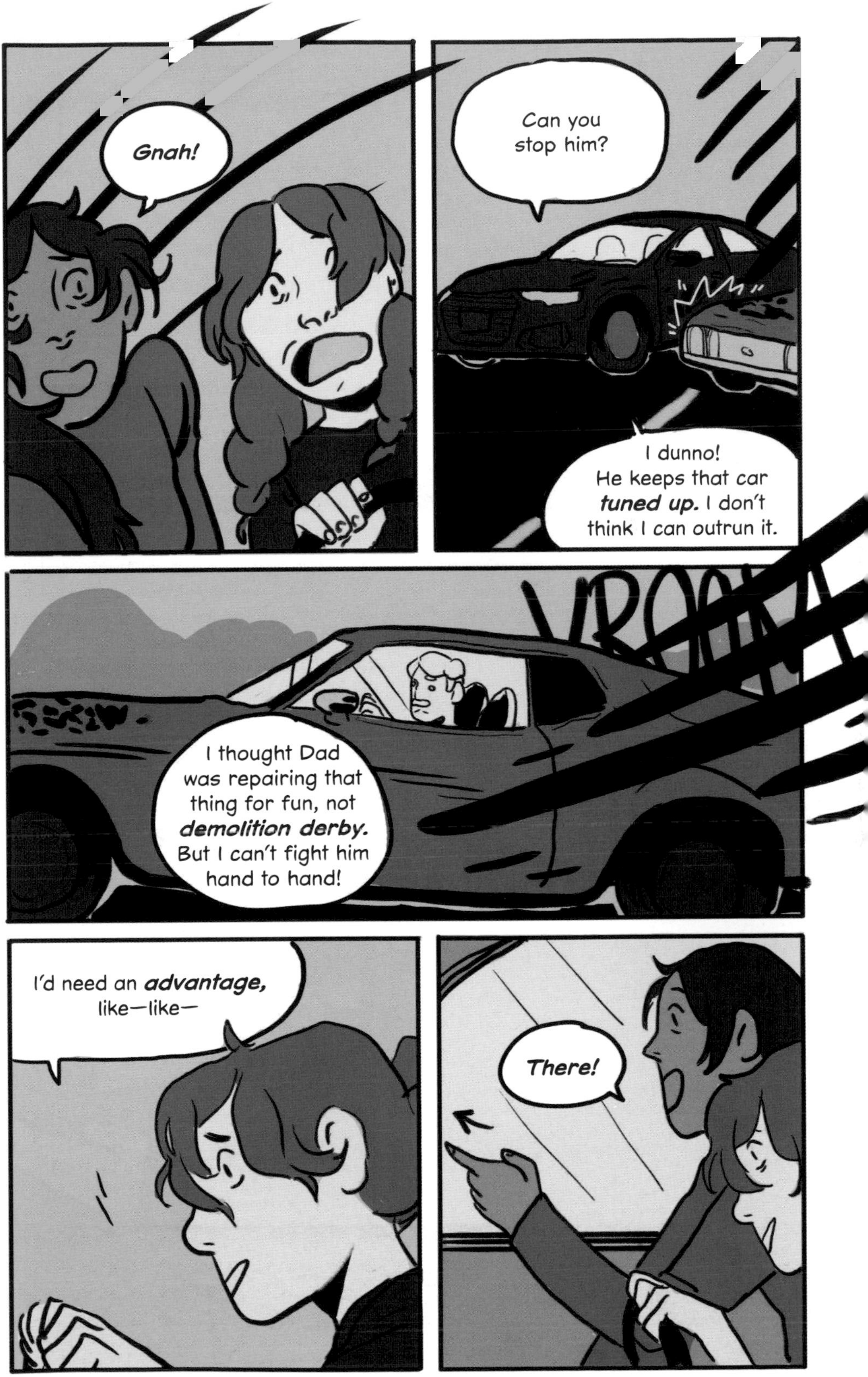
Gnah!
Can you stop him?
I dunno! He keeps that car *tuned up.* I don't think I can outrun it.
VROOM
I thought Dad was repairing that thing for fun, not *demolition derby.* But I can't fight him hand to hand!
I'd need an *advantage,* like—like—
There!

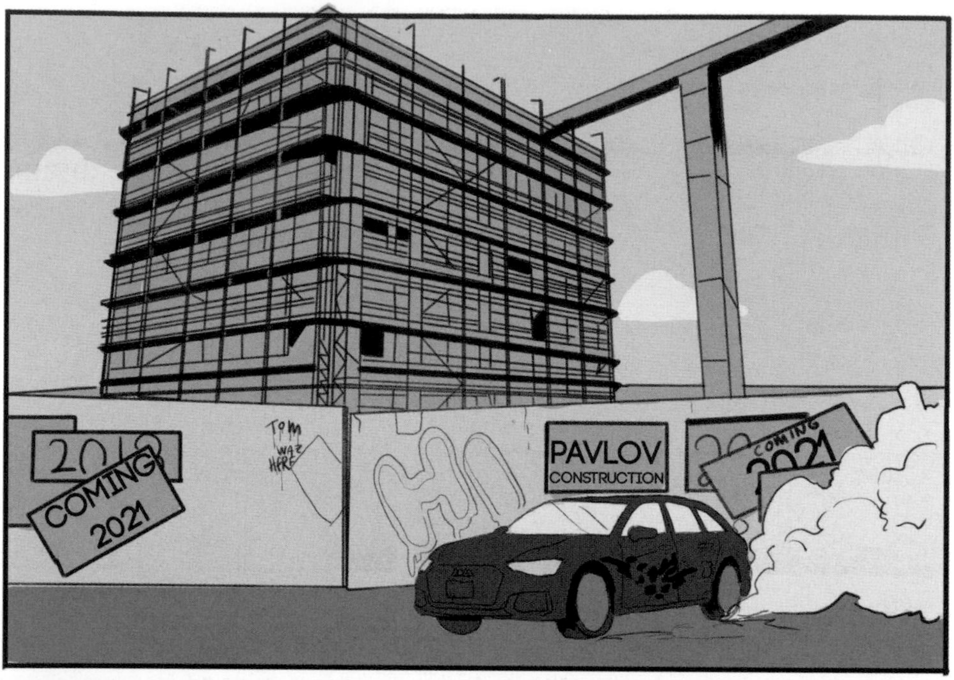
COMING
2021
TOM
WAZ
HERE
PAVLOV
CONSTRUCTION
COMING
2021

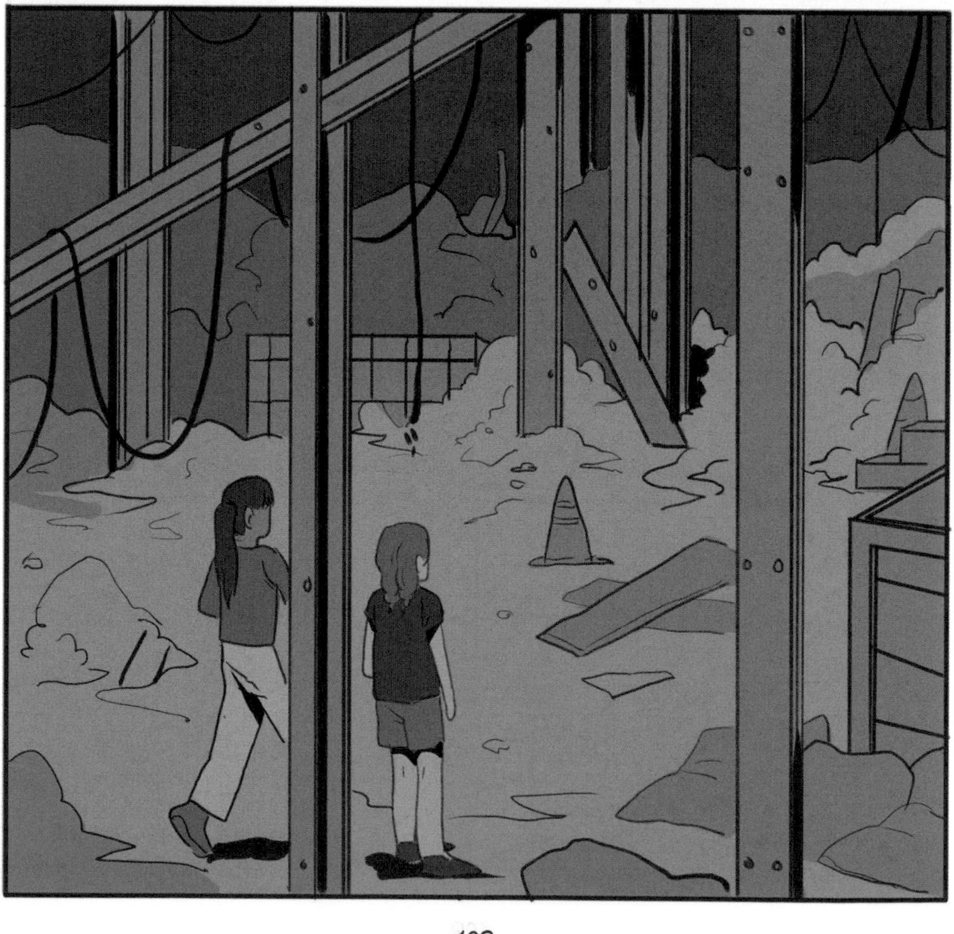

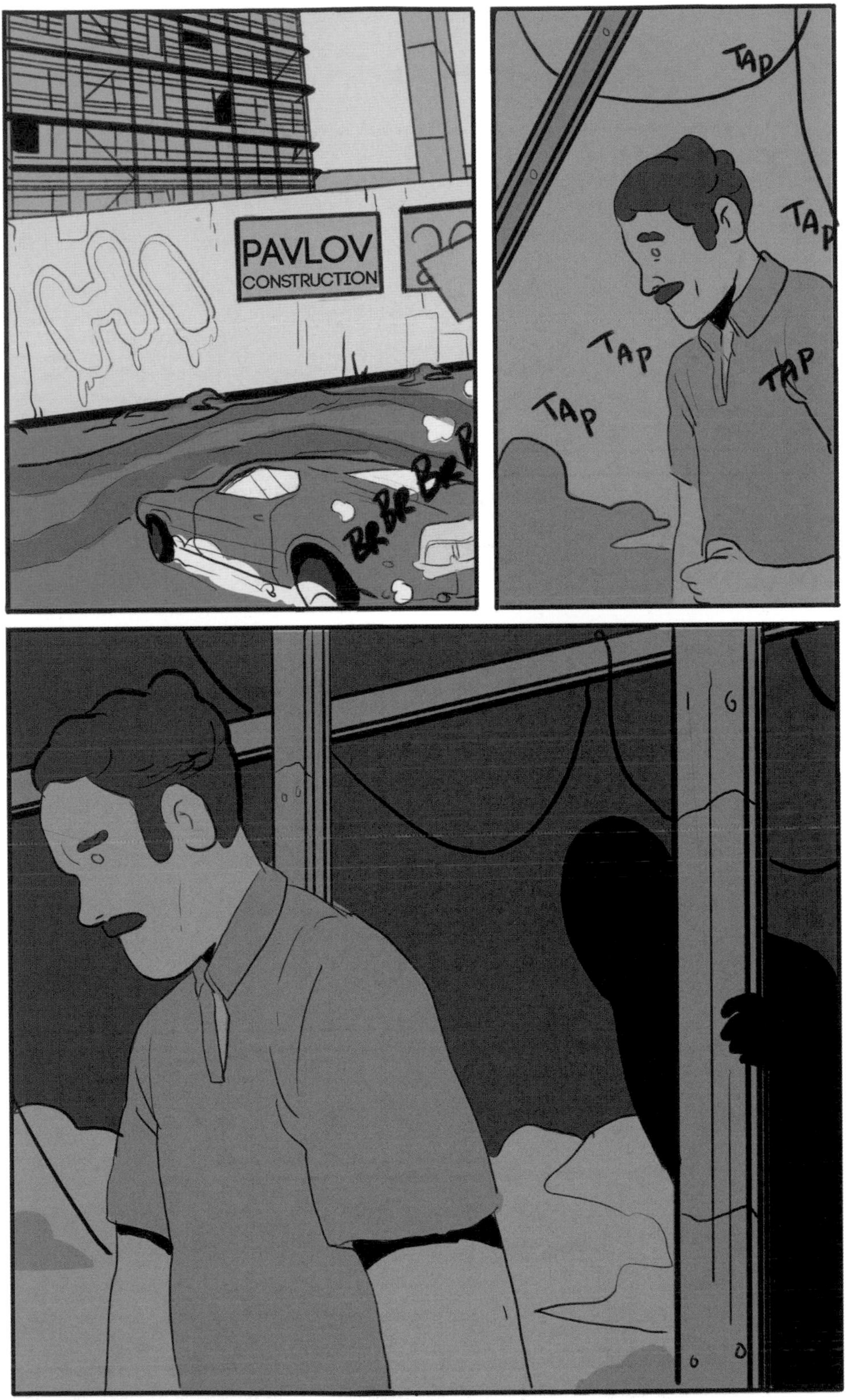
PAVLOV
CONSTRUCTION
BR BR BR BR
TAP
TAP
TAP
TAP
TAP

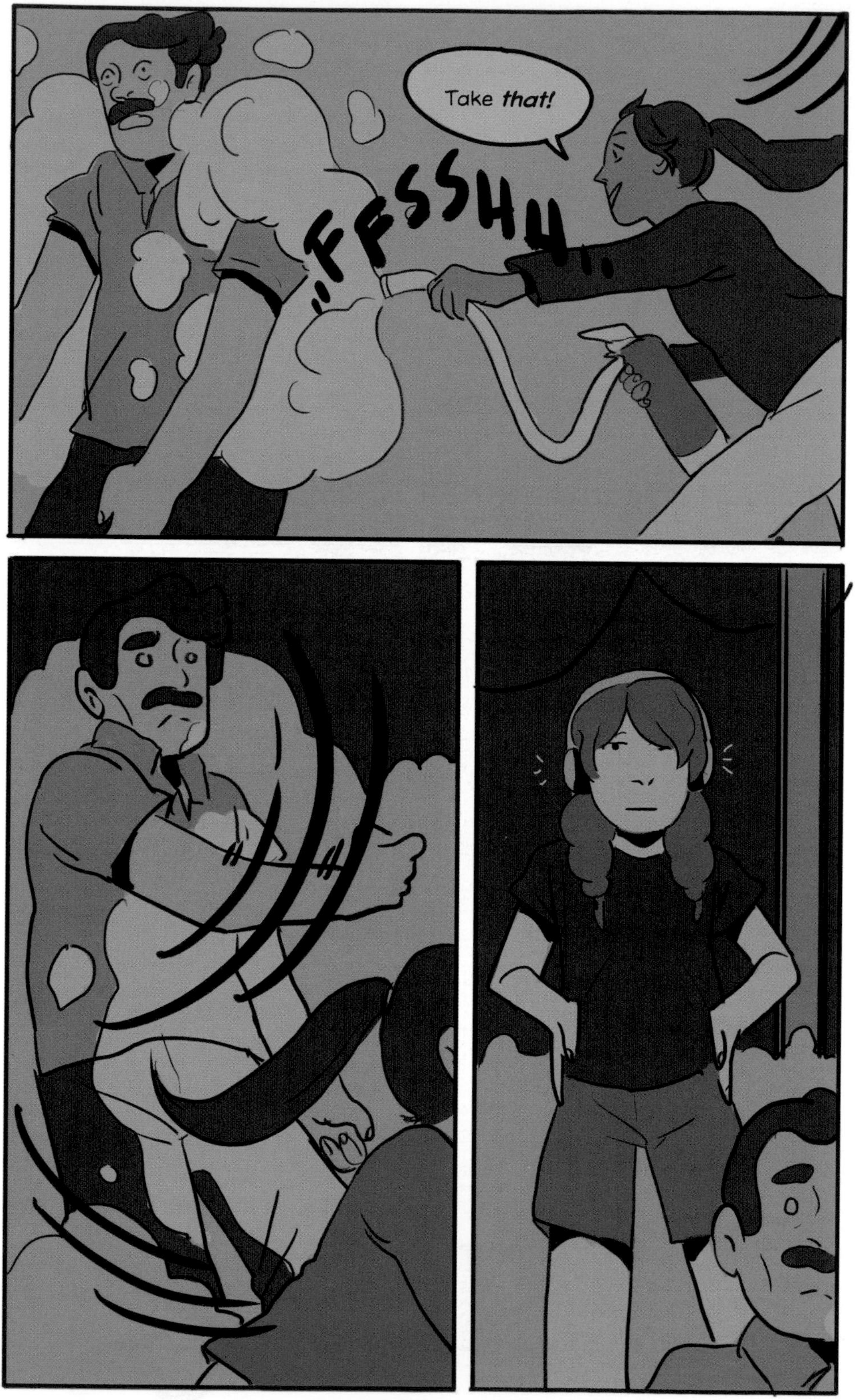
Take that!
FFSSHH

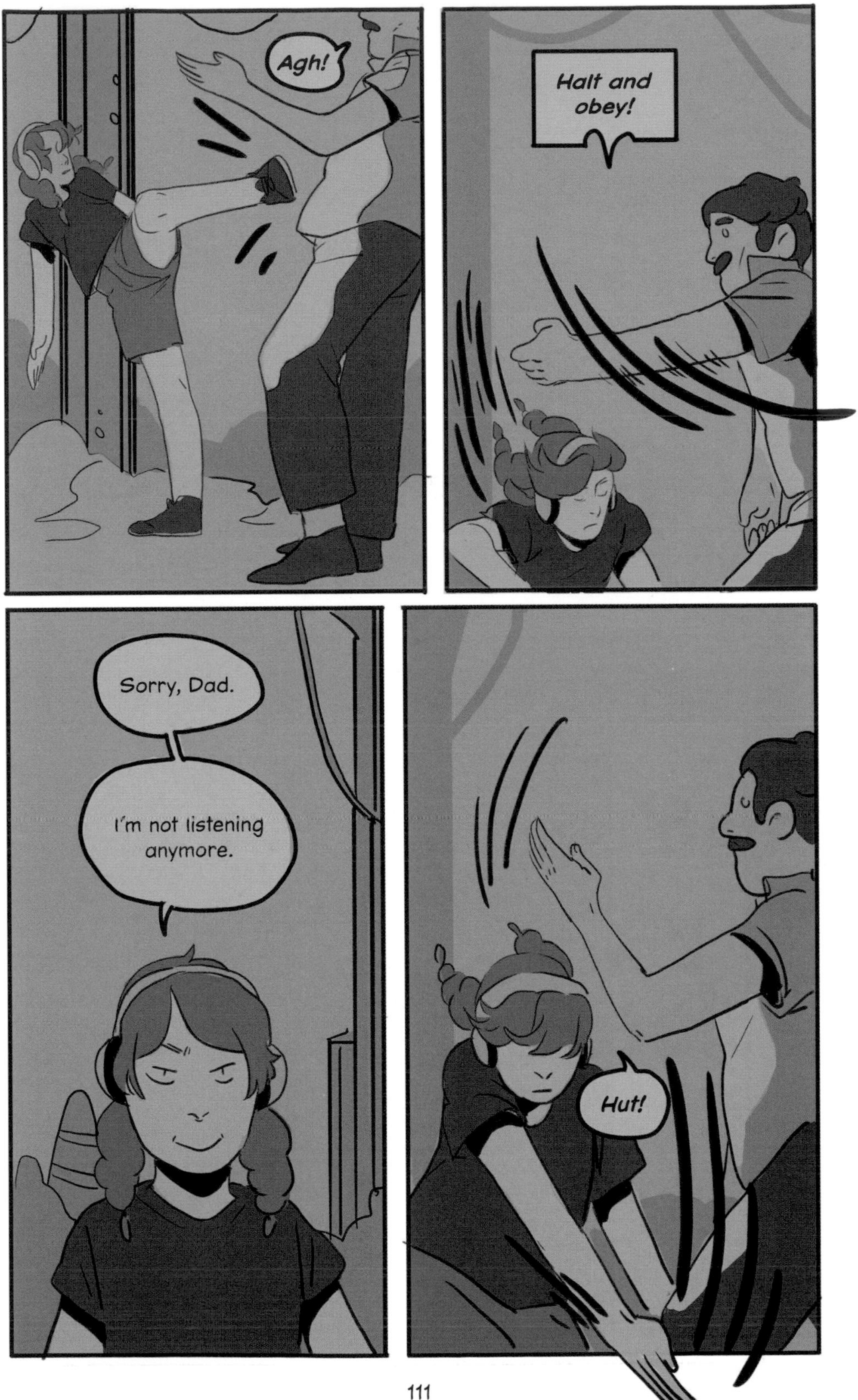
Agh!
Halt and obey!
Sorry, Dad.
I'm not listening anymore.
Hut!

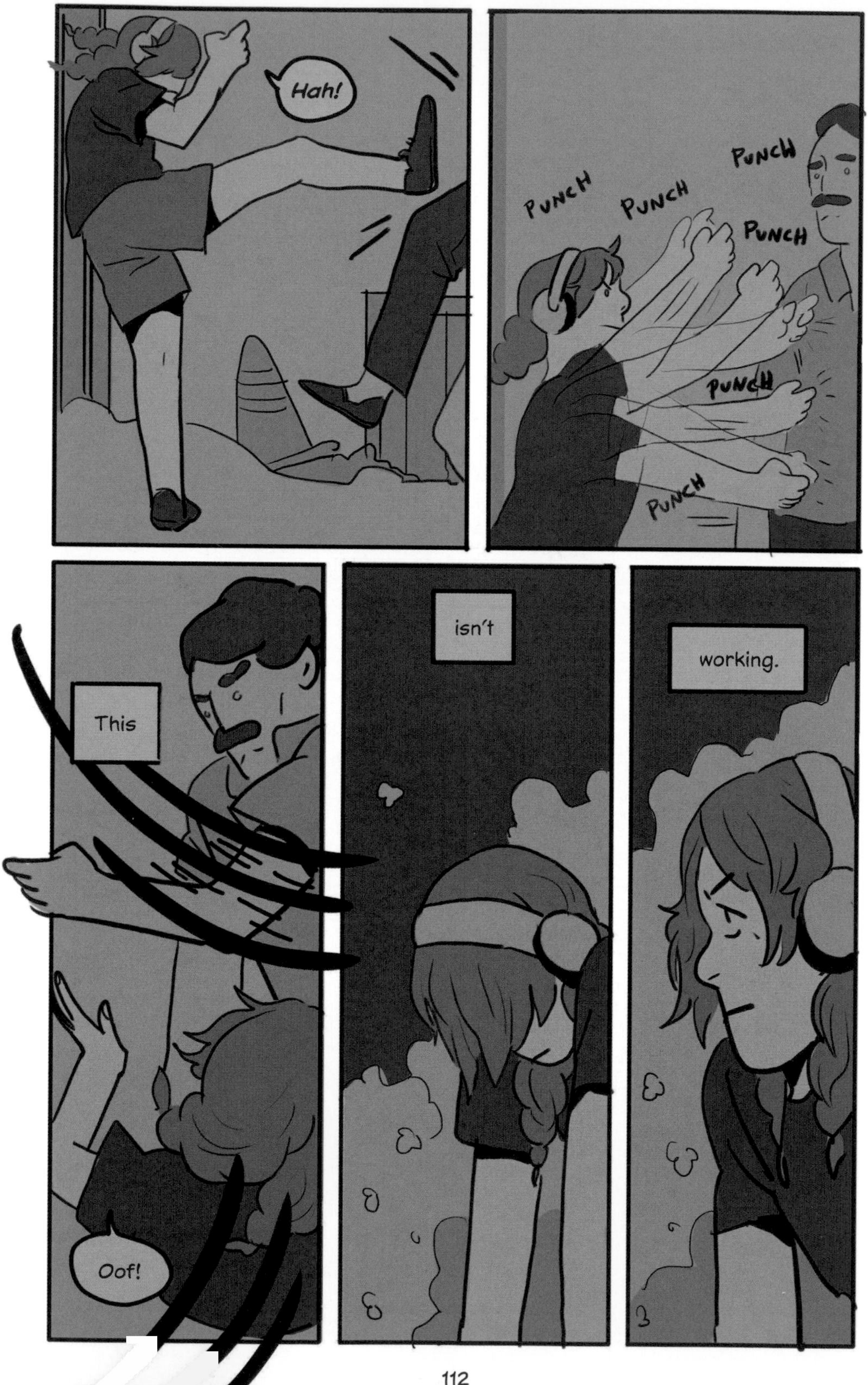
Hah!
PUNCH
PUNCH
PUNCH
PUNCH
PUNCH
PUNCH
This
Oof!
isn't
working.

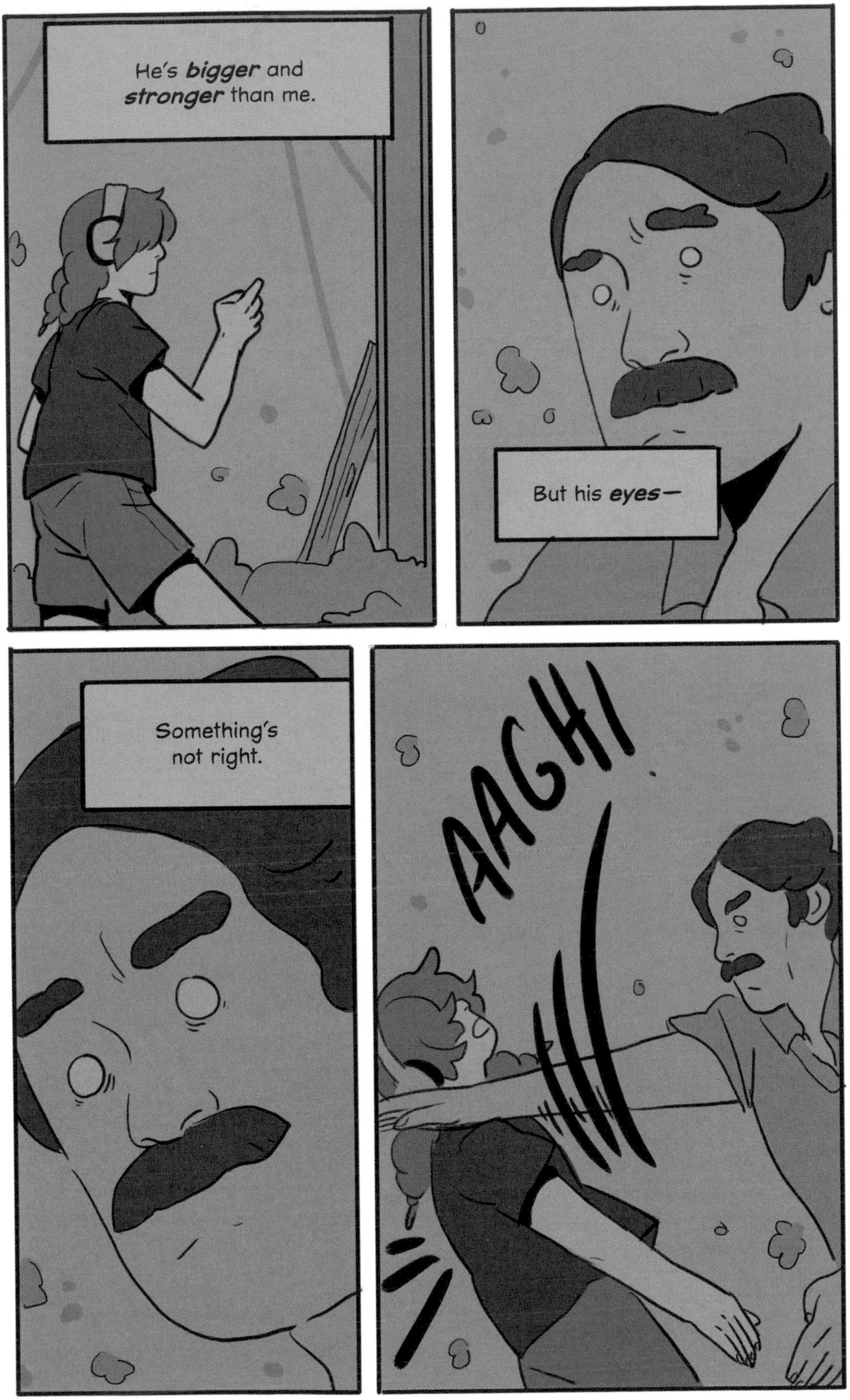
He's *bigger* and *stronger* than me.
But his *eyes*—
Something's not right.
AAGH!

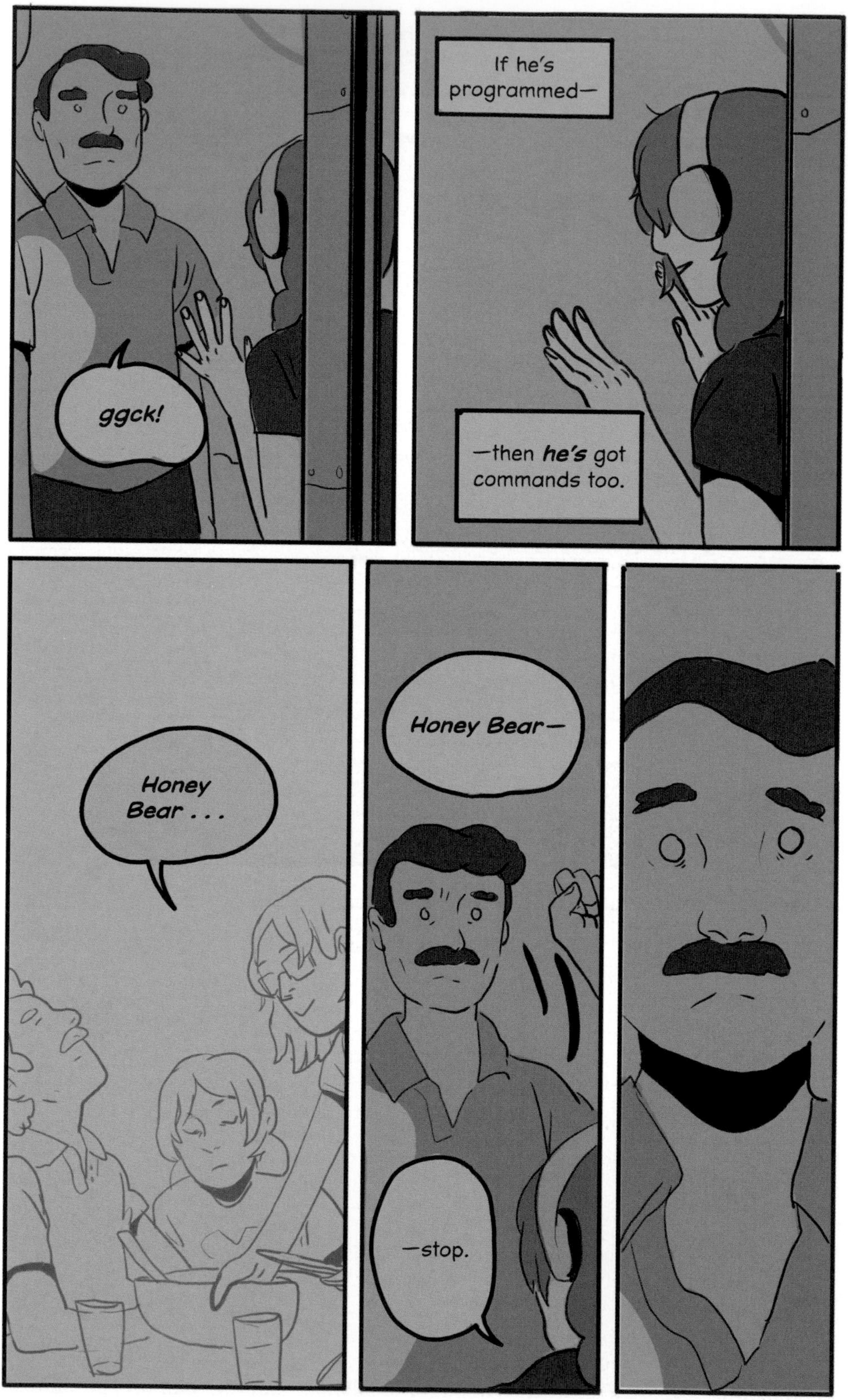
ggck!
If he's programmed—
—then **he's** got commands too.
Honey Bear . . .
Honey Bear—
—stop.

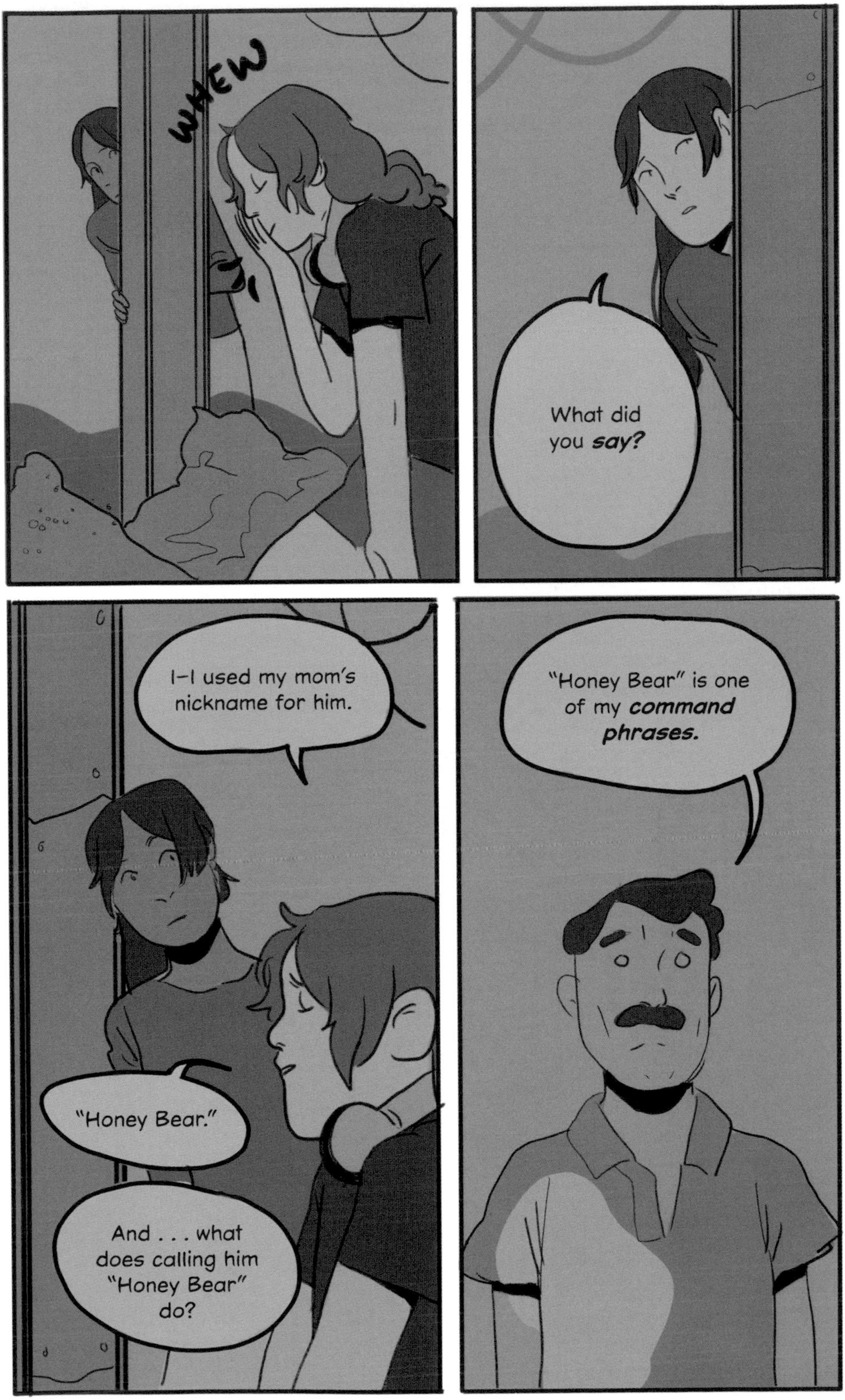
WHEW
What did you *say?*
I-I used my mom's nickname for him.
"Honey Bear."
And . . . what does calling him "Honey Bear" do?
"Honey Bear" is one of my *command phrases.*

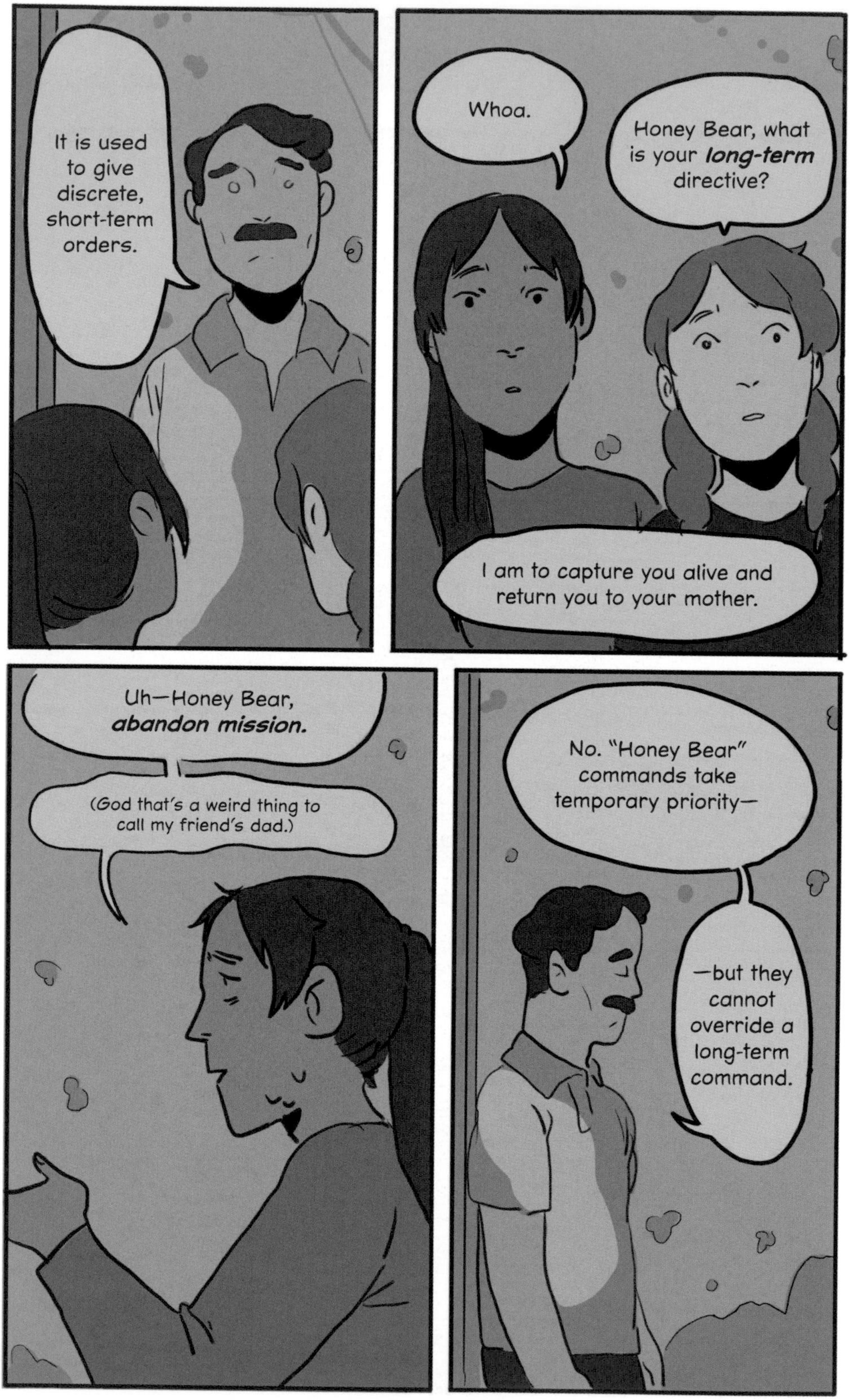
It is used to give discrete, short-term orders.
Whoa.
Honey Bear, what is your ***long-term*** directive?
I am to capture you alive and return you to your mother.
Uh—Honey Bear, ***abandon mission.***
(God that's a weird thing to call my friend's dad.)
No. "Honey Bear" commands take temporary priority—
—but they cannot override a long-term command.

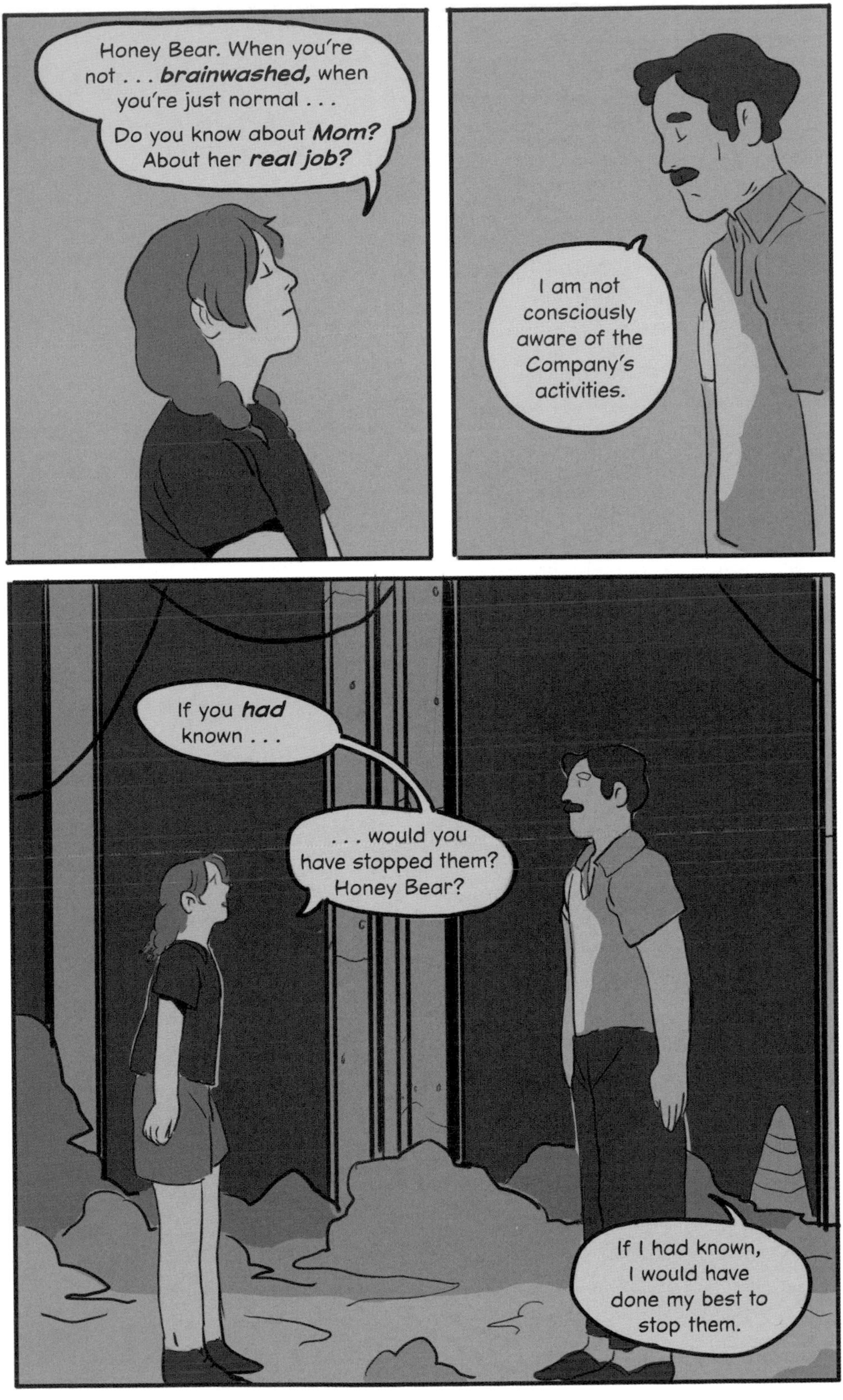
Honey Bear. When you're not . . . **brainwashed,** when you're just normal . . .
Do you know about **Mom?** About her **real job?**
I am not consciously aware of the Company's activities.
If you **had** known . . .
. . . would you have stopped them? Honey Bear?
If I had known, I would have done my best to stop them.

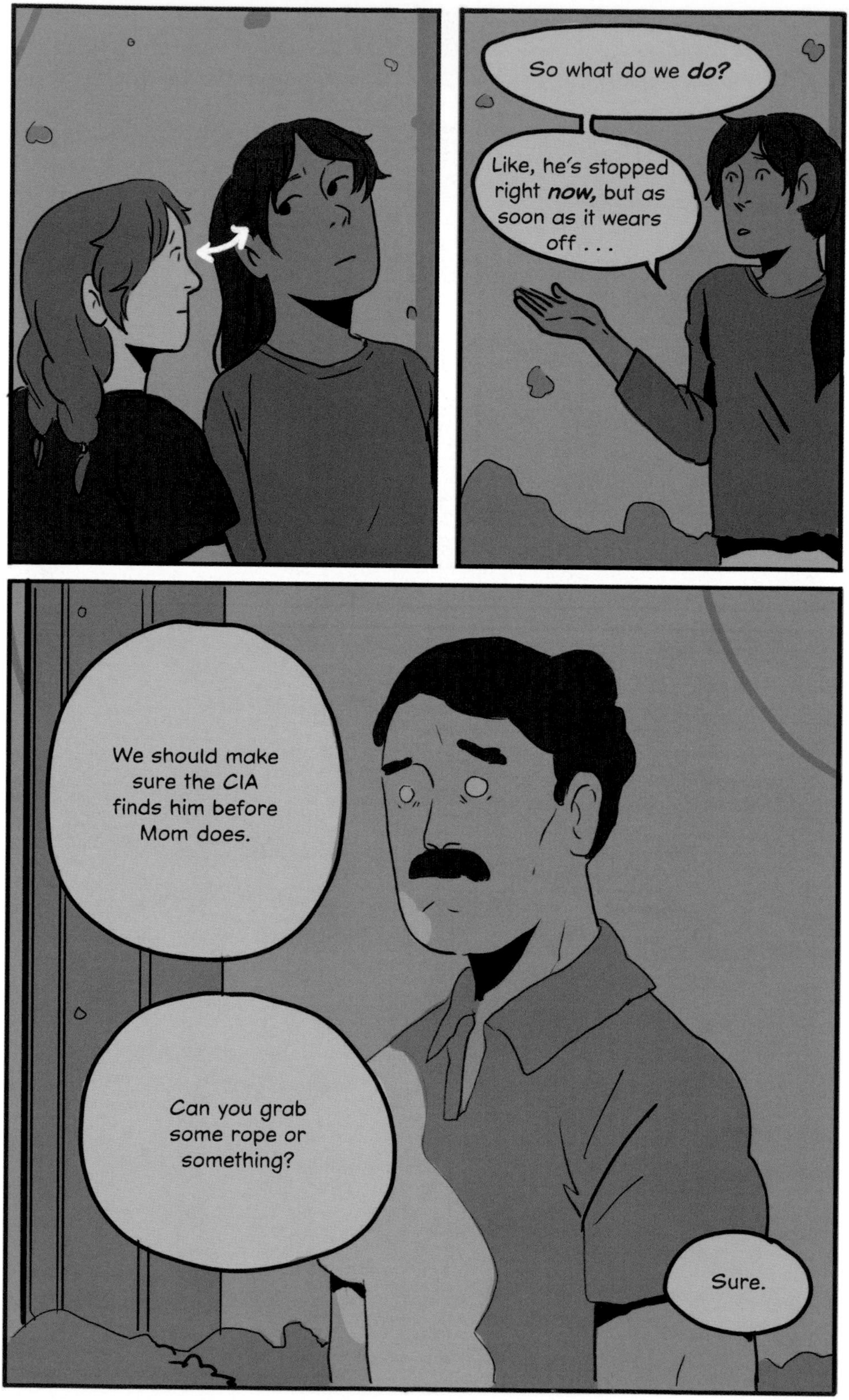
So what do we ***do?***
Like, he's stopped right ***now,*** but as soon as it wears off . . .
We should make sure the CIA finds him before Mom does.
Can you grab some rope or something?
Sure.

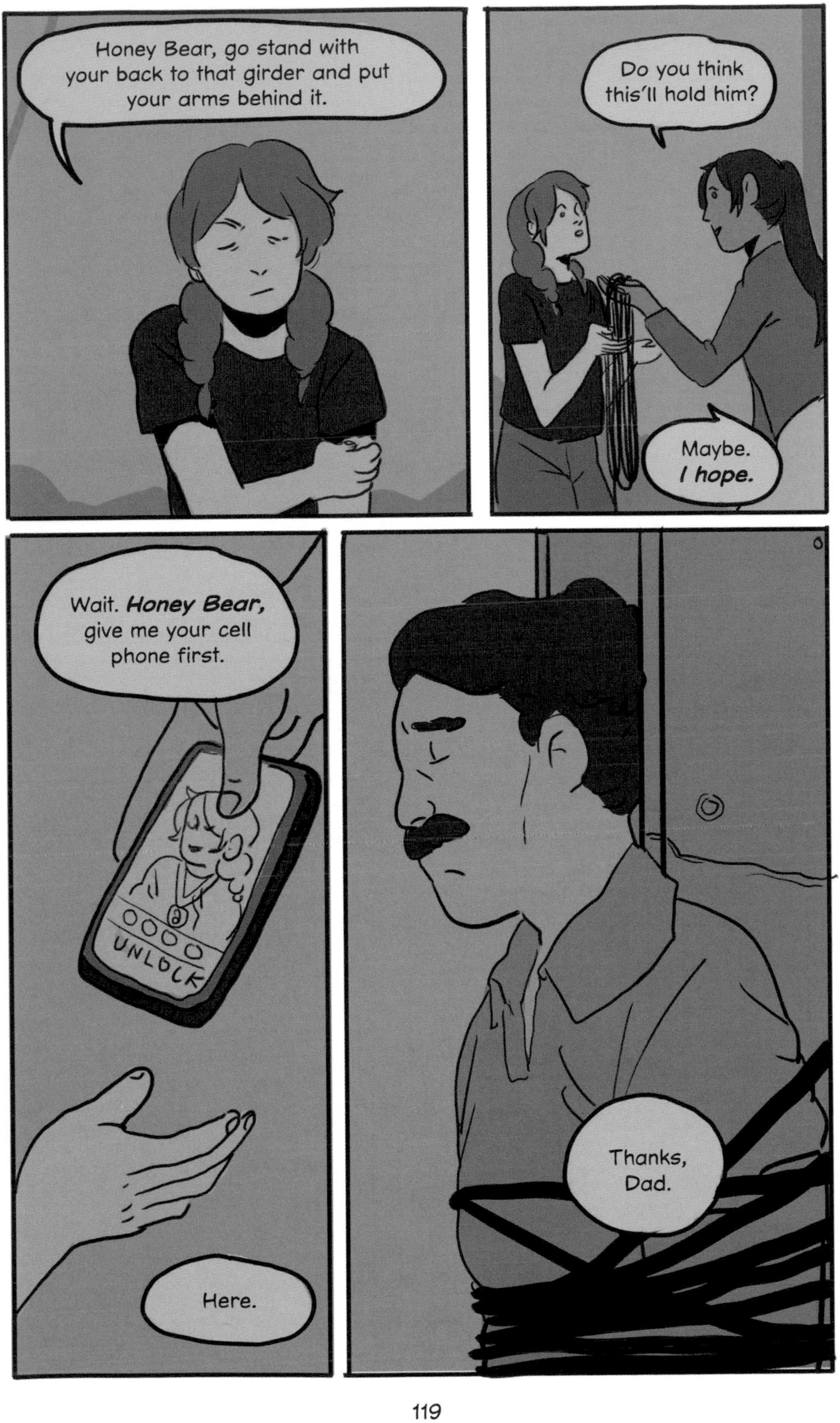
Honey Bear, go stand with your back to that girder and put your arms behind it.
Do you think this'll hold him?
Maybe. *I hope.*
Wait. ***Honey Bear,*** give me your cell phone first.
UNLOCK
Here.
Thanks, Dad.

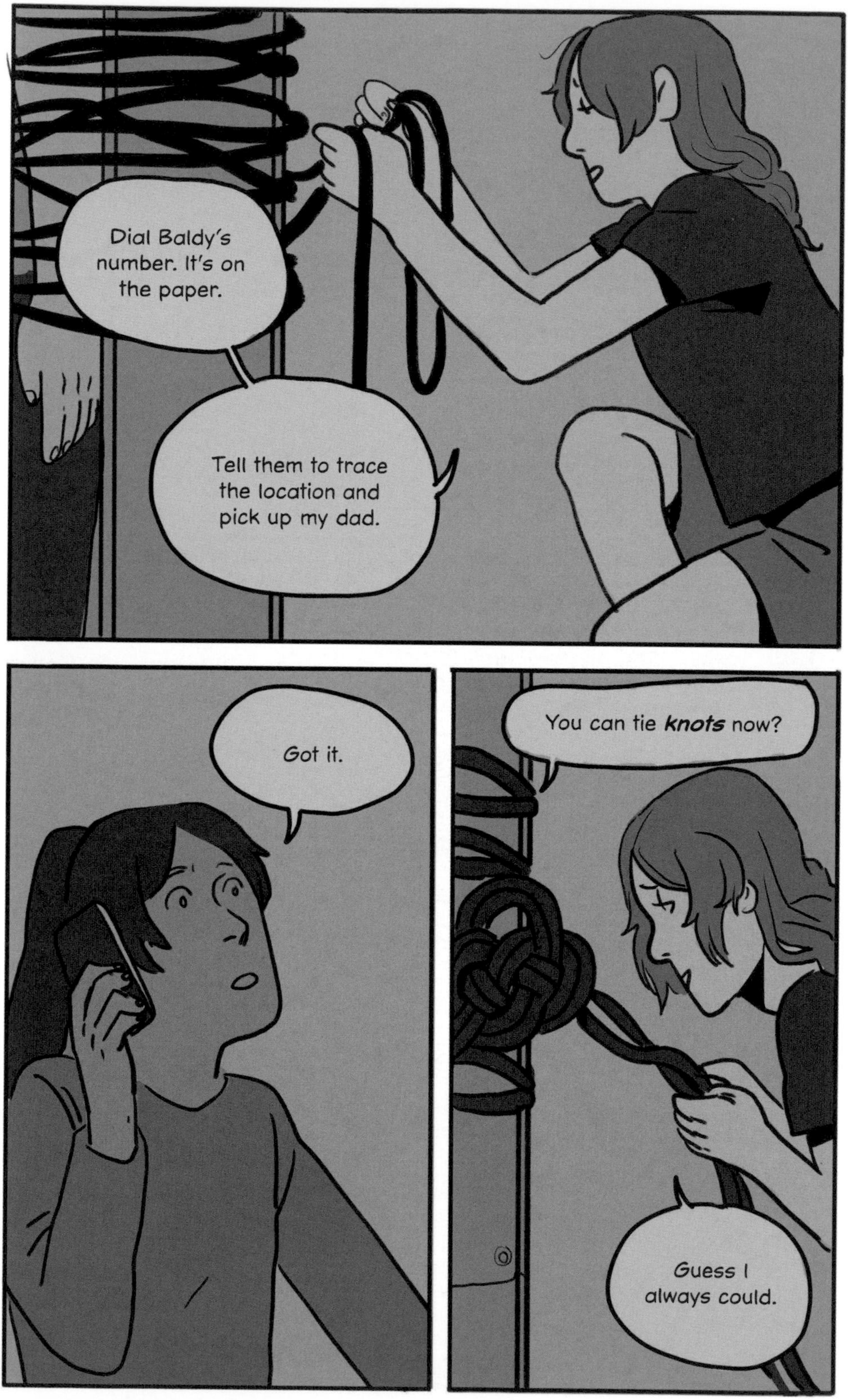
Dial Baldy's number. It's on the paper.
Tell them to trace the location and pick up my dad.
Got it.
You can tie **knots** now?
Guess I always could.

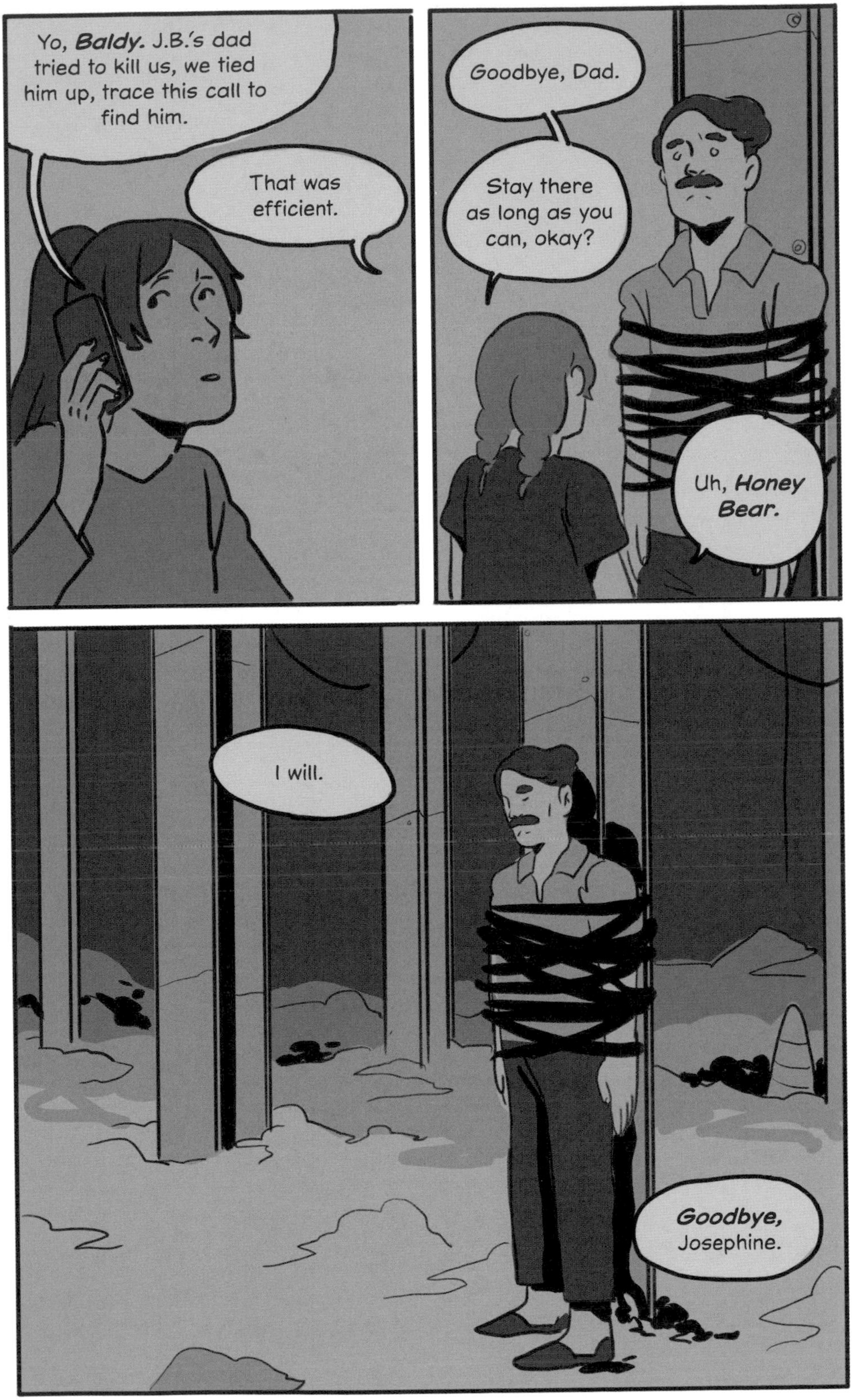
Yo, **Baldy.** J.B.'s dad tried to kill us, we tied him up, trace this call to find him.
That was efficient.
Goodbye, Dad.
Stay there as long as you can, okay?
Uh, ***Honey Bear.***
I will.
Goodbye, Josephine.

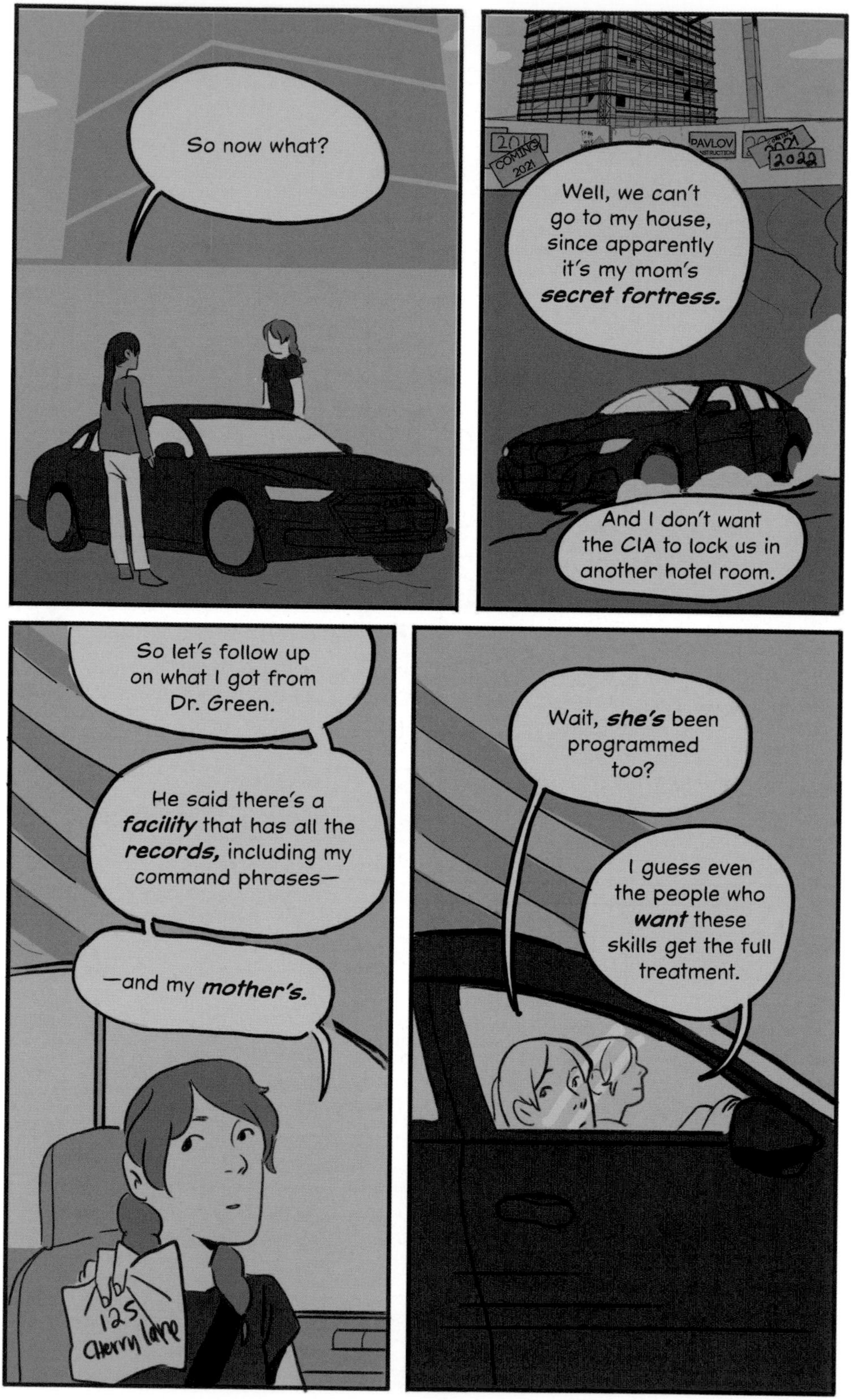
So now what?
COMING 2021
PAVLOV
2022
Well, we can't go to my house, since apparently it's my mom's ***secret fortress.***
And I don't want the CIA to lock us in another hotel room.
So let's follow up on what I got from Dr. Green.
He said there's a ***facility*** that has all the ***records,*** including my command phrases—
—and my ***mother's.***
125 Cherry Lane
Wait, ***she's*** been programmed too?
I guess even the people who ***want*** these skills get the full treatment.

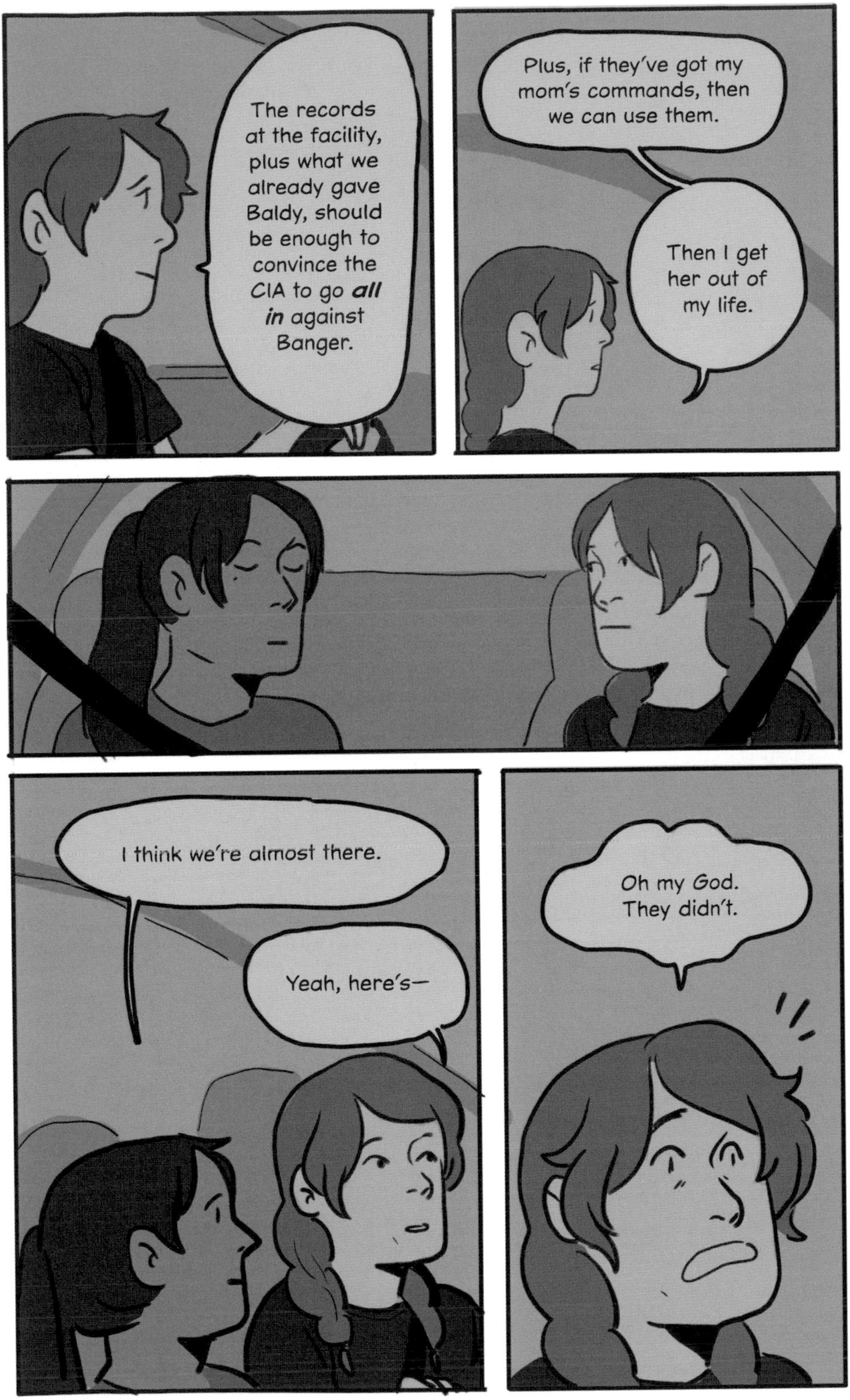
The records at the facility, plus what we already gave Baldy, should be enough to convince the CIA to go ***all in*** against Banger.
Plus, if they've got my mom's commands, then we can use them.
Then I get her out of my life.
I think we're almost there.
Yeah, here's—
Oh my God. They didn't.

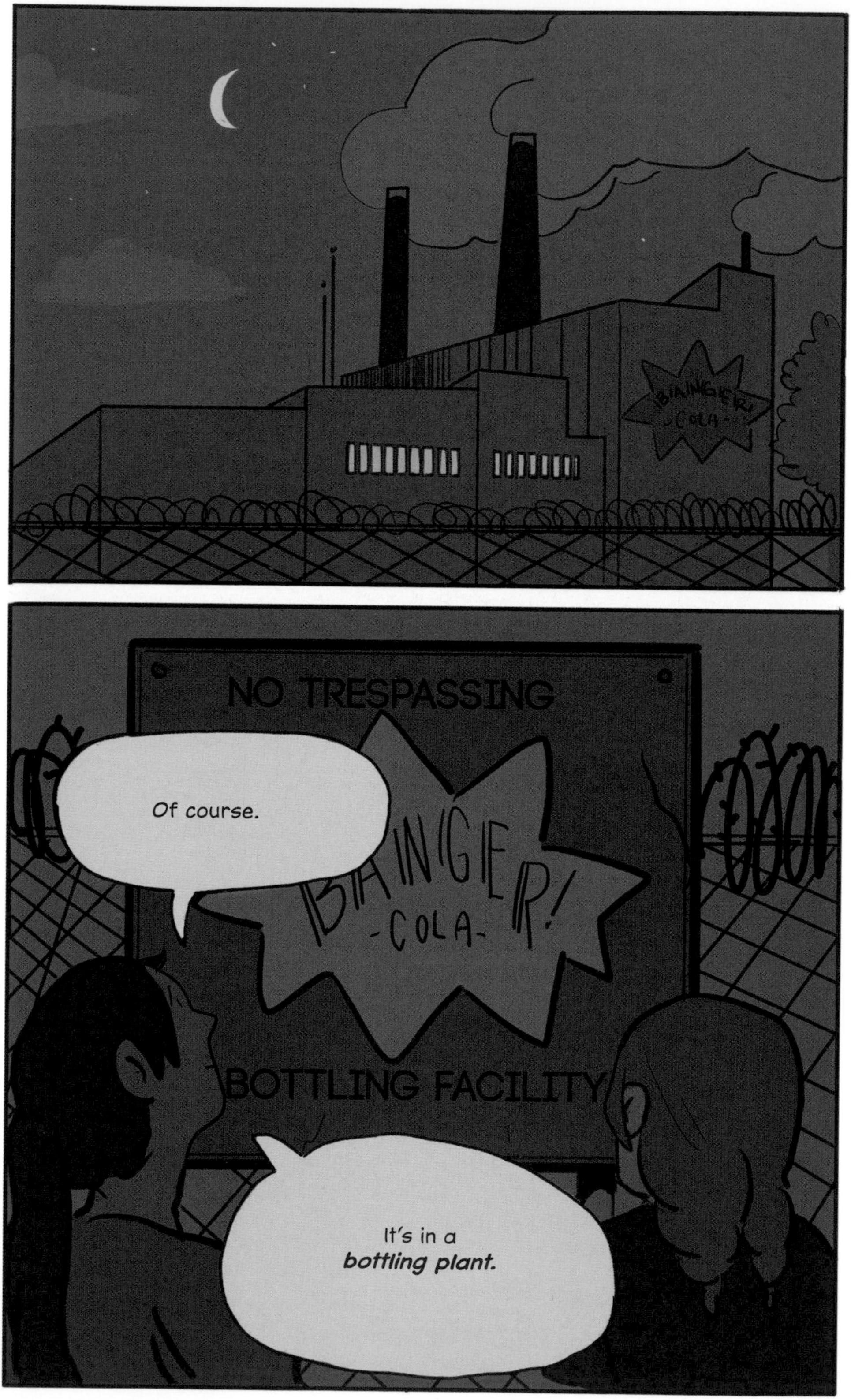
BANGER! COLA
NO TRESPASSING
BANGER! -COLA-
BOTTLING FACILITY
Of course.
It's in a *bottling plant.*

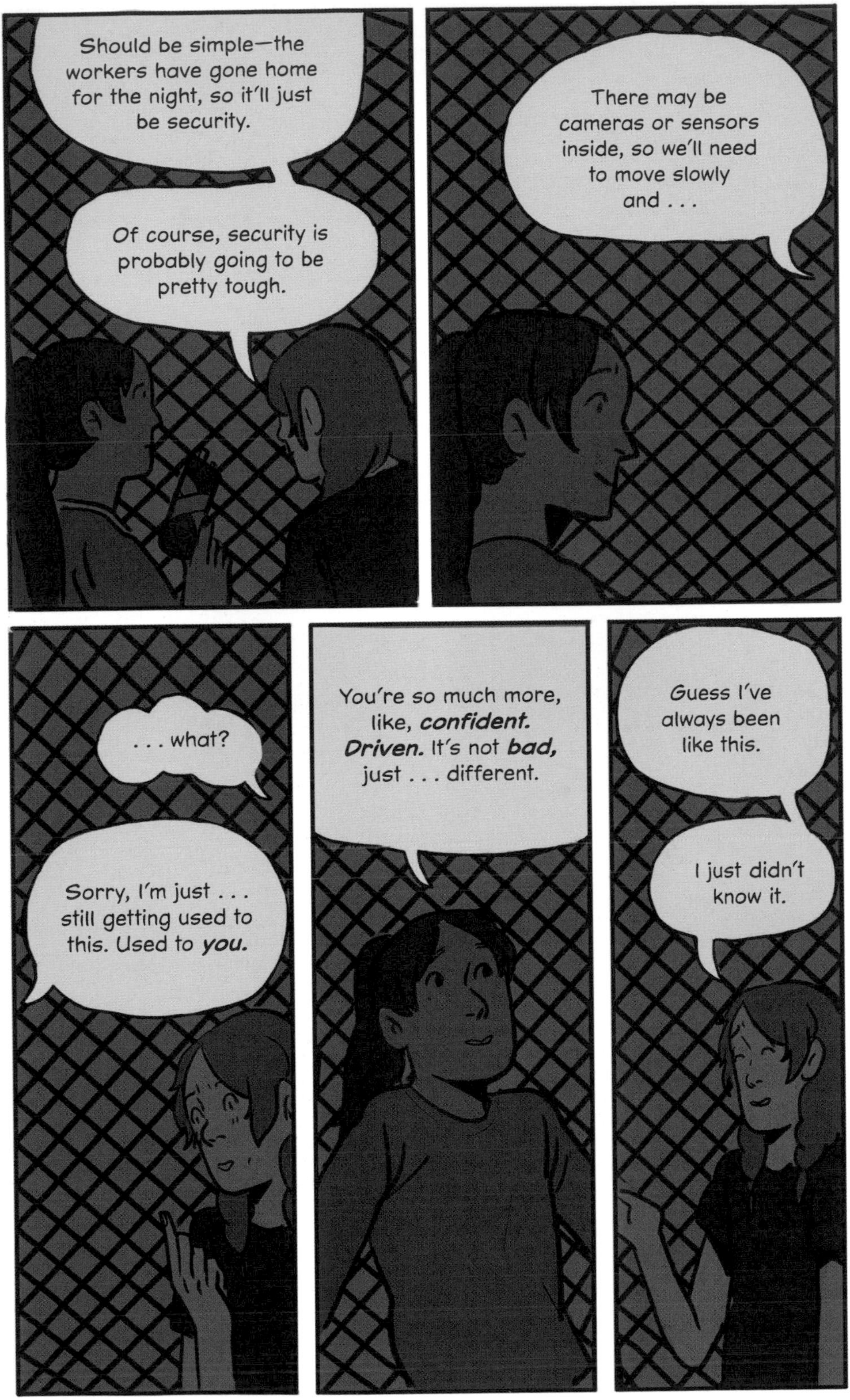
Should be simple—the workers have gone home for the night, so it'll just be security.
Of course, security is probably going to be pretty tough.
There may be cameras or sensors inside, so we'll need to move slowly and . . .
. . . what?
Sorry, I'm just . . . still getting used to this. Used to *you.*
You're so much more, like, ***confident. Driven.*** It's not ***bad,*** just . . . different.
Guess I've always been like this.
I just didn't know it.

SNEAK
SNEAK
Hm.

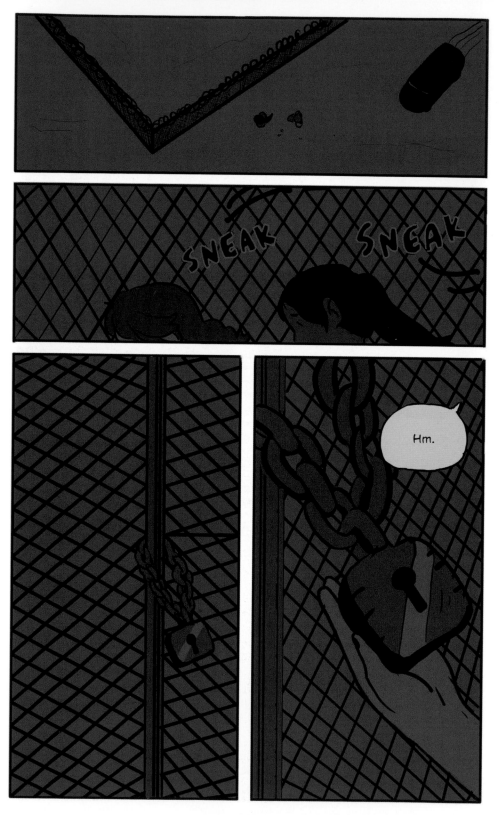

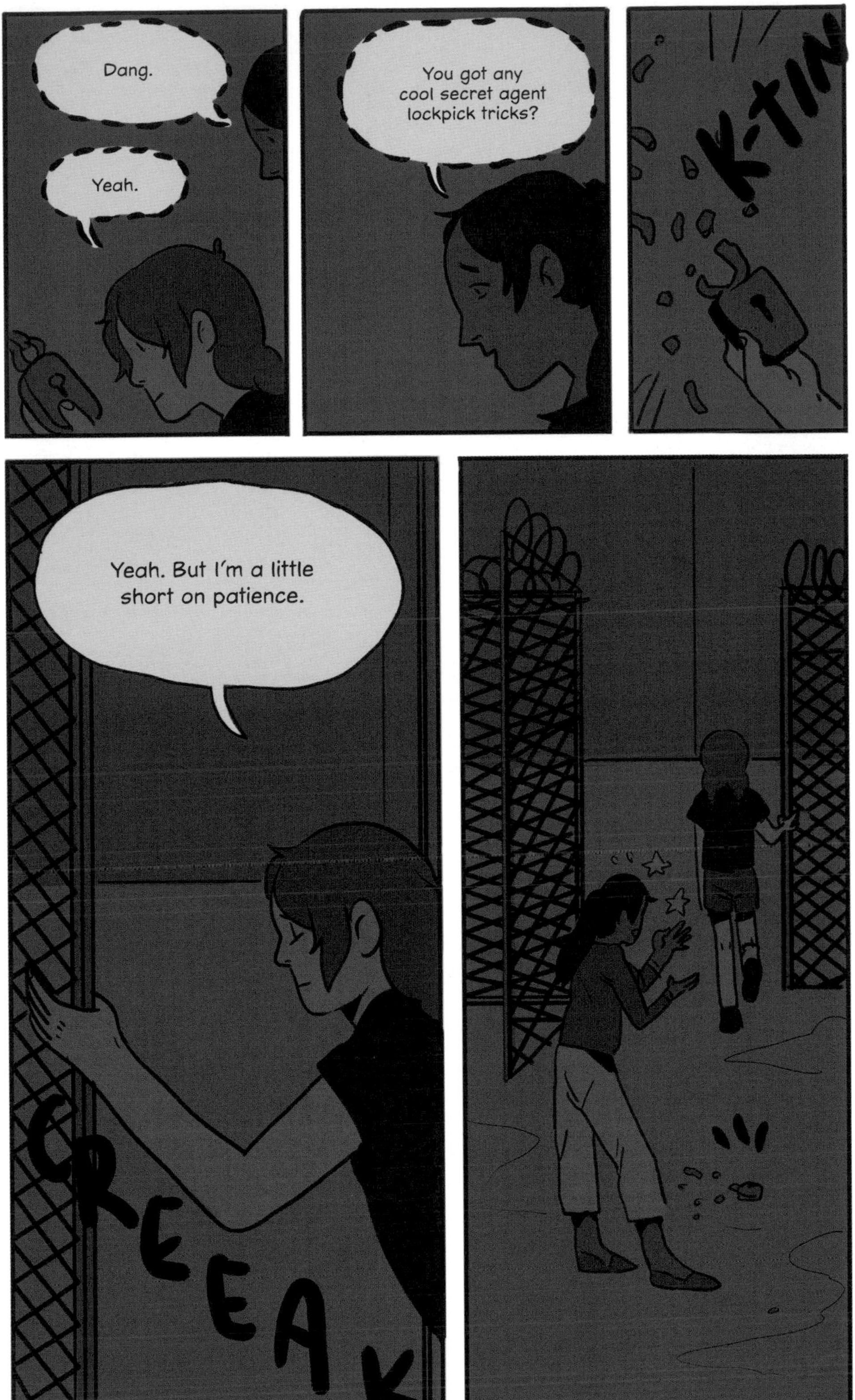
Dang.
Yeah.
You got any cool secret agent lockpick tricks?
K-TIN
Yeah. But I'm a little short on patience.
CREEAK

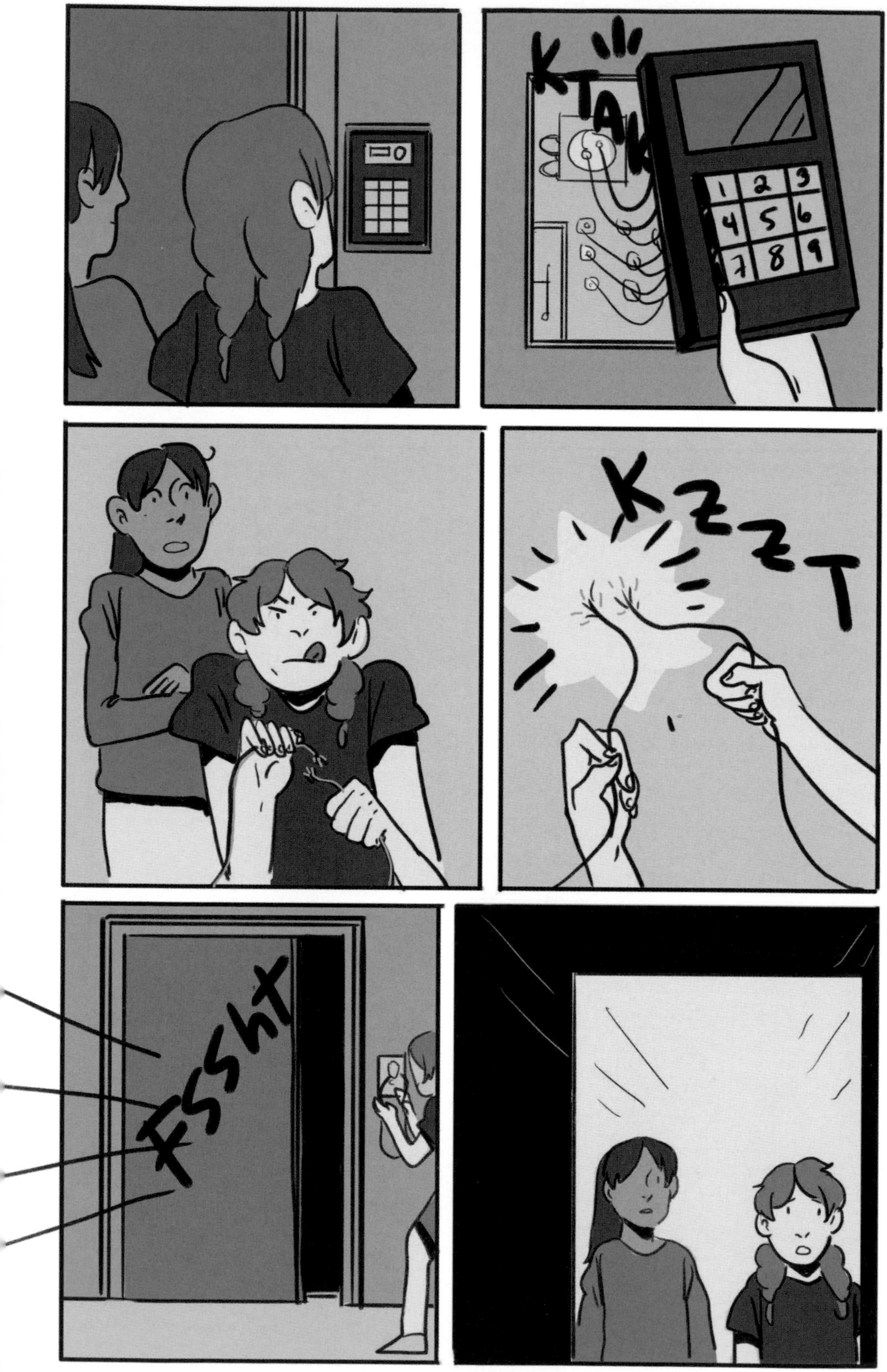

KTAK
1 2 3
4 5 6
7 8 9
KZZZT
FSSHT

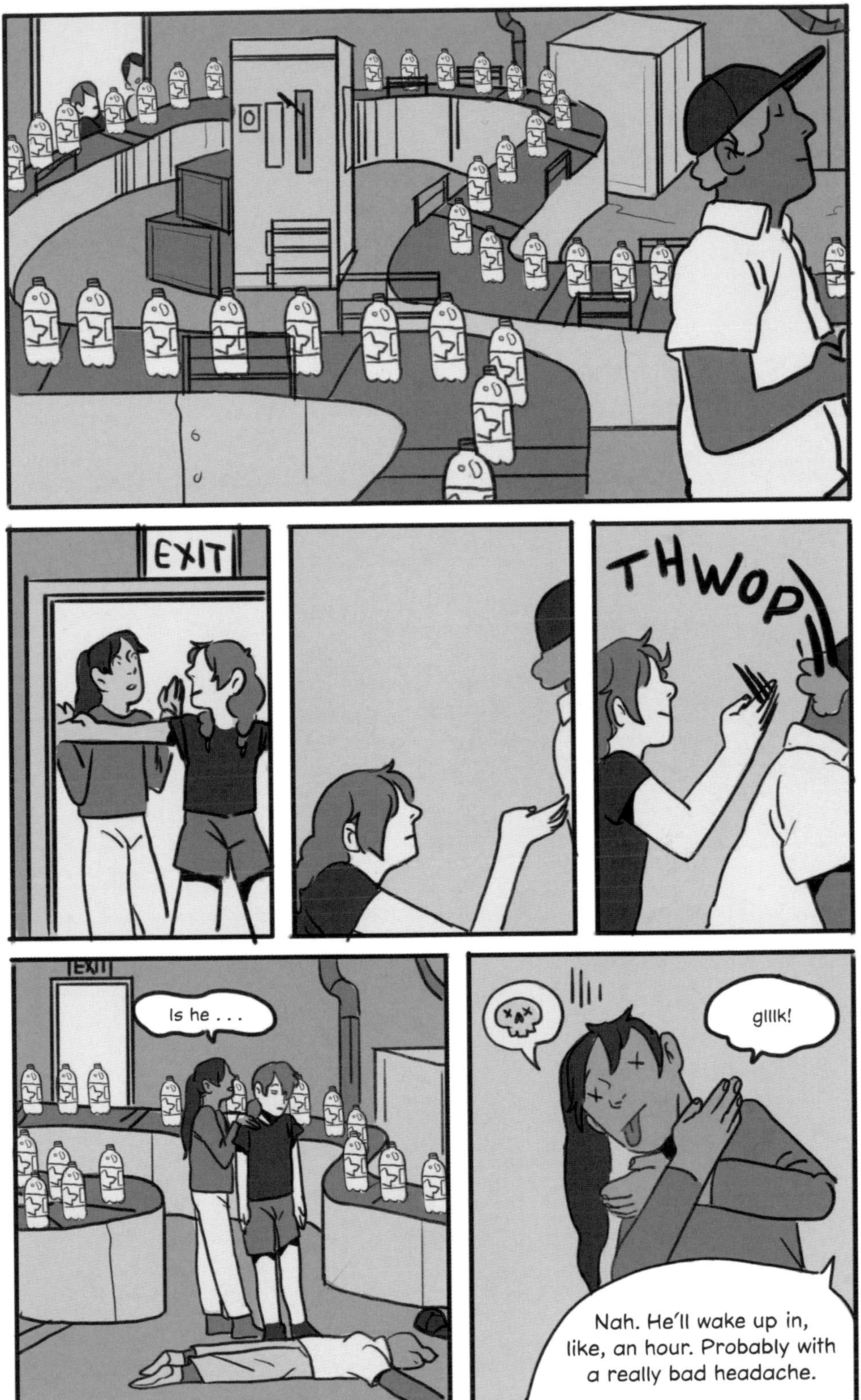
EXIT
THWOP
EXIT
Is he . . .
gllk!
Nah. He'll wake up in, like, an hour. Probably with a really bad headache.

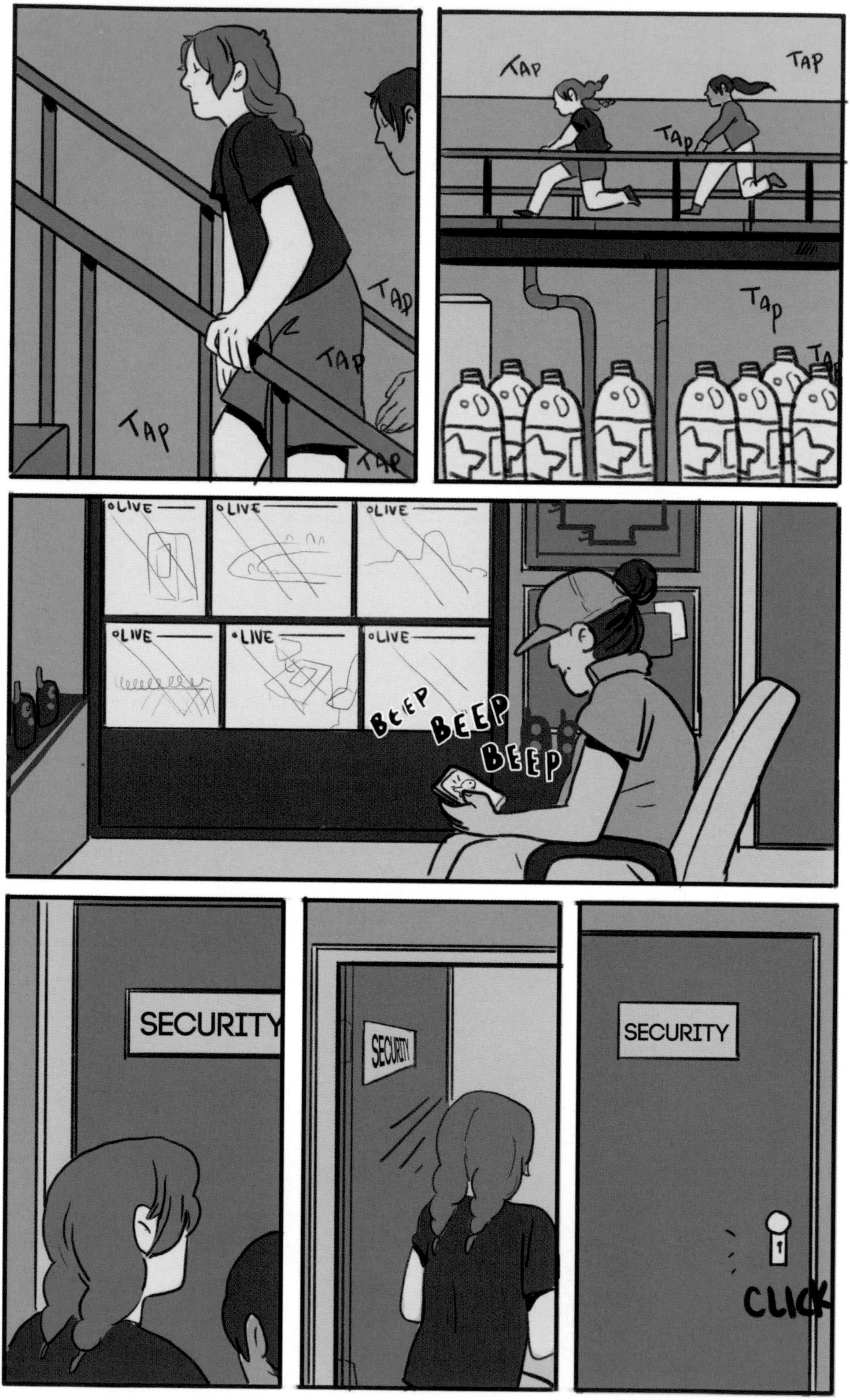
TAP
TAP
TAP
TAP
TAP
TAP
TAP
TAP
LIVE
LIVE
LIVE
LIVE
LIVE
LIVE
BEEP
BEEP
BEEP
SECURITY
SECURITY
SECURITY
CLICK

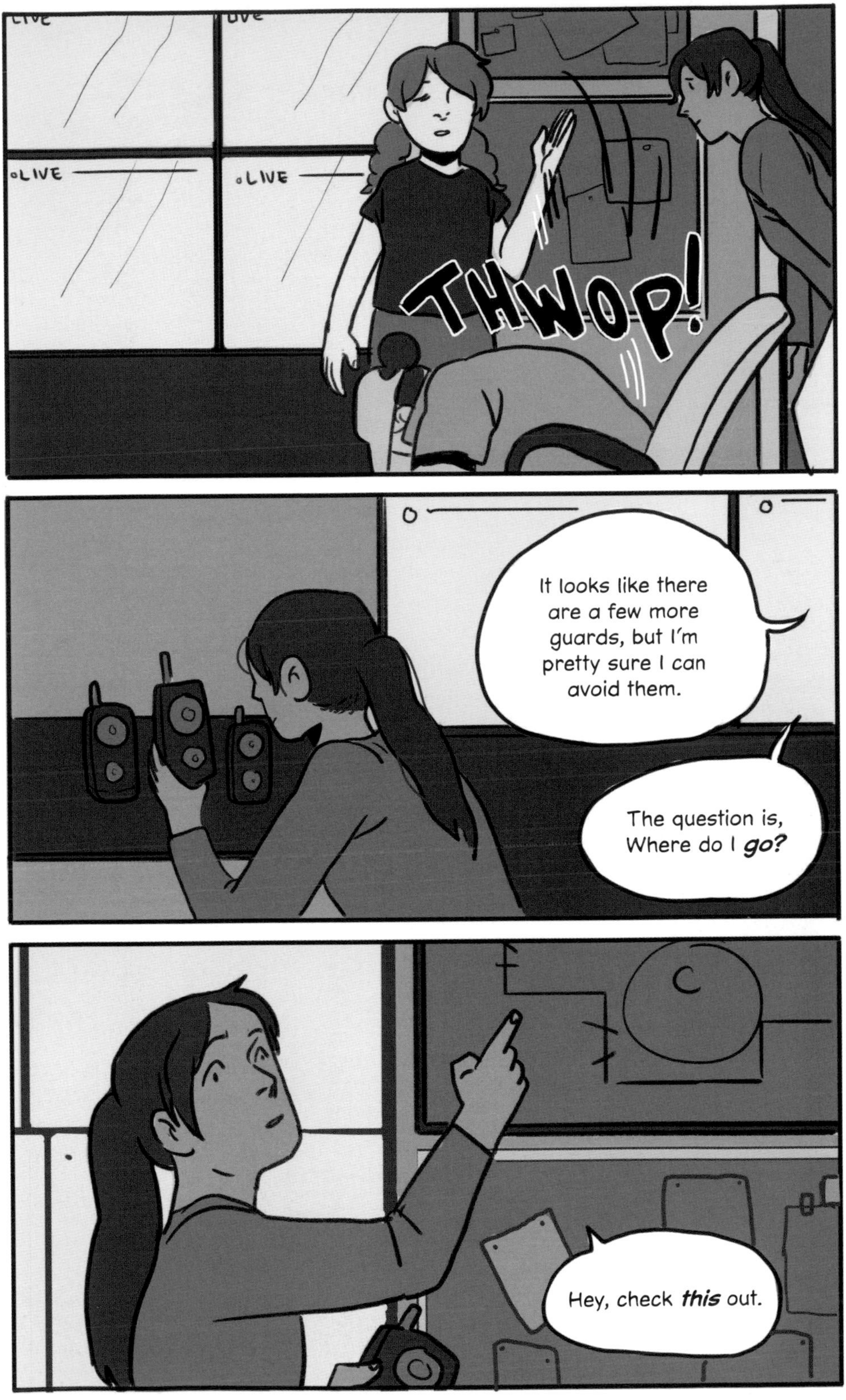
LIVE
LIVE
THWOP!
It looks like there are a few more guards, but I'm pretty sure I can avoid them.
The question is, Where do I *go?*
Hey, check *this* out.

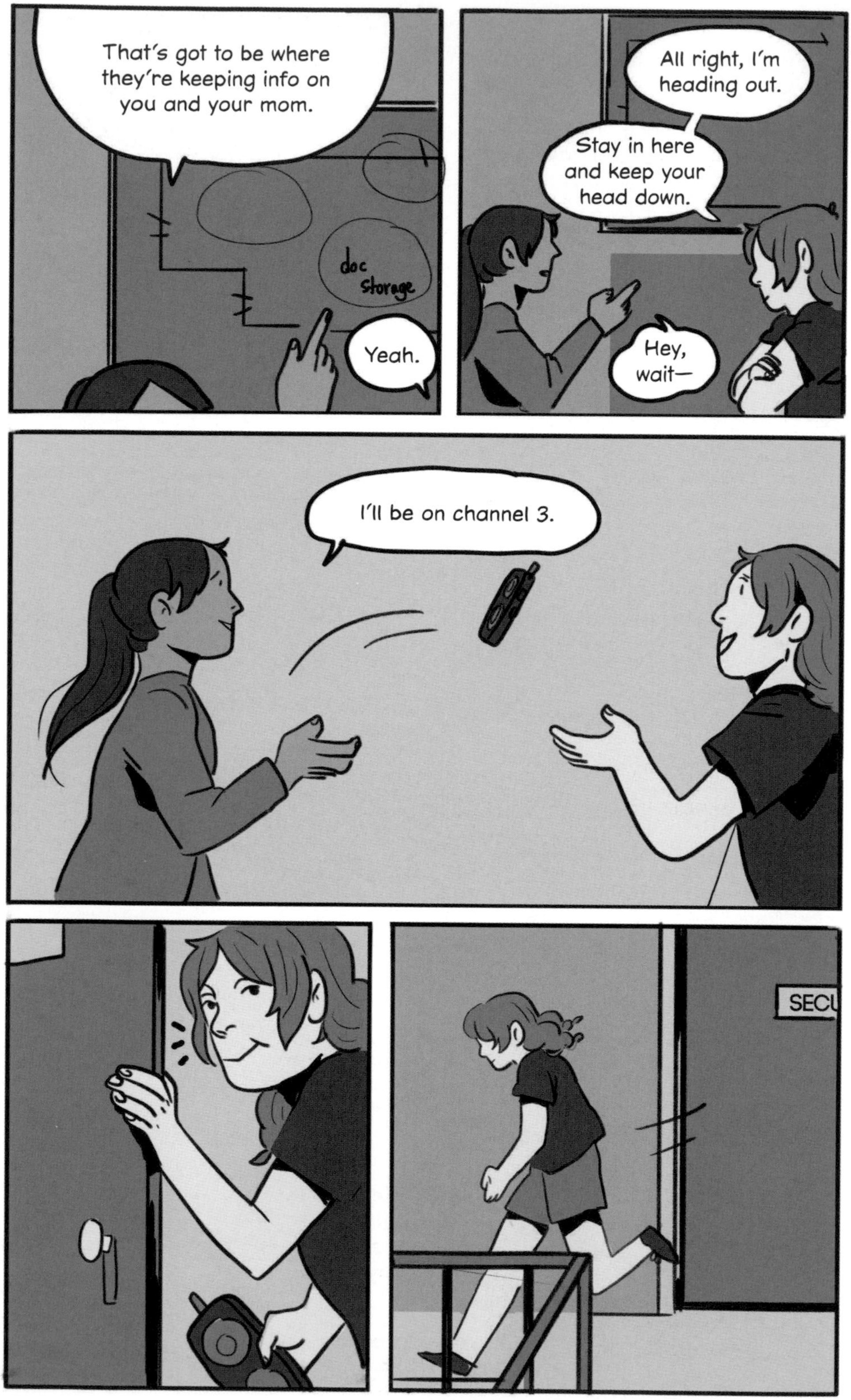
That's got to be where they're keeping info on you and your mom.
doc storage
Yeah.
All right, I'm heading out.
Stay in here and keep your head down.
Hey, wait—
I'll be on channel 3.
SECU

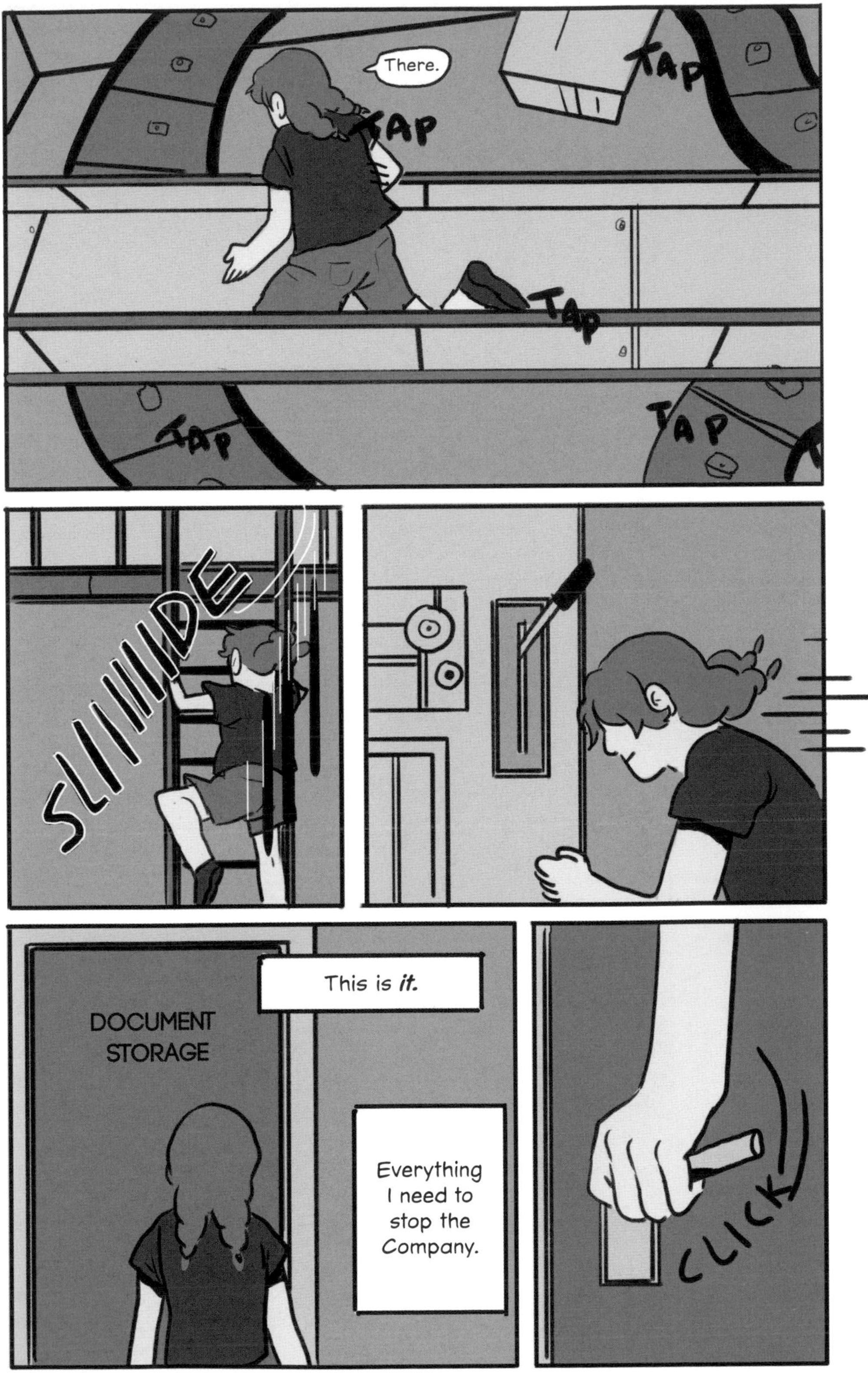
There.
TAP
TAP
TAP
TAP
TAP
SLIIIIIDE
This is it.
DOCUMENT STORAGE
Everything I need to stop the Company.
CLICK

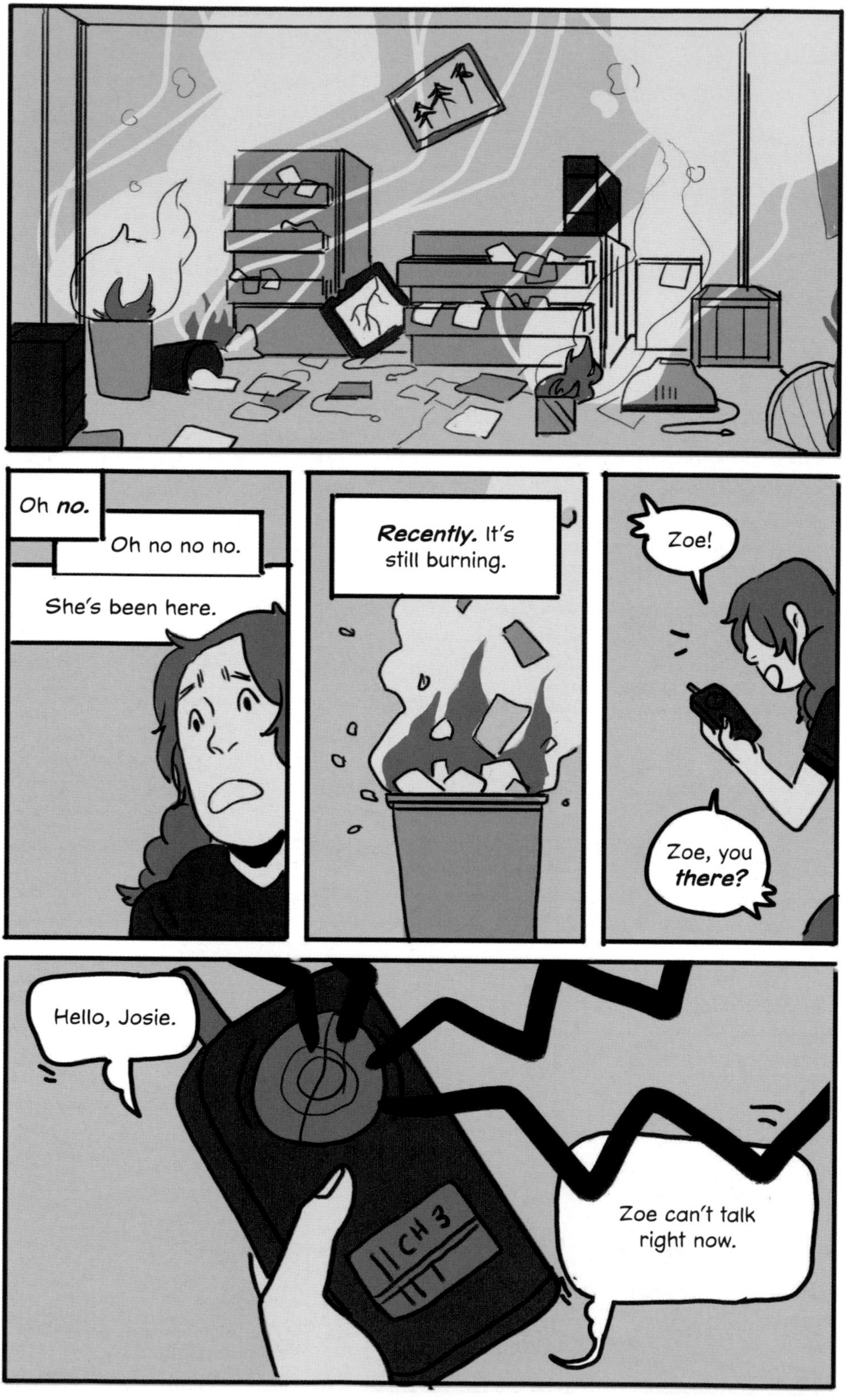
Oh no.
Oh no no no.
She's been here.
Recently. It's still burning.
Zoe!
Zoe, you there?
Hello, Josie.
Zoe can't talk right now.
CH 3

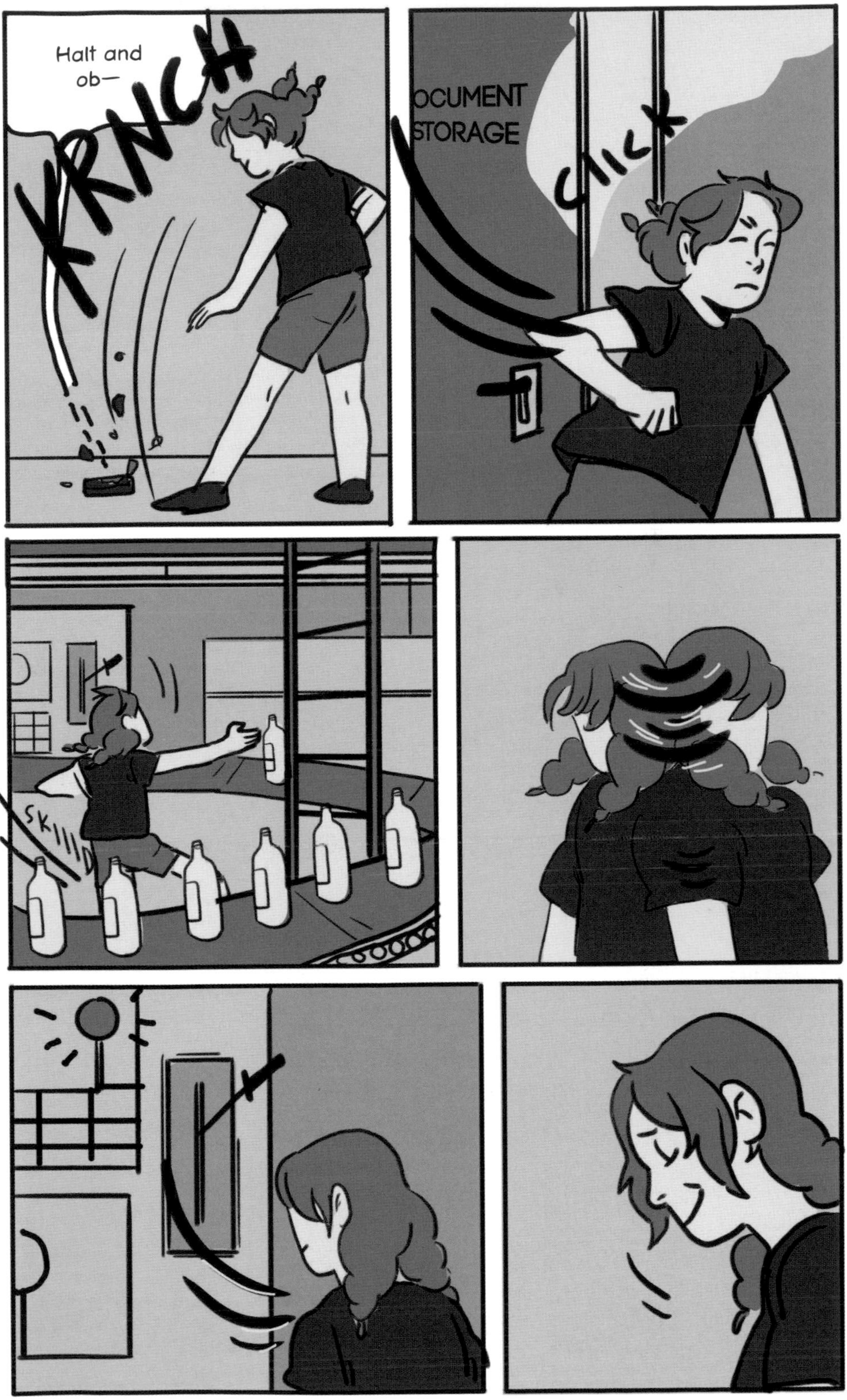

Halt and ob—
KRNCH
OCUMENT STORAGE
CLICK
SKIIID

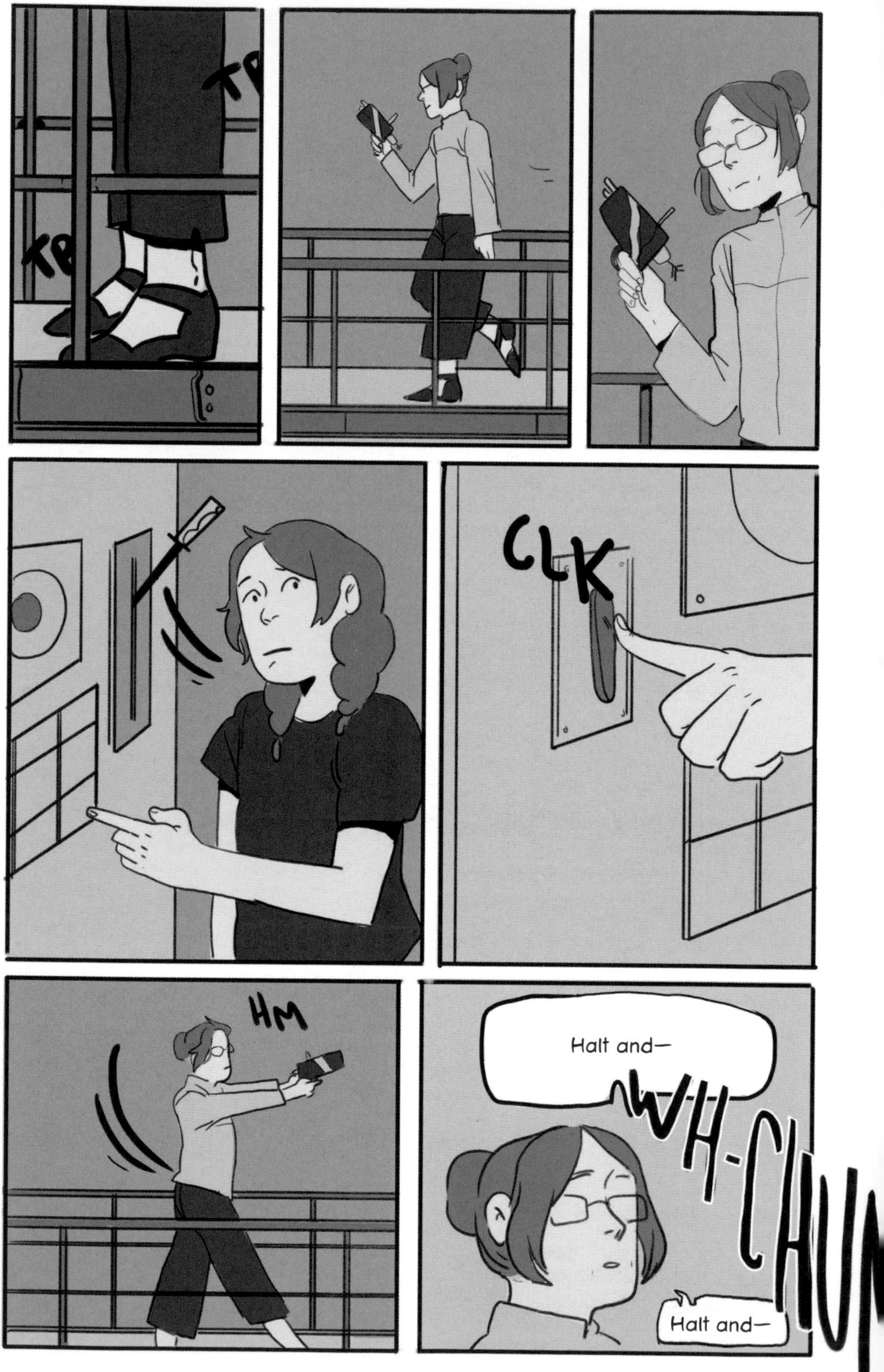
TP
TP
CLK
HM
Halt and—
WH-CHUN
Halt and—

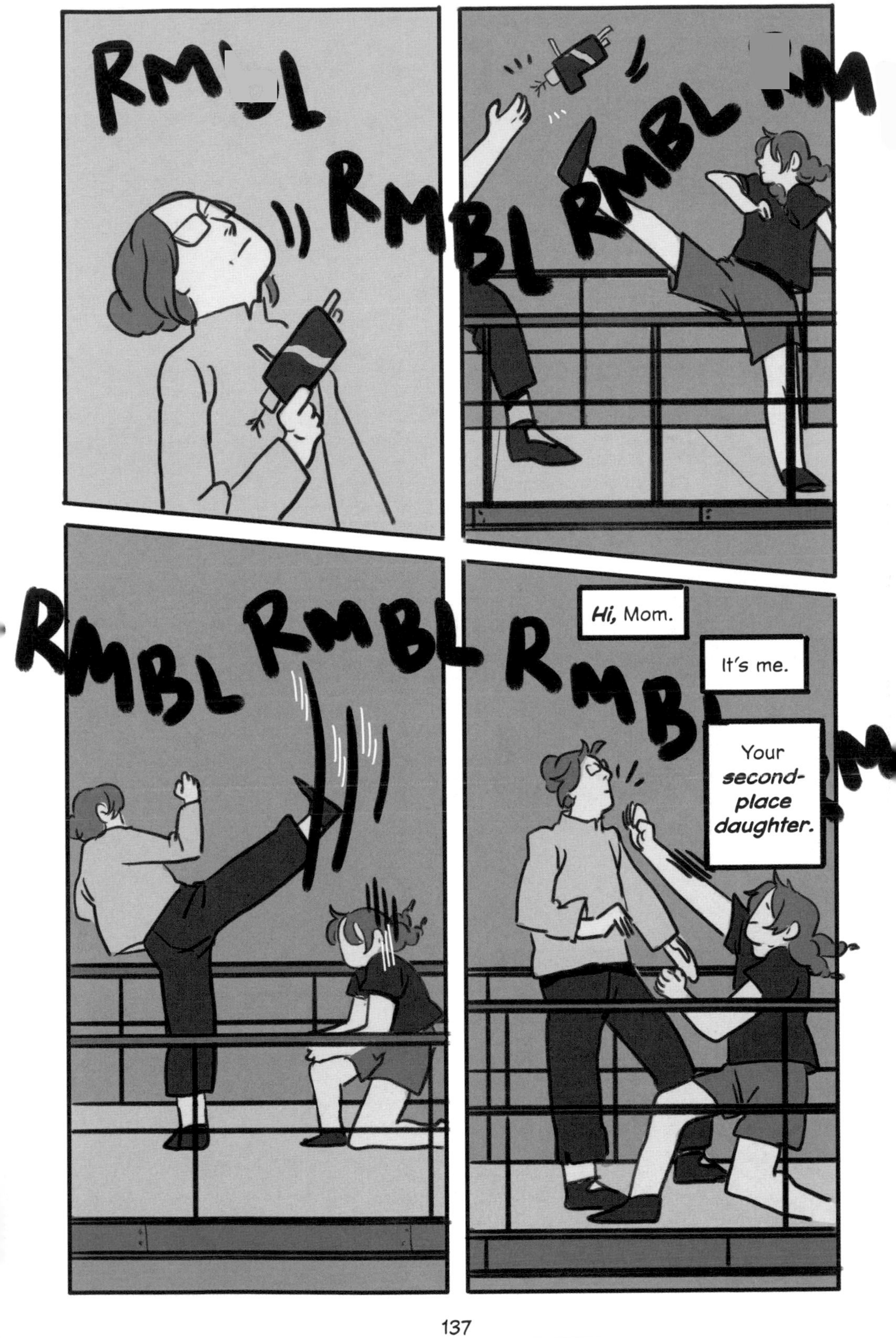
RMBL
RMBL
RMBL
RMBL
RMBL
RMBL
RMBL
Hi, Mom.
It's me.
Your second-place daughter.

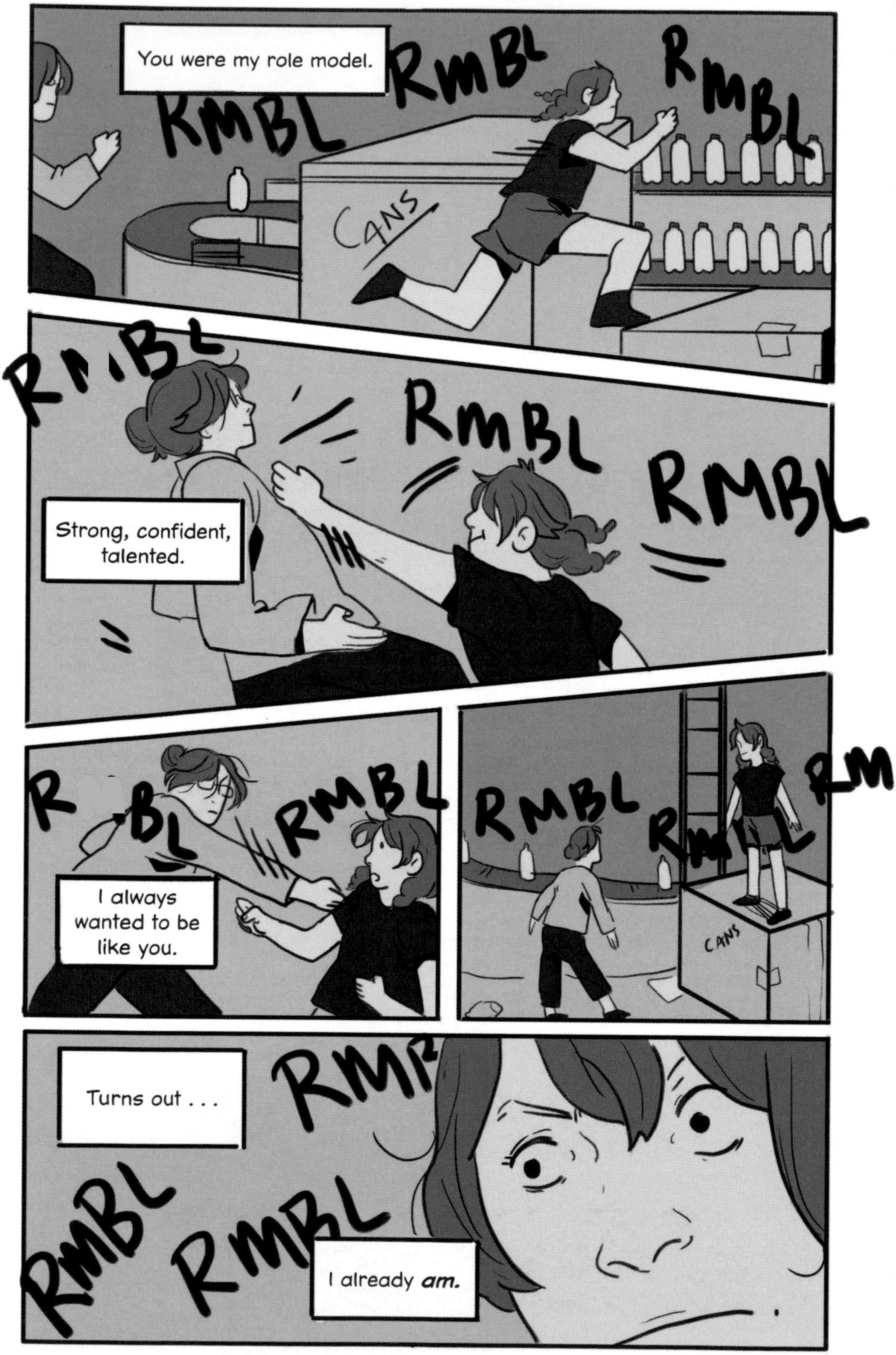
You were my role model.
RMBL
RMBL
RMBL
RMBL
RMBL
Strong, confident, talented.
RMBL
I always wanted to be like you.
RMBL
RM
Turns out . . .
RMBL
RMBL
I already *am.*

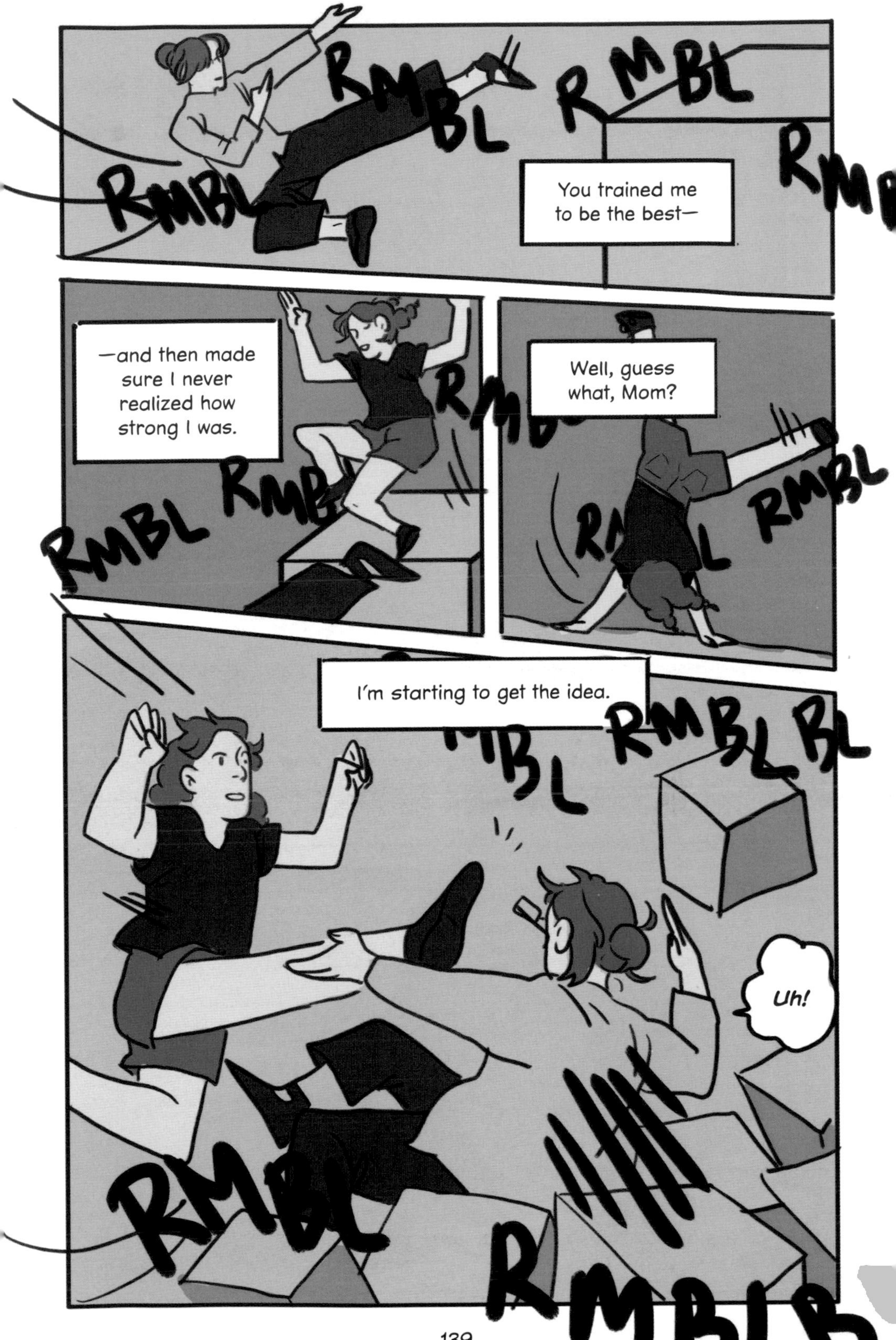
RMBL
RMBL
RMBL
RMBL
You trained me to be the best—
—and then made sure I never realized how strong I was.
RMBL
RMBL
Well, guess what, Mom?
RMBL
I'm starting to get the idea.
RMBL
Uh!
RMBL

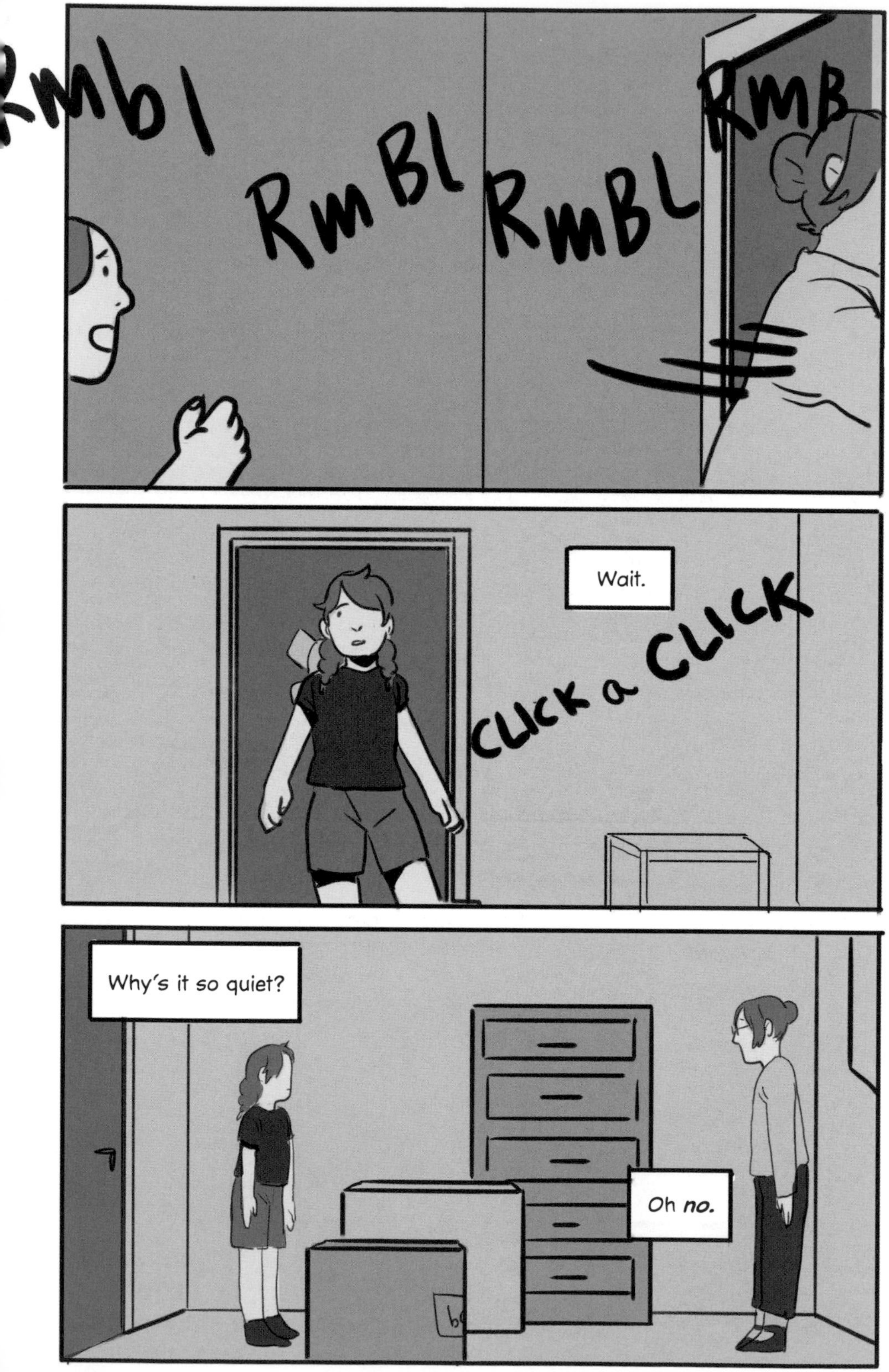
Rmbl
RmBl
RmBL
RmB
Wait.
CLICK a CLICK
Why's it so quiet?
Oh *no.*

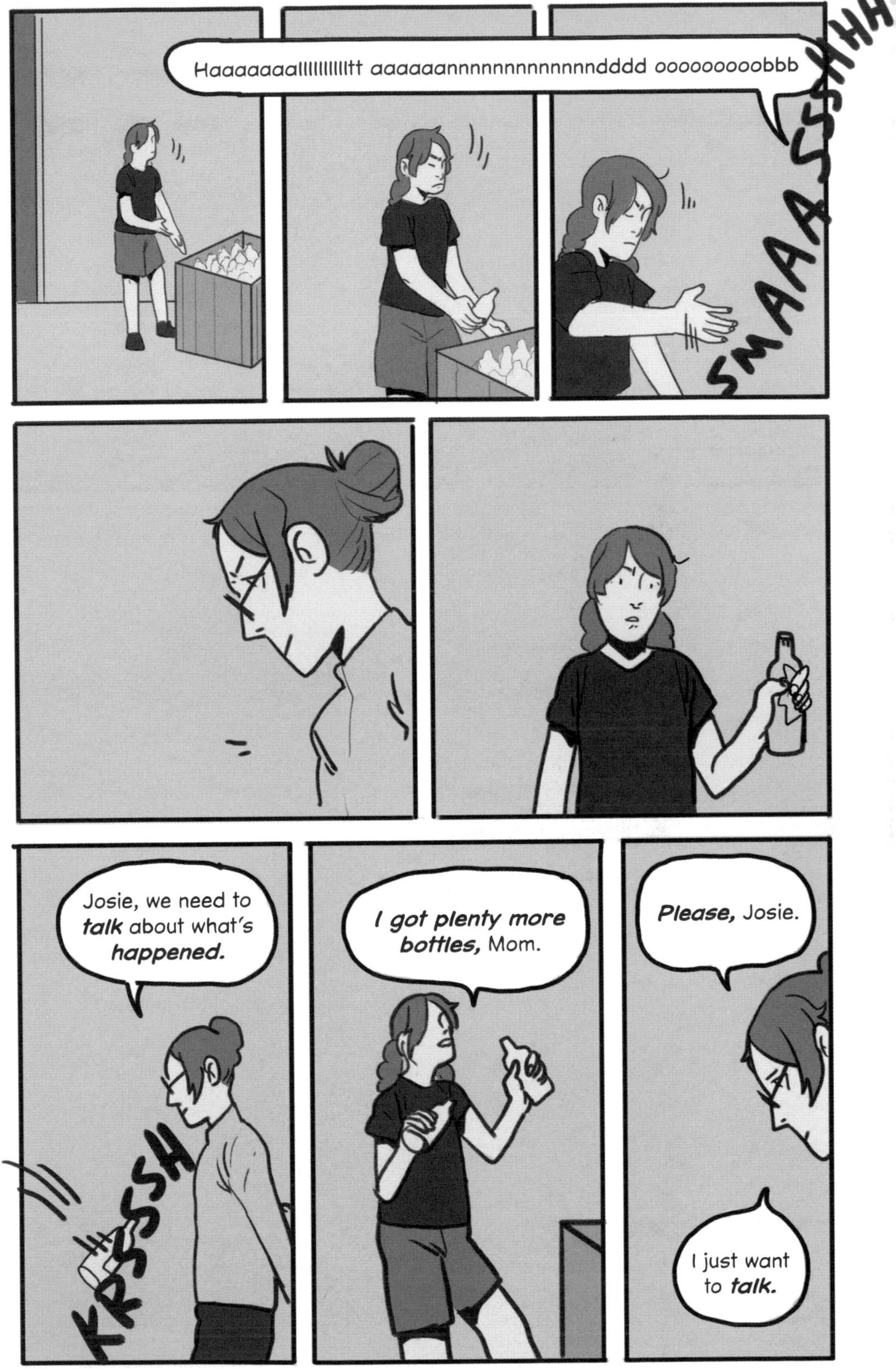
Haaaaaaallllllllllltt aaaaaannnnnnnnnnnnnndddd ooooooooobbb
SMAASSHHH
Josie, we need to **talk** about what's **happened.**
KRSSH
I got plenty more bottles, Mom.
Please, Josie.
I just want to ***talk.***

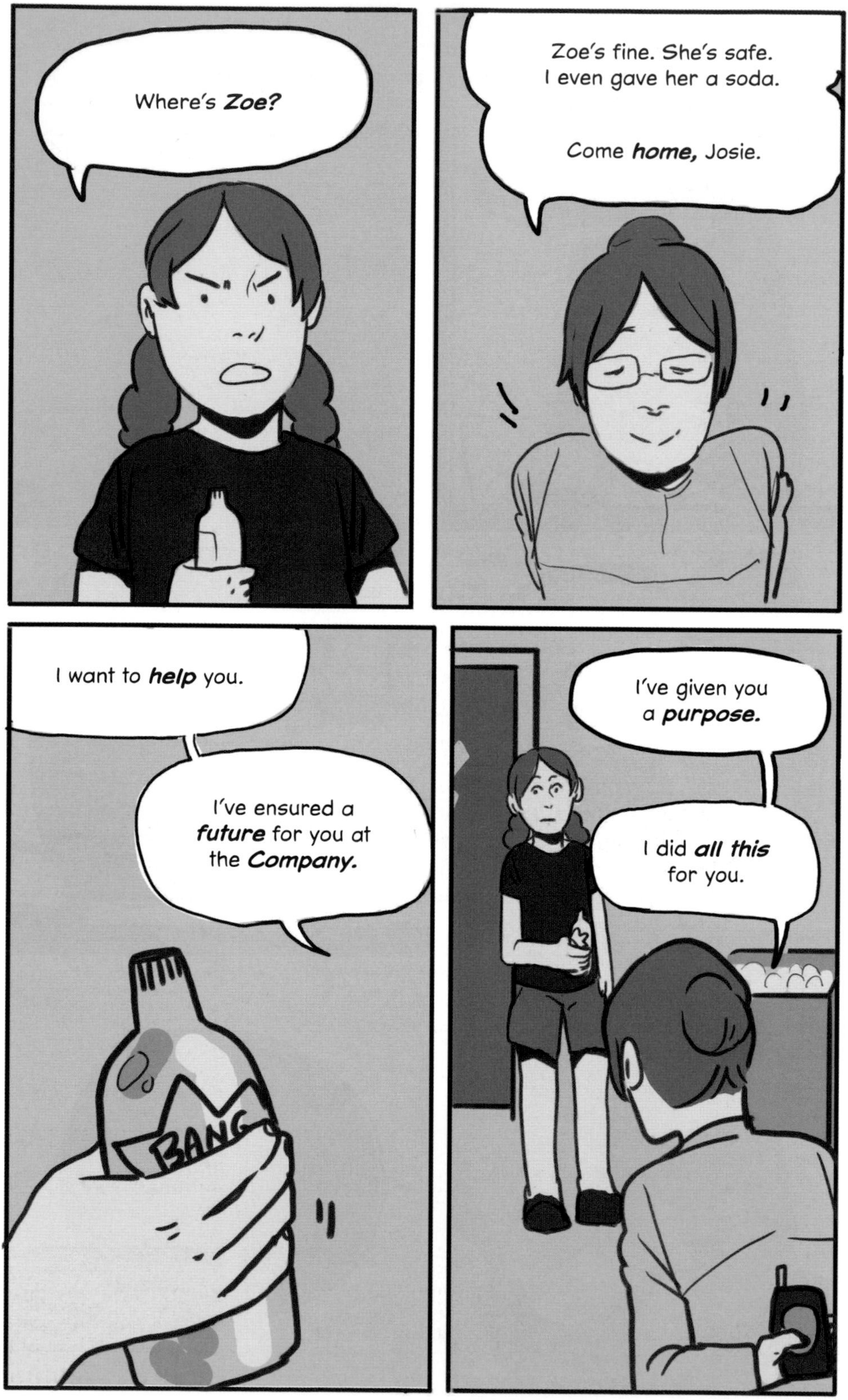
Where's ***Zoe?***
Zoe's fine. She's safe. I even gave her a soda.
Come ***home,*** Josie.
I want to ***help*** you.
I've ensured a ***future*** for you at the ***Company.***
BANG
I've given you a ***purpose.***
I did ***all this*** for you.

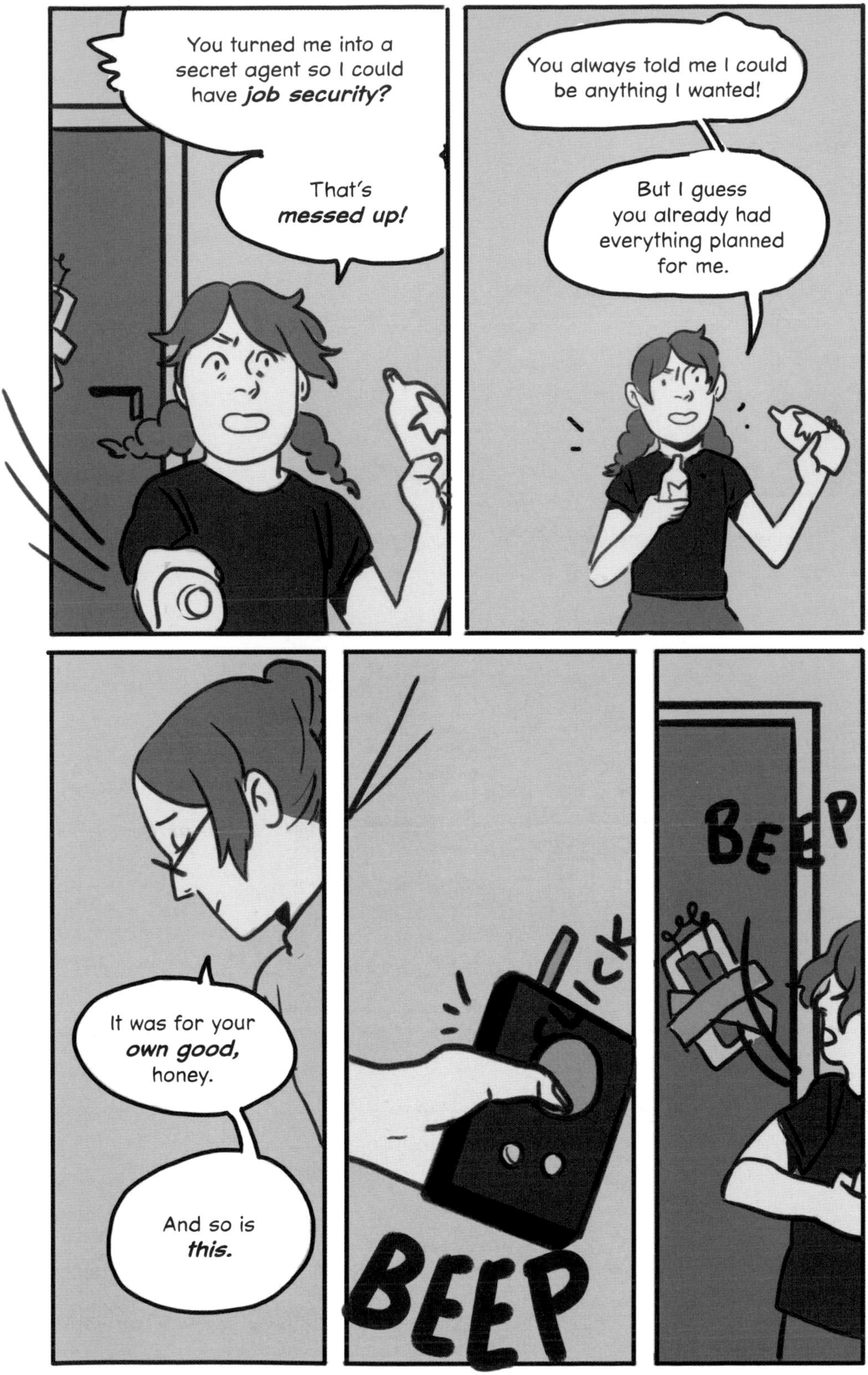
You turned me into a secret agent so I could have ***job security?***
That's ***messed up!***
You always told me I could be anything I wanted!
But I guess you already had everything planned for me.
It was for your ***own good,*** honey.
And so is ***this.***
CLICK
BEEP
BEEP

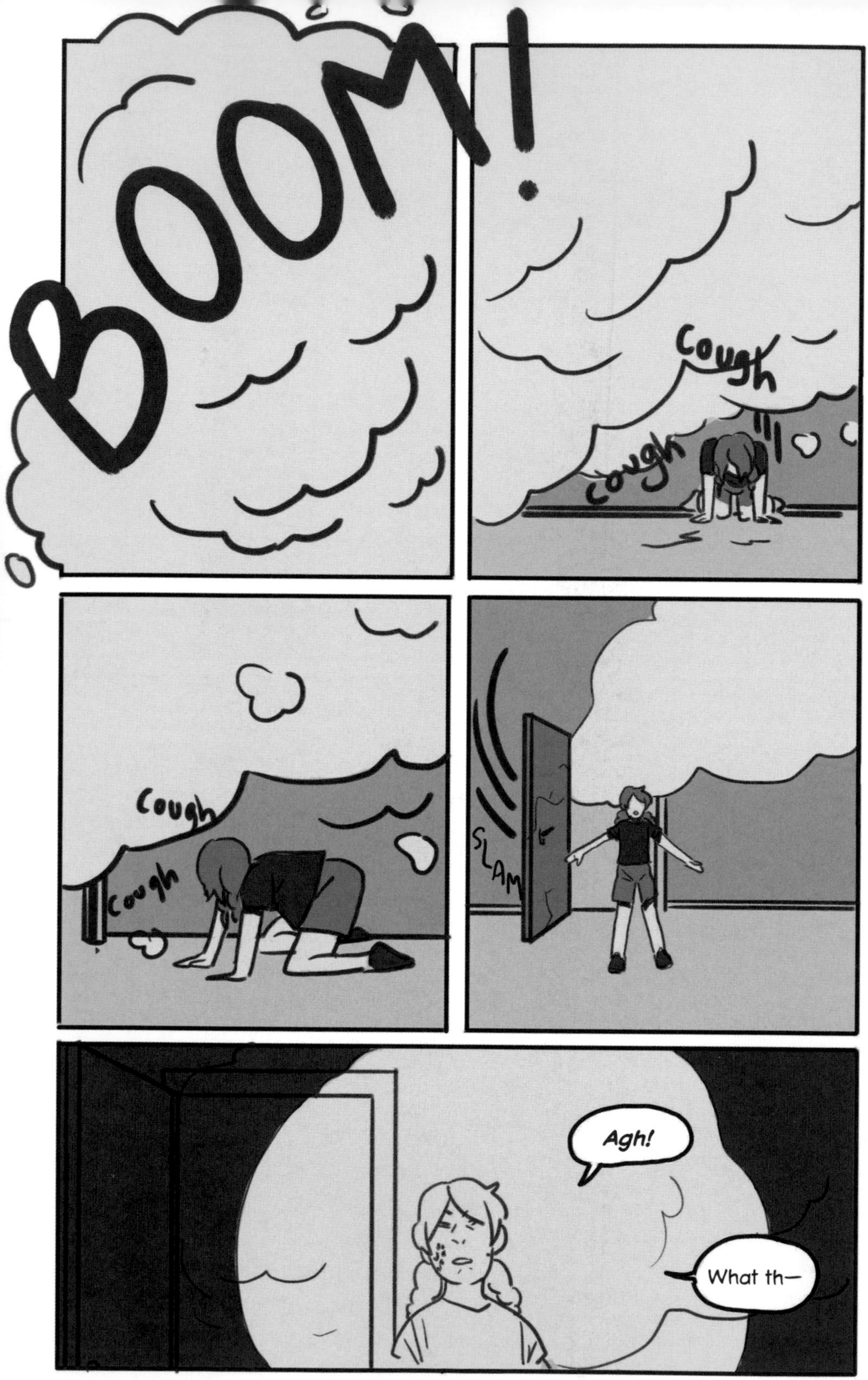
BOOM!
cough
cough
cough
cough
SLAM
Agh!
What th—

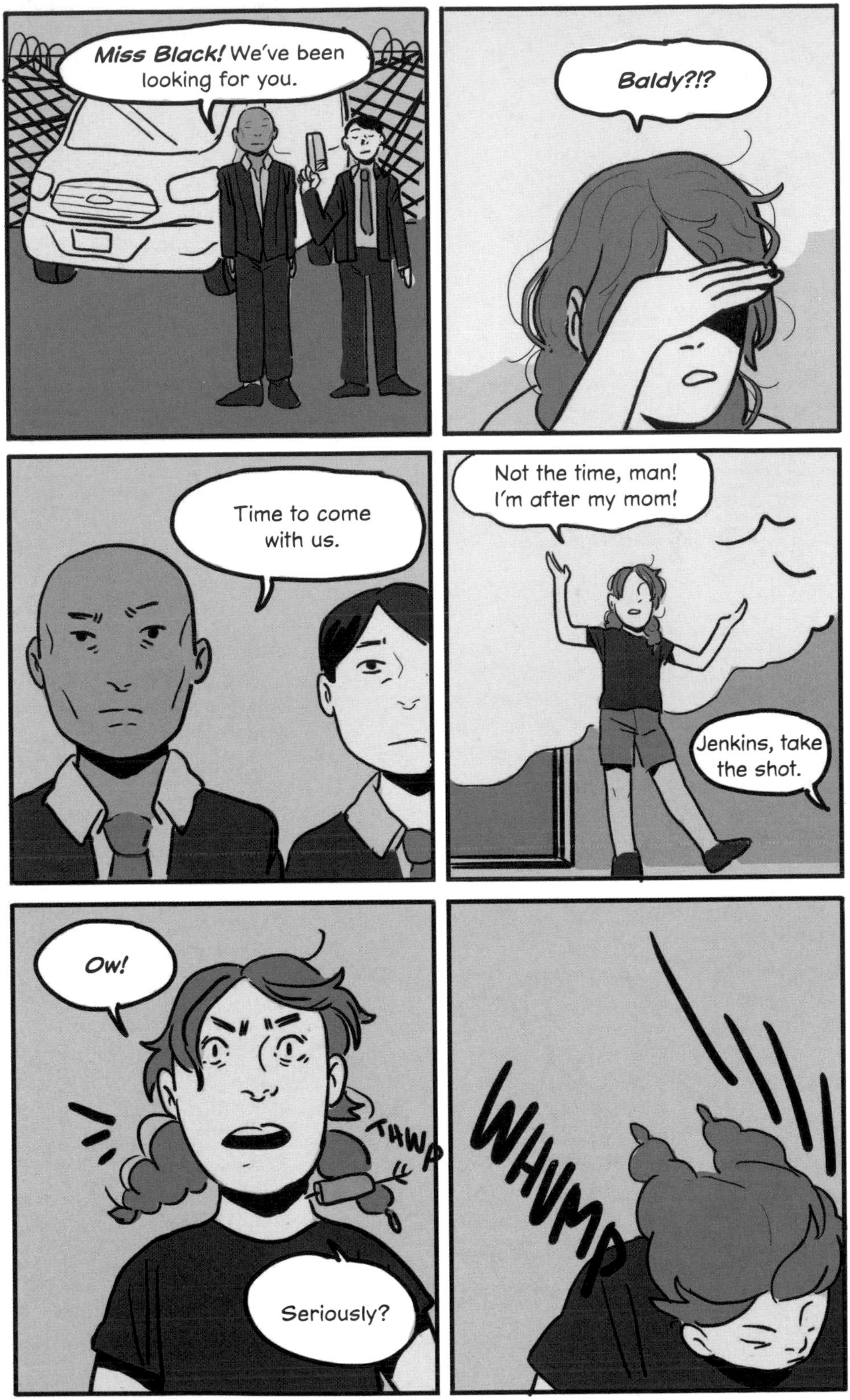
Miss Black! We've been looking for you.
Baldy?!?
Time to come with us.
Not the time, man! I'm after my mom!
Jenkins, take the shot.
Ow!
THWAP
Seriously?
WHUMP

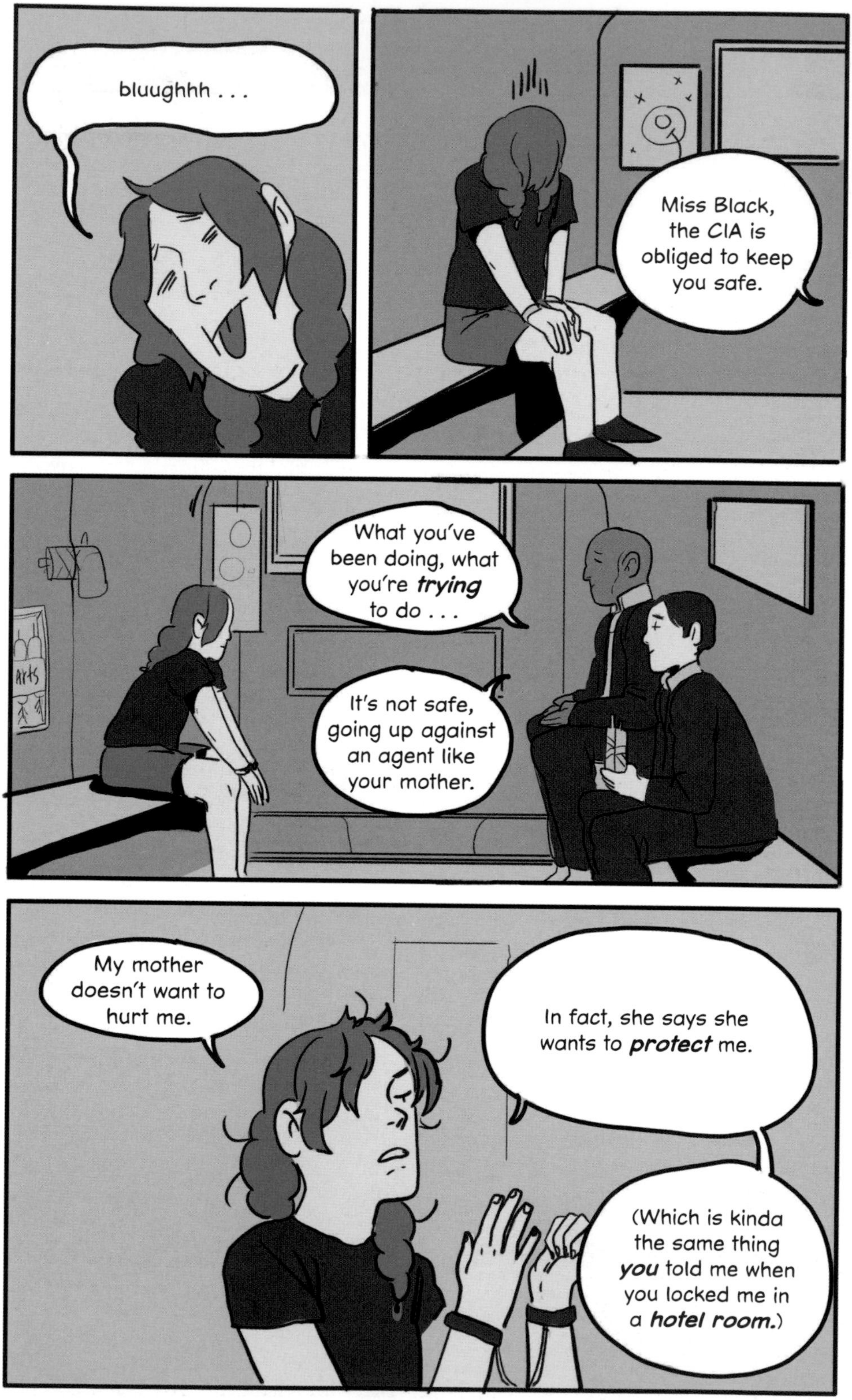
bluughhh . . .
Miss Black, the CIA is obliged to keep you safe.
What you've been doing, what you're ***trying*** to do . . .
It's not safe, going up against an agent like your mother.
Arts
My mother doesn't want to hurt me.
In fact, she says she wants to ***protect*** me.
(Which is kinda the same thing ***you*** told me when you locked me in a ***hotel room.***)

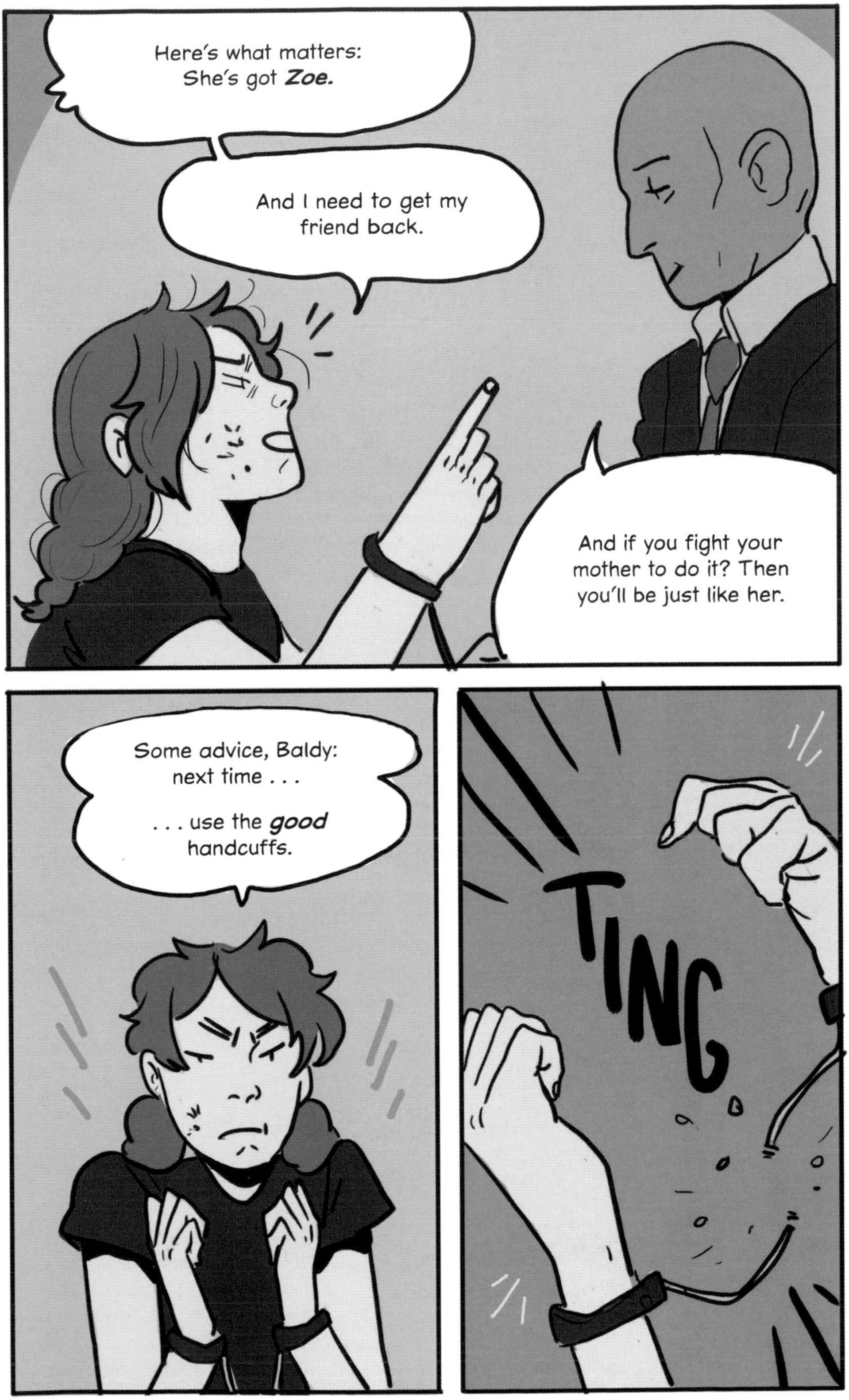

Here's what matters: She's got *Zoe.*
And I need to get my friend back.
And if you fight your mother to do it? Then you'll be just like her.
Some advice, Baldy: next time . . .
. . . use the *good* handcuffs.
TING

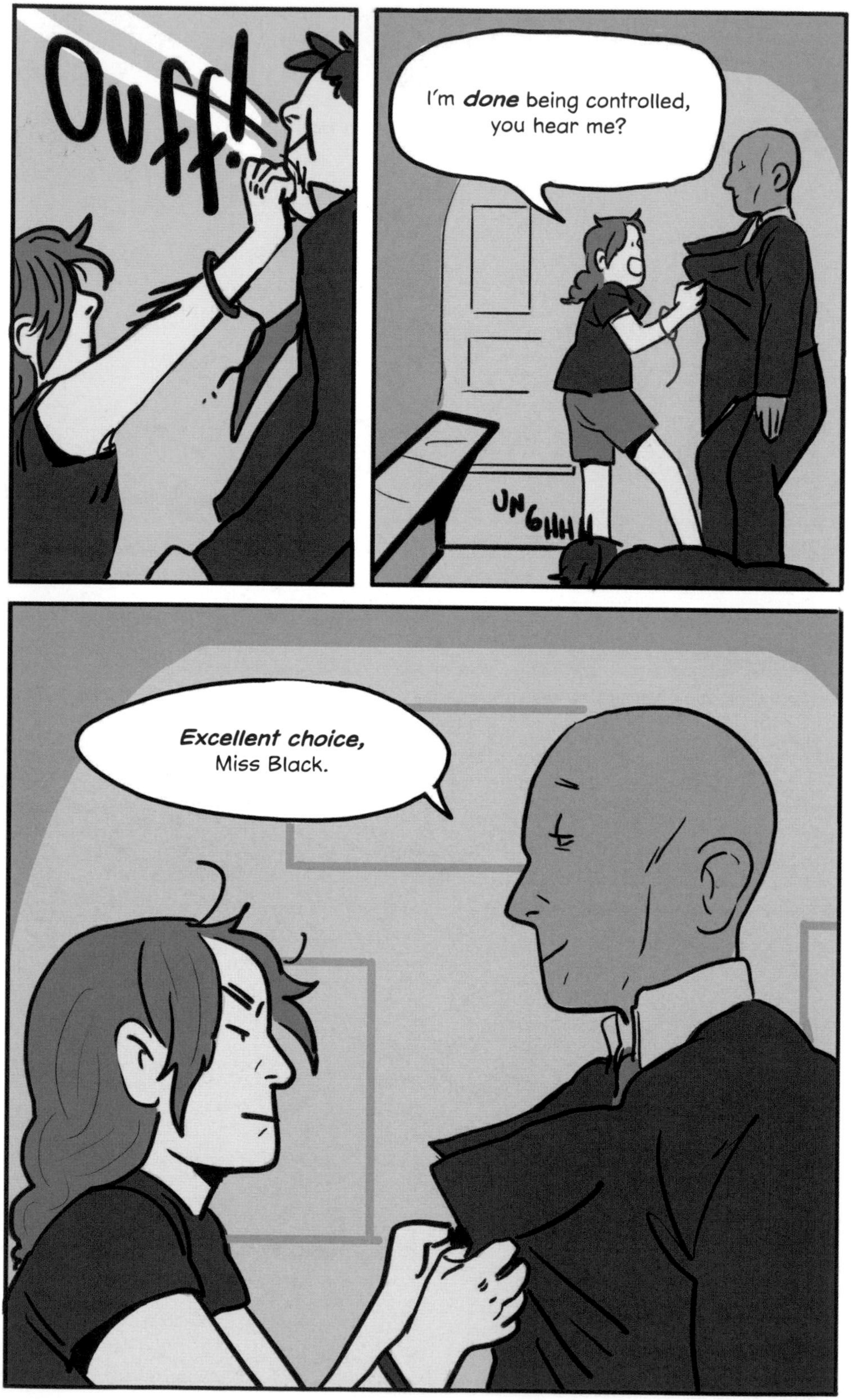
OUFF!
I'm *done* being controlled, you hear me?
UNGHHH
Excellent choice, Miss Black.

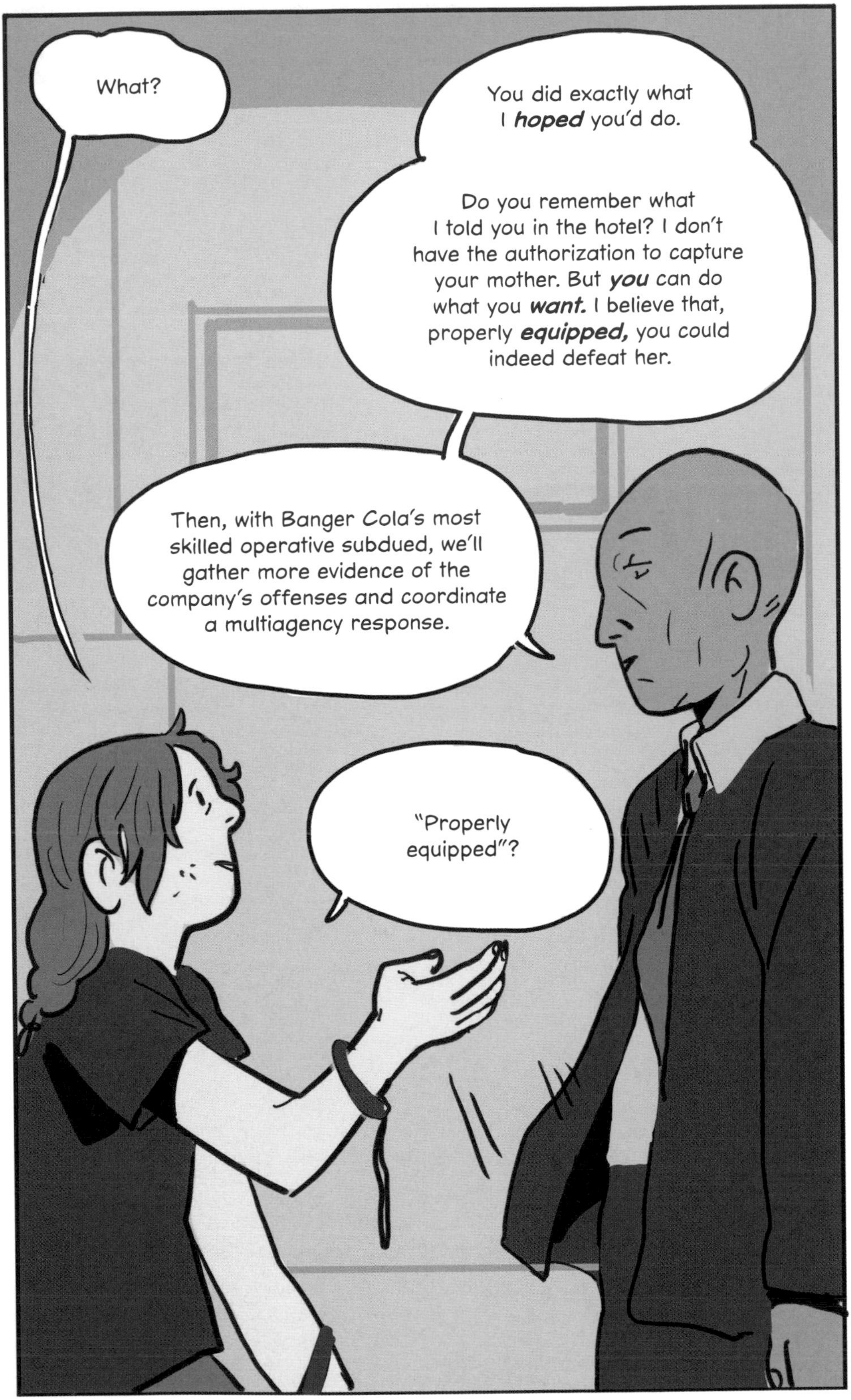
What?
You did exactly what I *hoped* you'd do.
Do you remember what I told you in the hotel? I don't have the authorization to capture your mother. But *you* can do what you *want.* I believe that, properly *equipped,* you could indeed defeat her.
Then, with Banger Cola's most skilled operative subdued, we'll gather more evidence of the company's offenses and coordinate a multiagency response.
"Properly equipped"?

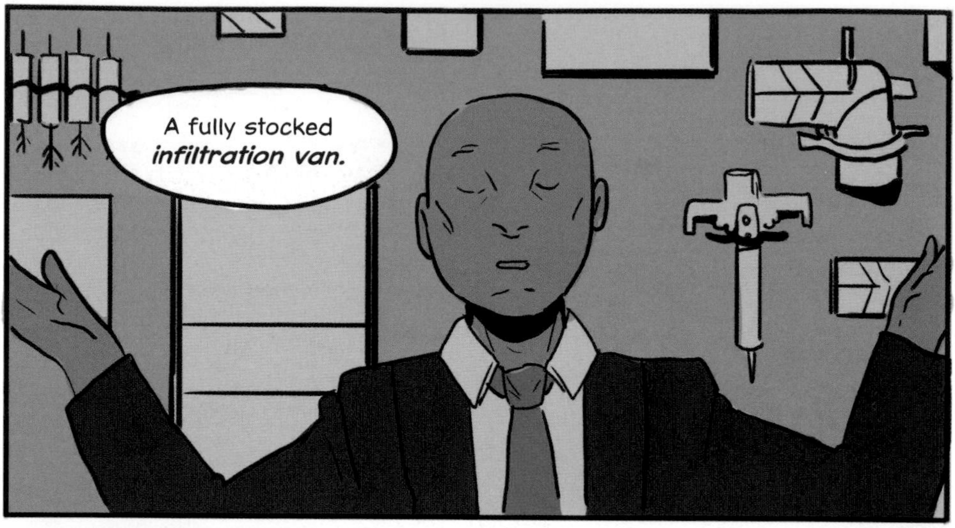
A fully stocked *infiltration van.*

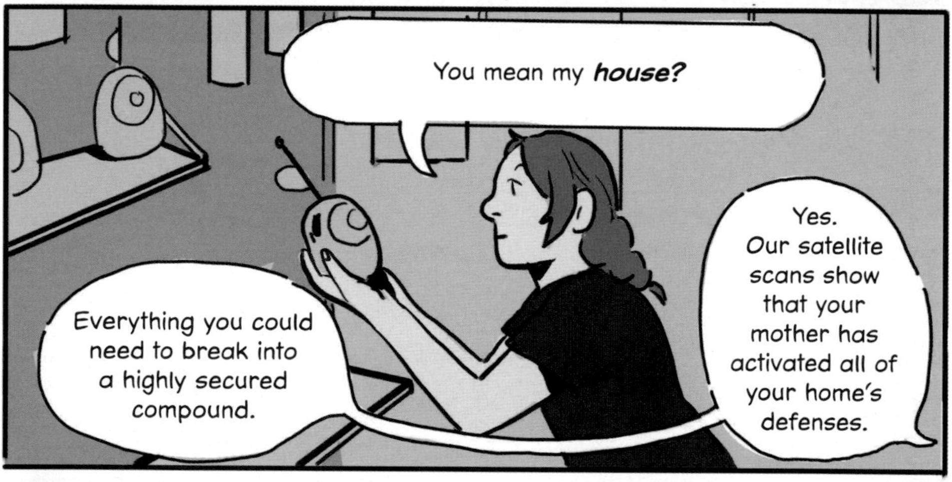
You mean my ***house?***
Everything you could need to break into a highly secured compound.
Yes. Our satellite scans show that your mother has activated all of your home's defenses.

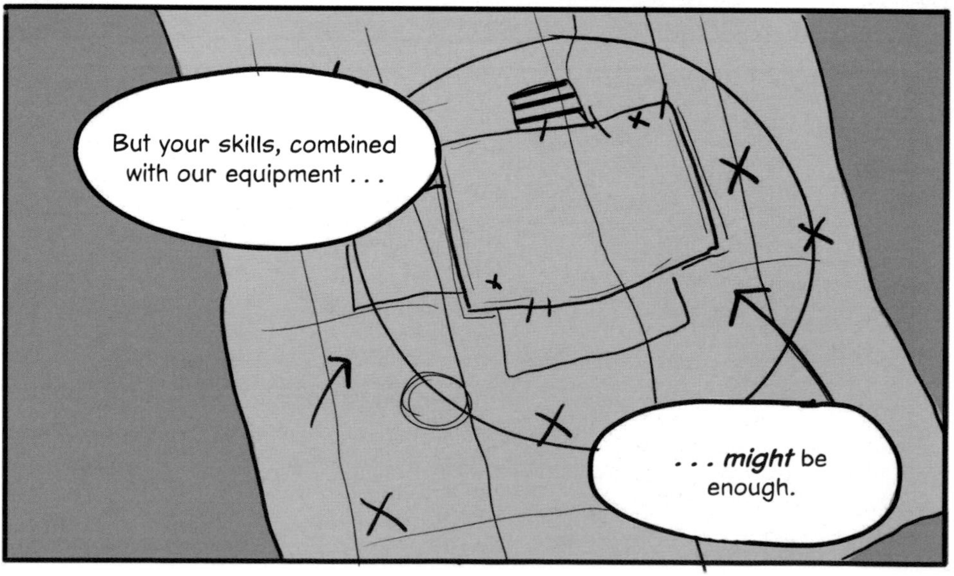
But your skills, combined with our equipment . . .
. . . ***might*** be enough.

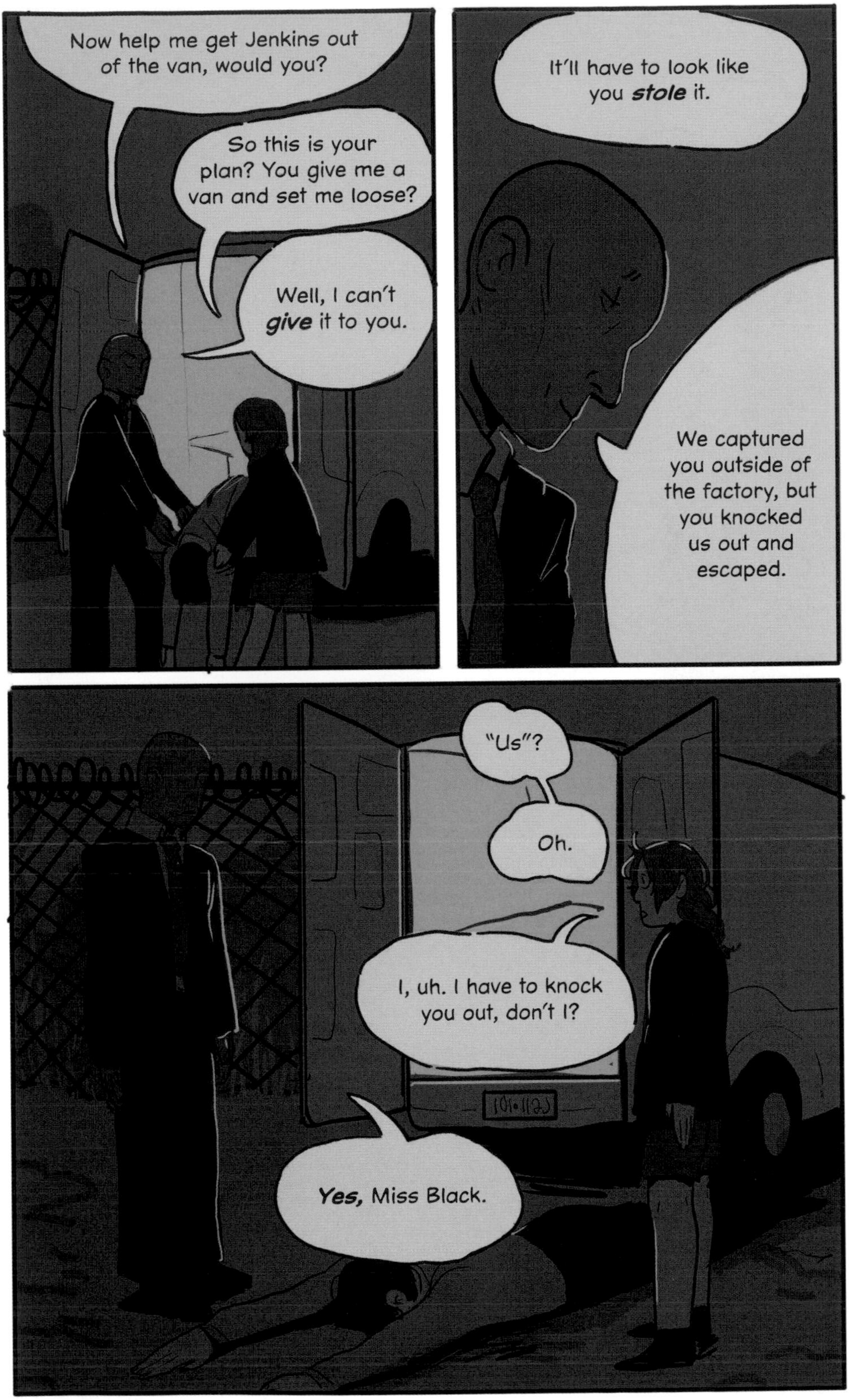
Now help me get Jenkins out of the van, would you?
So this is your plan? You give me a van and set me loose?
Well, I can't *give* it to you.
It'll have to look like you *stole* it.
We captured you outside of the factory, but you knocked us out and escaped.
"Us"?
Oh.
I, uh. I have to knock you out, don't I?
Yes, Miss Black.

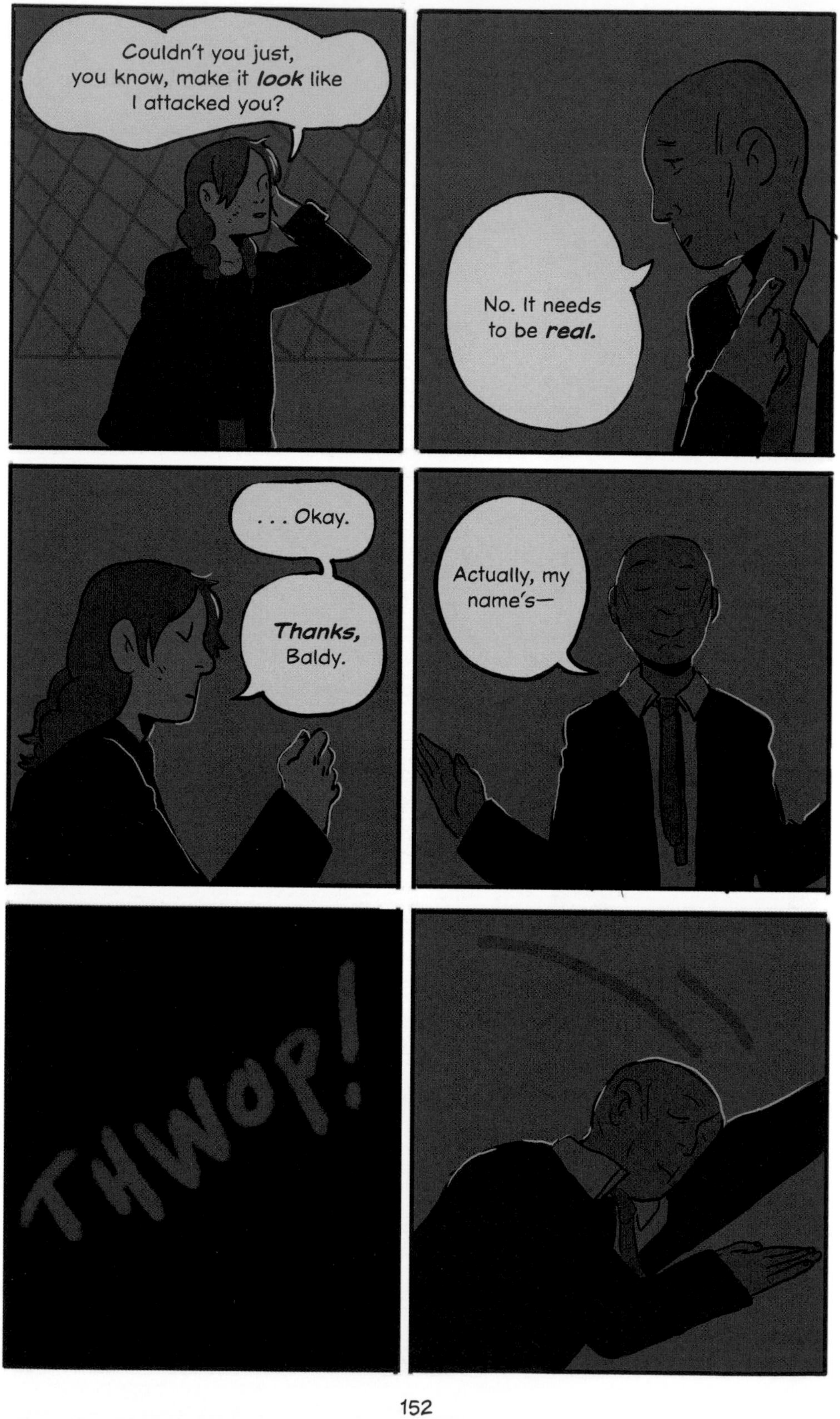
Couldn't you just, you know, make it *look* like I attacked you?
No. It needs to be *real.*
. . . Okay.
Thanks, Baldy.
Actually, my name's—
THWOP!

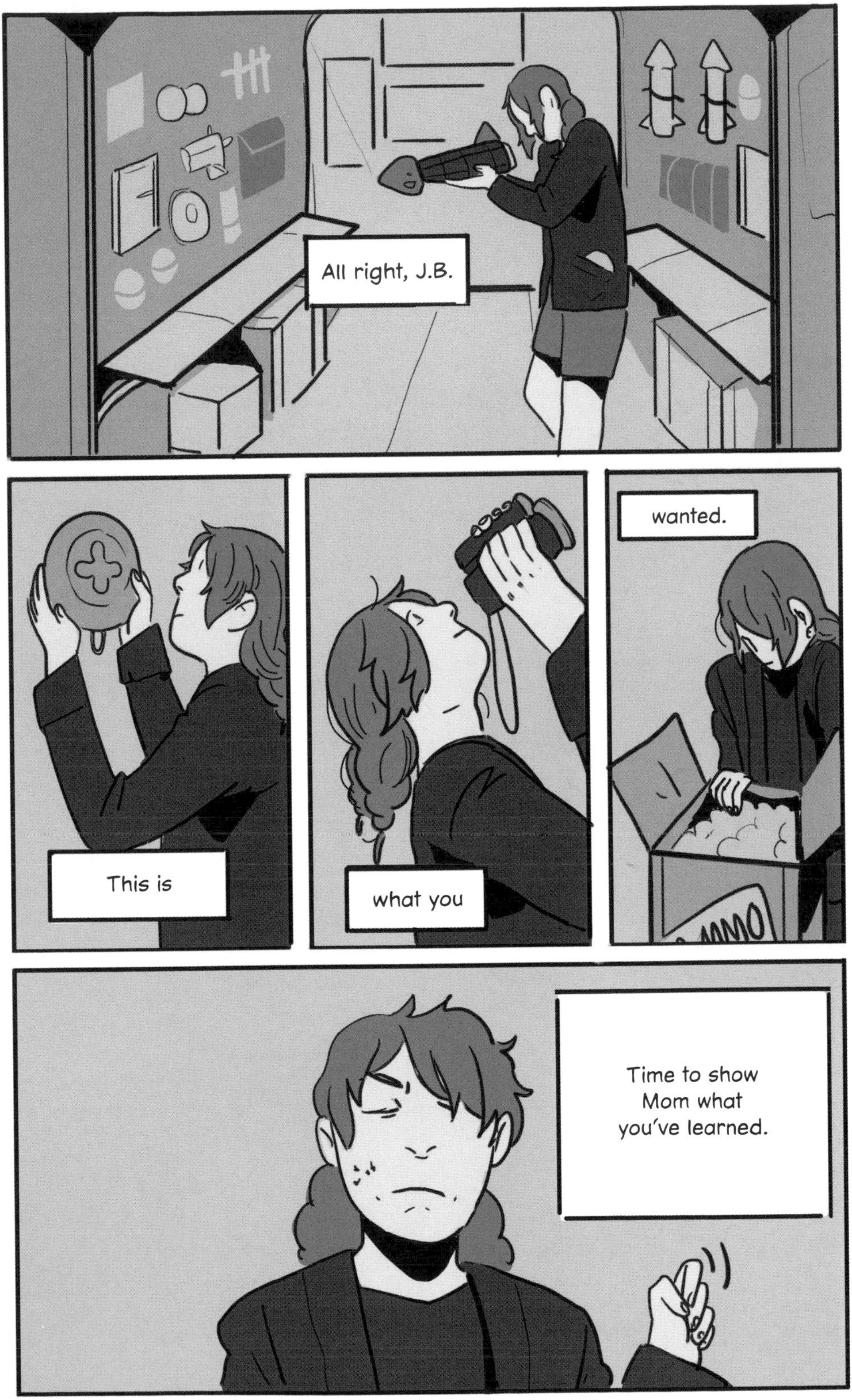
All right, J.B.
This is
what you
wanted.
Time to show Mom what you've learned.

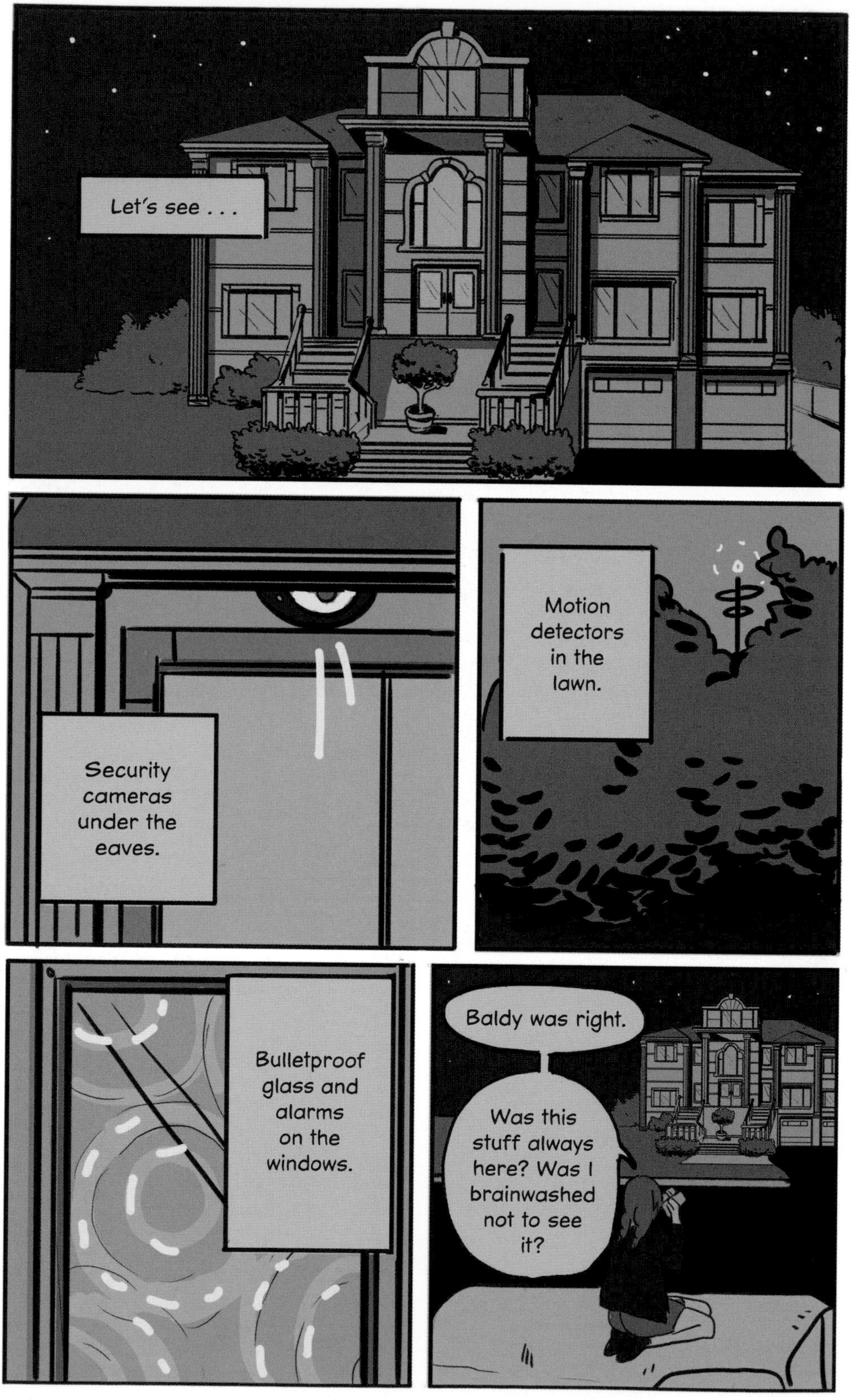
Let's see . . .
Security cameras under the eaves.
Motion detectors in the lawn.
Bulletproof glass and alarms on the windows.
Baldy was right.
Was this stuff always here? Was I brainwashed not to see it?

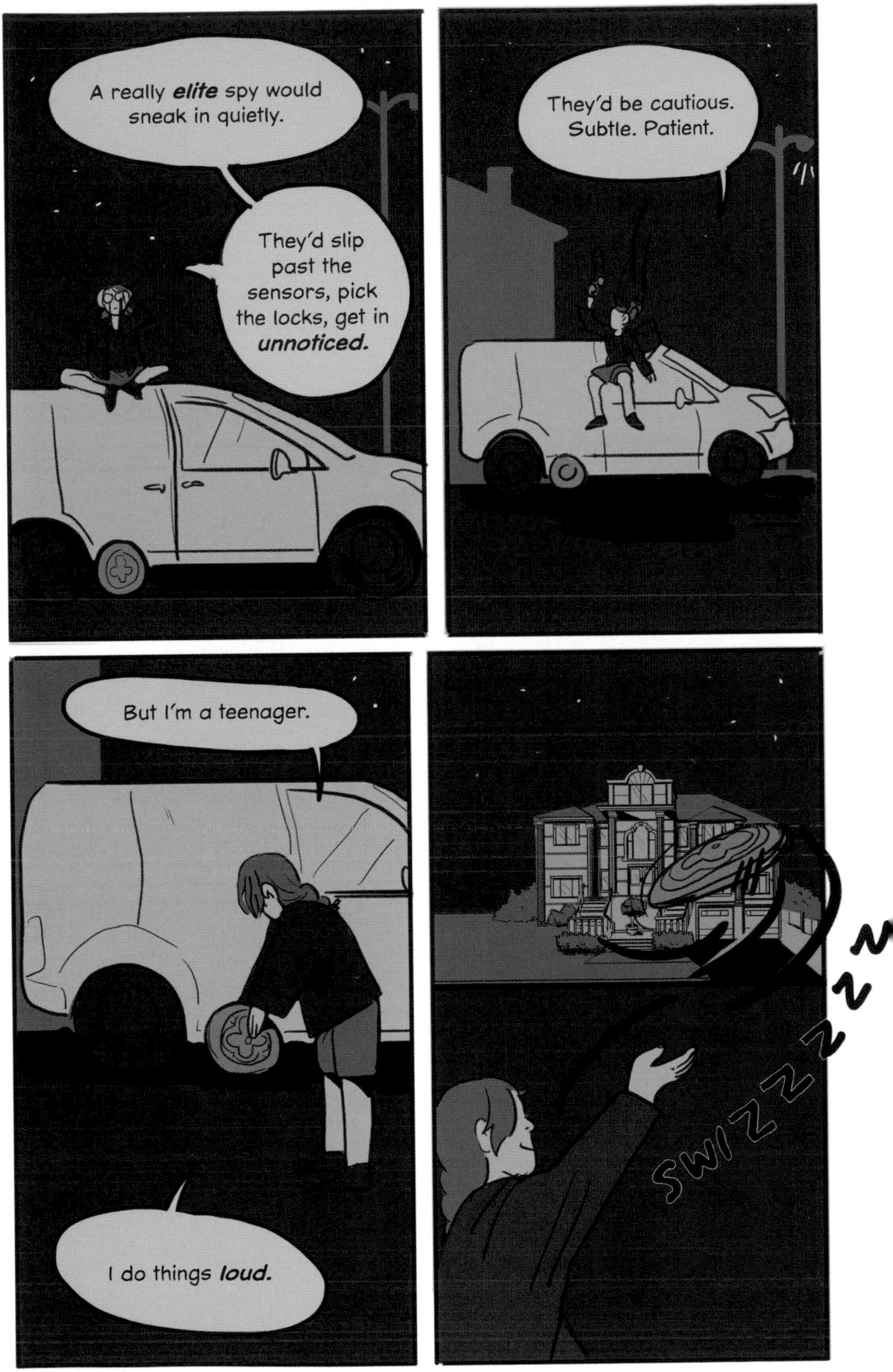

A really *elite* spy would sneak in quietly.
They'd slip past the sensors, pick the locks, get in *unnoticed.*
They'd be cautious. Subtle. Patient.
But I'm a teenager.
I do things *loud.*
SWIZZZZZ

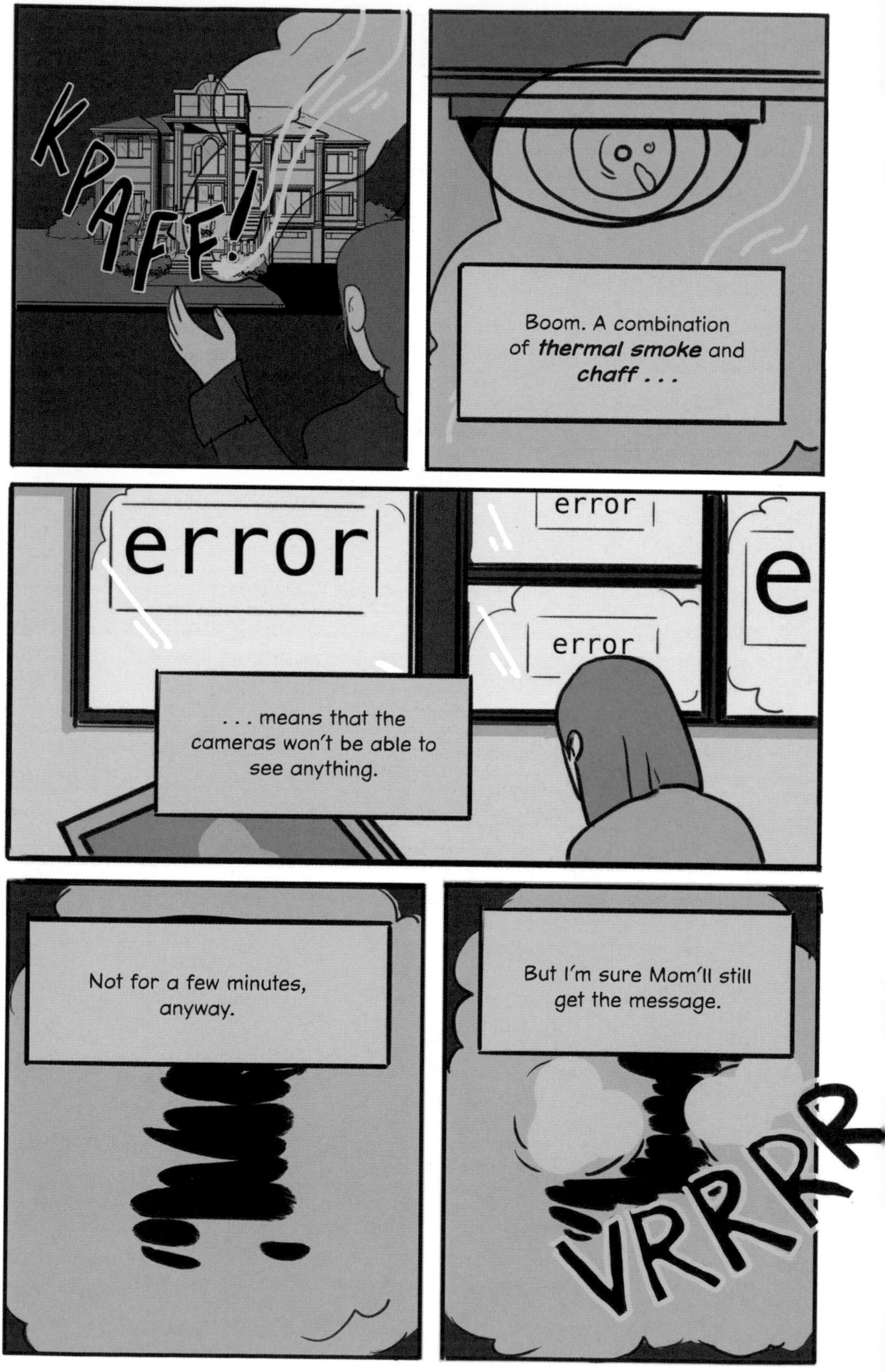
KPAFF!
Boom. A combination of ***thermal smoke*** and ***chaff . . .***
error
error
e
error
. . . means that the cameras won't be able to see anything.
Not for a few minutes, anyway.
But I'm sure Mom'll still get the message.
VRRRR

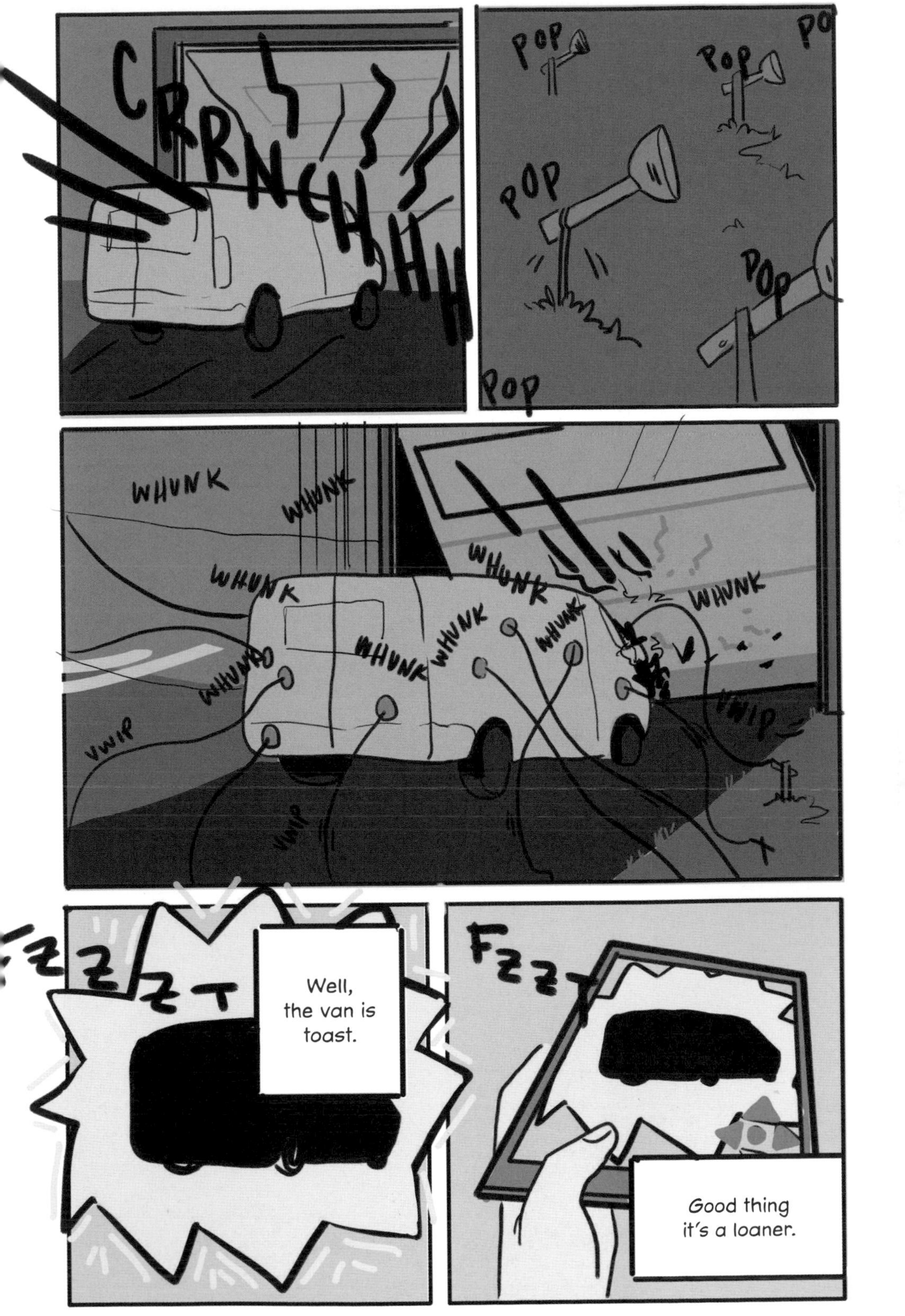
CRRNCHHHH
POP
POP
POP
POP
POP
POP
WHUNK
WHUNK
WHUNK
WHUNK
WHUNK
WHUNK
WHUNK
WHUNK
WHUNK
VWIP
VWIP
VWIP
ZZZZT
Well, the van is toast.
FZZZT
Good thing it's a loaner.

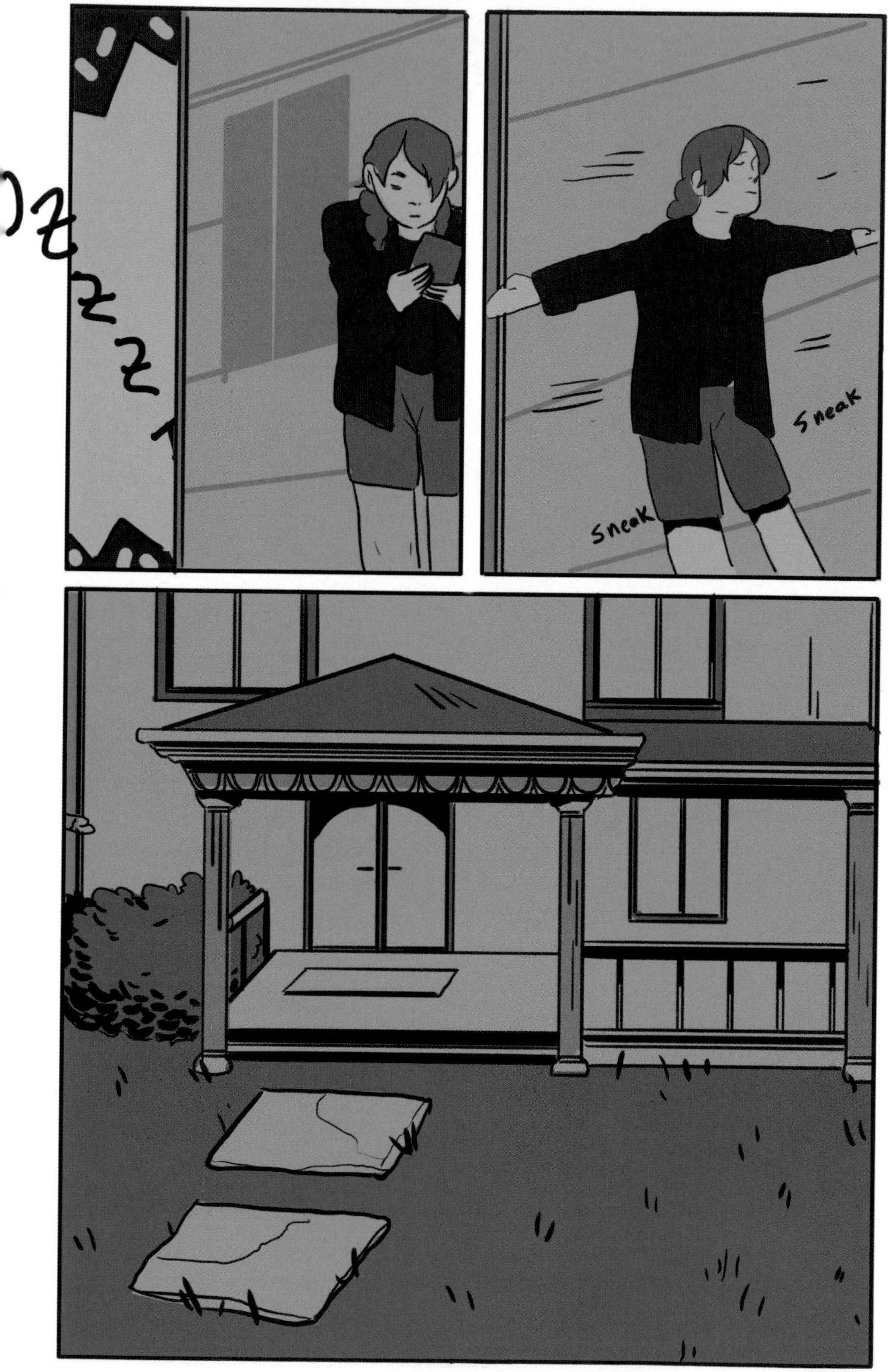
Sneak
Sneak

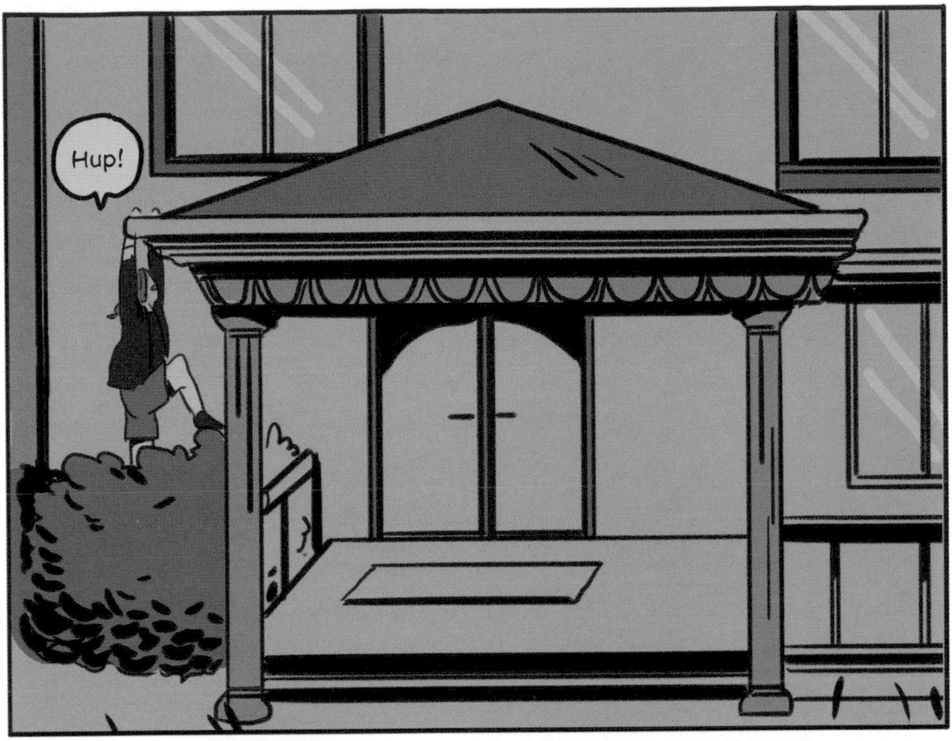
Hup!

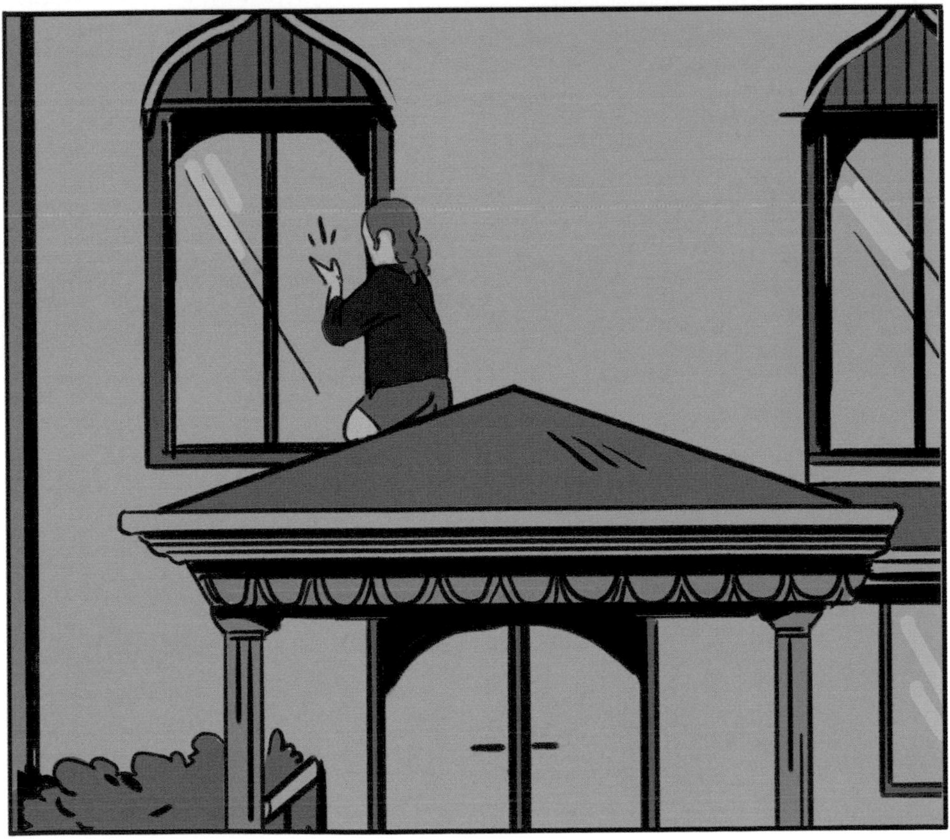

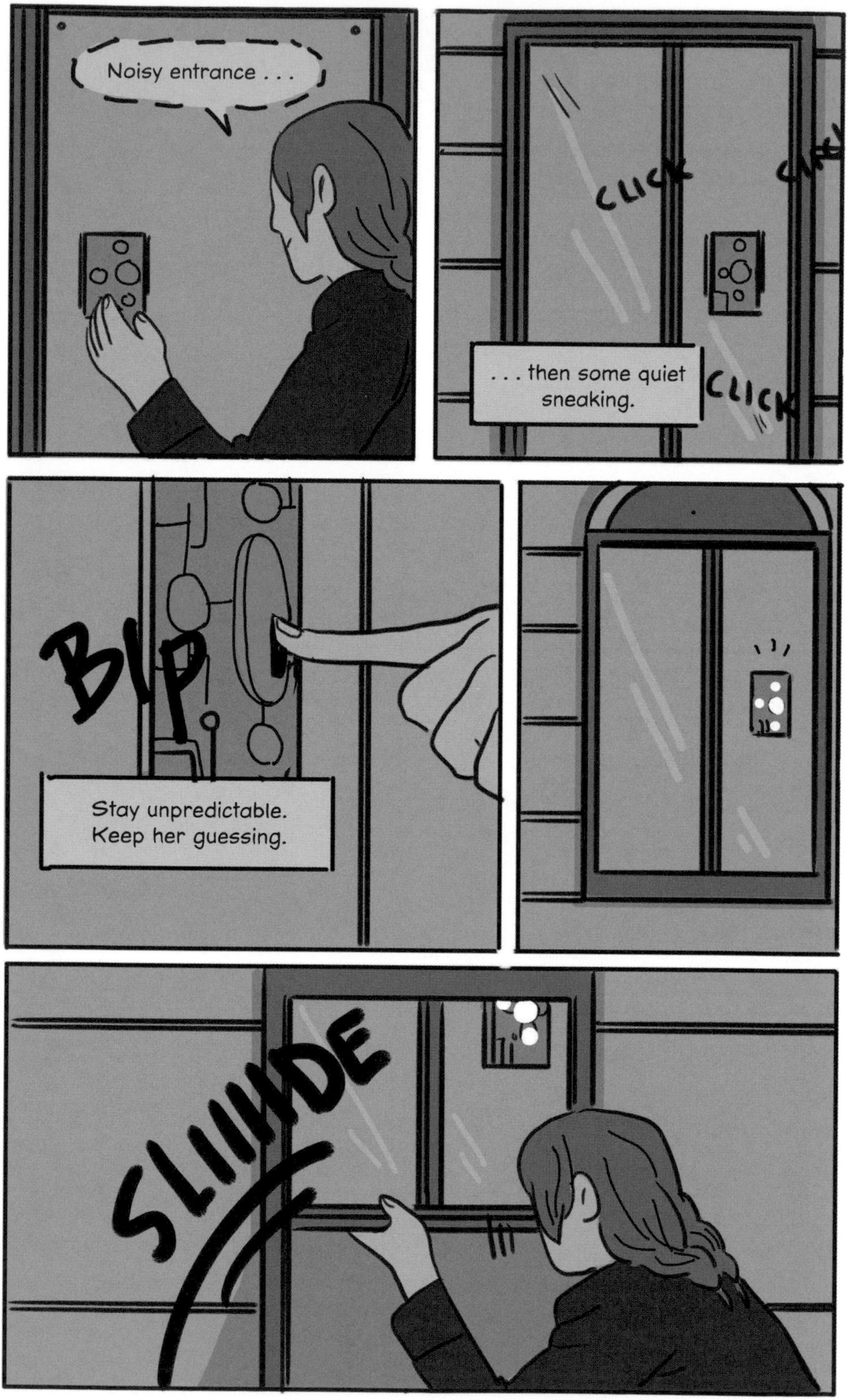
Noisy entrance . . .
CLICK
. . . then some quiet sneaking.
CLICK
BIP
Stay unpredictable. Keep her guessing.
SLIIIIDE

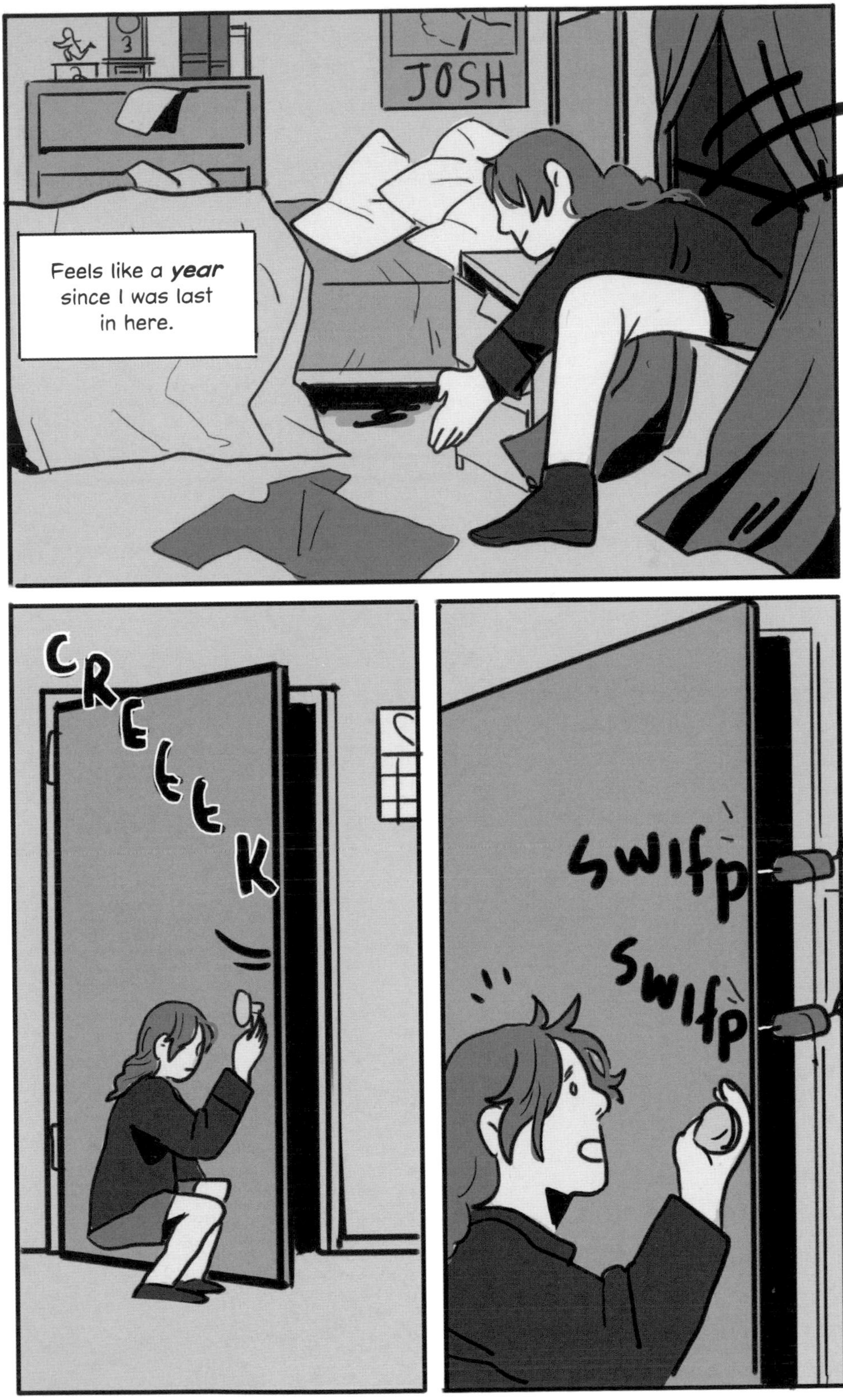
JOSH
Feels like a ***year*** since I was last in here.
CREEEK
SWIFP
SWIFP

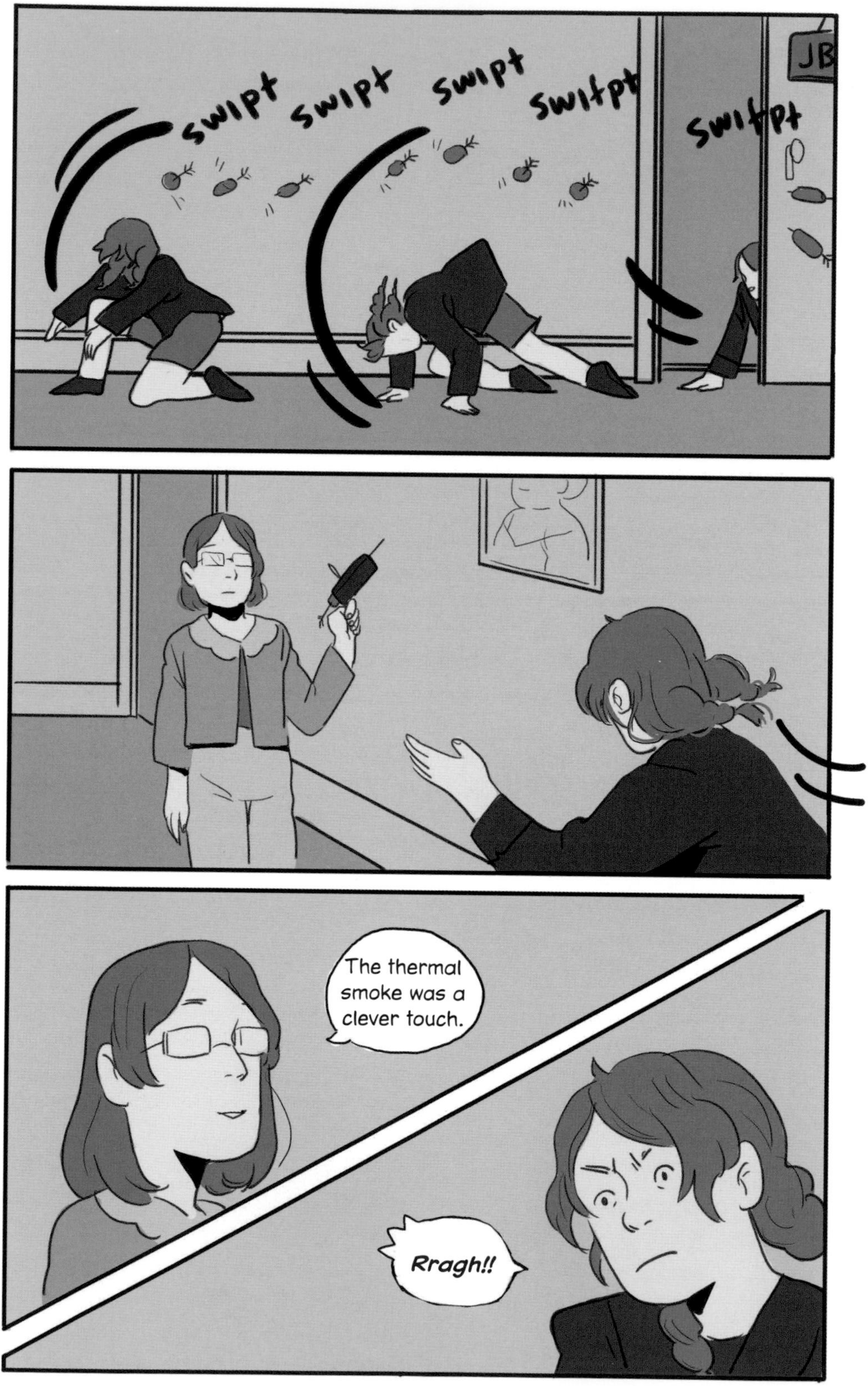
swipt
swipt
swipt
swiftpt
swiftpt
JB
The thermal smoke was a clever touch.
Rragh!!

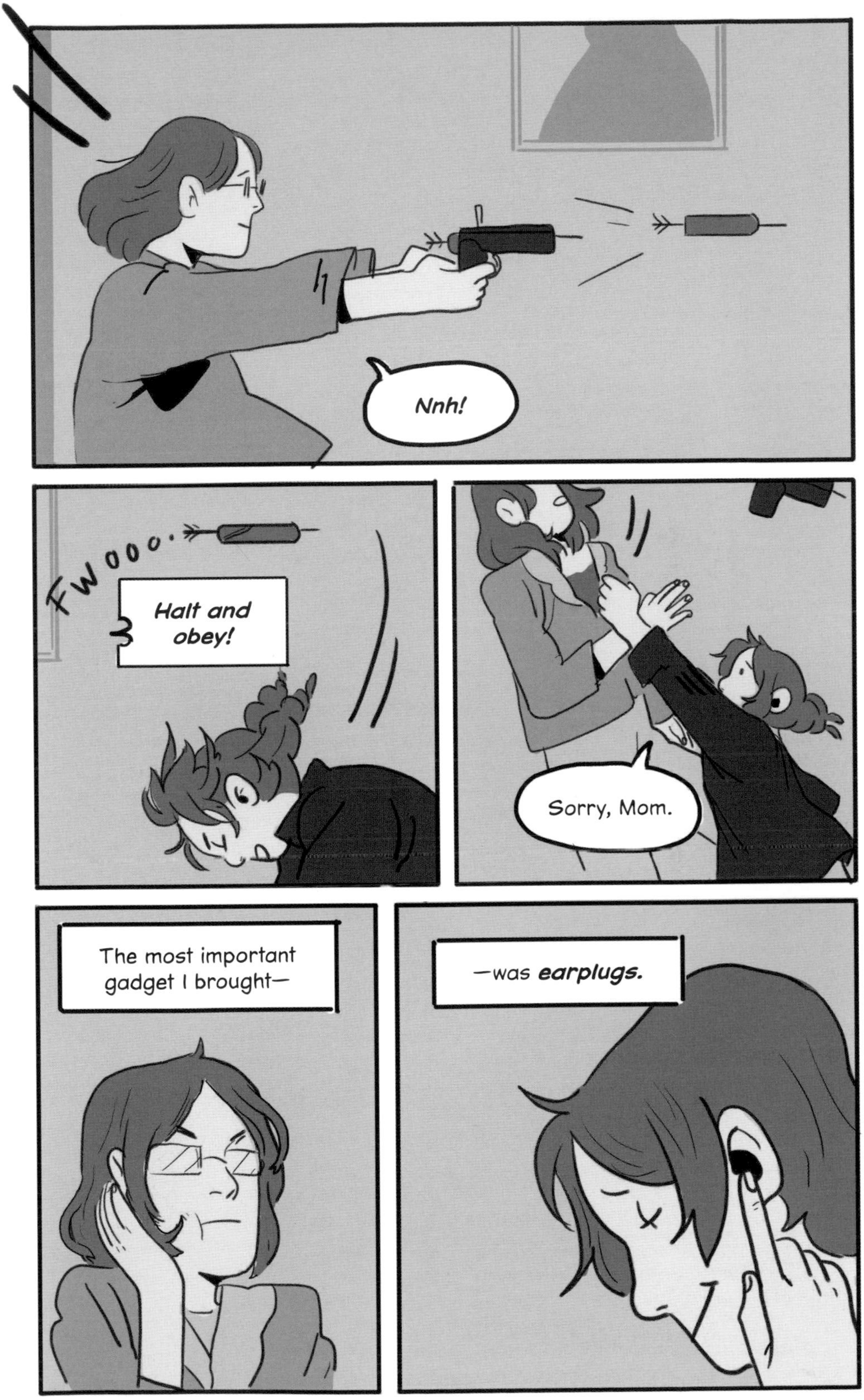
Nnh!
FWooo..
Halt and obey!
Sorry, Mom.
The most important gadget I brought—
—was earplugs.

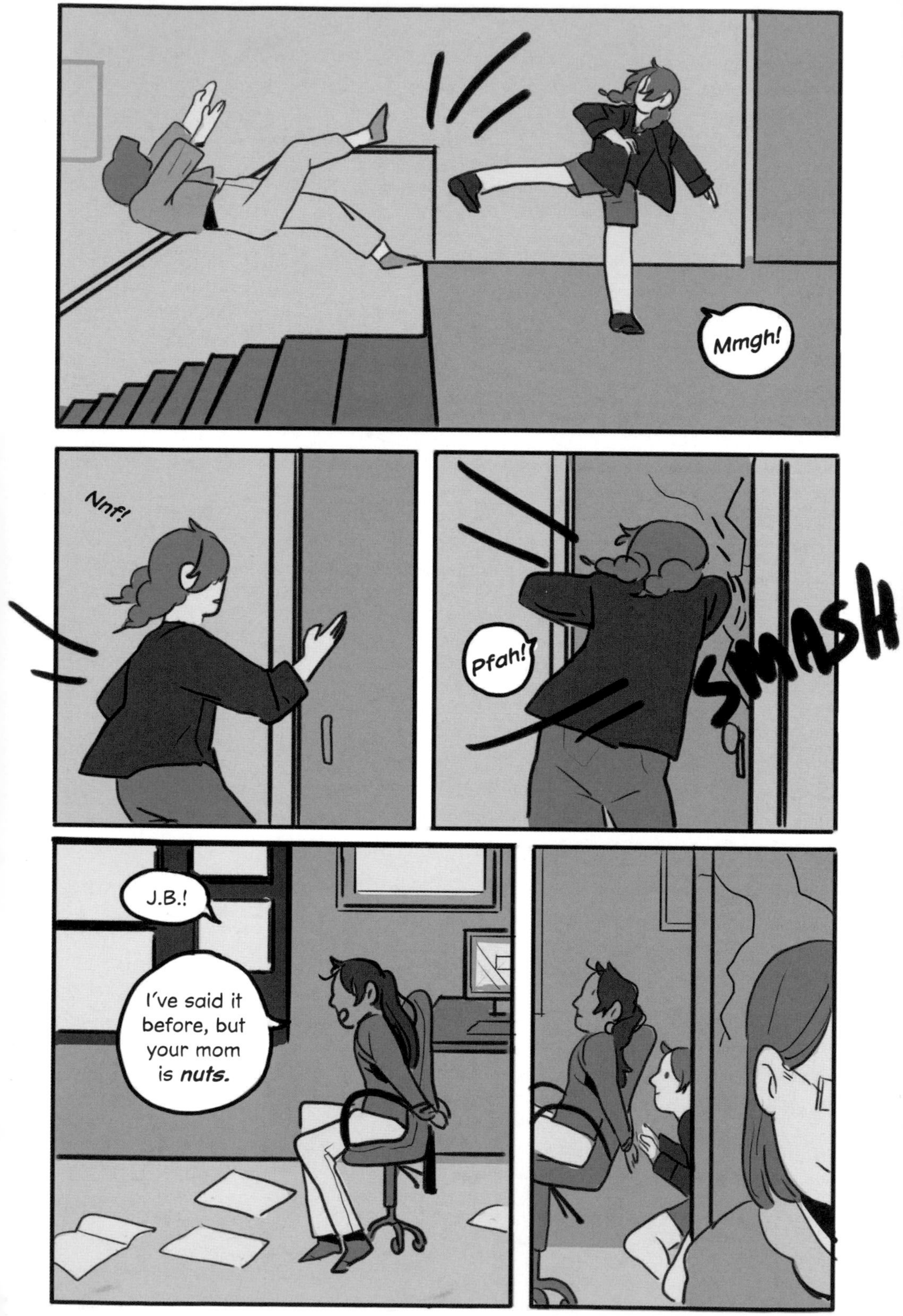
Mmgh!
Nnf!
Pfah!
SMASH
J.B.!
I've said it before, but your mom is ***nuts.***

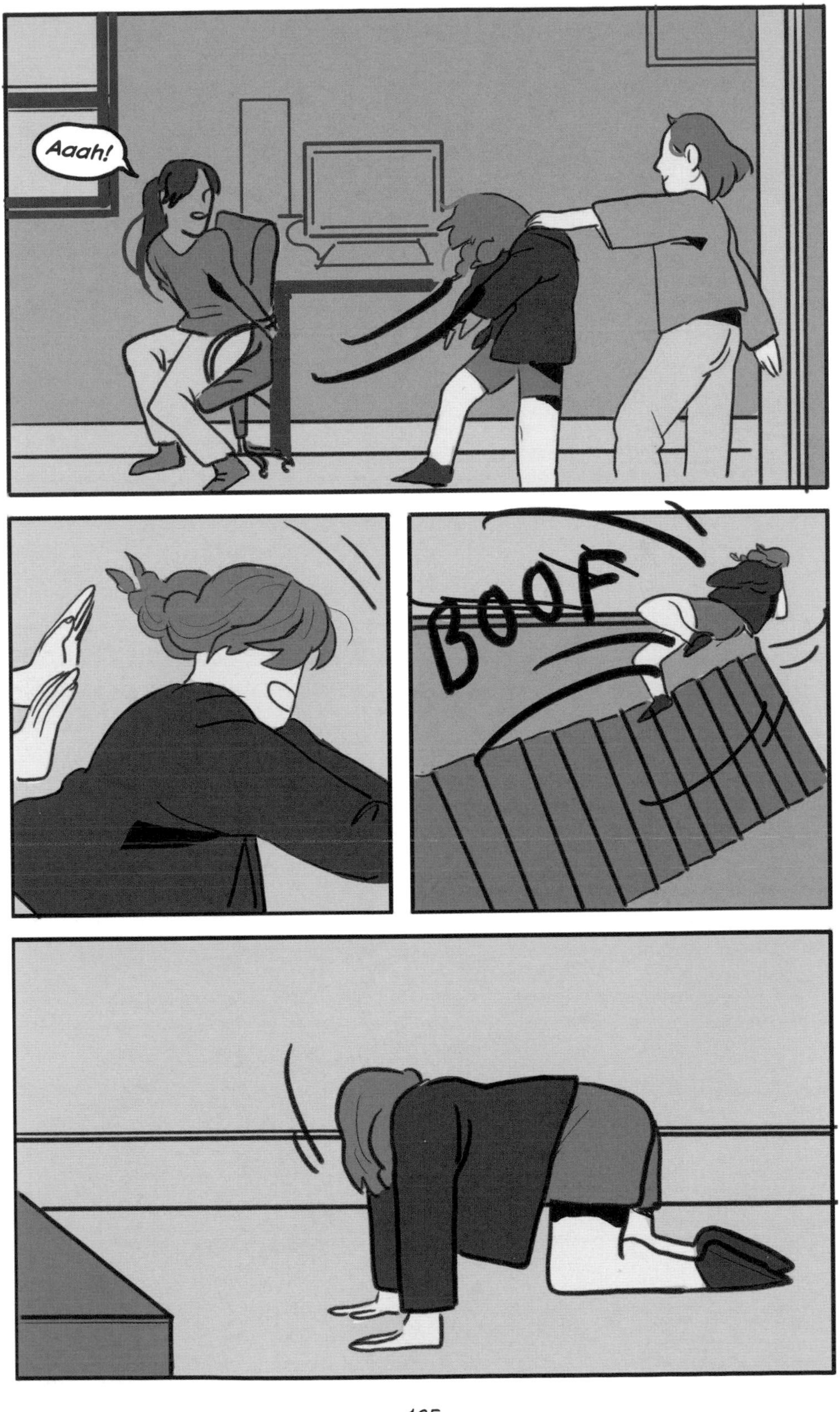
Aaah!
BOOF

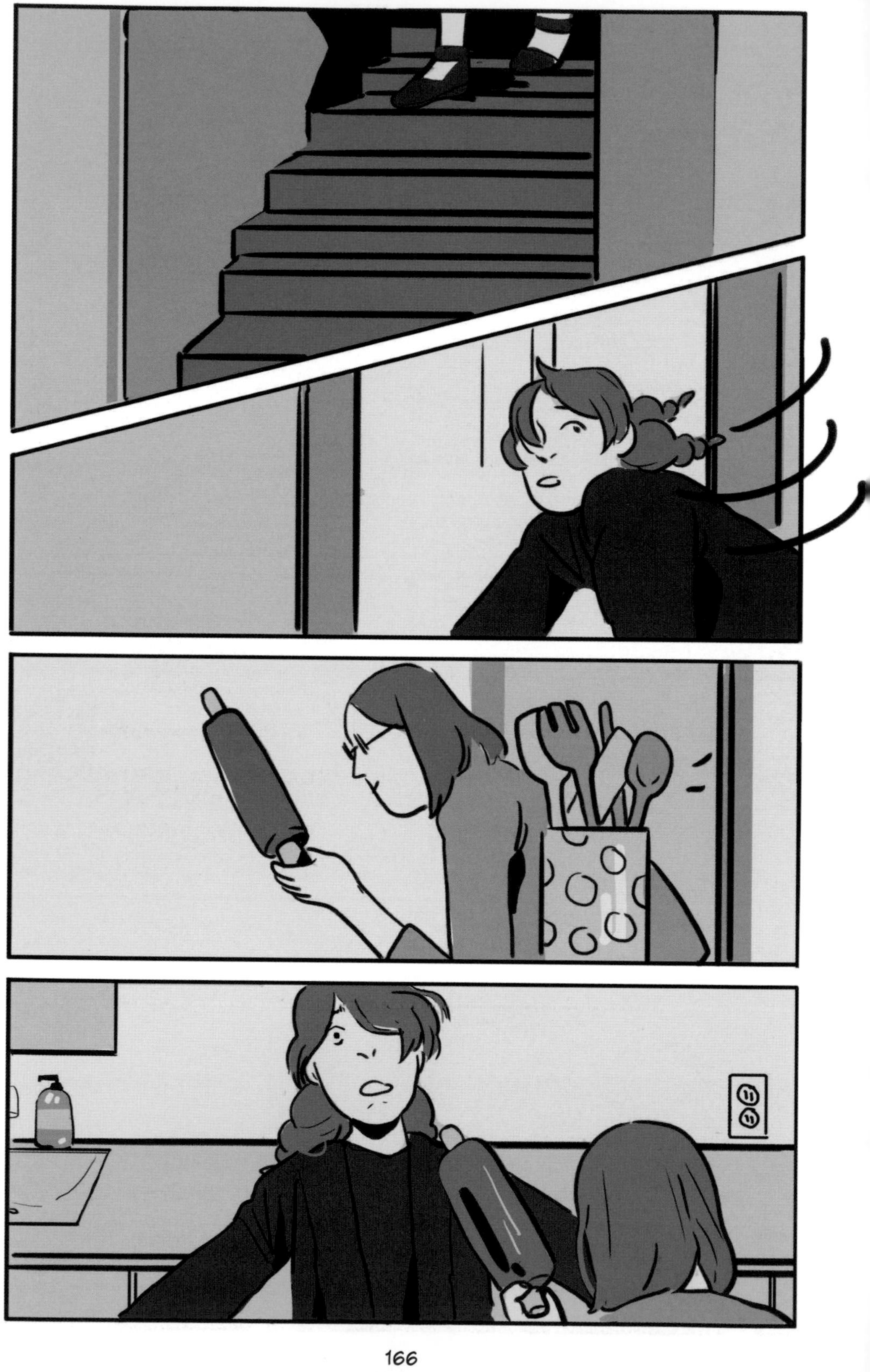

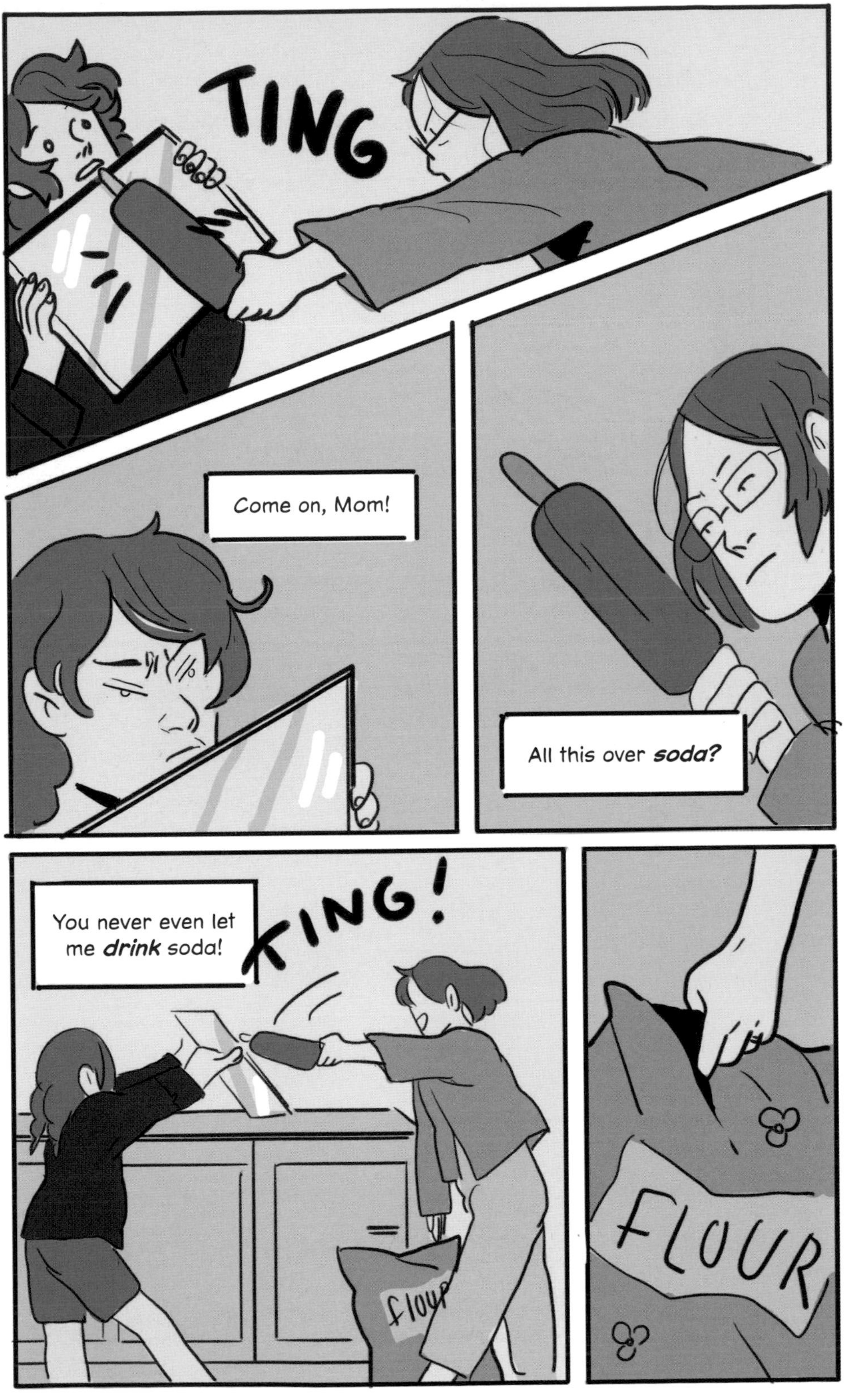
TING
Come on, Mom!
All this over soda?
You never even let me drink soda!
TING!
FLOUR
FLOUR

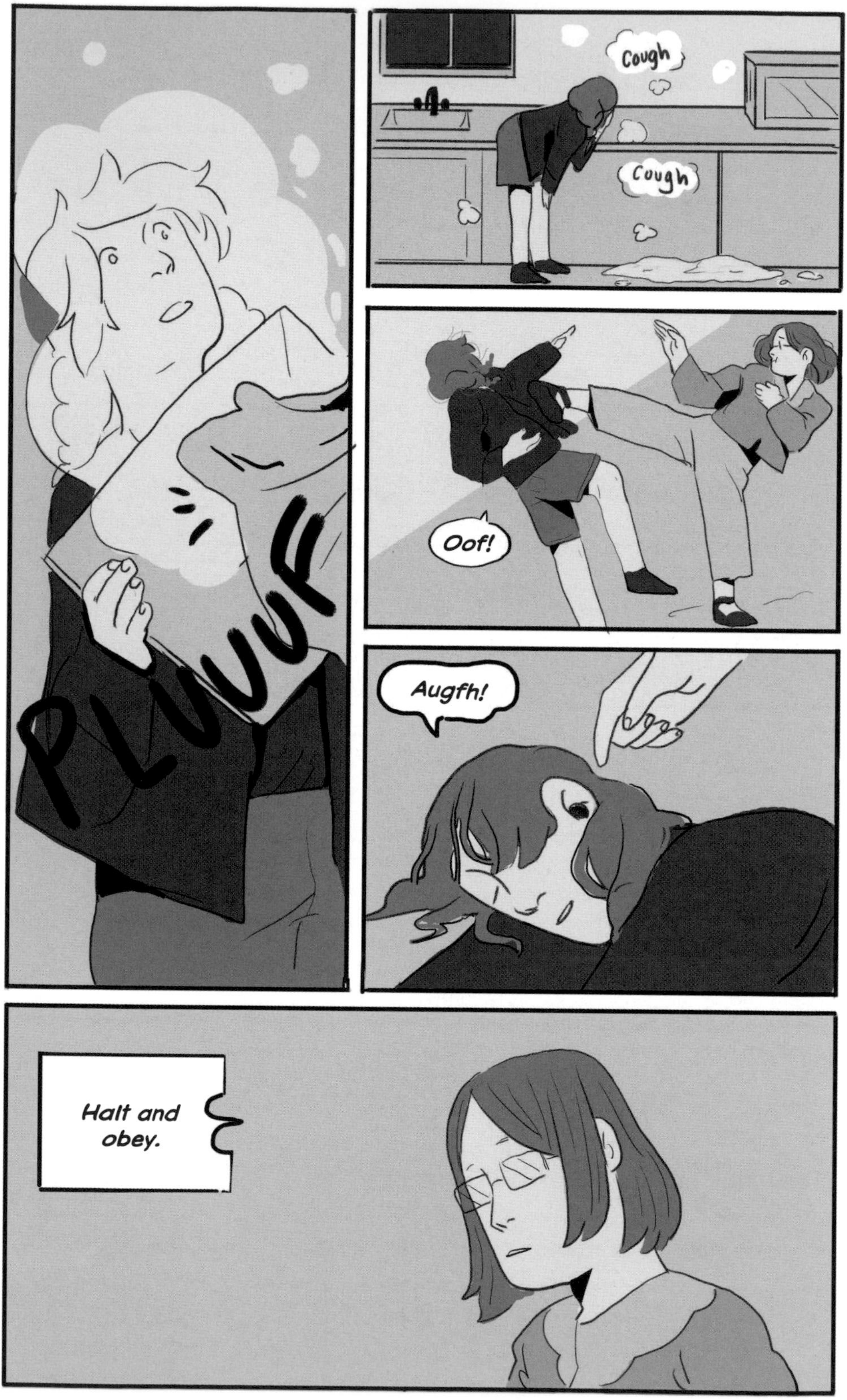
PLUUUF
Cough
Cough
Oof!
Augfh!
Halt and obey.

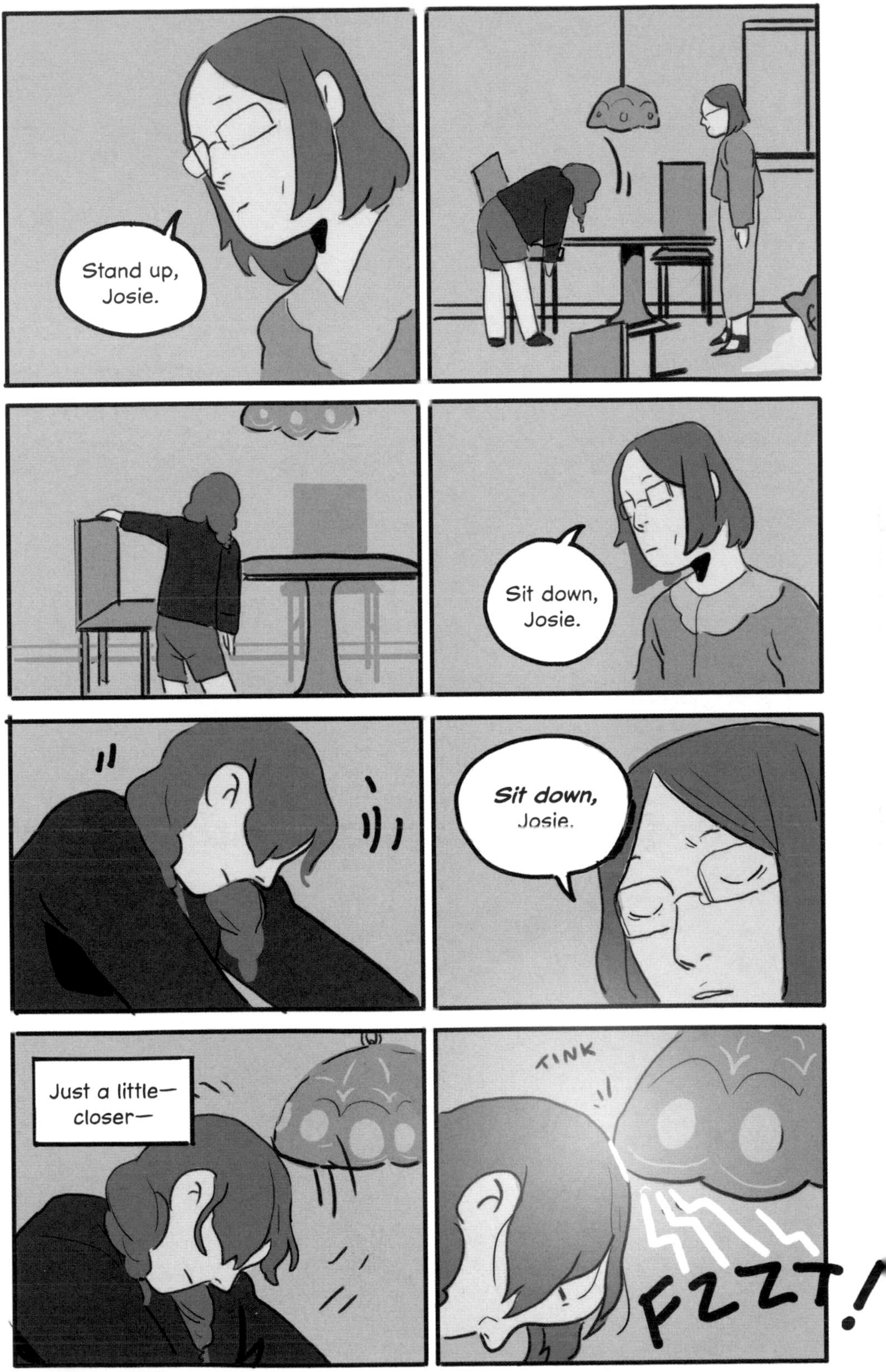

Stand up, Josie.
Sit down, Josie.
Sit down, Josie.
Just a little— closer—
TINK
FZZT!

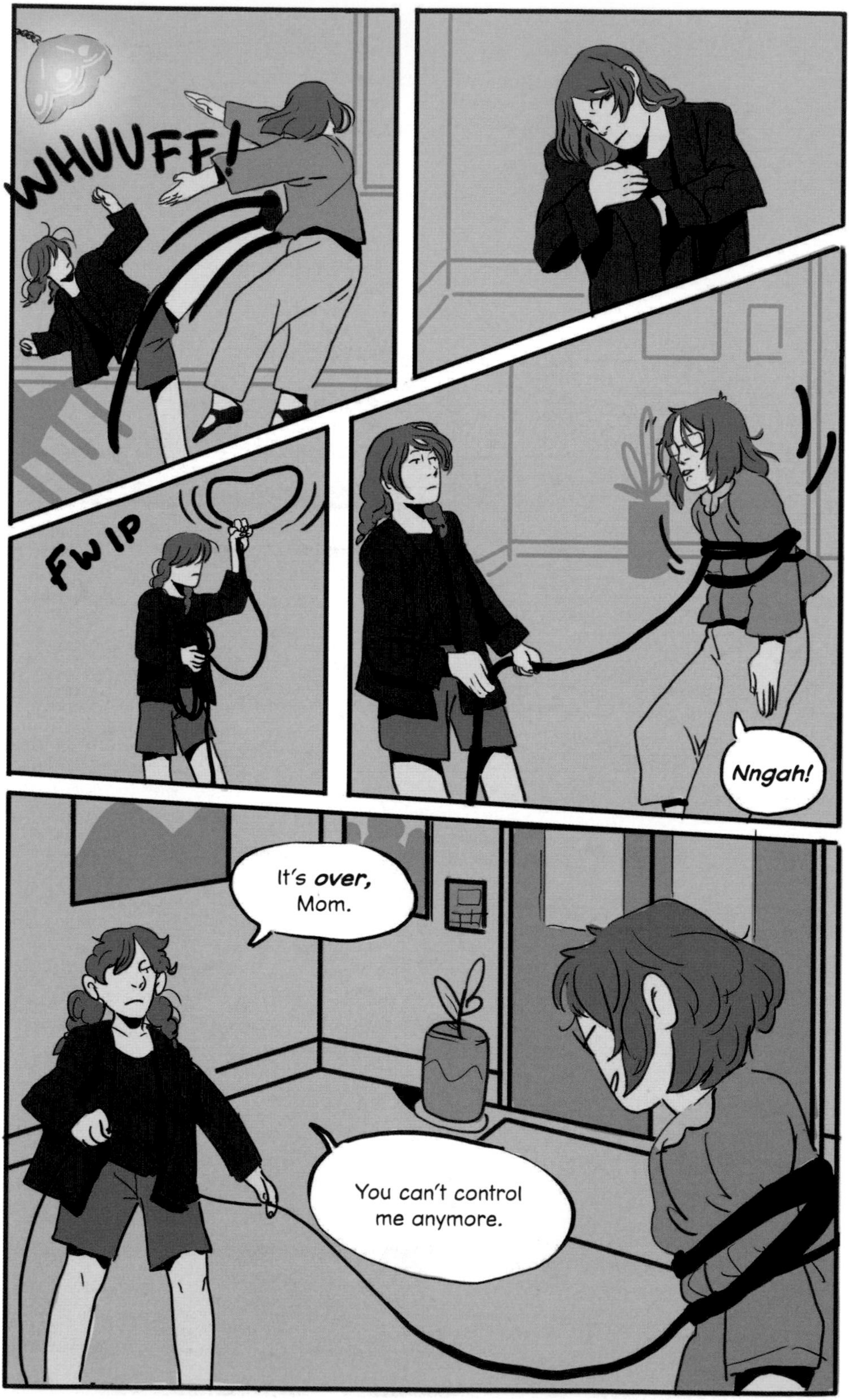

WHUUFF!
FWIP
Nngah!
It's *over,* Mom.
You can't control me anymore.

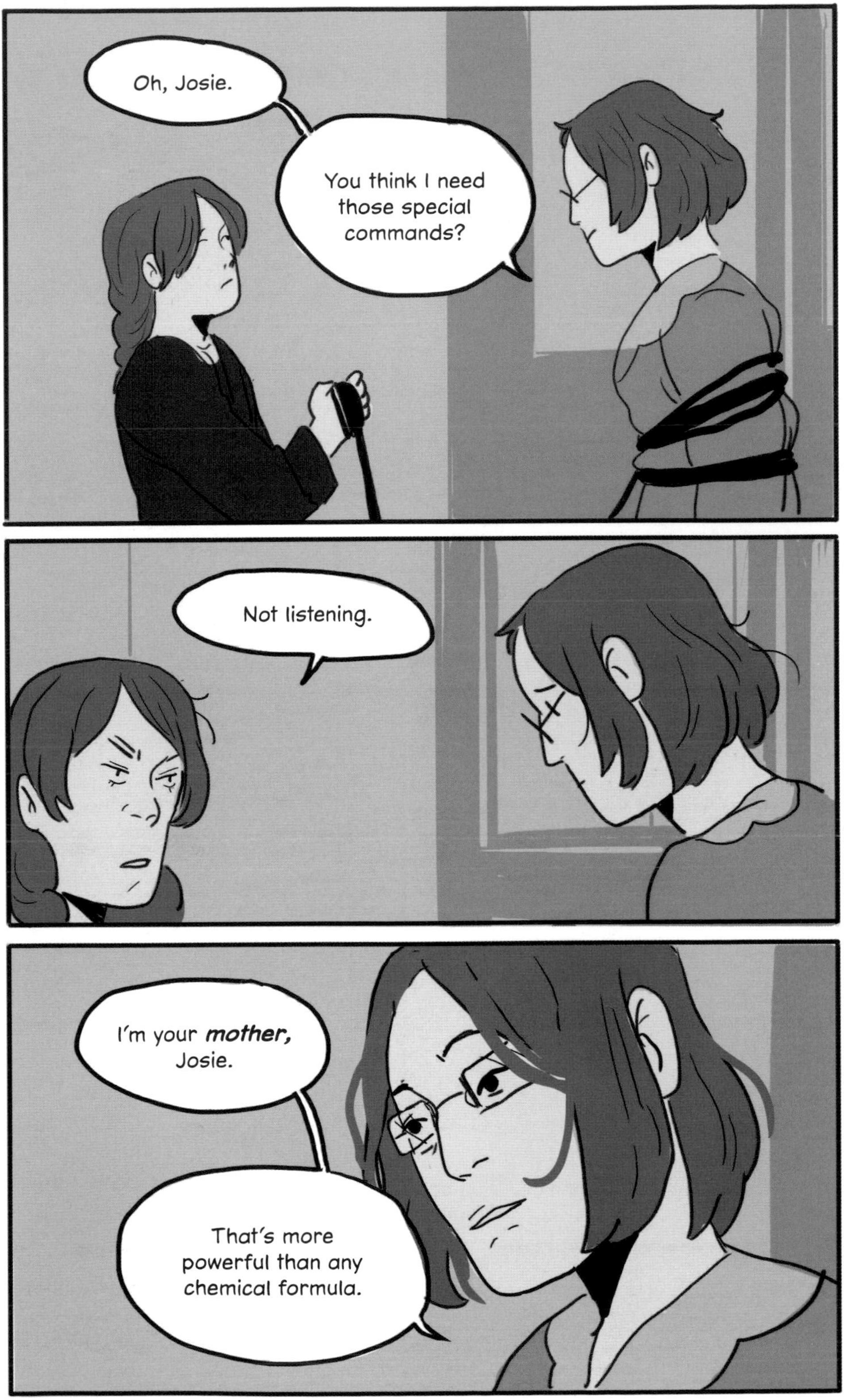
Oh, Josie.
You think I need those special commands?
Not listening.
I'm your ***mother,*** Josie.
That's more powerful than any chemical formula.

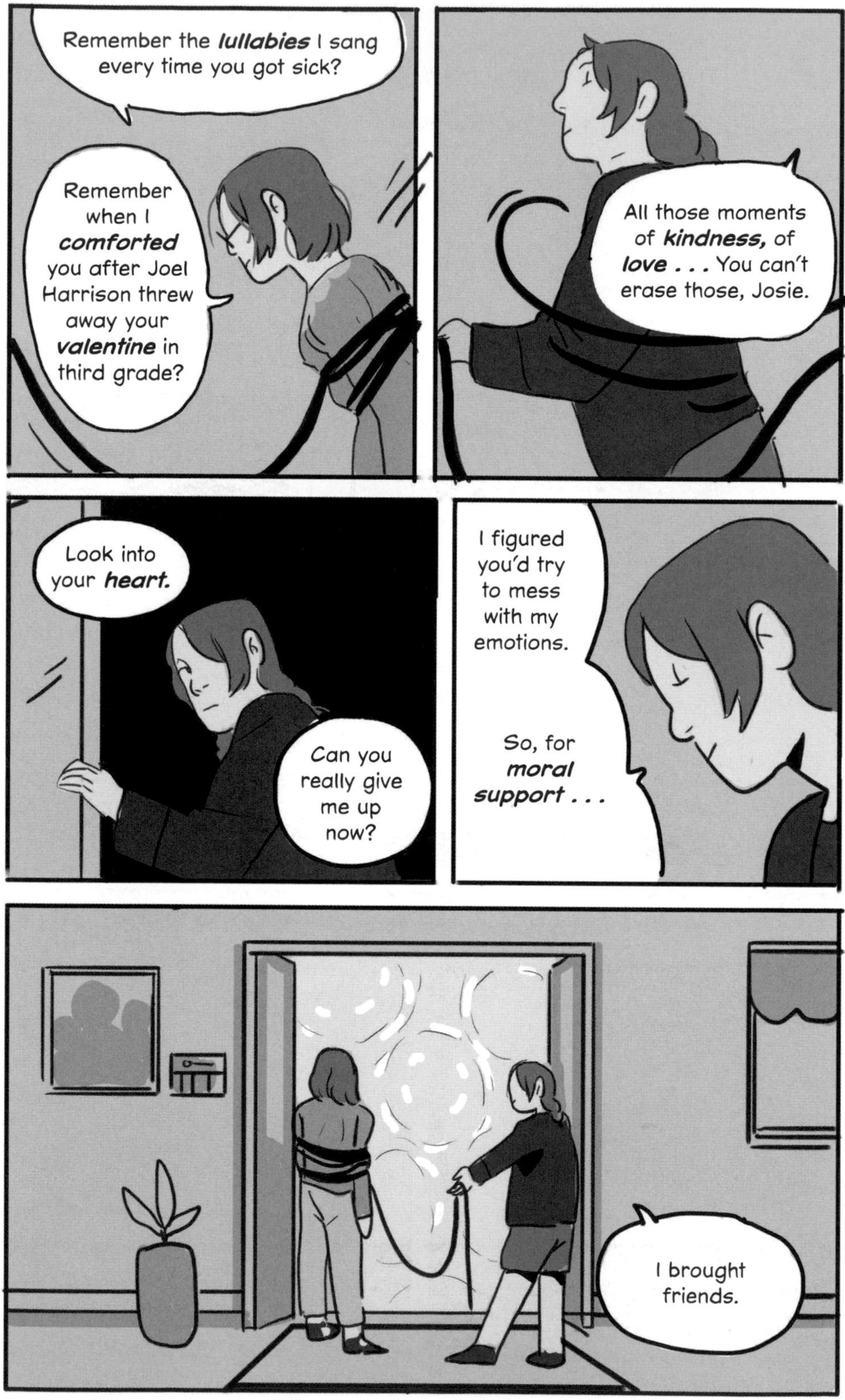
Remember the ***lullabies*** I sang every time you got sick?
Remember when I ***comforted*** you after Joel Harrison threw away your ***valentine*** in third grade?
All those moments of ***kindness,*** of ***love . . .*** You can't erase those, Josie.
Look into your ***heart.***
Can you really give me up now?
I figured you'd try to mess with my emotions.
So, for ***moral support . . .***
I brought friends.

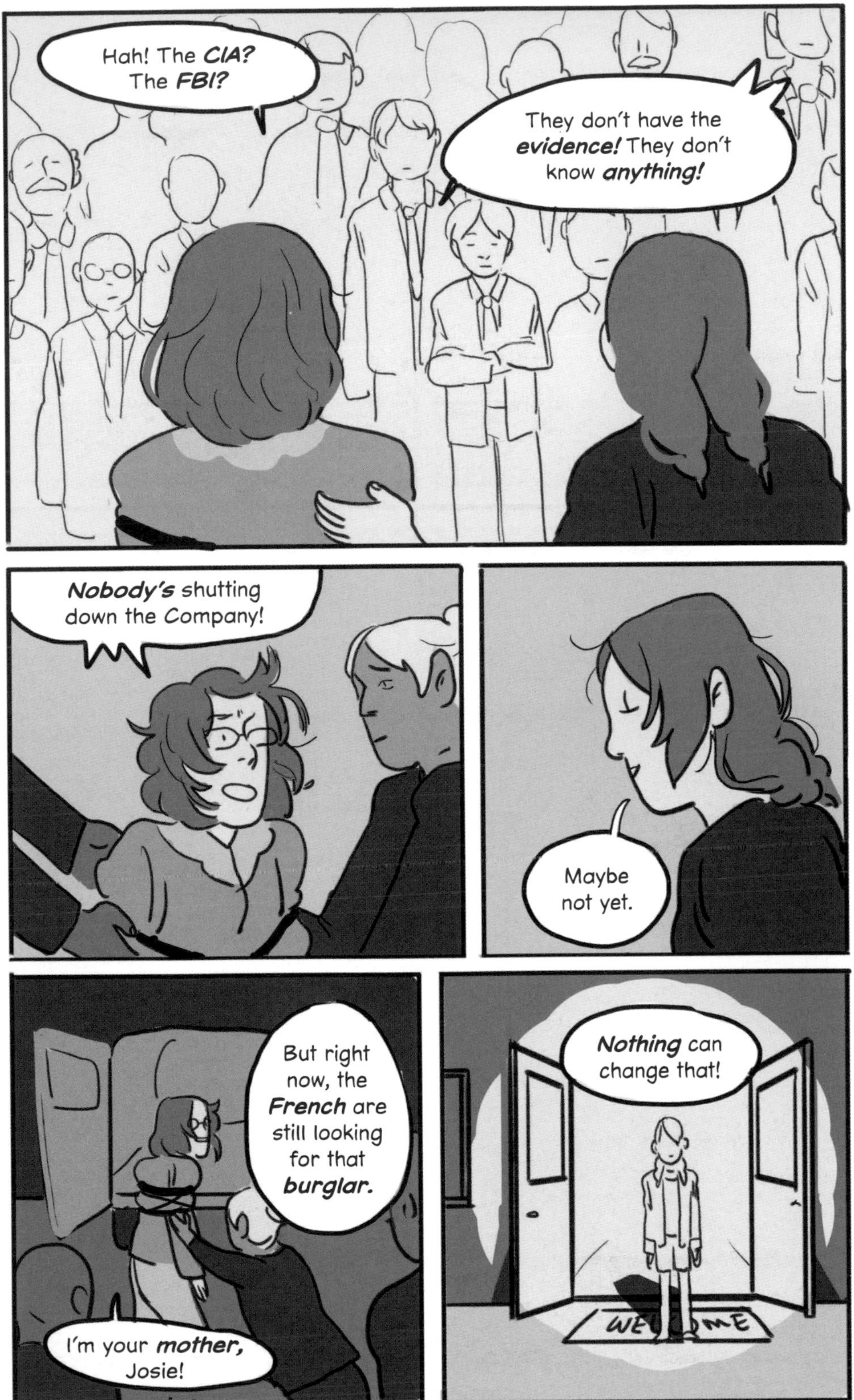
Hah! The *CIA?* The *FBI?*
They don't have the *evidence!* They don't know *anything!*
Nobody's shutting down the Company!
Maybe not yet.
But right now, the *French* are still looking for that *burglar.*
I'm your *mother,* Josie!
Nothing can change that!
WELCOME

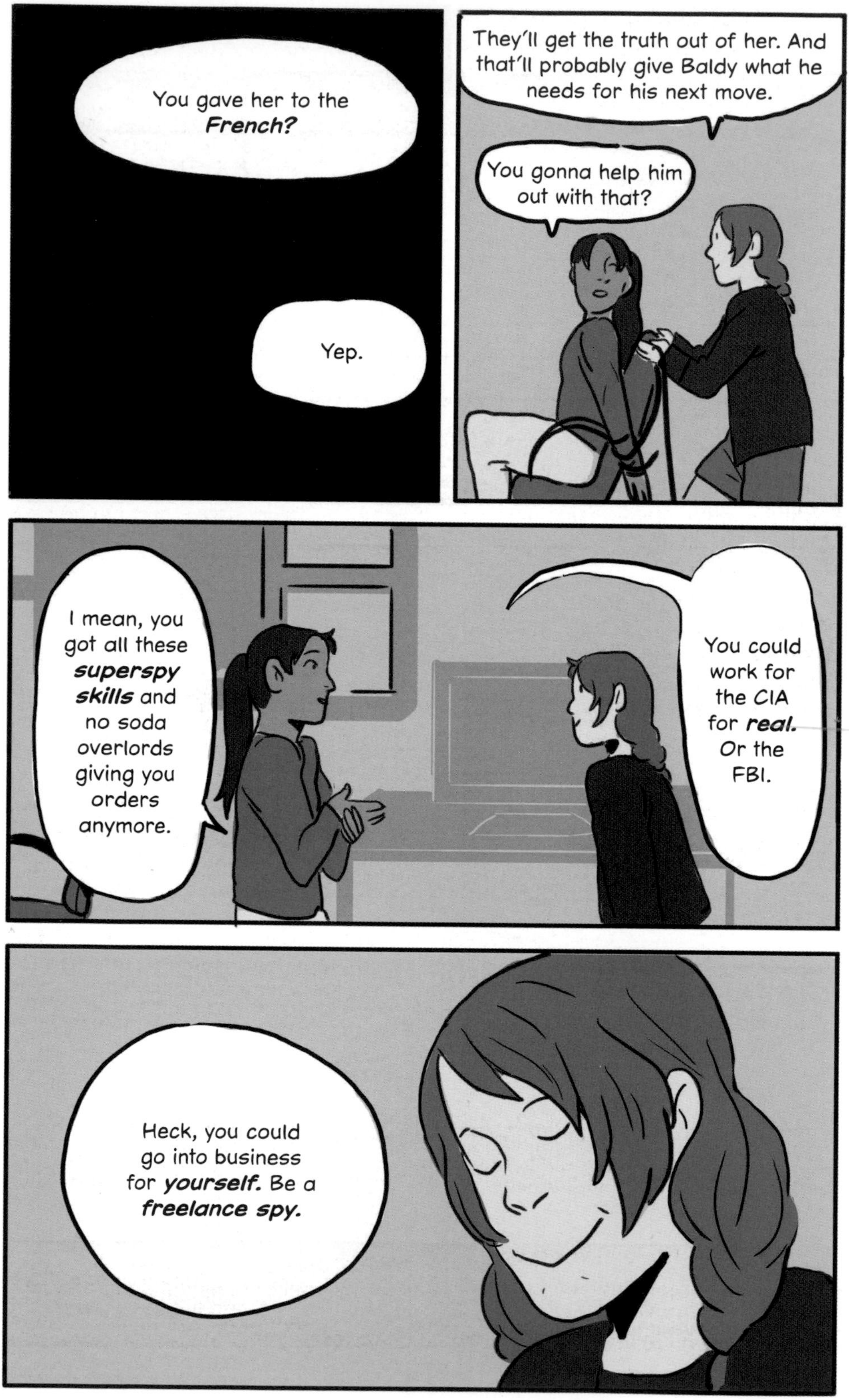
You gave her to the *French?*
Yep.
They'll get the truth out of her. And that'll probably give Baldy what he needs for his next move.
You gonna help him out with that?
I mean, you got all these *superspy skills* and no soda overlords giving you orders anymore.
You could work for the CIA for *real.* Or the FBI.
Heck, you could go into business for *yourself.* Be a *freelance spy.*

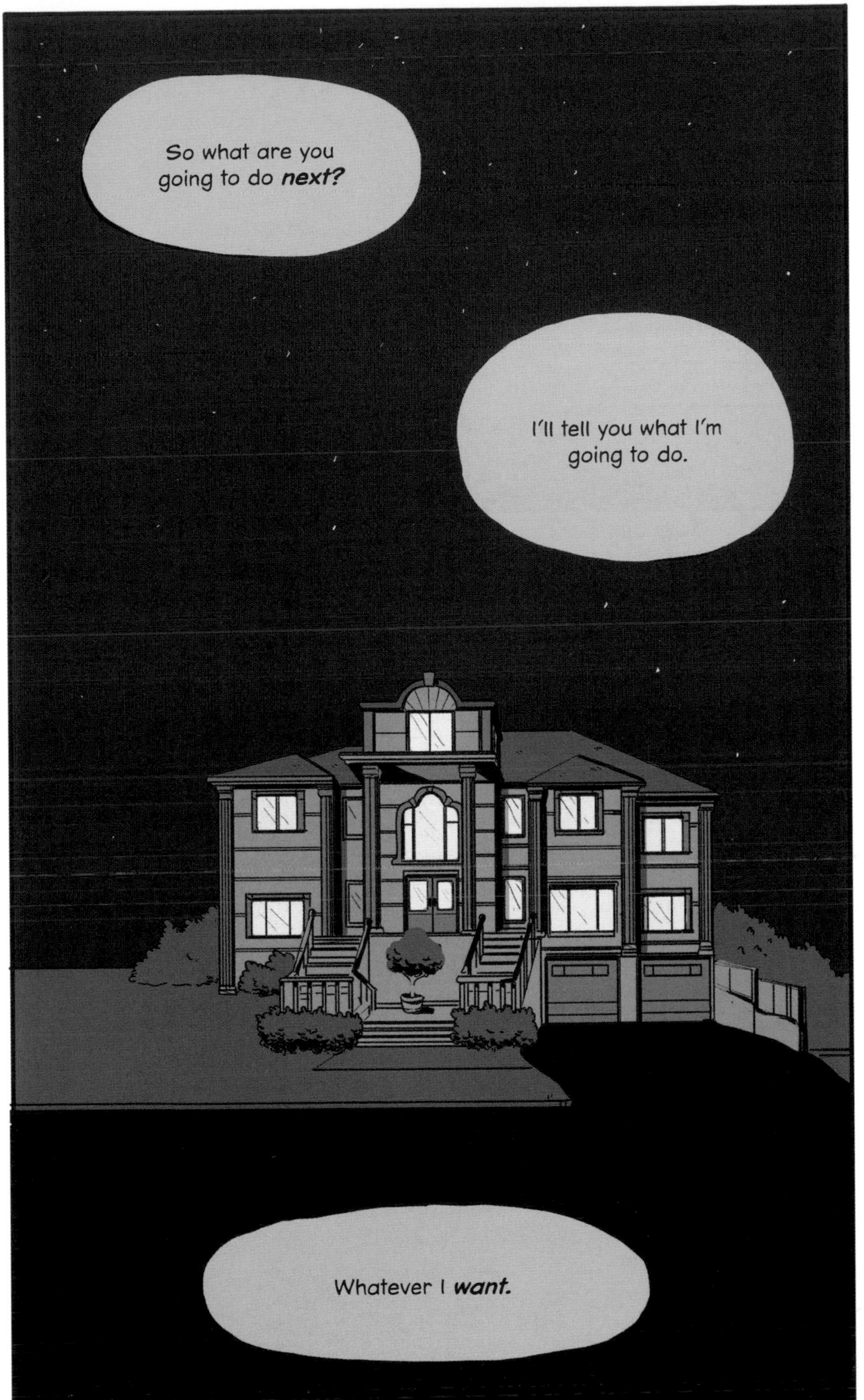
So what are you going to do ***next?***
I'll tell you what I'm going to do.
Whatever I ***want.***

ABOUT THE AUTHOR

TED ANDERSON is a librarian, educator, and comics writer from Minnesota. He has written licensed and creator-owned comics for multiple publishers, including BOOM! Studios, IDW Publishing, and Aftershock Comics. *The Spy Who Raised Me* is his first book for Graphic Universe. He lives in Minneapolis with several plants and zero regrets. To the best of his knowledge, he is *not* an internationally renowned spy.

ABOUT THE ARTIST

GIANNA MEOLA is a freelance illustrator and cartoonist from New York, currently living in Brooklyn. Her work has appeared in the anthologies *Comics for Choice* and *Group Chat*. She also draws storyboards and makes prints. In her spare time, she likes to volunteer with animals. Her website is GiannaMeola.com.

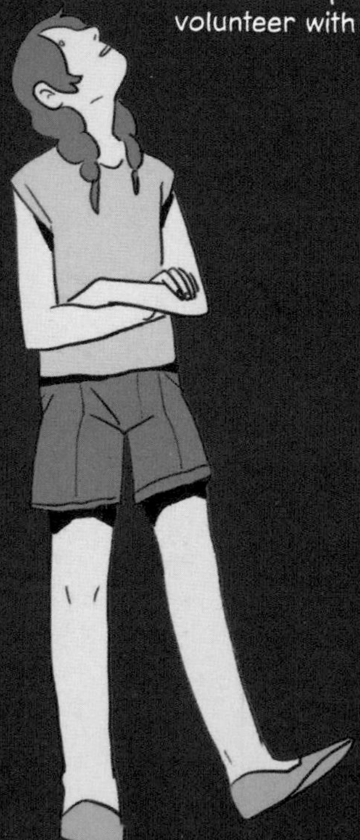